Praise for F

"In Mayer's deft hands, quarter-life burnout and the weirdness
of celeb culture are compulsively fascinating. Like a good tabloid
scandal, I couldn't turn away. So twisted. So fun."
—Goldy Moldavsky, *New York Times* bestselling author
of *The Mary Shelley Club*

"With prose that smacks your ear with its originality, debut
author Erin Mayer bursts onto the scene as a fresh new voice
with something to say. In *Fan Club*, Mayer casts a relentless eye
on a bored and lonely millennial's destructive infatuation with
an international superstar. In the process, Mayer lays bare the
terrible destiny of a society obsessed with social media stalking and
celebrity relationships that exist only through the glow of a screen."
—Julia Heaberlin, bestselling author
of *We Are All the Same in the Dark*

FAN CLUB

ERIN MAYER

mira™

ISBN-13: 978-0-7783-1159-1

Recycling programs
for this product may
not exist in your area.

Fan Club

This edition published by arrangement with Harlequin Books S.A.

For questions and comments about the quality of this book, please contact us at
CustomerService@Harlequin.com.

Mira
22 Adelaide St. West, 40th Floor
Toronto, Ontario M5H 4E3, Canada
BookClubbish.com

Printed in U.S.A.

To Mom, Steve and Benjamin—for all the pep talks.

FAN CLUB

"How do you like the Queen?" said the Cat in a low voice. "Not at all," said Alice: "she's so extremely—" Just then she noticed that the Queen was close behind her, listening: so she went on "—likely to win, that it's hardly worth while finishing the game."

—*Alice in Wonderland*, Lewis Carroll

1

I'm outside for a cumulative ten minutes each day before work. Five to walk from my apartment to the subway, another five to go from the subway to the anemic obelisk that houses my office. I try to breathe as deeply as I can in those minutes, because I never know how long it will be until I take fresh air into my lungs again. Not that the city air is all that fresh, tinged with the sharp stench of old garbage, pollution's metallic swirl. But it beats the stale oxygen of the office, already filtered through distant respiratory systems. Sometimes, during slow moments at my desk, I inhale and try to imagine those other nostrils and lungs that have already processed this same air. I'm not sure how it works in reality, any knowledge I once had of the intricacies of breathing having long been discarded by more useful information, but the image comforts me. Usually, I picture a middle-aged man with graying temples, a fringe of visible nose hair, and a coffee stain on the collar of his baby-blue button-down. He looks nothing and everything like my father. An every-father, if you will.

My office is populated by dyed-blonde or pierced brunette

women in their mid-to-late twenties and early thirties. The occasional man, a touch older than most of the women, but still young enough to give off the faint impression that he DJs at Meatpacking nightclubs for extra cash on the weekends.

We are the new corporate Americans, the offspring of the gray-templed men. We wear tastefully ripped jeans and cozy sweaters to the office instead of blazers and trousers. Display a tattoo here and there—our supervisors don't mind; in fact, they have the most ink. We eat yogurt for breakfast, work through lunch, leave the office at six if we're lucky, arriving home with just enough time to order dinner from an app and watch two or three hours of Netflix before collapsing into bed from exhaustion we haven't earned. Exhaustion that lives in the brain, not the body, and cannot be relieved by a mere eight hours of sleep.

Nobody understands exactly what it is we do here, and neither do we.

I push through a revolving glass door, run my wallet over the card reader, which beeps as my ID scans through the stiff leather, and half wave in the direction of the uniformed security guard behind the desk, whose face my eyes never quite reach so I can't tell you what he looks like. He's just one of the many set pieces staging the scene of my days.

The elevator ride to the eleventh floor is long enough to skim one third of a long-form article on my phone. I barely register what it's about, something loosely political, or who is standing next to me in the cramped elevator.

When the doors slide open on eleven, we both get off.

In the dim eleventh-floor lobby, a humming neon light shaping the company logo assaults my sleep-swollen eyes like the prick of a dozen tiny needles. Today, a small section has burned out, creating a skip in the letter *w*. Below the logo is a tufted cerulean velvet couch where guests wait to be welcomed. To the left there's a mirrored wall reflecting the vestibule; people sometimes pause there to take photos on the way to and from the office, usually on the Friday afternoon before a long weekend. I see the photos later while scrolling through my various feeds at home in bed. They hit me one after another like shots of tequila: *See ya Tuesday!* *margarita emoji* *Peace out for the long weekend!* *palm tree emoji* *Byeeeeee!* *peace sign emoji*

She steps in front of me, my elevator companion. Black Rag & Bone ankle boots gleaming, blade-tipped pixie cut grazing her ears. Her neck piercings taunt me, those winking silver balls on either side of her spine. She's Lexi O' Connell, the website's senior editor. She walks ahead with her head angled down, thumb working her phone's keyboard, and doesn't look up as she shoves the interior door open, palm to the glass.

I trip over the back of one clunky winter boot with the other as I speed up, considering whether to call out for her attention. It's what a good web producer, one who is eager to move on from the endless drudgery of copy-pasting and resizing and into the slightly more thrilling drudgery of writing and rewriting, would do.

By the time I regain my footing, I come face-to-face with the smear of her handprint as the door glides shut in front of me.

Monday.

I work at a website.

It's like most other websites. We publish content, mostly articles: news stories, essays, interviews, glossed over with the polished opalescent sheen of commercialized feminism. The occasional quiz, video, or photo shoot rounds out our offerings. This is how websites work in the age of ad revenue: each provides a slightly varied selection of mindless entertainment, news updates, and watered-down hot takes about everything from climate change to plus-size fashion, hawking their wares on the digital marketplace, leaving The Reader to wander drunkenly through the bazaar, wielding her cursor like an Amex. You can find everything you'd want to read in one place online, dozens of times over. The algorithms have erased choice. Search engines and social media platforms, they know what you want before you do.

As a web producer, my job is to input article text into the website's proprietary content management system, or CMS. I'm a digitized high school janitor: I clean up the small messes, the litter that misses the rim of the garbage can. I make sure the links are working and the images are high-resolution. When anything bigger comes up, it goes to an editor or IT. I'm an expert in nothing, a master of the miniscule fixes.

There are five of us who produce for the entire website, each handling about twenty articles a day. We sit at a long gray table on display at the very center of the open office, surrounded on all sides by editors and writers.

The web producers' bullpen, Lexi calls it.

The light fixture above the table buzzes loudly like a nest of bees is trapped inside the fluorescent tubing. I drop my bag on the floor and take a seat, shedding my coat like a layer of skin. My chair faces the beauty editor's desk, the cruelest seat in the house. All day long, I watch Charlotte Miller receive package after package stuffed with pastel tissue paper. Inside those packages: lipstick, foundation, perfume, happiness. A thousand simulacrums of Christmas morning spread across the two hundred and sixty-one workdays of the year. She has piled the trappings of Brooklyn hipsterdom on top of her blond, big-toothed prettiness. Wire-framed glasses, a tattoo of a constellation on her inner left forearm, a rose-gold nose ring. She seems Texan, but she's actually from some wholesome upper Midwestern state; I can never remember which one. Right now, she applies red lipstick from a warm golden tube in the flat gleam of the mirror next to her monitor. Everything about her is color-coordinated.

I open my laptop. The screen blinks twice and prompts me for my password. I type it in, and the CMS appears, open to where I left it when I signed off the previous evening. Our CMS is called LIZZIE. There's a rumor that it was named after Lizzie Borden, christened during the prelaunch party when the tech team pounded too many shots after they finished coding. As in, *"Lizzie Borden took an ax and gave her mother forty whacks."* Lizzie Borden rebranded in the twenty-first century as a symbol of righteous feminine anger. LIZZIE, my best friend, my closest confidant. She's an equally comforting and infuriating presence, constant in her bland attention. She gazes at me, always emotionless, saying nothing as she watches me teeter on the edge, fighting tears or trying not to doze at my desk or simply staring, in search of answers she cannot provide.

My eyes droop in their sockets as I scan the articles that were submitted before I arrived this morning. The whites threaten to turn liquid and splash onto my keyboard, pool between the keys and jiggle like eggs minus the yolks. Thinking of this causes a tiny laugh to slip out from between my clenched lips. Charlotte slides the cap onto her lipstick, glares at me over the lip of the mirror.

"Morning."

That's Tom, the only male web producer, who sits across and slightly left of me, keeping my view of Charlotte's towering wonderland of boxes and bags clear. He's four years older than me, twenty-eight, but the plush chipmunk curve of his cheeks makes him appear much younger, like he's about to graduate high school. He's cute, though, in the way of a movie star who always gets cast as the geek in teen comedies. Definitely hot, but dress him in an argyle sweater and glasses and he could be a Hollywood nerd. I've always wanted to ask him why he works here, doing *this*. There isn't really a web producer archetype. We're all different, a true island of misfit toys. But if there *is* a type, Tom doesn't fit it. He seems smart and driven. He's consistently the only person who attends company book club meetings having read that month's selection from cover to cover. I've never asked him why he works here because we don't talk much. No one in our office talks much. Not out loud, anyway. We communicate through a private Morse code, fingers dancing on keys, expressions scanned and evaluated from a distance.

Sometimes I think about flirting with Tom, for something to do, but he wears a wedding ring. Not that I care about his wife; it's more the fear of rebuff and rejection, of hearing the low-voiced *Sorry, I'm married*, that stops me. He usually sails in a few minutes after I do, smelling like his bodega coffee and the egg sandwich he carefully unwraps and eats at his desk. He nods in my direction. *Morning* is the only word we've exchanged the entire time I've worked here, which is coming up on a year in January. It's not even a greeting, merely a statement of fact. *It is morning and we're both here. Again.*

Three hundred and sixty-five days lost to the hum and twitch and click. I can't seem to remember how I got here. It all feels like a dream. The mundane kind, full of banal details, but something slightly off about it all. I don't remember applying for the job, or interviewing. One day, an offer letter appeared in my inbox and I signed.

And here I am. Day after day, I wait for someone to need me. I open articles. I tweak the formatting, check the links, correct the occasional typo that catches my eye. It isn't really my job to copyedit, or even to read closely, but sometimes I notice things, grammatical errors or awkward phrasings, and I then can't *not* notice them; I have to put them right or else they nag like a paper cut on the soft webbing connecting two fingers. The brain wants to be useful. It craves activity, even after almost three hundred and sixty-five days of operating at its lowest frequency.

I open emails. I download attachments. I insert numbers into spreadsheets. I email those spreadsheets to Lexi and my direct boss, Ashley, who manages the home page.

None of it ever seems to add up to anything.

The other thing I do is take coffee breaks.

Four of them, evenly spaced throughout the day: midmorning, pre-lunch, post-lunch, and midafternoon. The times are recorded as recurring appointments in my digital calendar, all of them titled "Meeting," in case Ashley takes a sudden interest in my schedule. She can check my calendar appointments anytime she wants, which I know because the privilege goes both ways.

When a reminder flashes across my screen, I stop what I'm doing and rise from my desk chair, ergonomic yet still somehow horrific. I walk the thirty-five paces to the kitchen and insert a hazelnut pod into the single-serve coffee maker on the counter beside the refrigerator. I watch a stream of brown liquid splatter into the cat-shaped mug I keep at my desk instead of in the cabinet of communal mugs above the coffee machine. The sound of coffee spitting against the clean white mug never ceases to remind me of a man urinating.

As I wait for the coffee to "brew," I think about the row of identical office kitchens extending above and below me along the fifteen-story building. Fifteen floors, fifteen gray kitchens with zany futuristic couches and circular tables with brushed metal surfaces, furnishings that appear to have been designed by aliens who crash-landed in an IKEA and thought *yes, this must be human.* Fifteen pantries stuffed with Day-Glo snacks: Cheez-Its, PopCorners, Kind bars.

I sometimes imagine that in one of those kitchens, the love of my life also prepares his morning or afternoon or midafternoon coffee, his movements matching my movements, arm reach for arm reach. My idea of him changes with my mood. Some days he's big and bearded, his checkered shirt barely containing bulging biceps fine-tuned at the gym in the evenings. Other times he's thin and tattooed, with wire-framed glasses to match his sharply pointed elbows and elegant wrists that echo the curve of a violin's neck.

Next comes the milk, a heavy splash to drown out the bitter edge of the mass-produced coffee. Then, cat mug in hand, I forgo the stiff purple couches, and, leaving my drained pod in the coffee machine, a quiet rebellion, my contribution to the anti-capitalist cause, I go around the corner to the bathroom, locking myself in the largest stall, the handicap stall. I always feel like an asshole for hogging this space meant for someone who needs it more, but the feeling isn't enough to make me stop.

Pressing my back against the tiled wall, making myself nearly invisible in case anyone else comes into the bathroom and wonders why someone is standing three feet from the toilet, I take tiny sips and meditate on the peeling pink paint on the metal divider separating this stall from the next. There's an elaborate pencil sketch of a rose above the trash bin for pads and tampons. The illustration has been here for as long as I've worked at the company; I know because I came here to hyperventilate on my very first day.

At some point I inevitably give up on going unnoticed, cross the tile, and trace the miniscule lines forming the petals with a fingertip, wondering about the woman who sat here and painstakingly scratched a flower into bloom on this grimy fake-cheerful fake wall. Did it take only a few minutes? Or did she return to it day after day, a gardener tending to a garden of one? What dreams did she have or let go of that led her to the spot where I stand now? Does she still work here? I think I'd like to meet her. Maybe she's in Accounting, or Sales.

My coffee cup empty, I flush for cover and leave the warmth of the stall, wash my hands at the sink, scrubbing fiercely behind each knuckle. Back at the web producers' bullpen, I wonder if Tom and the others can smell the coffee and bathroom stink clinging to my skin like wet cellophane. I surreptitiously dab a bit of solid perfume on my wrists and behind my ears before I return to my typing.

On this particular Monday, I've run out of articles to produce thirty minutes before it's time for the second coffee. I consider going early, but routine is the important thing, it's what holds me together.

The light above my head flickers milky blue, blinks brighter, settles, and continues its steady vibration. My eyes are dry and heavy now. I can feel the sinews fighting to hold them in place. I check Piger, the office chat service the entire company uses to communicate so we don't have to speak. There's a direct message from Charlotte asking me to prioritize an article about influencer Karlie Kaletta's new clothing line for Macy's.

We have the exclusive, Charlotte's avatar of a pink female symbol tells me.

On it!! I write back, then wonder if the second exclamation point was too much, if it made me seem disingenuous instead of eager.

I get on it.

The story is three hundred words with two ad campaign images, clearly provided by a publicist. I use the preview button to see what the article will look like when it goes live, scan the text for obvious errors, and click all the links, making sure each one opens in a separate tab. Then I hit Publish. The entire thing takes less than five minutes. I open Piger again. No new messages. In the Editorial chat room a lively debate about sushi, whether it's delicious or disgusting, has broken out. I wonder if it's racist to call a central facet of another culture's cuisine disgusting, decide that it is at least a little bit racist.

I love sushi, I type, delete, retype, hit Enter.

Bored, I open a new tab on my internet browser and type the letters *tw*.

Google autofills the URL, and I watch as my Twitter timeline floods the page in a wash of text. Scrolling through the steady stream of internal detritus writ large, my eyes dart to the Trending sidebar. A bunch of names I vaguely recognize— a famous athlete (baseball, I think), a historical monument in Europe, ISIS. Then the Meeting banner scrolls across the upper right-hand corner of my screen, and I drop everything.

How do people decide what to do with their lives?

I wasn't one of the golden kids. You know the ones. They were there, hitting the ice rink at five a.m. before school, or hunched over Bunsen burners in the science lab while everyone else was home eating dinner. The ones who were kept so busy with their passions they never had to stop and consider *is this what I really want?*

I never had any passion at all, real, imagined, or parentally enforced. The only thing that made me feel truly special growing up, the detail I still break out when asked to share a fact about myself at happy hours and networking events and parties, is that I taught myself to read before I entered kindergarten. I don't remember how. All I remember is that one day there was gibberish and the next there were words.

I've always loved reading, turning to books in the foggy hours of boredom that peppered my childhood. Fantasy lives, the magical wizards and troubled yet intelligent orphans, kept me going through summer afternoons and winter mornings. I left one foot dipped in the golden glow of fictional worlds, the other propelling me along reality's linoleum hallways. I never learned to live in the real world completely, to make choices about how my life should go. I let myself be carried, planless, until the day they shoved me off the auditorium stage with nothing but a useless English degree and a greasy polyester robe I had to return for use at next year's graduation, already obsolete before the ceremony was officially over.

I had no career aspirations or goals. But I did have Edith.

Frozen in black and white, hands poised elegantly above the keys of an old-fashioned typewriter, the stack of pages next to her appearing to have been ruffled by a light breeze, Edith wears a tailored jacket, nipped in at the waist, and smiles to herself like she just swallowed a secret.

She looks like a writer, but most likely she is *a typist*.

I found the photograph while researching a paper on women in the workplace for my gender studies class junior year of college. She was printed in a book called *The History of the Typewriter*. Something stirred in my chest as my eyes flicked across the image for the first time, squinting in a recessed cavern of old books, trying to bring this woman's life into shape, who she would be once the camera lens turned away. She looked utterly unbothered. *Satisfied.*

In the half dark of the library basement, I photocopied the page, tucking the still-warm sheet carefully between the cover and the title page of a textbook at the bottom of my backpack. At the dorm, I taped the photo to the wall beside my bed to glance at whenever I panicked about the future. I decided she looked like she could be named Edith, and, privately, that's what I called her. When people asked, I told them she was my grandmother.

I guess that's how I wound up here, at the website: I'm chasing whatever it is that Edith had when she posed for the picture, which still hangs by my bed. Whatever it is that enabled her to be, nothing as frivolous as happy, but content.

In my self-important moments, I fancy myself a language doula, birthing other people's words into the world, crafting a flawless user experience.

The rest of the time I simply feel invisible.

A voice interrupts while I'm stirring milk into the third coffee of Monday.

"Hey there," the voice says.

I almost don't respond, but there's no one else in the kitchen, so they must be talking to me. I turn. She's standing a few feet away, approaching with caution, like I'm a bear she doesn't want to startle for fear of her life. I knead my face into a smile, easing the muscles, working the dough.

"Hello," I say.

"Sorry, I'm new here? And I don't know where I need to go?" she says. Each sentence is a question. She looks about my age, freckles smattering her nose and cheeks. Her chin-length hair is dishwater blond and fringed with heavy bangs that cover her forehead. Her body is narrow from her chin to her hips to her calves, visible under the hem of her pencil skirt. Beneath the gauze of her pale pantyhose, I make out a hazy outline, a strand of greenery tattooed on her skin. Possibly climbing ivy, or a snake. She holds a tufted coat in one hand and a too-shiny briefcase in the other.

"You really are new here," I say. I can't help it; she looks like she stumbled in from an all-night bender at Ann Taylor.

We stare at each other until she blushes.

"I'm Meghan."

Of course. She looks like a Meghan. That, at least, I do not say out loud.

"Who are you here to see?" I ask.

She transfers the briefcase to the opposite hand and pulls an iPhone from somewhere within the starched folds of her blazer. Squinting, she plucks at her phone with a bouncy fingertip. "Karen Thomas in HR," she says, finally.

I point down a grayscale corridor.

"Third door on the left."

The space between Meghan's brows softens and she says through a smile, "Thanks *so* much! I owe you one."

I watch the origami creases of her wrinkled skirt disappear on their way to be onboarded, and then I return to the task at hand. My cat mug is still sitting on the metal grate under the coffee machine, rapidly cooling. I add milk and take a long, deep inhale of hazelnut essence, all the while wondering, *owe me one of what?*

The afternoon trickles by. Kathleen Morris, the lifestyle editor, asks me to enter a freelancer's essay on her late-term abortion into LIZZIE and schedule it for publication on Friday, which is National Share Your Abortion Story Day. It's treacly and overwrought, but I find my eyes watering anyway at the thought of all that loss. I finish and google the writer, spend half an hour clicking various links on her website, each story packaged under increasingly desperate headlines:

"*On Dating without Apps*"

"*My Year of Insomnia: a Journey in Sleep Aids*"

"*What My Mom's Death Taught Me about Surviving on My Own*"

I know she didn't choose these titles herself—that's the editor's job—and this depresses me more than her cliché-ridden prose. Here is someone so obviously trying to take control of her narrative, to own the worst parts of her history. Yet, at the top of each essay, a bold reminder that someone else is holding the frame.

At three o'clock I get another Meeting reminder. This time it's for an actual meeting, the monthly web production all-hands held in the glass-walled Emerald conference room behind Charlotte's desk. Nothing about the room suits its name—not the table and chairs, which are matching slate-gray, nor the mournful blank cyclops eye of a television mounted on the wall. Even the decaled quote affixed to one glass panel (*"You have the same twenty-four hours in a day as Beyoncé,"* no attribution) is rendered in black. If they really want us *not* to contemplate launching our bodies through an open window before noon, they could try to make the place look less like a morgue with a decent entertainment system.

All five of us on the production team sit scattered around the table in the center, deflated, like crumpled fast-food wrappers. There's Tom, Mariah, Carly, Emily and me. We have our laptops propped open in front of us, as if the fucking world will burn down if an editor needs to wait fifteen minutes for her *breaking news* to go live. Like we're the goddamn *New York Times*.

I lower my screen halfway, so I won't be too distracted by the constant twitch of Piger notifications and incoming emails in the upper right-hand corner.

Lexi and Ashley enter the room next, their conflicting energies creating a tornado of chaos. Where Lexi is sharp, all edges, Ashley is cotton candy fluff, tufted and teased. Just looking at her honey-colored curls is enough to give you a toothache. While Lexi takes a seat in the swivel chair at the head of the table, Ashley sets up screen-sharing on her laptop so we can see the home page on the television.

These meetings are far and away the most pointless part of my month, but I enjoy them. I never quite believe the people who loudly protest meetings, as if they'd rather be working head down at their desks, ants carrying torso-sized bread crumbs back to the nest, than sitting around a conference table spacing out. At the very least, meetings are an excuse to look out the window at the blue-green of the building across the street, to imagine the rippling surface to be water instead of glass, the pigeons like inquisitive koi fish with suckling mouths in place of beaks. Which is what I'm doing when Ashley says, "This has been a great month for our team. Home page traffic is up thirty percent."

My bosses are always talking about home page traffic. Home page traffic, they say, demonstrates the brand loyalty of our readership. It tells us how many people are coming to the website without a clear goal, just to see what we've published lately, because they value our unique take on the news of the moment, rather than because they typed some key words into a search bar and our article happened to be the top result. They share the numbers as if they have anything to do with us, as if our tweaks and adjustments make the difference. I suspect it's just to help us feel invested in the website's success. But the truth is, there's not much we can do to influence the figures one way or another.

For the next twenty-five minutes, we listen as Ashley talks us through the stats from the past few weeks. Lexi stares and blinks, her eyes two lasers pointed at the side of Ashley's head. I almost expect to see smoke leaking out from behind her ear. I can tell Lexi intimidates Ashley, because whenever Lexi attends these meetings, Ashley's skin shines like half-melted wax and her voice reaches the height of sucked helium, each sentence drawing up a nervous octave at the end.

We are *all* a little bit afraid of Lexi. I think it's because she feels no pressure to smile, nod or coo reassuringly as she listens to you talk. She is still and silent until your mouth stops moving, and sometimes even for several seconds after, as if what you'd just said was so utterly disappointing that you couldn't possibly be finished. Right now, as Ashley reads off the top-performing articles from the end of November, a list we can plainly see for ourselves since it's currently blasted on the large screen behind her golden-hour hair, Lexi sits with elbows jabbing the armrests, fingers steepled under her chin. She hasn't moved in a full minute, not even to blink.

Ashley concludes her speech with a single hopeful sigh. One finely threaded eyebrow migrates an inch closer to her honeyed hairline. When Lexi doesn't immediately respond, Ashley turns to the rest of us for encouragement. I stop just short of giving her a thumbs-up, settling for a wan smile. Ashley's optimistic oval face droops slightly, but she recovers.

"Keep up the great work!" she shouts, too loud, her words an air punch.

Lexi pushes her chair back and stands.

"Good job, team," she says flatly, as if we're all her teenage daughters and we've disappointed her by bringing home a C minus on our math test. She glides out the door, an Olympian on ice skates. Ashley's gaze follows Lexi's retreating oatmeal cashmere silhouette with such longing on her face that I actually start to feel a little bad for hating her as much as I do. But she notices me watching and narrows her eyes, a thin smirk ironing her glossed lips.

"You are free to go," she says.

And I do.

2

Most nights I go straight home at 6:01, dodging eye contact with anyone who appears overly friendly on my way to the elevator. But when Mariah Walker, the web producer with soft brown eyes and a shy smile who sits next to me at the bullpen, messages to invite me to happy hour, something inside me glitches and I say yes.

It's not that I'm against friendship. I crave it like anyone else. More. I'm needy as an addict, thirsting for that shy, punch-drunk intimacy that's so easy for girls to stumble upon in high school and college and gets harder and harder to come by in the years following graduation. But I've always thought of coworkers like the dusty porcelain dolls you inherit from the great-grandmother you visited twice before she died: you didn't choose them, yet you're saddled with them, 'til death or untimely resignation do you part.

I don't know what makes me agree to a drink (*just one*, I pledge) on this, the Monday-ist of Mondays. Maybe it's the drab sameness of everything, from the space-age couches to the empty sky to the deadened expressions on all of our faces as we type, type, type into oblivion. Or maybe it's the utter disdain I clock in Ashley's eyes before she dismisses us from the team check-in, like she's suddenly realized what we've implicitly understood this whole time—that Lexi doesn't give a shit about her and never will. That all of this effort is for nothing.

All I know is I feel myself evaporating like the top layer of water from a glass left out too long in the heat of a July afternoon. My edges blend into the atmosphere and I need something, preferably alcohol-based, to keep me from spiraling into the ether.

I zip my laptop into my backpack and my body into my jacket as I wait for the others. Together we march down the aisle, past the two distinct after-six camps: the editors and writers with spines balled over their keyboards, showing no sign of packing up even though it's five-past, and the account managers from Sales who ring the kitchen island, topaz beer bottles sweating in their hands and off-the-clock grins plastered on their faces.

As I press the button to call the elevator to our floor, Mariah leans close.

"I'm glad you're coming," she whispers, her voice a scratch against my eardrum.

I see us in the wall mirror; I look pleased, if a bit startled. The elevator arrives and we climb on.

Blinkers is a few blocks downtown from our office, a dingy, ripped hole of a place. The walls are crowded with photos of prizewinning horses in mid-race and tabloid covers from the '90s and early '00s. *National Enquirer* and Seabiscuit. Monica Lewinsky and Anna Nicole Smith. We pile into a booth in the back, pulling over a chair at the head of the table for Tom. He offers to buy the first round, takes our requests, and shunts off to the bar. Chivalry might be dead, but Tom is leaping onto the casket just before it lowers into the ground.

The entire web production team is here, all five of us. Besides Mariah, Tom, and me, nestled next to a framed *New York Daily Mirror* dated June 1997 featuring a photo of JonBenét Ramsey in her bridal white pageant dress, there's Carly Aster and Emily Blandino, two small dark-haired girls from Los Angeles who are practically identical, except Emily is half-Japanese with more refined facial features. Today they wear flared black jeans on their toothpick legs, black leather mules, and oversized sweaters in slightly different shades of beige.

Carly and Emily are both aspiring social media influencers; as Tom places their spicy margaritas on the table, they pull out their cell phones and take turns snapping photos with the flashlights hovering like fireflies. First, Emily lifts the glass to her lips and licks the salt rim, a mischievous glint in her eye, while Carly takes her picture. Then they trade places, setting up for Carly's shot. She balances the frosty glass on her head, holding it in place with one hand. Finally, they bring their heads together and hold out both phones at the same time. Satisfied with the options, they duck and squint at the photo-editing apps pulled up on their screens.

Mariah clears her throat. "I'm glad we all got together like this; it's been a while."

I know this is directed toward me. The rest, the girls at least, go out for drinks about once a month. They always ask me to join, and usually I say no. The last time I said yes was almost eight months ago, when I was still new enough and desperate enough to try.

"Me too," I say, lifting my wine toward the center of the group in a loose gesture. The pinot noir I requested has been poured so heavily it nearly sloshes over the lip of the glass.

"How about that meeting today?" Carly asks. Her phone is now on the table beside her margarita, intermittently lighting up.

"Lexi is *such* a bitch, and Ashley is so desperate for her approval. I can't watch it anymore," Mariah says. She's sweet in a leader-of-a-suburban-book-club sort of way, but there's bite to her, especially when she's talking about our bosses, who none of us can stand. Ashley and Lexi clash on a deep, chemical level. You can feel it in the air when they are in the same room, like the charge before a thunderstorm.

"It's fucking embarrassing," Emily says, shaking her head.

I take another sip of wine. Raising my eyes over the lip of the glass, I notice Tom watching me, and not the way a man with a wife normally would or should. There is no trace of his grunting daytime personality here. He looks serious and focused as he licks a line of beer foam off his top lip with all the determination of a promise.

"So," he says.

"So," I say.

The other girls are too busy diagnosing Lexi and Ashley with a variety of psychological disorders to pay attention to us. Their conversation is risky and offensive, and I'm glad to be tucked away from it, cordoned off by Tom's unrelenting focus. Music and voices cymbal-crash above us. The noise has a cushioning effect; I could say anything and only he would hear.

"Why do you do it?" I ask. As the question waterfalls from my mouth, I make a decision: if he says anything along the lines of *"Do what?"* I will get up and go home. If he understands, I will finish my drink, and maybe have another.

Tom sighs. "I wanted to be an editor when I was younger. Like the head of *Esquire* or *GQ*, that was the big dream. But life happened, you know? The death of print, student loans. Paying rent and getting married. It all just kind of hit me around the same time. I started producing, because it was steady work, and the only kind I could get in this field without any impressive internships. Sometimes I pitch articles to the vertical editors at the website, or other places. I've gotten a few clips, nothing major. Still hoping for that big break, I guess.

"How about you?" he adds.

I lower my eyes into the reflective surface of my pinot noir. Edith is there, smiling up at me over the rim of her typewriter, elbows jauntily tucked into her sides. I swirl the liquid and the image dissolves. The wine settles and rearranges to show me my own murky silhouette.

I laugh nervously. "Yeah, me too. Well, without the marriage part."

Tom rubs at his wedding ring, polishing the gold with his right thumb. I can't tell if he's sending me a subtle message, *stop this now*, or if it's an unconscious gesture. Maybe he doesn't even feel the ring anymore, it's become such a part of him, like a birthmark or a scar. While I'm thinking about the ring, I realize that he really is handsome, with his strawberry blond hair flopping boyishly over his forehead.

"You're low," Tom says, and it takes me a few seconds to realize he's talking about my wine. "Want another drink?"

I drain the contents of the glass.

"Sure."

The room turns syrupy sometime after my third glass, all the lights and colors running together. Sensory overload. Mariah has her arm around my shoulder, and we've switched places so that JonBenét's cherubic face now floats next to her deep tan one.

"I am *so* glad you came! This is so much fun!" Mariah scream-whispers at me.

To Emily and Carly, she shouts, "I fucking love this girl!"

They let out a *whoop*, toss their arms in the air, and clink glasses. Margarita chutes down their forearms. Emily licks at hers. I wonder where Tom is and then he appears, sliding into the booth next to me so the three of us are squished together on the bench, with me in the middle. The pleather under us makes little mouse squeaks whenever we adjust. The air is sticky and warm, heavy with breath and sweat and beer.

My head feels heavy, too, and I long for a pillow. I wilt, lolling gently in the crook of Mariah's neck, burying my cheek in her tangled braids.

I've been drunker, but not for a long time.

Another arm snakes around my neck and Tom leans in. I can't make out what he's saying at first, but each word becomes clear on a slight delay, like dock lights blinking on in the dusk over a lake: "Do. You. Want. To. Dance. With. Me?"

Before I can respond, he has me by the waist and is guiding me through the crowd of clean-shaven men in slacks and crisp shirts, women in dresses so tight their flesh oozes out on either side, reminding me of toothpaste. I giggle at a blonde girl's jiggly cleavage and she glares at me.

Tom leads me to a small clearing at the back of the bar. Not really a dance floor, but a few couples are using it as one. They sway, holding each other up like blocks in a doomed Jenga tower. This part of the room is quieter, the music more clearly audible. I can now see that it's coming from two speakers high above the arched doorway leading to the bathrooms. Even in my fuzzy state I manage one distinct thought: *I can't believe so many people are here on a Monday night.*

Tom whirls me around and pulls me smack into his chest, not an inch of space between us. At the moment of our collision, I think not of Tom's wife, but of Lexi from work. Of what she would say if she saw me like this, sloppy. Probably nothing, but it would be the soul-destroying form of nothing. Tom's heartbeat leaps in time with the music, yo-yoing softly against my breastbone. I feel my heart yo-yoing in response.

We bob gently to the beat, out of time with the lively tempo. It's almost romantic.

Then the thumping dance track ends and the room takes a breath.

When the next song starts, it seems, just for an instant, to come from inside my head. Like maybe I'm dead and this is what happens, an angel chorus trapped between the ears, welcoming you to the afterlife. It starts slow, like a ballad. The singer's voice is liquid crystal. After a few bars, a catchy garage beat kicks in, the snare drum boasting an idiosyncratic thump. And over that beat, all the time, leading the charge, that voice. That voice is lifting me up, turning me upside down, dismantling my skeleton and putting the bones back together in a new and improved orientation. Restructuring me.

The words don't register, just the saintly quality of the vocal cords vibrating in the singer's swanlike throat. She sounds familiar in a way I can't place, like an aria once memorized and long forgotten, a church hymn from bygone days of attempted piety. It makes me think of Edith again, typing eternally in the photo next to my sleeping head, forever frozen in time. The song, the voice, they both have the same effervescent quality as Edith's smile, whatever it is that I keep chasing.

Tom tugs at my hips and I realize I've stopped dancing. She's saying the same phrase. Over and over again, a chant or a prayer. Tom's mouth is moving but I can't hear him, or I don't want to. I shake my head and he repeats himself, louder, forcing me to comprehend. "What's wrong?"

He has his hands wrapped around my forearms now, and I can feel his wedding ring, the metal cold and hard against my skin. I shake him off and yell, "I have to go! Tell the girls I said bye!"

And then I'm running, ignoring the *heys* and *watch outs*

from the people I slam into on my way out the door, those toothpaste girls and their sloppy men, and into the brisk night.

The whole cab ride to Brooklyn I hope to hear the song on the radio, proof I didn't dream it, like a message from whatever god is out there. *I'll believe in you if you show me a miracle*, I think. But the driver is blasting reggae. He mumbles, watching me in the rearview mirror. I shake my head; I can't hear.

He turns the stereo dial. "Anything you want to listen to instead?"

I shake my head again. "This is fine."

The driver turns up the volume knob but keeps it several notches lower than before. The song from the bar wiggles back into my skull. An earworm: a song that swarms. But I only remember the outline, the general shape of the instrumentals. The rest slips easily out of my mind's grasp.

The city glides by, buildings scattered against the starless night. Soon we're traversing the bridge and descending into the quiet alleys of my borough. My section of Brooklyn is nearly suburban, shadowed with brownstones on tree-lined streets, only the occasional desperate siren or troubled shout punctuating the air.

The car pulls up outside my building. I climb out, mumbling an ill-formed *thank you*. I unlock the front door and take the crumbling stairs two at a time until I reach the third floor, apartment 3A. Inside I kick my Vans off by the shoe rack. The living room light is on, but my roommate is not there. I hit the switch and go straight into my bedroom, shutting the door as best I can. My room, the bigger of the two because I'm the one who found the apartment and secured the lease, is sealed off from the rest of the unit by a set of French doors that don't close properly. They give the room a certain romance, a pleasing draftiness that lets me pretend, on temperate nights, that I am the heroine of an arthouse movie, an ambiance further aided by the sheer white curtains I hung over the glass panels for a modicum of privacy, and the tarnished gold knobs that came with the place. Otherwise, it's a mess of clutter. Clothing climbing the furniture and torn-edge posters—old favorite bands, Tarantino and Coppola (Sofia, not Francis) films—on the walls.

I strip off my sweater, nestle into bed still wearing my jeans, and dig my ancient MacBook, a gift from my parents for high school graduation, out from underneath a towering stack of books on the floor. Edith smiles in the pool of streetlight that reaches my room from three floors down. I flick on the lamp next to the bed and the light bathes her in a warm glow, a warped floral pattern from a scarf tied around the shade stretching across her face and creating shadows on the wall.

The laptop takes a few wheezing moments to power up, another minute to load the browser. I attempt to plug combinations of words into the search bar. The cursor lags a few steps behind me, and then the letters flood the empty field in a mad rush.

I recognize her as soon as her photo loads on the sidebar— her sharp ponytail and pointed chin. Adriana Argento is one of those celebrities everyone is aware of even if they think they aren't. She got her start on some cable show for tweens when I was in high school, too old to have paid attention, though I absorbed knowledge of her through cultural osmosis. The show was canceled after two seasons and, free of her sugary on-screen image, her airheaded persona, Adriana aggressively restyled herself as a serious musical artist. The song I heard at Blinkers is her newest single. I click on a Pitchfork review, skip the text, and find the music video embedded at the bottom of the page. It buffers for a second and then opens on an electrified cityscape at night, much like the one I watched from the taxi window not an hour earlier. A kind of skewed, apocalyptic New York. The words *Adriana Argento* are skywritten above the buildings in soft pink letters and as the camera zooms, the letters spiral outward. I slip through a rose window and find Adriana gazing mournfully out another window at the end of a rootless corridor. It stretches into infinity. The camera tracks toward her, I'm *walking* toward her, as she breaks into that celestial introduction.

The tempo picks up and Adriana climbs down from the window ledge, trailing a platinum blond braid and oily black skirt. She makes searing eye contact with the camera, with me, before jumping straight through the floor. A web of fairy lights, the same ones that decorate millions of college dorm rooms and first adult apartments, places she has never lived, break her fall. She kicks one razor-heeled boot as she hangs there, a mystical spider caught in its own miraculous web.

I watch the rest with chills running down the back of my arms, feeling ridiculous and smeary-eyed drunk. The camera pans in and out of different buildings and we see different Adrianas engaged in curious activities: Adriana hangs from scaffolding in a tulle dress, her wrists looking far too fragile to keep her from falling. Adriana dances on an empty stage. Floats in a hot-air balloon. Stomps on a dollhouse. Sits cross-legged on the floor of a room as white and bland as a hospital corridor. Holds up masks of her own face, each one blinking false eyelashes and mouthing the lyrics through shellacked lips.

I should hate this. It's bombastic and it bears no resemblance to the stripped-down guitar ballads, the sad boys and girls I plug my ears with when I can no longer stand to hear myself think or when I walk home from the subway or when I need to be reminded of love or heartbreak because any real memories of those feelings as I have known them evade me.

And yet, this *does* resemble those songs, in a way. It is similarly raw and honest.

According to Pitchfork, this is her first song since Sophie Heffernan was murdered near the Staples Center during Adriana's Los Angeles stop on her last tour. Sophie was fifteen, blonde and blue-eyed, the platonic ideal of the victim. The tickets were a birthday gift from her mom, and she attended with a friend, whose name was withheld by the media because of her status as a minor.

Between the end of the opening act and the start of Adriana's set, Sophie went to the bathroom and never came back to her seat. Her friend stayed through the entire show, so dazed by Adriana's presence she could hardly remember when Sophie left. Her body was found nestled against a dumpster a block away from the arena, a knife stuck through her thrown-back hand, giving the illusion of being pinned into place. The word *Hazardous*, Adriana's latest album, was written in blood beside her body, a bag from the merch stand and a blood-soaked Adriana Argento T-shirt tucked under her head like a pillow.

Strangest of all was the ivy coiled around Sophie's wrists and ankles, a reference to the nickname for the Adriana fandom—the Ivies, an homage to her first number one hit, "Poisoned Ivy."

The description of her death is familiar; it was the first major news story to break after I started at the website, when I was still training. I shied away from the details then, as I always do when dealing in real tragedy. Tonight, alone in my bedroom, the song on repeat, I look closer.

My head rocks against the closed subway door between stops. A deep ache pulses between my eyes, and my stomach churns every time I'm jostled by a stranger, which is often, because it's rush hour on the Q. I slept weird, gory nightmares and a dry mouth shaking me awake every few hours.

The web producers' bullpen is empty when I arrive. Mariah comes in first, clutching a venti from Starbucks. Emily and Carly slump in next like a pair of used Kleenex, translucent and shriveled. They remove bug-eyed sunglasses to reveal sunken purple eyes shipwrecked in the middle of pale, bland faces. None of us speak. We are hungover, not only from the alcohol, but from the awkward intimacy of a late night at a crowded bar. I sink lower in my torturous chair, every lump stabbing at my hips and spine, and shove my headphones deeper into my ears, avoiding everyone. Tom still hasn't shown up by nine fifteen. As I take note of his absence, my computer dings. A Piger notification dances across the screen.

Tom Powell has posted in #editorial.

Despite myself, I check his message: not feeling so great, WFH!

If it's possible, Carly goes a shade paler. She shrinks and then vaults from her seat in the direction of the bathroom. I glance at Emily, then Mariah. They focus hard on their computer screens. I open a direct message.

Hey. What happened after I left?

An ellipsis flits for a few agonizing seconds before Mariah's response comes through.

Got weird. Carly and Tom disappeared for an hour.

Dot dot dot.

Still glad u came, tho! We should do it again soon.

I minimize the conversation without replying. The knowledge of Tom and Carly, an alliance between them, twitches in my hands. I don't know Tom's wife and I owe her nothing. Yet I feel like this is my fault, as if by leaving when I did, I

somehow pushed them together, created the cosmic circum-
stances that led to their union. Maybe if I'd stayed, things
would've been different. I imagine myself exercising the pious
restraint of a straight-backed nun, dancing a friendly distance
away from Tom, pecking him on the cheek before ferrying
myself home, alone.

But then I remember the heady clamminess of the steamy
bar, the electric jolt of his wedding ring on the skin under my
pushed-up sweater. Who the fuck am I kidding?

I work harder than I have all year to keep my mind off of
everything. I even manage to eke out a small sense of pride
in how polished the website looks, how lifelike and crisp the
images are, how all the links open in a new tab, everything
in its proper order.

Is this what it feels like, to enjoy what you do?

I'm deleting emails after my final coffee of the day, striving
for the elusive Inbox Zero, when a chat box appears on the
screen, headlined by Tom's full name. It's blank, so I think
maybe it's a glitch, or the product of some bored technologi-
cal deity who likes toying with people's emotions during the
afternoon slump and probably sits at a blank slate desk just like
mine, without even a cubicle for the illusion of privacy, until
I see that telltale ellipsis pulsing next to the photo of Tom in
lumberjack plaid, an ax jauntily tossed over one shoulder and
a field of trees flooding the background.

He types for nearly a minute, the symbol skipping like a
heartbeat. Then it disappears and the text box remains empty.
I watch the blank field for a few seconds before bouncing my
cursor on the X.

3

Tom keeps a framed photo of his wife next to the large monitor plugged into his laptop. The image faces away from me, but I saw it up close once, very early in my time at the website, a late night when I'd ended up in the office alone, having spent all day too overwhelmed to get any work done. Touching nothing, I crept around to various workstations, taking in the rubble of other people's work lives, their staplers and day planners, pen cups lined with dust, everything decorated with an inspirational slogan, wondering what life would be like if we didn't need platitudes to convince us it was all worth it.

Slowly, I worked my way into a large circle, ending up at Tom's side of the bullpen, his chair directly opposite mine. In the picture, Tom's wife sits alone at a kitchen table, her face tilted to the right as if she's speaking to the photographer. She is pretty but plain, with long blond hair and a chunky Irish fisherman sweater, roomy so as to illustrate just how petite she is. Prettier than Carly, certainly, and likely prettier than me, too, though I've never been confident in evaluating my own physical appearance. Sometimes I forget that I even have a body, a face. I move uneasily, walking into traffic, creating narrow misses, all because I don't keep track of where I am in space, or the fact that others can see me. Tom's wife rests her elbows on the table alongside a milk carton and a cereal bowl, the contents partially eaten. There's a spoon perched in her left hand, and her eyes are tight-lined with black liner. Otherwise, her face appears bare and natural.

There's something about the photo that I noticed right away, a blurred quality; it seemed obvious to me that Tom was the one behind the camera, the candidness of the snapshot showing off just how in love they really were, and I wonder what happened.

Adriana Argento, born in 1991, was raised in Sacramento, and made her Broadway debut at age fourteen in a musical called *One Summer*. She played the lead role of Summer Smith, a high school freshman struggling with first love and her parents' divorce over—yes—a single summer.

Her biography collects like coins in my mind's dull corners, all the facts of this stranger's life mounting together. Her social media accounts are as full of glamour shots and tour videos as they are slice-of-life moments: being silly with friends, snuggling her dog, singing in the car, kissing her boyfriend, Nolan Lynch, a white rapper who goes by the stage name Dr. No.

I don't care about celebrities and I'm proud of not caring. I don't follow the dating lives of the rich and famous or stalk their upcoming projects. I believe the art I love is entirely separate from the people who created that art. It has never been about the people behind the scenes.

And yet. *Her.*

One photo in particular snags my attention. In it, Adriana and Nolan crouch on either side of the yellow line down a dark street, meeting to kiss in the middle. Her tall ponytail is a shot of sepia against the blackness. Her sweatshirt sags off one fine-boned shoulder. He has a white baseball cap pulled low on his forehead, light brown stubble sprayed across his chin. They look almost normal, if normal were glazed over with the frosting of fame. Traffic doesn't stop for just anyone.

So, I have to wonder: What must it be like, to be so damn sure?

And this is how I find myself on a Wednesday afternoon using the website's Wi-Fi to watch clips of Adriana Argento interviews on the late-night, midday talk show circuit. It doesn't really matter; everyone in the office browses the internet constantly, for work purposes or otherwise. Being pop culture savvy is part of the job. Just in case, I minimize the screen anytime Lexi stands up from her desk, perpetually visible out of the corner of my eye. Only the editor-in-chief, the CEO, and the HR department have their own offices. The rest of us, editors and web producers and interns alike, share open-plan real estate.

I'm so absorbed in Adriana's conversation with Poppy Yates on *Nightly with Poppy* that I skip my second coffee break, then my third.

She's wearing a pink strapless dress that poofs dramatically under the bust, tan boots that trellis up her thighs. Today, the ponytail is high on the crown of her head with a braid down the center. "I look like a gumdrop, don't I?" she giggles, tugging at the dress's abbreviated hem, flashing dimples and white teeth, and sitting on her hands.

"Stop, you're stunning," Poppy says in her clipped British accent.

She does, and she is. This put-upon ignorance, this denial of her beauty should be irritating, but it further endears me to her. I find her self-deprecation relatable, if unearned. Not everyone looks like that, but we all feel like that.

"So, don't keep us waiting! Tell us about the new song."

"It's sort of a response, you know? To everything that happened on my last tour." She raises big eyes to the rafters and fans away tears with her false lashes. The way her mouth puckers, as if she's tasted something sour, I can tell the emotion behind the gesture is real.

"It's been almost two years since your last album, *Hazardous*. Are we getting close to another release?" Poppy asks.

"Yes, yes. My album, *solstice*, is coming this summer." She's interrupted by applause, which she rides out with a polite smile. "The title is supposed to invoke that feeling of the light and warmth that comes after a long winter. You know, like that first day when you realize it's still light out after seven p.m. That's the feeling."

A laugh bubbles up from her throat and she curls at the waist, hiding her giddy face behind her hands as another wave of excitement erupts from the audience. There's no sign of the tears from earlier; she's been flipped over as easily as a new penny.

"I like that—*solstice*," Poppy echoes, allowing the full weight to settle.

In another clip from the same taping, Adriana takes the stage suspended in a rainbow prism. The lyrics, now committed to my memory, embody the kind of happiness and freedom that can only come after a period of extreme hopelessness. The music, which I previously dismissed as trite in comparison to the vocals, calls to mind the scattering of clouds following a great rainstorm, that extreme and fleeting sensation of clarity, that moment after a break in your atmosphere, when you believe that you finally know everything and there can be no other surprises. Her voice, clear as a church bell, sends little tremors down my spine. She closes her eyes and sways with the music, and I sway along in my rock-hard chair. She could be any girl, locked in her bedroom, singing her heart into a hairbrush. I nearly turn away to grant her privacy.

A tap on my shoulder startles me and I slam the Enter key. Adriana freezes, her jaw clenched. The new girl, Meghan, stands on my left. She's retired the Ann Taylor business attire for a pair of dark wash jeans and a loose emerald-green silk button-down. A circular gold necklace glints on her décolletage. Squinting, I realize the pendant is embossed with the silhouette of Athena holding a bow and arrow.

"Hello," she says.

"Um, hi."

"I just wanted to thank you for helping me get my bearings the other day." Meghan's eyes skip over to my computer screen. "You an Ivy?"

"A what?"

"An Adriana Argento fan."

"Oh. Uh. Not really?" This feels like a lie, so I continue, "I like her new song."

"She can really sing, huh?" Meghan says.

"Yeah."

An awkward silence hangs in the air.

"Well, anyway. I'd love to get lunch sometime."

"No one takes lunch around here." As soon as the words clear my lips, I wish I could take them back. Do I always have to be such a bitch?

Meghan laughs. "I've noticed. But that doesn't mean we can't, right?"

"I…guess. I mean, that'd be nice."

"Cool, so. I'll see you around."

She jerks her wrist in a shallow wave, mirroring the curve of her fingers with a little eye roll that turns her away from my desk. I swivel around in my chair, feeling stupid. There's a flurry of movement across the table: Tom, lowering his eyes.

I think *What do you want from me?*

I think *Leave me alone.*

I don't say anything.

It takes me a long time to commit. I check her Instagram at least once a day for several weeks, but I don't follow her or like any of the photos. At work, on my commute, late nights, early mornings, I listen to her music. All of it, in order, a forced march, skipping nothing until I'm humming the tunes interchangeably during the moments when I don't have my headphones in, yet I don't buy any of the albums.

All three of Adriana Argento's studio records have charted in the top ten on the Billboard 200. She has 150 million followers on Instagram and 35 million YouTube subscribers. She routinely sells out the biggest venues in the biggest cities, tens of thousands of people, all ages, screaming every word, mimicking the intake of her breath.

At first, I resist being grouped in with her sea of fans. I cling to my individuality. By virtue of my upbringing, I had long believed in my own specialness. My parents taught me that I could do anything, be anything. Yet I'd always felt unoriginal at my core. The drive to stand out was stifling. So, in the end, it's the sense of anonymous belonging that attracts me. There's a certain appeal in shedding the burden of uniqueness, in accepting that you are one of millions, a cog in the wheel of her stardom. Each time I stream a song, watch a video, click a heart icon, the count ticks up by one: a single number, a drop, a particle. That's all I will ever be to Adriana Argento—a symbol on a screen, an inconsequential dash of money in a bank account she pays someone else to handle, a singular adoring light in an arena of thousands.

It's when I lean into it entirely, when I finally click Follow, click Subscribe, click Download, that I understand the appeal.

The most efficient way to lose yourself is to idolize somebody else.

Adriana and Nolan are baking cookies. There are two tubs of raw dough set on the counter. Nolan lifts the lids off gingerly with his tattooed hands, taking all the care of a jeweler displaying precious stones on a velvet cushion. Adriana's eggshell acrylics creep into the frame like bleach-tipped spider's legs, and her laugh trills in the background as Nolan waves his hands over the open containers, a magician presenting his assistant for audience consumption. They roll the raw dough into tight, moist balls with the palms of their hands.

"Nice balls," Adriana cracks in her heady soprano. More laughter, the full-throated kind, comes from them both. They're two kids finding themselves much funnier than they are, and I'm intoxicated on their energy, curled on my side on the sagging living room couch, the one I dragged up three flights of stairs from the sidewalk when I first moved into this apartment, before I really understood bed bugs. Luckily, the couch was a rare curbside gem—clean, in good condition, could be from West Elm if you squint and tilt your head to the right.

A door creaks and my roommate, Sasha, appears in the kitchenette. I slam my laptop closed on instinct, as if she just caught me watching porn, which it feels like she did. Sasha took a gap year before college to follow Conor Oberst on tour; there's no way she'd understand this *thing*. She pads toward the sink and turns on the faucet, letting water trickle on her wrist as she waits for it to cool. Our kitchen sink has the opposite problem of most New York sinks; it runs hot, even when only the cold tap is on.

I sit up and watch as she pulls a lidless mason jar out of the cabinet, fills it to the brim with water. She turns away from the sink and yelps when she notices me sitting there. Water splashes down the front of her ribbed gray tank top. "Dammit, make a *noise*."

"Sorry. I didn't mean to scare you."

"What are you doing out here?"

I glance down at my closed laptop, still humming with the memory of Nolan and Adriana, their confessional laughter. "Just catching up on some…news."

"Do it louder next time," Sasha says, dabbing at her shirt with a paper towel.

We're not friends, exactly, but she's not always this much of a cunt. Work must've been bad today. Sasha is a production assistant at a daytime television show that films in Rockefeller Plaza, and her job is even worse than mine.

Mostly, we ignore each other, but sometimes our dynamic develops the antagonistic edge of a popular girl encountering a band geek in an empty high school hallway. I tolerate it because she is quiet, rarely home, and always able to pay the rent on time.

Discarding the paper towel on the counter, Sasha opens the refrigerator, ducks to retrieve a Chobani from her stash on the top shelf and pops the foil lid. She bangs around in the silverware drawer for a spoon, making more noise than necessary, as though to illustrate her point. With a resounding slam of her bedroom door, she's gone. I push the computer off my lap and stand, slowly crossing the room. When I reach the counter, I lift the damp paper towel with two fingers and drop it into the trash.

The cookies come out of the oven twenty minutes later. Bronzed, with chocolate chips the color of wet asphalt. Nolan loosens them from the baking sheet with a metal spatula. My mouth waters. Adriana holds the camera up close with one hand as she pours milk into a mug with the other. In the next video, the largest cookie links their two hands. Her fingers are delicate as handblown glass, his are charcoal-etched with tattoo ink and nicotine. Together, they dip the cookie into the milk. I fall asleep without dinner, sheets twisted around my legs, utterly alone and dreaming of dessert.

4

Tom follows me when I go to the kitchen for my first coffee on Friday morning. We haven't spoken since the night last week at Blinkers. The silence is merely circumstantial on my end; I'm simply not sure what there is to say. I concentrate hard on the stirring of milk into coffee, squinting at the center whirlpool like a scientist examining a rare specimen, even as I feel Tom come up behind me, his breath on the back of my neck, the shift of his weight creaking the flooring. He reaches past me to rinse his mug in the sink, his arm hovering a few inches over my shoulder. Several water droplets collect on the cuff of my shirt. He stands there, watching.

"How many cups do you drink a day?"

I tug my eyes away from the rhythmic swirl of the spoon to take him in. They resist, landing somewhere in the amorphous valley between the collar of his shirt and the blush-pink corner of his mouth. "Four."

"Me too. At least that many. Sometimes I lose count." He swallows. I'm disturbed by how easy it is for me to picture the coffee going down the hidden machinery of his throat.

"Listen, uh, about the other night? At Blinkers? If I made you uncomfortable…"

"Uncomfortable? Why would I be uncomfortable?"

"Well, we were dancing, and you ran off? Figured I must've done something to chase you away."

Could he really still be flirting with me? I can't explain why I left when I did. Sure, I knew dancing with him was a bad idea. The wedding ring, the wife it symbolizes. But it's not that simple. I was drunk enough not to fully grasp the difference between right and wrong, drunk enough to be ready to make some mistakes. When that Adriana Argento song came on, it pierced me in the heart with stunning lucidity. But I can't tell Tom any of that.

I shake my head. "It wasn't you."

"That's what they always say," he says, and his laugh is dry as a thumb scratching sandpaper.

What I think is: *Aren't you married?*

What I say is: "Are you bringing your wife to the holiday party?"

He looks momentarily stunned but recovers.

"Nah, just me," he says.

"Cool. Guess I'll see you there."

I take my coffee into the handicap stall and lock the door. A smile traces the mug's curve as I drink.

Nolan Lynch has been in love with Adriana since they met on the set of the music video for "Poisoned Ivy," on which he is featured. It's obvious in the barely contained glee splashed on his face as he watches her singing and dancing. He teases her throughout the video, a schoolboy tugging at a pretty classmate's hair without any menace. In one scene he comes up behind her as she's pouting at the camera and hooks an arm across her waist. They both laugh as she falls into the cush-

ion of his oversized sweater. He does his verse up close. Their
mouths almost touch. She pulls away suddenly, swiping the hat
off his head and lowering it over her glossy, cascading curls.
Everything about her was softer back then: her sound, her lip
gloss, her curled hair ribbons and coquettish skirts.

They move closer and closer as the song begins its long fade.
I find I'm holding my breath. I release only when they do,
finally, kiss. You can see, in the working of his jaw, the press
of her lips, how much they both mean it. I wonder what it's
like to have your first kiss with your future boyfriend viewed
by over 400 million strangers.

I've never been in love. Maybe I thought I was, once. So
long ago it happened in a dream, to someone else. But no one
has ever kissed me like that.

Carly leans down to pull a black pump over the hump of her
heel. She sits on the bathroom counter, one bare foot braced
in front of her hip, the heeled foot dangling like a fishing line
toward the floor. Emily checks her lip gloss in the mirror. I'm
next in line for a stall, holding my black velvet dress in one
hand and a Ziploc bag bulging with makeup in the other. I'm
tapping my foot to dispel my nervous energy.

A door swings open and the room stands still. Lexi steps
out of the handicap stall, a midnight-blue dress clinging to her
hips and flowing all the way down to the gold straps gilding
her ankles. A pearl-studded barrette holds her piecey bangs
off her face. She pauses to wash her hands next to Emily, who
lowers her tube of gloss. Lexi fixes a nonexistent smudge of
red lipstick with a moist finger, like a Grecian statue examining her own beauty. Then she saunters out, taking the tension with her.

Her musky perfume lingers in the stall when I step in and
lock the door.

★ ★ ★

The office is trashed, work clothes and bags strewn about on every available surface like dead fish after an oil spill. There's a dystopian energy in the air, the festive shouts and the smell of alcohol from open beers and bottles of tequila only adding to the strangeness of seeing my daily surroundings upended by unusual factors.

The three of us pick our way back to the web producers' bullpen to collect our jackets, stash our extra makeup and day-time shoes for the night. The website's holiday party is held every year at the same trendy hotel on the Lower East Side. The pictures online show a geometric tower of glass and a rooftop with sculptural views of Lower Manhattan.

Anticipation courses through me. For one night, I am eager to act like someone who loves her job, at least enough to dance in front of a picture window facing the East River at her first company holiday party.

A cluster of people are pre-gaming in the kitchen, clutching plastic cups full of sticky, sour liquor. Meghan is among them, standing outside the circle with her mouth gaping open, as if waiting for a moment to speak. I decide I don't need to get started this early and head downstairs to the main lobby with Carly and Emily, where Mariah is waiting.

"Where's Tom?" I ask as I slide into the back of the cab.

"He's meeting us there," Carly calls from the front seat. She turns to the driver and says, "Corner of Rivington and Essex, please."

As the car pulls away from the curb, I get the urge to hang my head out the window like a puppy, to taste the groggy city air as it rushes past my outstretched tongue. But Emily is next to me, and though she's absorbed in whatever she's looking at on her phone, I don't want to draw her attention. I settle for pressing my forehead to the window and watching the streetlights reveal my reflection. I got up early that morning and scraped my hair into a tall ponytail, using a picture of Adriana on the *Billboard Music Awards* red carpet as a guide. I even smoothed the ends with Sasha's expensive straightener, carefully rewrapping the cord and slipping it back under the sink so she wouldn't notice. That was hours ago, and now the static from my coat causes the bottom of the ponytail to frizz. The back seat is cramped. Carly fiddles with the dial on the radio, flicking from one station to the next, taking a selfie at every traffic light. I wouldn't blame the driver if he opened the door and pushed her onto the street like I can tell he wants to, but he stares straight ahead as if he's alone.

After about twenty minutes stalling through traffic, the cab pulls up in front of the hotel, and we tumble onto the sidewalk. We're already acting kind of drunk, talking too loudly and smiling at nothing. This is how the most dangerous nights start, giddy and loose. And why shouldn't tonight get a little dangerous? We work hard all year. Or, if not *hard*, then we work tough, subjugating ourselves for the good of this website. This is our one moment, when we walk into a thumping room and set ourselves free on the company's dime. We earned this.

We're greeted by the concierge, crammed into an elevator with a bunch of blondes from Sales, and sent flying several floors above the city. My first thought, when the doors glide open like parting curtains, is that we're at the wrong party, on the wrong floor, at the wrong hotel. There are too many beautiful people, too many chandeliers, for this to be ours.

I recognize Charlotte first, vampiric in red glitter lipstick and a diaphanous cream slip dress, a diagonal seam bisecting her from left hip to right thigh. She and Ashley, Glinda-like in sparkling ruffles, sip flutes of champagne by the bar. Lexi stands apart at the hors d'oeuvres table, carefully selecting a stuffed mushroom.

"Let's get a drink!" Carly says brightly, tugging Emily by the wrist.

Mariah and I follow. At the bar we all order red wine. Emily and Carly take turns photographing each other, glasses aloft, in front of a wide window that divulges the glistening Lower Manhattan backsplash. Camera flashes draw the attention of a few people clustered nearby. A man I don't recognize with gelled black hair and a green velvet sport coat offers to take a shot on his tablet-sized iPhone, and Emily and Carly draw together at the hip.

Embarrassed, I turn toward Mariah.

"Cheers!" We clink and drink. This feels like what I remember of new friendship, the small ways you begin to align yourselves against the outer world, creating a sealed unit. The first sip of wine liquefies me, softening my muscles as the booze travels down my throat, burning. The room shimmers briefly before returning to normal, everything just a touch wilder and more vibrant. This is the best part of a night out, I think. The beginning, the first few sips.

Emily and Carly finish taking photos and dive into the crowd, where a large group that is either already intoxicated or doesn't need to be in order to dance has assembled. The music is loud, the song not particularly distinguishable from everything else in the current Top 40, yet everyone seems to know the words. I watch as they throw their bodies around. I can practically see sparks shooting off their shiny hair, their fringed skirts, their illuminated cheekbones, and a stab of envy shudders through me.

Then Tom appears at Mariah's side and my self-consciousness deepens a shade. I guzzle more wine as he says, "Hey."

There's something different about him tonight. Maybe it's the gray suit jacket, open over a partially unbuttoned blue shirt that highlights the dip of his throat. Maybe it's the clandestine flash of his eyes. Whatever it is, it pulls me in. I tilt toward him, squaring my shoulders parallel to his. I glance at his left hand, but it's tucked deep into a trouser pocket. The placement feels purposeful, for my particular benefit.

Mariah notices the change in my energy. She raises an eyebrow and says, "Hi, Tom."

"Ready to celebrate another year at this giant trash fire of a company?"

"You forget, it's my *first* year here. It's only, like, a miniature trash fire from my perspective," I say. It sounds better than my bitter, ugly truth, which is that I die a small death when I walk through the door each Monday morning.

"Just wait," Mariah adds. "It'll get worse."

"Worse than *that*?"

We follow Tom's gaze. The CEO, one of only a handful of men in the room, gyrates against a pencil-thin brunette I've never seen before. The buttons on his lavender shirt strain over his beer belly, and his tongue hangs out of his mouth. He resembles the dog I imagined myself imitating in the taxi.

"Does she even work with us?" I say.

"I *hope* not," Mariah mutters. "That's gotta be an HR violation."

We watch them for a few seconds longer until it becomes too awkward. A server twirls by, offering a silver platter of bacon-wrapped dates. I pop one into my mouth to avoid coming up with something else to say. Mariah's eyes flick from Tom to me to Tom and back to me, and then she excuses herself to get more wine. She's forcing me to make a choice while I'm still capable of rational thought. I picture Nolan Lynch and Adriana Argento, kissing urgently for the camera crew, hiding nothing. She was dating someone else at the time, another musician, a forgettable boy with an acoustic guitar. Her kiss with

Nolan was art-directed for public consumption. That doesn't make it less of a betrayal.

It's not that I fancy Tom to be my Nolan Lynch. There's nothing of that innocence between us, the sense that we are two trains destined to collide on the track. It's just that his mouth looks so soft in the amber light hanging over the bar and I've been so lonely.

I drain my beverage. The wine leaves my mouth dry. I feel the beginnings of a headache, a beast waking behind my skull, opening its furry eyes.

Tom is watching expectantly, like he's waiting for me to give him a sign.

I gesture with the empty glass, the bowl stained red. "Are you ready for another?"

Mostly, there are snippets.

Blue and purple lights. A salty, human smell. Someone bumps my elbow and I spill whatever I'm drinking. I can no longer tell the difference between red wine, white wine, rosé. My palate is sugared numb. It all tastes the same and I didn't eat enough dinner, but who eats real dinner at these things?

I think: *what's enough?*

I think: *how many stuffed mushrooms make a meal?*

I think: *why not?*

I'm dancing at the center of a circle and the song is playing or maybe I'm hallucinating and it's any other song. Every song is becoming that one song to me. Charlotte's teeth glow in the dark as she laughs. Lexi spins me around in a circle under myself and I must be dreaming. *I hate you!!* I think. I laugh out loud and so does Lexi, her mouth dripping wet, a cave I almost fall into. Then I think, *Wait, what's funny?*

I'm about to ask.

But then, arms around my waist. But then, cologne. But

then, a hand closing around mine. I see a tattooed wrist. *Nolan?* I think, stupidly. *What is he doing here? I knew I was at the wrong party.*

No, it's Tom. Cuffs rolled up. Had I really never seen him in short sleeves? It's at once impossible and so obvious, like everything about his arms pulling me into the tunnel of him and his lips grazing my hairline.

I knew the ponytail was a good idea.

We wind up on the roof. It's nearly empty, which is, initially, a surprise, before the cold begins to register, first held at a distance, and then I feel it sink into my skin layer by layer. Ah, yes. December. I picture my coat, fleetingly. Somewhere downstairs, which might as well be another galaxy. How will I ever get my coat back? If I once had a ticket for the coat check, it's likely gone by now. I can't bring myself to care, though I must be freezing. My dress is cheap, flimsy fake velvet and my arms are bare. I feel the chill, but it is removed, theoretical. I know I should be cold, so I'm cold. But I'm floating above, or below, the concept of temperature. The alcohol pads my senses, cushioning me from my temporal reality. Beetle-black sky, the watery lights on the horizon, and Tom's hand pushing into the small of my back, guiding me forward. Nothing is real, nothing is real, nothing is real.

I should be asking more questions. Instead, I sit down on the blocky couch he leads me toward. It faces the edge of the roof, that impressive view. My head feels heavy. I rest it on his shoulder as we look out. We lost the other three hours ago, or what feels like hours. Last time I saw them they were writhing in a tight knot on the dance floor, even Mariah, as Justin Bieber serenaded them over the DJ's throbbing speakers.

"That's what you pay for." I point to the shimmering skyline, think of Adriana climbing the scaffolding, her dress a disco ball, her body twisting away from the safety of the metal framework and into the sky. The city flattens and it's like a green screen, no dimension. At the other end of the roof deck, illuminated by the flicker of a heat lamp, elbows resting on the railing, is a solitary figure. Meghan. Her bangs are pushed to the side of her forehead, her metallic suit creased. From this angle she seems to be smoking, a cool puff emanating from her lips. When she moves her hand from her mouth, I realize she's just breathing, and the smoke is air. She doesn't look over, but I can feel her attention on us.

Tom inhales. I realize, with mild horror and amusement, that he is, in fact, smelling my hair.

"You're so…perplexing," he says, tongue tripping over the second *p*.

Where is your wife? This would be the time to say it. I should run like I did the last time we were this close. I should absolutely not turn my head so that our noses touch, so that we're breathing into each other, our lips parted, trading oxygen, keeping each other alive. Tom's eyes are so big and open from this angle, like pleading twin moons. He knocks a comma-shaped lock of hair off his forehead, and the sideways movement of his head lands in a kiss that sucks the breath out of my lungs for real. When I start to breathe normally again, I hear the sounds I make loud and gasping against his mouth. Tom's lips move thirstily. He's the desert, I'm the water. The kiss sobers me a little. Enough for me to notice he tastes like champagne and the gourmet pizza bagel he swallowed in one bite just before we climbed up onto the roof. Who eats a pizza bagel if they're planning to kiss someone? The sheer humanity of it wrenches me out of the moment. I'm not being fair, I know. I bet even Nolan Lynch—hell, even Adriana Argento— tastes like pizza sometimes. But it takes the magic right out of the kiss. I pull back and Tom shifts forward with me, reluctant to let me go.

"What is it?"

"Nothing, I just…shouldn't you be at home? You know, with your wife?"

A shadow crosses Tom's face, drawing his features inward. "I guess I misread what was going on here," he says.

"Maybe you should go find Carly."

It's the cruelest thing I could say, and by saying it, I've likely shattered any possibility that I will find myself in this situation, with this person, again. That's for the best, and yet. It was a good kiss, wasn't it? Before my quest for perfection and my skewed, belated morality got in the way. A good kiss, not a great kiss. If it had been a great kiss, I wouldn't have ruined it.

Tom looks confused, then ashamed. "Carly," he says. "Nothing happened with Carly."

I'm completely sober now and I don't believe him. I can see it so vividly, how he would have followed her outside after I left Blinkers. Pushed her against the wall and kissed her. He was so drunk he probably wouldn't have been able to tell that she wasn't me. All I want is to be home, wearing sweatpants, watching Adriana Argento videos on YouTube. If that makes me a fan, a cliché, an *Ivy*, so be it. Tom opens his mouth, but I'm up and moving before he can speak. I don't turn back, not even when I start to feel guilty. *He'll be fine*, I remind myself, *he is loved*. I see a mirage of his wife, her image from the photo on his desk, hovering in the reflection on the door's circular window, and I push my way inside.

Downstairs, I slink around the edge of the vibrating dance floor toward the coat check. As soon as Tom kissed me, when our mouths were still locked, I'd remembered where I left my ticket. Sure enough, the little orange cardboard square is zippered neatly into a pocket in the lining of my clutch. This is who I am—a woman who thinks through the possibilities, a woman incapable of spontaneity unless she's planned for it. A woman who puts her coat check ticket somewhere safe before she's too drunk.

I slip the coat check girl a dollar and leave without saying goodbye to anyone.

Hand thrust in the air to hail a taxi, I feel the first flakes hit my face. Pinpricks of cold melting on contact with my cheeks, bringing me to the surface of my body. I imagine myself from the perspective of a driver in a car, flushed and pretty, one leg cocked behind me, a dancer in a snow globe.

On the ride to Brooklyn I watch as the snowfall becomes steadily thicker and begins to blanket the ground, washing my city clean.

It's going to stick.

"She's—she's like a saint."

Nolan Lynch talks like the bottom of his mouth is weighed down with pebbles. The interview is a couple years old, shot around the time the "Poisoned Ivy" video came out, before they were a couple. He's twenty-one in the clip, baby-faced, and he keeps looking down at the ground, avoiding the off-camera reporter's face. He seems shy and far too innocent to be the same man who made his name rapping about doing so much cocaine, his "nose running redder than that red ass sea."

That line about Adriana being a saint, it's the last thing I hear before sleep overtakes me. I close my eyes, surrendering. I'm still wearing my party dress.

Ughhhhhh.

There's a staple in my hair.

Not enough coffee in the world to get me through this day.

I'm on cup number three already.

How can you even think about consuming anything?

What time did y'all get home last night?

IT'S SNOWING!!!!

The vibrations of my cell phone, entombed in the tangled bedding, wake me in lieu of my alarm clock, which I neglected to set before passing out. When I finally unearth the phone from the vise grip of a tossed-aside sheet, I'm greeted by a handful of new messages from the web producers' group chat. First, I take note of the time; by some divine miracle, it's only about thirty minutes later than my usual alarm. My head is throbbing. My stomach lurches toward my throat when I try to sit up. Are you guys working from home? I write, ignoring the previous conversation.

Girl check your email!

Look outside!

The first new message in my inbox is from Lexi. It's titled SNOW DAY. Thank god. Her email, sent at nearly six o'clock in the morning, is joyless. The office is closed due to the storm, but we are expected to work a full day. Not a complete twenty-four-hour period has passed since I started at the website without some sort of "urgent" communication from one of my bosses. We are technically allowed sick days, of course, but no one takes them, unless there's severe vomiting or hospitalization involved, and sometimes not even then. Most editors are on email all weekend. If they're going to be unavailable for a few hours, they announce it in the #editorial channel on Piger, as if the company is owed all of their time. Mariah got a DM from Ashley on Christmas Day last year, about a typo a self-publishing writer made in the headline of an article no one read. There's a rumor that Lexi pauses sex with her boyfriend to answer Piger messages when she hears her phone ding. Vacation days are "unlimited," which means you'd better not request more than a week or so every twelve months, lest you give the impression you're *not a team player.*

Regardless, I'm grateful to have an entire day away from my coworkers. It's Friday of the week before Christmas; the whole website will be operating remotely from now through New Year's Day, and soon the amorphous hours of working from my couch will give way to the amorphous hours of the weekend, and then the holiday week, which I will spend at home, an unremarkable town in New Jersey, with my parents and two sisters.

I peek outside the bedroom window to see my fire escape blanketed with snow. Exchanging my sleep-dampened dress for a pair of sweatpants and a tank top, I leave my devices in the bedroom, make coffee, and drink it sitting at the kitchen table with my feet propped on an opposite chair, indulging in the rare modern luxury of staring at nothing. The white curtains on the living room windows are so threadbare I can usually make out the dark green shapes of trash cans in the alley below, when I take the time to look. It's like peering at the world through a ballerina's skirt, the suggestion of transparency.

Today, though, it's just a square of pure, milky white.

My cell phone twitches in the other room, with texts and

Piger messages, emails and whatever else. I can't bring myself to care.

This is the thing about working from home: it's kind of the
same and also different. Yes, you're still bored. Yes, you're still
tethered to your computer or phone the entire time, perhaps
more so than when you're in the office because you can't risk
going too long without responding to messages, in case they
come to suspect you of committing the ultimate white-collar
crime—being too obvious about doing anything other than
work on company time. But there are more ways to make the
day bearable. You can watch TV, for instance, prepare elaborate lunches using the contents of your own refrigerator, pee
as often as you'd like without raising suspicion, even take a
surreptitious shower. Sasha left early in the morning, so it's
just the ladies from *The View* and me. After a few hours, *The
View* blends into reruns of a reality show about famous sisters with matching expensive fillers. I wonder who, exactly,
these episodes are for, imagine them playing to empty living
rooms, company for lonely house pets, the sisters' uniformly
tanned and plumped faces forming warped projections onto
curved fish tanks. Their voices create a comforting dial tone
pitch that soothes me as I copy-and-paste freelance articles
into LIZZIE and swap out some images for less fuzzy versions
of those same images. I fix a dozen typos. I refresh the home
page, then refresh it again. I read a few essays, just for fun. I
forget every word as soon as I close the tabs.

My phone continues to jump with updates to the web producer chat, tidbits from last night: Gavin from IT puked in
the bathroom sink at the after-party, held at a club near the
hotel called Pogo. Lexi and Ashley slow danced to Adele
(There was no room for Jesus, reports Emily), and Ashley may
have cried and begged Lexi for a promotion. Carly says the
CEO possibly grabbed her ass, she can't really remember, so

she doesn't think she'll tell HR. Mariah left the earliest, before even me, and only had three drinks. Emily doesn't think she'll ever be able to fully open her eyes again, which might actually be a decent vibe for selfies. My new personal brand—sexy and asleep, she writes.

They ask what happened to me and I deflect: I didn't feel great. Too much wine, not much food.

Other than that, no one mentions Tom. Is it possible no one saw us going up to the roof together? Or, and this seems more likely, they all saw and are discussing it in a secret group chat made specifically for the purpose of talking shit about me.

I stare at the green dot next to Tom's name on Piger, the one that indicates he's online. When I look away, my eyes are branded.

5

Adriana's three studio albums build on the pop-meets-R & B sound she established early on in her career. The first, *Sincerely, Adriana*, is bubbly, packed with upbeat love songs and the occasional mournful ballad. Upon release, critics compared her to the greats: Mariah Carey, Whitney Houston, and The Supremes. Her follow-up, *My Whole Heart*, debuted the next year. Despite the sweet name, it's more overtly sexual and less lyrically complex, my least favorite, though I listen to the whole thing anyway, for authenticity's sake. Then, there's *Hazardous*, her breakthrough record, the reigning fan favorite, with a sultry pure-pop sound and singles created by the iconic producer Sterling Starlight.

Some members of the forum for Adriana fans on which I've been lurking are nervous about *solstice* after hearing the new single; others are confident it will be the best thing she's ever done:

"It's still high pop, ballad x dance track mashup, but it's definitely a new sound."

"Idk about this, guys, seems like she's moving away from the Haz-ardous vibe that made me a stan."

"Come on, we all knew we weren't getting Hazard pt 2 with this album. She loves R & B and has just been waiting til she gets more successful to make the kind of music she wants."

"Personally, this is what I've always wanted from Adriana. She has plenty of bops, but she's never done something so personal."

"It's exactly what she needed to release after Sophie. A beautiful comeback and tribute."

The first January afternoon after I've returned to the city, there is a pizza-making class in the office kitchen led by the executive chef from a Michelin-starred place in Williamsburg with a miles-long waitlist. This is the kind of access that al-most makes this job feel worthwhile: the access you get when you say you work *here*. Never mind that you do nothing of relevance, that you're not responsible for shaping the voice or the coverage, that your health insurance is negligible. You can replace your entire identity with one word—the name of a company—if it's impressive enough.

Here I am, wrist-deep in dough dust, the counter splashed with sauce like a crime scene. I'm kneading and kneading and kneading. The muscles in my hands ache; they are not used to this push and pull, the physicality of using my forearms. I can already sense that they will be sore tomorrow.

Carly and Emily are next to me in gray knit and stove-pipe denim, arms hovering above the flour-dusted table like a multinecked snake with two cell phones for heads. Mariah is still at the bullpen finishing up some work. *Maybe I'll catch you for the "eating pizza" part*, she'd said. Truthfully, she's not missing much. If I learn anything, it will be by accident.

The executive chef, with his tattoo sleeves and diamond-studded nose, directs us to put our pizzas in the improbable brick oven built into the corner of the office kitchen. The sky is dark outside the floor-to-ceiling windows. Carly spins away from the table and returns with three beers in one hand, placing one down in front of me. She used to be a waitress, and it shows in the flourish of her wrists. Lexi is at the head of the island, nose resting on the arrow point of her extended index fingers, pressed together like a gun pointing straight up her nasal cavity. She stares into the barrel, fearless. Her face stiffens, the skin tightening around bone, and her eyes flick up to meet mine. For an excruciating second, I feel as though she might do something. The options flicker like a time lapse fanning out from the real Lexi. Shadow Lexi points the finger gun at me, clicks her tongue, and winks. Or she points the finger gun at me, clicks her tongue, and fires, the bullet gliding straight into my third eye. Or she tilts her head and I know once and for all that she sees me for what I really am: a fraud who cares about nothing, least of all her stupid fucking website. The Lexi clones melt back into the singular Lexi, and then her one mouth does the most surprising thing—smiles.

A timer goes off, indicating that the first round of pizzas is ready to be pulled from the oven. My mouth waters as the sous-chefs, two women bright as copper wire, lay each pizza down on the counter, bubbling cheese and ponds of sauce fenced in by puffy dough. They have a telepathic sense of which pizza belongs to which employee, and they work with assembly-line precision. The first woman pulls a pizza from the innards of the oven, and the other lowers her white-blond head several inches toward the burbling surface, cocks an eyebrow, and listens. The pizza crackles and pops, sizzling in a secret language. After a few seconds, she straightens, palms the pizza with a gloved hand, and strides confidently to place it in front of its rightful owner. Parsley dandruff belongs to

Charlie Carson in Sales. Cheese running over the crust is
Anna McLemore, the senior social editor. Charlotte's pizza
has lakes of sunset orange puddled between open cauldrons
of mozzarella.

A cutting wheel makes its way around. Charlotte lifts a slice
to her rosebud mouth and closes her eyes. The reverence with
which she bites down is humiliating to behold, like she's inhaling the powdered scent of her baby's head. I cut into my
pizza's fleshy crust with the sharp rolling blade, feeling like
Edith when her typewriter hits the end of the page. As I bring
the first bite to my lips, a flurry of movement catches my gaze,
and I see Meghan next to Charlotte, waving. She toasts with
the soggy end of a pizza slice, delivering a disconcerting smile.
A knowing smile, that says she's been watching me. The halting way she chews, then swallows, makes me feel raw, and
hunted. I drop my pizza, no longer hungry.

I lied: I've always cared about celebrities.

The ones that came before Adriana were all men with gui-
tars and papery voices that turned to dust and vanished at the
end of each note. Cranking the volume on my iPod, I would
walk down the streets of my New Jersey suburb, imagining
their poetic turns of phrase directed at me, every song a love
song even if it was clearly about something else, politics or
war or drugs. Because there's only love when you're fifteen,
sixteen. There is only a boy, looking at a girl. Someone looking at someone else. I pictured them picking me out from the
crowd at a concert, these beloved singer-songwriters, my longing so Herculean it became tangible, a pillar shooting through
the center of the room and cracking the ceiling.

I wanted to be impossible to ignore.

In high school and college, my friends and I concocted elaborate schemes to get our favorite singers to notice us. Signs

decorated with Shakespearean proclamations, bundles of sexy underwear to lob at the stage, so different from the cotton daisy-dotted Hanes we wore in real life. Detailed maps drawn in glitter pen that led right to the stage door.

At the shows, our courage died in our throats. We hovered at the perimeter, near the bathrooms, afraid to approach the stage, singing along so softly we couldn't hear ourselves over the din of hysteria, watching the prettiest girls push their way to the front and strain against the barricades, reaching, reaching. The violence with which they rattled the metal bars, the crazed varnish across their eyes, terrified me. They were prisoners trying to break free. Seeing them losing control made me both nervous and jealous. During my favorite songs, I'd feel the energy drain from the room, stranding me in profound seclusion. I'd think, *no one will ever feel that way about me.*

I realize, looking back, it's not the fame I craved, or even the musicians themselves. It was the adoration on either side of the barricade. The infatuation in the lyrics mirrored in the hysterical eyes of the girls in the pit.

Perhaps what I feel for Adriana is not so different from what I felt for those scratchy-voiced crooners in the cramped, yeasty concert venues of my adolescence. Fandom, at its root, is the desire to possess, to become, to consume. It is only the meal that changes.

Stephanie is at the usual table at the usual place when I arrive. We have been best friends since childhood, the inseparable kind, always touching, trying to mold our bodies into one ungainly, unstoppable girl. Grew up two houses apart, attended the same schools from elementary through college. Our friendship has continued into our midtwenties more out of habit than any remaining passion for each other's company. Yet I'm comfortable in her boringness, like the old, worn-in sweatshirt with our alma mater's name stamped on the front that I wear to sleep.

We meet about once a month for nostalgia-tinged dinners at a candlelit bistro in Tribeca. The food is decent, not too expensive, and it's midway between our two offices, so we can both leave work at six and arrive at a quarter after, then catch the yellow line in opposite directions when we head to our disparate apartments, hers in Yorkville, mine in Brooklyn. Before these dinners, on the way there, I play out in my head exactly how it will happen. What Stephanie will say, how I'll respond. Life has been like that recently. So predictable I could sleep through it and still know how it ends.

Stephanie is an assistant editor at a publishing house, and, since starting this job six months ago, she has begun to carry herself with the blunt-edged superiority I've come to expect from the moderately powerful. I put my bag on the floor under the table, hoping she won't sense the copy of *The Goldfinch* she lent me months ago nestled unread at the bottom, carpeted with old receipts.

Tonight, the air is frigid, and my cheek thaws gently as Stephanie presses her candle-warmed skin against it. She asks me how I am, and I pretend to examine the wine list. Eye contact with Stephanie is dangerous when I have a secret. "Fine. Work still sucks." *Oh, and I kissed a married man at the office holiday party.*

"Have you applied for anything else? I told you, there's that internship program at Booklight. It's paid."

I continue scanning the wine list. "I'm not about to be the elderly intern at your office."

Stephanie sighs her mom sigh, the one that makes me want to tip the flame from a nearby votive onto her flammable blowout. "A better job is not going to land in your lap when you're not paying attention. You have to look for it. Kind of like a relationship." Oh yes, how could I forget that Stephanie is also extremely, vocally *taken* by a Murray Hill banker who I'm convinced sleeps, showers, and has sex in his uniform of pressed blue-and-white-checked button-downs from J. Crew and Brooks Brothers slacks?

I wrinkle my nose, but she won't be deterred. "What about the technique I told you about?" The main problem with Stephanie is that she has adopted the law of attraction as religion. She read *The Secret* last December and, within a year, she had the boyfriend, the job, and the slimmer waistline. Since then, everything wrong in my life, she blames it on my lack of vision.

"Close your eyes and visualize," Stephanie says.

The waiter arrives to take the drink order—red for me, white for Stephanie—and when she leaves, I try to change the subject.

"How's work for you?"

Steph refuses, however, to veer from her script. "You will never get what you want if you don't know what you want." This is one of the things I have always hated about her, and it has only gotten worse—her tendency to speak like she's reading from a self-help pamphlet at a psychologist's office, the canned responses that make it clear she's never listening to what I've actually said, only what she expects me to say.

"Steph, it's not so easy."

The waiter returns and places two glasses in front of us. Stephanie swirls her chardonnay a few times, the level wavering perilously towards the edge of the glass. She dips her nose, inhaling with the seriousness of a sommelier. The movement calls up a memory: Stephanie kneeling on a dirty bathroom floor, tugging at the rising hem of a tight spandex dress, vomiting as I hold her hair, flat-iron-fried compared to the smooth follicles that peacock out from her head in the flickering light of the restaurant. The gestures are distortions of each other: a similar dip of the nose accompanied by a retching breath. A jarring before-and-after that leaves me hollowed out and missing that version of Stephanie, so much less polished, not yet a master of her emotions.

We stew in loaded silence like a married couple with too much between us and nothing left to say. "I just want to see you happy," she says after long pause, and then I feel bad.

Our food arrives while I'm thinking of something nice to say, maybe something about the first ten pages of *The Goldfinch*, but I can't picture a single detail beyond the cover.

Stephanie's other thing is a form of food exposure therapy wherein she orders french fries but does not eat them. Something about the scent and their essence infusing the plate. She says it's like eating fries without triggering her potato addiction, which I know is just the excuse she's made for denying herself. Craving is not the same as addiction, I want to tell her, but I refrain. She pokes at a fry with a cocked eyebrow and takes a bite of her veggie burger. The burger is couched in a sheath of lettuce and it crunches loudly. Toppings spill from the sides, stinging onion and a violent squirt of ketchup. Watching the grind of her jaw as she chews, I wonder how we've made it this far as friends. It's not the first time I've had this thought; I've had it many times over the past few years, often while watching her not eat fries from across tables in restaurants like this one. When we were younger, friendship was merely a matter of proximity; we lived on the same street and we both loved reading books. But even the weight of shared history doesn't seem to be enough to sustain us.

I ask if she's heard the new Adriana song, for something to talk about. It's the first time I've said her name aloud, and it feels clumsy in my mouth. She brushes me off with a comment about only listening to classical music and instrumental movie scores because it helps her concentrate. "I can send you my playlist. It might give you some direction," she says. She swishes wine around her mouth. "Isn't she dating that greasy guy with all the neck tattoos? She's so hot. She can do *so much* better."

"Nolan Lynch. I think he's kind of cute, actually."

"Figures." Stephanie pauses to chew. "You've always had terrible taste." Then, I swear, she pinches a fry between her fingertips, lifts it to her nose, sniffs, and drops it back onto the plate.

I hate her for not understanding, and me for not being able to explain. I bury my fork into the salmon filet, and a too-large piece flakes off. I pop the whole thing in my mouth and cough a little as I swallow.

"Since when do you care about celebrity gossip, anyway?" Stephanie says.

I don't answer right away, instead pluck the longest fry off of Stephanie's plate and grin as I chew, all teeth and gluey potato residue. "I took your advice to find a hobby," I say.

"There are a couple openings at my company," Stephanie continues, as if the previous few minutes never occurred. "Entry-level stuff, not just internships. We're looking for passion above experience. Take a look at our career page; if you see something you're interested in, let me know. I'll put in a word."

The plates are cleared, we decline dessert, and the waiter brings the check. As we say goodbye outside the restaurant, dispelling kisses into the night, Stephanie grips my shoulder with sudden urgency and whispers, "Nothing worth having comes easy." She trots down the steps to catch the subway, and I spend a moment on the corner, watching her blowout bounce and disappear underground. My bag digs into my shoulder. I lower the strap to my elbow, undo the clasp, and lift out Stephanie's book. The bird on the cover looks out with beady, accusatory eyes. I toss *The Goldfinch* into a trash can by the Q entrance and leave feeling much lighter.

6

My cat mug is missing.

It's not in my filing cabinet. It's not on the floor underneath the filing cabinet. It's not upside down on the desk, where I sometimes leave it to dry overnight, the mouth forming a perfect O on the paper towel.

I've recommitted to treating my Meeting reminders as sacred. Holy appointments, as unmissable as daily prayer. I've been lost for weeks in the fandom, spending my precious free moments wrapped up in Adriana and Nolan, their lives and their music, their love story. They are imprinted like holograms on the inside of my eyelids. They are more me than I am. I need regulation. Which is why I'm crawling around on all fours in the square of space where my legs slot neatly beneath the web producers' bullpen, as if it were designed just for me, my nose mere inches from Tom's khaki-coated knees. There's a spot of dirt on one cuff, and I battle with my desire to lick the pad of my finger and wipe it off. No mug.

There's one place I've yet to look, perhaps the most obvious. I stand, brushing the dust from my pant legs. The meeting reminder continues its militaristic scroll across the upper corner of my screen. I hit Ignore and go into the kitchen.

I see them right away. Two lacquered black eyes staring vacantly. Two white ears like snowcapped mountains. My mug, sitting on the counter by the coffee machine where I did not put it, a wooden stirrer sticking out the top, a hand that is not mine wound in and around the handle.

And above the smiling mug's face floats Meghan. "Hi there," she says.

I stand rooted to the floor, mouth agape, and watch as she continues trailing the stirrer through her coffee. There's something about Meghan that unsettles me. Her bangs gathered like straw on her freckled forehead, maybe. Or, perhaps, her smile, which is so wide it exposes slimy pink stripes of gum on either side and both full rows of teeth. Or maybe it's that she smiles like she knows me. As if she suspects that, under the buried layers of my resentment and boredom, we're more similar than we appear. I take a step toward her, keeping the mug in my sights.

"You never took me up on my lunch offer," she says.

"I've been, uh, busy. Is that my mug?"

"We all need to eat."

Meghan turns away from the counter, cat nestled in her cupped palms, fingers threaded beneath its adorable ceramic chin. She takes a slow sip and the black eyes peer over the tops of her fingertips, pleading. Meghan's nails are short and unpainted, but neatly groomed. She knows her way around a nail file. I want to reach out and grab the mug from her, splashing us both with the hot coffee.

Instead, I say: "Tell that to everyone else who works here. Hey, did you find that mug in the cabinet? Because I think it's mine. Not sure how it wound up in there. I keep it at my desk."

"You don't have to be like everyone else, you know."

The need for caffeine, the desire to end this conversation, wins out. I pull a different mug, this one stamped with the company logo, from the communal shelf. Place it on the grate, insert a hazelnut pod, and slam the lever. There's a crunch and brown liquid spits from the nozzle. That image creeps up again, a man's hot, acidic piss leaking into the welcoming maw of a urinal.

I keep my tone polite. "How about today? For lunch. One o'clock?"

"It's a date. And, yeah, someone left your mug out on the counter. Figured it was up for grabs. Sorry. I'll get it back to you." She saunters away with a little wave over her shoulder.

"Well, it's not," I mutter to the Meghan-shaped space.

I suggest a Japanese place around the corner from the office. I've ordered from them a few times; the food is serviceable, standard medium-quality sushi bar fare. More importantly, it's quick. We sit side by side at the counter and watch as two chefs pack pearly seaweed full of jewel-toned sashimi, avocado, and imitation crab. Their movements are a studied, rhythmic choreography. Each reach and grab, each flex of the fingers, serves a divine purpose.

Though the restaurant itself is empty, the lone waiter shuffles back and forth, arms laden with take-out bags.

"I'm glad we're finally doing this," Meghan says, taking a swig of green tea.

I concentrate too hard on filling the soy sauce dish.

"I suspect we have quite a lot in common," she continues in her odd, formal manner. "For instance, I also love cats." The scene has the mood of a meeting, like she's about to launch into a presentation about why we should be friends. I feel her watching as the murky soy sauce stream trembles in my shaking hand. Again, I'm struck by that skin-crawling sensation. Like each sentence she utters has a double meaning just beyond my grasp.

"I really do want my mug back," I say. "It's…special."

"Of course. It's such a cute mug. And I really am sorry about the mix-up. I didn't know it was yours. Someone from the cleaning crew must've left it in the kitchen. God, being new around here is weird. It's like high school all over again. So many unspoken rules. I'm always failing."

I think of the other web producers with their heads bowed over our shared desk, and how I told Meghan I'd meet her by the ugly yellow painting in the lobby, that poor approximation of pointillism, so the others wouldn't see us leaving together. And how it's not because I like them all that much, but just that I don't want to lose my place among them, the ranking that gives my life shape.

"I guess the website is a little cliquey."

"A little? You're the only person besides Lexi, my literal boss, who's spoken to me, like, using their vocal cords, the entire time I've worked here. Unless someone needs me to do something, it's like I don't exist. It's *bizarre*."

I think: *Maybe it's because you're irritating and clingy.* But truthfully, I am surprised to hear her say all that. I was under the impression that editors were the privileged class. The chosen ones, the ones with *a platform* and *something to say.* I didn't expect one of them to be lonely and confused, like me.

The sushi chefs stack our plates on the glass-topped bar, and the overworked waiter flurries to arrange them in front of us, even though we could have easily reached over and taken them ourselves. The gesture, it reminds me of web producing, in a way.

Suddenly starving, I tweeze a salmon avocado roll between my chopsticks. I want to ask Meghan why she chose me, if it's only that I happened to be the first person she encountered on her first day.

"So, when did you get into Adriana Argento?" Meghan asks, surprising me. The roll becomes a fine paste between my grinding teeth. She calmly sweeps a layer of neon wasabi across a tongue-shaped piece of tuna, betraying nothing.

"It's a recent thing. Since her new single came out."

"I've been a fan for years. From way back, during her Disney days. I was a little too old for the show, but I saw her singing live with the cast on *Good Morning America* and it blew me away. That *voice*." Meghan's eyes go a little glassy as she meditates upon the display of unprepared fish running the length of the bar.

"Isn't she so talented?" Meghan addresses the luminescent slabs like she actually expects them to answer.

"I'm not usually a big pop music fan, but there's something about her," I concede. Meghan's silence is encouraging. "It's like, these past few years, I've been dying off piece by piece. Becoming numb. And that song, the first time I heard it, it brought me back to life. Does that sound crazy?"

Meghan's head draws back sharply, only briefly, like a bow drawn across cello strings. Then her neck relaxes, and she smiles, bends down to inch up the ankle of her jeans, revealing the dark curve of her tattoo, the one I noticed peeking through her tights when we met in the office kitchen. It's a strand of ivy. "It goes up my whole leg. We all have them. Her most dedicated fans. What you're saying doesn't sound crazy at all."

"Everyone in the fandom has that tattoo?"

Meghan shakes her head, laughs. "Oh god, *no*. Everyone in our little group. Five of us who meet once a month. I know how that sounds, but it's totally not weird. We all have jobs and lives, other friends. We just *love* Adriana, and we love hanging out with other people who do, too.

"It's so hard to make friends once you leave school, don't you think? But youth really can last forever, the good parts, anyway. Like friendship and good music. If you find the right people to share it with."

Growing up, shedding your younger self, the skin cells you no longer have a use for—it's supposed to be a good thing. But I can't help thinking fondly about that crushed girl in those crowded, beer-slicked concert halls. I miss her. I want her back. I want her, only better. Her, as she always should have been.

"Yes," I say. "I love that."

A shift has occurred. The silence we settle into now is comfortable. My annoyance, my brain's automatic response to Meghan, as if she's a splinter wedged into the prefrontal cortex that I'm trying to muscle out, has vanished. We finish the last bites of our meal and request the check. On the walk back to the office, we chat about the work we need to get done before six o'clock, hers more interesting than mine, but I try to keep up. I find myself wanting to impress her, this Adriana fan who seems so together, so *grounded*.

As we turn the corner, Meghan puts a hand on my shoulder, forcing me to stop in the middle of the sidewalk. A haggard woman steps around us, huffing, but Meghan doesn't even notice, or pretends she doesn't. She stares at me and I feel I'm caught in the heat of a floodlight. "Thank you for coming out to lunch with me. It means the world."

"You're...welcome. I mean, it was fun."

"And hey, you should come to the Ivies meeting next week. They'll love you. Here, what's your number? I'll text you the details." She already has her phone out. I dutifully recite my number, guilt pooling in the bottom of my stomach. Even if

I like Meghan now, I'm still not going to join her adult Adriana Argento fan club.

Meghan pockets her phone in her jacket. "Done!"

We lock eyes, and the longer our mutual gaze holds, the more her grin collapses at the edges. She's reaching out for something, an analog friendship. I'm not sure I can give it, but I'm hit with the unexpected realization that I might want to try.

Stepping into the lobby, I'm almost surprised to see the yellow painting still hanging along the eastern wall, right where I left it, the splashes of red and blue marking the tranquil surface. The lobby, the art, is unchanged. But I am, in ways I can't quite determine.

The next morning, from all the way across the room I spot a hunched white shape on my desk. My cat mug placed carefully on a square of paper towel, upside down, the way I usually dry it. A yellow Post-it stuck to the bottom, the edges soaked through. *Apologies again. Thx for doing lunch. Xx Meghan.*

The inside of the mug is spotless, not a trace of leftover coffee circling the bottom or a single lip print kissing the edge. The note crumples easily in my tense fist. With a flick of the wrist, I send it bouncing off the shiny surface of the desk. It hits the floor. I kick it aside and sit down.

Nineteen bullets hit the desk in nineteen scattered, explosive thuds. Charlotte is opening a package. She doesn't flinch, just sits there calmly as if she's alone in her living room, and not sitting in the middle of an office with no walls, no soundproofing. I watch her flip a couple of the lipsticks over and read the labels on the bottom, select one, tuck a white-blond strand of hair behind a triple-pierced ear, and pitch towards the desk mirror so that I can see her face only from the nose upward. When she pulls back, her lips are fuchsia.

I bounce my fingers up and down, typing nonsense into an email with no intended recipient. Tom is working from home again, as he's done at least once a week since the holiday party, otherwise I'd be hiding in the corner of an empty conference room or in the last booth by the kitchen windows, hunched over my laptop like it's a still body of water I can disappear into. We haven't spoken since the party, not even to exchange the customary morning greeting, and I miss it more than I would've guessed, that little anchor to my day. I'm beginning to understand how adulthood is stringing together small pleasures that make an average life—so much less spectacular than anyone bargains for when they are very young—bearable. Things like coffee, idle chatter with co-workers, a clear-blue song on the radio. *Morning.*

My new pre-coffee routine involves watching. Charlotte turns to read something on her monitor, her mouth a garish neon slash in the wan light, the rest of her features depressed by the contrast. She looks like a cardboard sign. I crank the volume on the next Adriana song that comes up on shuffle. It's a challenge: I will not look at Charlotte again until the song ends. I focus on my screen and get back to pulling the traffic numbers for the past week, a new task Ashley bestowed on me like it was a compliment. Charlotte, so bright and so blonde, remains a vivid splash on my peripheral vision, impossible to tune out. Her hair streaks and blurs around the side of my laptop, an eruption of starlight. Still, I don't turn my head.

When the song ends, my gaze slides back to Charlotte. She smirks while she types, as if something vaguely funny but not hilarious, a meme or a message, has popped onto her screen. Only her expression hardly changes, that frozen smile remaining as if freshly sprouted for nine hours a day, every day. Her face wavers periodically into mild displeasure, but, for the most part, it holds that grin steady.

And can I blame her? I might be that self-satisfied if I, too, received a lifetime supply of free makeup every day before noon. Then again, how much foundation does one person with one face, one stubbornly smooth and unblemished and young face, really need?

The editorial intern, Rae, an eager college senior who began haunting the edges of our department after the holidays, materializes at Charlotte's side and offers to take the new lipsticks to the beauty closet, a tiny room shoehorned in the cramped hallway next to the bathroom. Rae is always appearing at Charlotte's desk, summoned forth by the alarm bells of crinkling paper, the sharp punctuation of staples tearing through plastic coating.

Sure enough, Charlotte hands her a canvas tote straining at the handles, and Rae limps down the narrow hallway, emerging less than a minute later, empty-handed.

I wait until she's settled in her seat—interns sit on a pair of couches by the windows with a coffee table between them instead of at the desks with staff, because there's simply no space for them among all the wide-open space—before I retrace her steps. Making like I'm about to enter the bathroom, laying my warm palm on the cool handle, I duck into the beauty closet when I'm sure no one is looking. The room is lined with Ikea shelves overflowing with baskets. This is where Charlotte stores the products sent for review that she does not immediately take home with her. Though it all sits here, slowly rotting in this windowless cubby, no one is allowed to touch it without her permission. I feel a certain kinship with the languishing makeup, these bottles of foundation iced over with dust and these crumbling, ashy eyeshadows. The baskets boast handwritten labels in neat, feminine script that reeks of Rae; the one nearest my eye level says *Perfume*. I pull it out a few inches and tip the opening toward my face, peering at the contents. Bottles clink as they slide down the incline, some luxe and expensive, others the sugary body mists that decorate the aisles of CVS. Pale pink and blue and violet liquids tinged with sparkle.

I reach for a cloud-shaped cap, lifting the bottle to read the gold embossing: Cumulus by Adriana Argento. My heart thumps in my ears. This must be a sign. I spritz a dash of perfume and it hits the veined underside of my wrist, filling the room with lavender, bergamot and vanilla. Girlish, with a hint of mystery. Beguiling.

There's a pile of canvas totes wedged between the corner legs of two shelving units. The bag Rae carried in is settled on top. Without overthinking, I extract it from the stack and slip in the perfume, a black liquid liner, and one of the lipsticks housed in thick black shell casing. I wrap the handles twice around the sagging belly of the bag, tuck the bundle out of sight behind a bin of hair products on the bottom shelf, and leave the closet. Shutting the door, I turn to find Meghan hovering at the mouth of the hallway. Her bangs are splayed like toothpicks, grazing her eyebrows.

"Oh, hi. I was grabbing some water." She grips a turquoise Hydro Flask. My hands are sweating. I rub a guilty palm on my jeans. Meghan moves closer, looks as though she is about to speak, inhales. I panic, thinking she'll smell it on me, Cumulus. Spinning backward and away, I bump into the closet door, hard, so that it quakes in its frame. Meghan smiles to hide a laugh and takes an uncertain step around me; that's when I realize I've been blocking the water fountain.

At my desk, I take a calming breath and start typing the name of the perfume into the Google search bar to check the price. Then I remember company Wi-Fi. I have no idea how trackable it is, and though I'm not sure taking one bottle of celebrity fragrance from the beauty closet is a fireable offense, I can't afford to take the chance.

At six o'clock, I stay in my seat, watch the clock count up five minutes, then ten. The rest of the web production team is long gone, always among the first to leave. Charlotte is still here, and Rae, her little shadow, watching Charlotte across the room with watering puppy eyes. Charlotte shifts in her chair and Rae's eyes dart away, fingers flexing over her laptop keys. I recognize the signs: she's trying to look busy.

I power down my own laptop, and gather my belongings, starting down the path toward the bank of elevators at the back of the office, on the opposite end from the neon lobby. At the last second, I turn, like I've realized I need to use the bathroom before my commute, which I do. First, I slip into the beauty closet, shutting the door behind me. The lights are on. This is an office; the lights are always on. I kneel, shins grazing the matted carpet as I scoot across the floor, grabbing for the bundle I hid earlier. I empty the contents into my open purse and stand, discarding the bag on the floor and kicking it like a deflated cow udder toward the other totes.

The hallway is empty this time. I adjust my purse strap, enjoying the new weight settling into my shoulder, and fling open the bathroom door. I pause with one hand still on the knob. Lexi is at the sink, holding a Q-tip, one end stained lightly black. A cotton swab, as we've been instructed to call them in articles. God forbid we imply something negative about *a brand name*, which is what Q-tip is, in case you forgot, which everyone does, because why would you remember when we all call them Q-tips?

For a second I truly forget that she can see me, that those Magic 8-Ball eyes in the mirror are, in fact, Lexi's own eyes. Her gaze runs over my body like whiskey hitting ice at the bottom of a glass, smoky irises lingering on my bag for a second too long before she turns her attention back to her reflection.

I must have imagined the suspicion in her eyes. There's nothing odd about an employee, a salaried employee, a valued *team member*, using the office bathroom at the tail end of a long day. Yet I feel her glare nipping at the nape of my neck the whole way home.

All night I jitter like a junkie until Sasha finally turns off the TV and goes into her room. When I hear the door click, I rush to my purse, casually discarded on the shoe bench by the apartment entrance, and drag it into my room. I arrange the beauty contraband on my dresser with care. I don't steal often, and only from the website when I do. Every three months or so, I take a few things small enough not to be missed from the closet. I've amassed a tiny collection in my first year: a lip pencil, a single eyeshadow, pink blush in a gold compact. This is my biggest haul, and the perfume is the riskiest item I've swiped. It's the opposite of what I usually go for: flashy, expensive. Adjacent to fame. The apartment is silent, but I can't shake the notion I'm about to be caught. I keep looking over my shoulder, hallucinating Meghan's wide smile.

I cue up a playlist I created over the weekend, a mash-up of Adriana's and Nolan's most popular songs, titled NA. I'd spent Saturday afternoon curating the order, playing around with variations on the name, separating the letters via ampersand or plus sign. But I found I preferred the first way, short and sweet, with so many potential meanings. *Not applicable* or *natrium* or *Narcotics Anonymous.* The playlist careens between soulful ballads and moody rap tracks and party anthems, carving wild sonic semicircles in the air. The first song is one of Adriana's big hits from *My Whole Heart.* She performed it at the Victoria's Secret Fashion Show the year the album came out, in a black sequined crop top and a matching A-line miniskirt, her tanned midriff bared as she pranced down the runway, darting between models tall as stilted circus performers, looking like Alice after drinking the first potion.

Bouncing to the beat, I squirt tufts of fragrance into the air with abandon, coating the room with the spicy musk of Cumulus. Did Adriana bend over lab samples for hours? Sniff perfume-soaked paper strips to find the exact right ratio of black pepper to vanilla bean? Or did she stamp her approval, her likeness, onto an already finished product? I'll wear it anyway, so long as the bottle bears her name. I'm that far gone.

Lancing the fragrant puffs with outstretched wrists the way my grandmother taught me when I was a little girl, I wonder how it feels to watch your signature, your face, become a symbol of a movement far beyond you. The mist cools my skin, soothing the rough itch from the heat pumping out of the radiator. I bop over to my half-open armoire, tossing clothes onto the bed. Stripping out of the boyfriend jeans and sweatshirt I wore all day, I paw through the rumpled pile and find a stretchy dress I haven't worn since senior year in college; it clings to my body like cellophane.

My reflection, framed by the chipped gold paint on the mirror that leans against the baseboard by the bed, comes as a shock. I have forgotten my own features since I last examined them, replaced them in my mind with someone else's. Not just anyone's, I suppose. I explore the ways in which she and I are different, searching in vain for similarity. Where Adriana is tanned and gleaming, I am sallow and pale. Where she's bony, I'm soft. I sing along with the song's climax and yes, there it is: where her voice soars, mine thins, snapping like a handful of twigs against the high notes I can't quite reach. The bass cuts out. The song ends with several seconds of a cappella harmony. I stop trying. But at least I smell like her.

Tom changed his relationship status to Single.

The web producers' chat blinks onto the wall above my bed, a silent fireworks display. I ignore the messages. The last thing I want to do is gossip about Tom's relationship status; he was obviously a terrible husband. His wife is lucky, or smart, or both, to finally have gotten rid of him. I feel no jealousy or excitement about this development. No emotion whatsoever besides a sprinkling of self-disgust.

I keep replaying our kiss, my mind slowing the film until the brief overlapping of our lips stretches to fill an hour, a day, my whole life. Wondering if I'm misremembering the tangy taste of him, the abundance of saliva on his flicking tongue. And shouldn't I be able to overlook everything—the pizza residue, the moisture, even the wife—if we were right?

He's already at work when I arrive, an egg sandwich weighing down an open wax paper square beside his mouse pad, spread wide like a cadaver's chest. A single bite is missing from one side. The sharp valleys left by his teeth bring a flood of memories shivering to the surface. The lights. The roof. The cold.

"Morning," he says. His lightly freckled jaw bunches as he chews, swallows, smiles.

I drop my bag on the floor and fall into my chair. This is the first time I've heard his voice outside of a meeting in weeks, and it absolutely levels me.

"Morning," I reply cautiously. The sound scrapes out of my mouth, an ugly clearing of the throat.

"How's it going?"

The energy around me crackles. "Things are…things are good."

"Good."

I bite my lip to keep from smiling and turn my computer on. There's a Piger message from Ashley waiting.

Will you handle the home page update this morning? I have back-to-back meetings.

Sure.

Other words that are brand names: Kleenex, Band-Aid, Bubble Wrap, Chapstick. Consider, instead: tissue, bandage, poppable plastic wrap, lip balm. There are words and then there are *words*, heavy with meaning. For the website, the most meaningful language is the kind that can lose us money.

The List comes out every Monday afternoon, an updated account of companies we must heap only with praise. No coverage exposing their CEOs' sexual misconduct, no essays about how depressing it is that their stores only carry up to a women's size eight, no jokes implying we'd rather eat wet sand than dine at one of their chain restaurants. I would love to ignore The List like I ignore so many things, but Ashley is always reminding us that *our team is the last line of defense.* And the only way I can really upset her is to cause problems with Sales.

So, I change *cheap* to *affordable* in a post about how to save money on itchy polyester thongs at Victoria's Secret. Anything I can do for the cause. It feels vaguely illegal. Dirty, at the very least. Editors aren't allowed to explicitly tell the freelancers that they can't write anything negative about these specific brands, imploring them instead to *focus on the positive* in general, and so I have to delete and delete and delete. Sometimes the sentences we cannot allow are the best ones, bright and funny and sharp. I hate to water them down, making our content weak and insipid to please some Midas-touched CEO or founder. If I think about it too hard, it actually makes me a little sick.

Sometimes I daydream about adding vile accusations to an article I'm producing, hitting Publish, and storming out of the building. Ignoring Ashley's frantic DMs, tossing my phone into the Hudson. But I'm no activist; I'd wind up jobless and just as miserable, and the website and all the corporations we dare not slander would have just as much power and one less pain in the ass to deal with.

The thesaurus is bookmarked at the top of my browser. I wonder who still shops at Victoria's Secret anyway as I refresh a preview of the article, make sure the photos are okay. Every other week there's a story about the company's impending bankruptcy. Sometimes I think about the things I hope to outlast, the useless celebrities, the war-happy world leaders, the brands. Imagine lying on your deathbed, thick with the knowledge that Victoria's Secret is going to live on. Worse yet, imagine dying *while* wearing Victoria's Secret, stiff elastic punctuating upper thigh, a reminder that your imperfections will endure.

I inch my jeans down to check the waistband on my underwear, just to be sure. Smooth black cotton from the overpriced minimalist basics brand the women in the office are always freaking out about, every launch of a new V-neck sweater or high-waisted jean an occasion.

I save the article I'm working on for the final time, hit Publish, and message Charlotte the link. She sends me a thumbs-up emoji. We are beyond language. I want to send something back, but I can't think of what, so I close Piger without responding. On Twitter, everyone is talking about a reality star who vomited in front of the paparazzi, on the sidewalk outside a Hollywood club. The pictures are splashed all over

TMZ and *People.com* and the *National Enquirer*. I think I'm
not going to look, I'm not going to look, but then I do. Her
highlighted head hovers over a puddle of chunky beige liquid, and her oily skin is so tan it's orange in the glare of the
camera flash. In the next shot, she sinks to her knees. In yet
another, she lifts her face, hair pushed wildly across her forehead, a trail of spittle winding down her chin. I stare and am
guilty, but I keep staring, binging on this woman's humiliation. Drinking it in.

This is what she gets for living her life in the spotlight, reads the
first comment, written by someone with a cartoon mouse avatar, someone who values their own privacy if no one else's,
and the flexibility it gives them to act like an asshole in public.
Because the internet *is* public. You can hide behind a screen
grab from an animated children's movie, you can use a fake
name, but when you're an asshole on the internet, you're just
an asshole.

I close Twitter. I open Facebook. More of the same.

Piger dings, briefly dimming Adriana's voice burrowed
into my ears. Sometimes I wonder how she got there; I hardly
ever remember opening the music player and plugging in my
headphones anymore.

The message is from Mariah: Blinkers after work?? She must
sense my hesitation because she presses on without waiting for
a response. Just the girls.

This means Tom's not coming. This also means she knows
I'd want to know whether Tom is coming, suspects the answer will impact my decision. She's right: I planned to say no,
but now I say yes. And I'm not even sure I want to, only that
I don't want to be alone, not yet.

JonBenét winks. No, that can't be right. JonBenét is dead.
JonBenét is an unsolved mystery. JonBenét is a picture in a

frame on the wall and the wall is next to my head and she is winking right at me, I swear.

We're in our usual booth at Blinkers and I'm too tipsy to be amazed that I am someone with a usual booth anywhere. I'm shoved all the way against the wall, my hairline grazing JonBenét's polished Mary Janes. Next to me, Mariah stirs her margarita with her pinky because we don't know where her tiny plastic cocktail straw has gone. Carly and Emily drink chilled rosé even though it's so cold out they had to flirt with the sleazy bartender to get it. He kept telling them they don't serve rosé in winter as they pushed their small breasts onto the glutinous counter. When he said *rosé*, you could tell he really meant his dick, which he would serve them anytime, anywhere. He just wanted to hear them beg.

I'm reflecting on all the ways we hurt ourselves and each other, and then I get so depressed I take a swig of wine like an eraser to my brain. Now the blackboard is blank and I'm flying.

"So, where's Tom tonight?" Carly asks.

I'm relieved she's said something, so I don't have to sit here fighting the urge all night, silently begging JonBenét's tabloid ghost to help me keep my mouth shut.

Mariah shrugs. "He said he's busy."

There's a hesitation in the way she says it, a space around the words that tells me she didn't invite him at all. That she did it for me. I squeeze her arm and slide closer, rest my chin on her shoulder. It's nice, like girl-closeness I remember from high school. Earlier, even. The primal memory of bonding formed as early as the womb.

As if she senses what I'm thinking, Mariah plants a kiss on my forehead.

"Awww you guys are so cute! Aren't they like us, Carl?" Emily nudges Carly in the rib cage, and Carly forces herself to look in my direction. Her eyes fall on Mariah and stay there. Her lashes are clumpy and her mouth a sour pucker.

"Just like us," Carly says. There's an edge to her voice that I take as a warning. A little tremor worms up my spine. *Oh, whatever,* says the voice in my head that sounds like Adriana and comes out when I'm drunk.

There's a movement in the corner of my eye. Could it be JonBenét shifting in her two-dimensional prison? I creep myself out thinking that maybe, when we die, we get trapped inside the pictures of ourselves for eternity. Maybe that's what purgatory is: every photo ever taken, a different fragment of the soul. I think about my phone's camera roll. I think about Adriana, all the photos of her that exist, millions and millions. Red carpet shots. Grainy concert footage. Coy selfies. All of them coming to life with her spirit, turning to me at once with an expression that says, *Hello, didn't see you there.*

"You look like you've seen a ghost."

I'm not sure who said it because they're all looking at me like I shouted something incomprehensible. Who knows, maybe I did. I sit up straighter. Clear my throat, take a sip of water. "Yeah, fine. I'm fine."

Carly and Emily exchange a look. Mariah avoids my eyes, curling her fingers in to examine her nails, and rubs at one of them like she's polishing it clean.

"Who's up for another round? On me."

It works. They shout orders and clap me on the shoulder, and I feel like the night's true savior. I push through the crush of the bar to get the drinks. Mariah helps me carry them to the table. I avoid looking at JonBenét as I put the drinks down and slide into the booth. Soon we're laughing like nothing happened, and whether it's a kindness or they've really forgotten doesn't matter.

Emily pulls out her phone, open to Sting. "It's a dating app for celebrities and creatives. You have to know someone to get invited and then the committee approves you."

"Have you matched with anyone famous?" Mariah asks.

"I have matched with some people you would know. But I can't, like, talk about it. Unless we actually go on a date. Then it's fair game, I guess. I literally had to sign an NDA. If you take a screenshot of someone's profile you get banned."

"What if someone sees over your shoulder? You know, while you're swiping?"

"I mean, it's impossible to keep all the users a complete secret. It's just, like, honor code."

Carly plays with her cocktail napkin, bored. Folds up one corner and smooths the crease with a polished beige nail. "That app is so stupid," she says, pressing down so hard that her nail breaks. She pops the offensive finger into her mouth and sucks.

"Don't you think certain elite people should have a smaller dating pool? I mean, Taylor Swift can't just *join Tinder.*" Emily spits *Tinder* out like a bug caught in her mouth. We ignore the fact that she just compared herself to Taylor Swift.

All but Mariah, who rolls her eyes. "Isn't that, like, eugenics or something?"

"That's *not* what *eugenics* means," Carly says, startled awake. She sits back against the booth and crosses her arms.

"Well, I don't think Nazis would object to a selective dating app. Especially if Taylor Swift were on it," Mariah says.

I laugh, too loud. I can't help it; it was funny. Carly's cheeks turn a deeper red under the artificial vermillion light. Emily folds her arms over her chest. The mood is suddenly sharp. I notice, for the first time all night, how thirsty I am. I need water. I need to be at home in the safety of my bed, shutting myself against the night that never fully darkens, listening to the city's continual death rattle. Only then will I be able to let the facade fall away. I close my eyes and I'm there, under those covers, releasing one muscle at a time, softening the space between my eyebrows. My eyeballs sink deeper into the sockets, that strange yank at the edges reminding me of the buried treasure of my anatomy.

"You okay?"

My eyes snap like quick-drawn blinds and I'm facing Carly. She hopes I'm not okay. The fact of my breathing is a disappointment. She hates me for stealing Tom, though she never had him. She hates me for laughing. I smile. "Yes, fine. Just fine."

A man is stretched across five seats. He seems to be asleep, or maybe dead. I'm trying not to think about the fact that we're hurtling toward the river in a metal tube suspended on century-old tracks. If I let myself remember, even for a second, my stomach clenches, threatening to squeeze half-digested cab sav up my throat like a glut of thick paint. I've never vomited on the subway and I don't want to start now. I don't want to be *that* girl, drunk to spilling her insides at eleven thirty on a weeknight, so obviously *not from around here*, not in any way that truly counts. I could have taken a cab, but I'm broke after the bar, queasy at the way I threw dollar bills at the counter like I was showering monetary praise on a thinly clad dancer at a gentleman's club. Besides, sometimes it's good to have the ground beneath your feet to remind you that you're really here, really living.

The train rocks, a steady rhythm that lulls me into stasis, a near trance. I am calm, breathing to keep it all down. Stomach fluids mixed with wine and forgotten fried pickles, a stinking mass. I feel it moving within me, too.

The sleeping man lets out a pillowy snore from beneath parted lips. One arm, slung across his face, blocks out the light. He could be anywhere—in a college dorm, a bachelor pad with a mattress on the floor. Instead he's passed out on a train, a garbage bag balled in one outstretched fist. I'm not close enough to smell him, but his clothes appear ratty and dank, as if soaked in one rainstorm after another with barely a moment to dry in between.

We shuttle over the bridge. I press my nose to the window, where someone has scratched *BITCH* into the glass. I rest a pad of cartilage in the hollow of the *C*. Although it's not possible, in my exaggerated state it seems like a message from Carly. I'm less horrified by the idea than I am honored. I see her, designer knee-points pressed into the orange plastic seat, finger grinding into the glass with fury. Nail polish particles spraying in all directions like something from a kids' cartoon, upper teeth working lower lip as she concentrates hard on making me pay for my sins. *I got it, thanks,* I think, running my hand over the word, toying with the ridges. Carly isn't wrong about me. I can admit it. I know what I am. The lights of Lower Manhattan smear under my palm. Rain drops cluster under the *BITCH* and I'm too drunk to care that I will have to walk the ten minutes home wet and freezing, without an umbrella. We disappear into the DeKalb Avenue station and I sit, head pressed to the *BITCH*, for the rest of the ride.

At my stop I stumble onto the empty platform, which is aboveground, cold. The air hurts immediately, like hundreds of jellyfish stingers sinking into my exposed flesh. The sleeping man stirs as the doors shut, and I fight the urge to wave goodbye, deciding to do it at the last minute, thrusting my arm toward the window above his head. He can't see me, anyway. His eyes are still covered.

Listing to one side, I start the last leg of the journey home, stopping at a bodega outside the train station to pick up an egg and cheddar on a roll. I eat as I walk, the spongy bread quieting the sloshing in my stomach. With the first bite something within me caves and I chew with a wild hunger, like I have no idea when I will eat again. My mind is racing with possible excuses to get me out of work tomorrow. But we have a meeting and then that tequila happy hour for a reality TV housewife's line of artisan cocktail mixers. So many things I shouldn't miss.

The walk feels forever. I know I'm almost to safety when I pass the DNA testing center with the baby poster out front, underlit by three eerie spotlights. The infant emerges from the dark like an angel, a promise: *Does she REALLY have her father's eyes?* I round my corner and run the last half block, shivering in my insubstantial coat. There was a scarf once, but it seems to have vanished. I crash into the warm, bright lobby. A woman rocking her baby to sleep on the interior steps looks up, startled. I give her my best *I'm not crazy* look and bolt up the opposite staircase.

My bed welcomes me and my unwashed face, my shivering body. I'll have raccoon eyes in the morning and an eyeshadow chin strap, but I'm too tired to care. I hold my phone above me, my head propped on a pillow, watching a parade of Adriana Argentos glide across the screen until my arm aches. Her mouth stretched open mid-belt. Her hand a fleshy web protecting her from the paparazzi. Her face in Nolan's neck. Her voice backstage at one of his shows, yelling, *That's right, that's my baby.*

And here I am, observing her life out of order, piecemeal. Her life is a public scrapbook, available to anyone who wants to rearrange the pictures and create a better story. The faster my finger pushes from one photo to the next, the more diluted her image becomes. How much of yourself can you scatter like confetti until you cease to exist?

I pause on a blurry shot from a concert. Adriana's flesh

puddles slightly between the rigid fabric of her crop-top and matching skirt. I experience naked relief—even pop stars have bad angles. But then I pull back and I notice how perfect she still is, without airbrushing, without Photoshop, without pinching and smoothing. Her chin sags slightly, filling out her face. Using my phone-free hand, I pinch the same section of my own jawline.

Then the phone slips from my grip and smacks me square between the brows.

In the dream, Adriana is clad in a floor-length powder-blue gown that Cinderella-poofs at the waist. Her hair, loosed from its ponytail, winds like a strand of pale ivy down one shoulder as she runs a brush through the ends, the flat plane flashing in the candlelight, counting one hundred strokes. She doesn't see me. I am a piece of furniture. I try to look down at my body, if I even have a body, but nothing moves. Adriana sets the brush on a mahogany table. Slowly, she stands and circles the room. Now we are face-to-face and she's preening in front of me, smoothing her polished edges. Her frizz-free hair, her ironed forehead, the stiff yet pliant fabric of her dress. As she presses and swipes, I feel the reverberation of her gestures tugging at my own limbs. That's when I realize what's happening: I am inside her mirror. I *am* her mirror. As I mimic her, I solidify. Become Adriana. Her chin is my chin, her dress is my dress. There's no floor underneath me; I vanish into blackness outside the mirror's frame. It's hard to determine who is controlling whom, whose hand lifts first to our shared face. Am I leading, or is she?

She examines every inch of us with her critical, discerning gaze. There's nothing wrong that I can see as I watch her watching, and it's the happiest I've been inside my body in as long as I can remember, perhaps since the moment I became aware of having a body.

A sudden violence flashes over Adriana. Her expression darkens. Her entire being seizes up. Her hand hovers an inch or two over her cheek and then it plunges downward, gathering the skin of her jaw—my jaw—between her index finger and thumb. She pulls at our face over and over again, clawing at the flesh until it gives like putty.

My vision goes hazy and Adriana, the reflection of her reflection, blurs, and I feel the wetness on my cheek, a little splash. I taste the salt or graphite. Whatever the liquid is, it burns my lips. My tongue darts out for a quick, definitive lick, a gesture that is distinctly mine even as I watch the pink muscle limp out of Adriana's mouth. Why are we crying or bleeding or both? I try to ask, but no sound comes out. The lips open and close, voiceless.

Adriana grips her throat. The muscles in my neck strain even as I comprehend the emptiness and start to understand that my vocal cords are missing. I want to tell her, I need to tell her she speaks for both of us, but the message isn't coming through. In my desperation, I fall forward, sending Adriana and me toppling inward, towards each other like a collapsed house of cards.

Our hands meet as the glass breaks.

7

A text from an unknown string of numbers comes the following Wednesday as I'm waiting for the train. A parade of horrors comes to mind, as it does whenever I receive correspondence from an unsaved contact: my mom is dead. My dad is dead. Both my parents are dead. Nuclear holocaust. Subway bombing. My grandparents are dead. Military coup. Everyone in New York City but my coworkers and me, the entire population of millions, is dead.

I open the message. Hey girl! Ivy meeting @ 7:30, 225 Driggs Ave. Off the Bedford L stop in Williamsburg. Let me know if you can make it! Xx.

In the pre-caffeinated haze of the morning, it takes a good thirty seconds. Meghan. The tattoo snaking up her calf. Lunch. The Ivies. Adriana Argento.

The Q comes. I wedge into a coveted against-the-door spot where I can lay my spine, as if I'm in bed standing up, and try and read the galley of a mystery novel I took from the office, keeping the book partially propped on the forearm of the bulky man holding the vertical pole by my head. My phone disappears into the bottomless pit of my tote bag, Meghan's text unanswered, but I can't focus on the page.

All morning, I try to put the invitation out of my mind. I'll have to decide eventually, but eventually might never come.

It's hard to say what puts me over the edge. Maybe it's the averageness of the day, so bland and uneventful it disappears into the whirlpool of eyestrain and constant, nagging thirst. Maybe it's Carly stirring her yogurt parfait until it turns liquid and tossing it, largely uneaten, into the trash. Maybe it's the photo I see later when scrolling through my feed as I wait for lunchtime coffee to brew, the parfait ringed with a granola halo. Caption: *YUM!!! @chobani.*

A DM comes in, Mariah asking about Blinkers tonight.

Can't, sorry. Plans!

I open Meghan's text again.

I'll be there!!

Then I save her to my contacts, so I won't worry about the apocalypse next time she gets in touch.

225 Driggs is a brick town house with a stoop large enough to sit on. I'm a little early, so I circle the block several times, staring at my phone to avoid being spotted by someone from work. They all live in Williamsburg.

At seven fifteen I enter a wine store on Bedford Avenue, spend ten luxurious minutes browsing the reds as if I could tell the difference. Eventually I pull the second cheapest bottle off the shelf and carry it over to the register. Make like I'm going to grab my ID, but the cashier doesn't ask, so I swipe my debit card and exit the store.

Back at 225 Driggs, I climb the short staircase and hesitate before ringing the bell. The chime echoes. I picture an empty interior, musical notes climbing the stairs. Seconds pass before I hear footsteps, seconds in which I consider retracing my steps and running underground into the warm, damp mouth of the subway, leaving the wine on the stoop like an offering or an abandoned baby.

But then the door is opening, the light from the foyer is flooding the stoop, and my eyes are adjusting to take in the overwhelming blondeness, the pink skirt suit, of the woman in the doorway. She's tall enough that I have to tilt my chin to see her face, and she smiles so broadly it makes me want to apologize.

"You must be Meghan's new girl! Come on in."

I'm swept inside and up a pale oak staircase, into an open living room with white floor-to-ceiling curtains blanketing one entire wall. The room is warm and smells of mulling spices. Candles flicker on the end tables, too many to count, their shadows skittering up the wall like insects on a loop. The room is already full of women draped languidly over various pieces of cream furniture like expensive afghans.

Something feels off about this space, a certain showroom quality. I'm considering the strange, colorless aura, when a shape vaults off a settee and into my arms. "We are *so* glad you could make it."

Meghan pulls away, wolfish teeth bared, and it hits me, what's so odd about the room. It's not an apartment. This is a house, and one that has not been subdivided into smaller pockets for multiple tenants to live in. Nothing bangs above us, no too-loud music pounding the floorboards from below. There is only the oppressive quiet, the gentle scrape of traffic on the avenue. A *home*.

Meghan breaks away, pulling me to the couch. "This is…

everyone." She gestures expansively at the other four women. I feel all eight eyes drilling into me. I shift uncomfortably on the cushion, still holding the wine. I thrust the bottle limply into the vague middle of the room. "Here, I brought this."

The blonde who greeted me rushes forward. "Thank you *so* much. I'll open it in the kitchen."

Without the bottle between these women and me, I feel exposed. I cross my arms, cross my legs, pretzel my limbs so I'm as small as I can make myself.

"So, you're Meghan's coworker," says a brunette. Part of her hair is shaved, the rest long and cresting over the crown of her head in a dramatic sigh. The exposed ear is reddened and barbed with piercings. She's wearing a pleated pink tulle dress that hides the shape of her body and explodes below her knees. The froth breaks away to reveal a tattoo identical to Meghan's lashing up her left leg, barely concealed by threadbare black stockings laddered with rips. I notice that they're all wearing dresses or skirts, displaying their shared ink, despite the cold outside. I feel stuffy and underdressed in my Uniqlo jeans.

"Yes, but her job is much more exciting than mine. I'm in web production."

The one that was just speaking slides her eyes, hooded by heavy liner, to the left. She's so bored she can't even look at me. "I don't know what that means."

Meghan chimes in. "It's a very important, key role in editorial. The web producers make an editor's job so much easier, believe me."

I try to smile, but it turns chalky and frail on my lips. The hostess returns, saving me with a glass of red wine, balanced on a tray with five other glasses. She passes them around, puts the tray on a glass-topped coffee table, and sits on an armchair embroidered with roses, the only patterned piece of furniture in the room.

"Welcome to our little group! I'm sure Meghan told you, but we call ourselves the Ivies. Our meetings are devoted to discussing the latest Adriana Argento news as well as what's going on in our personal lives. We *love* Adriana—" Here, the candied host, with her flushed cheeks and dew-tinged lashes, is interrupted by a chorus:

"*Love* her."

"Adore."

"She's a goddess."

The host waits for a respectful, honorific beat. "But you shouldn't be afraid to talk about yourself, too. We want to know the real you—if you end up joining us permanently, of course."

Permanently. The commitment of it seizes my diaphragm and I cough. Her short speech segues into introductions. The pink-tinged host's name is Veronica and she's an account executive for a PR firm that works with a number of major beauty brands, which means her parents definitely paid for this town house. The girl with the partially shaved head is Pearl, a bookstore manager and the lead singer of Tulips, a punk band that mostly plays open mic nights. The Black girl next to her is Crystal, muscled yet thin in a white tank top tucked into a high-waisted mini skirt, patent leather belt, and fishnets, a tuft of brown curls hemmed in by a small patch of cornrows above her left ear. She is a bartender/painter. Then there's Jessie, with black hair she wears in two low pigtails and a natural tan. She works in marketing and her teeth are slightly too big for her mouth, forcing her lips apart as if she is always on the verge of speaking. Finally, Meghan, the entertainment editor, and me, the lost one.

I nod placidly as we make our way around the circle, my eyebrows raised so as to promote the right level of interest. Veronica asks if I have any questions and, though I really want to know how soon I'll be expected to brand myself with tattooed greenery, I shake my head.

"Then let's get started! It's Crystal's turn for the gossip rundown."

Crystal opens a laptop and reads from a list of Adriana-related news items. Nothing is particularly exciting aside from the rumors about the impending release of the next single.

"We can only hope it's better than the last one," Veronica says with a little scoff. Everyone murmurs in agreement.

I sit up straighter. "Wait, you guys don't like the song?"

The other women begin to fidget. Crystal swirls her wine. Jessie crosses, uncrosses, recrosses her legs. Pearl bites her lower lip and avoids my eyes.

Finally, Meghan clears her throat. "It just...it wasn't what we expected. After... You know, right? About what happened with Sophie."

"The girl who was killed," I say.

"The girl who was killed," Meghan repeats. There's another soft murmur through the room, the others making solemn noises of muted respect. "We thought Adriana would honor her more explicitly. That was her first release since the murder, and it wasn't about Sophie at all. It was all about *her*."

They nod as one, marionettes operated by the same puppet master.

"That poor girl *died*," Veronica says. "She deserves *more*."

"Well, maybe Adriana thought it would be in poor taste to exploit a fan's murder for money," I say.

"But what about us? What about *the fans*? We made her who she is and then one of us *died*. For *her*. The least she can do is acknowledge that sacrifice. And it *was* a sacrifice," Pearl says. What she's saying, it doesn't match her detached, robotic tone or the calm way she finger-combs the long side of her hair so that it undulates.

I must look taken aback, because Meghan jumps in, placing a warm hand on my shoulder, addressing me as a kindergarten teacher would an unruly child. "I understand what you're saying. And it's not a *bad* song. After all, you told me it's what got you into Adriana's older music."

I nod.

"Tell us," Crystal says.

"Yes, tell us," Veronica purrs.

I tell them.

I tell them about Blinkers, the fuzzy lighting, the wine sliding down my throat. I tell them about Tom, his hot breath, his hands on me, holding me in place, the claustrophobia of it. I tell them about the wedding ring, an electric shock on my skin. And then the song, bursting in like a gospel choir to save me from myself, how I tasted it on my tongue like a communion wafer. I tell them how I ran out of the bar so fast I think I could've run all the way home. I tell them about diving into the cool water of her voice, an ocean I could drown in, happily gasping for oxygen, killing myself silently by swallowing.

They're all watching me, rapt. I think I see a few tears sparkling in more than one eye. I'm waiting for applause, for a standing ovation, when Veronica clasps her hands to her chest and says, "That was beautiful."

The mood in the room eases up; my origin story as an Adriana fan is good enough to make me one of them. I'm not sure I *want* to be one of them; they are odd, with stilted half smiles that look drawn on and scary intensity behind the eyes. But I want to be the one to decide. And it's calming to be in this posh living room, sipping wine with these women, knowing we all have one crucial thing in common, a fact that renders small talk obsolete.

Crystal cues up a playlist of Adriana songs, slides the laptop onto the floor by the couch. I listen as the others discuss their hopes for the next single, glasses clinking, words gently slurring. It seems they want a return to form, the bombastic big pop of *Hazardous*. They want high notes, vocal runs, whistle tones, inspirational lyrics, a message of hope for the fans. I'm afraid to admit that none of that is what I love about Adriana's music. That I prefer her lower register, her personal songs, the ones that sound like voice memos left on her phone in lieu of journal entries.

We drink more wine. I relax, my muscles unknotting. My shoulders have never been this loose. I wonder if I can do that yoga pose with hands linked at the cervical spine, the one all the together-looking women who have no problem meditating can do. I ease back on the couch, less anxious about spilling wine onto the pale fabric than I would be if I were sober. This is how accidents happen, I realize, when your guard is down.

But I am insulated from harm, cozy and flushed in this candlelit room, the kind of home I didn't believe existed in this city of steel beams.

A timer beeps. Veronica leaps from her floral chair and goes into the kitchen, returning with a delicate blue-trimmed serving plate loaded with steaming spanakopita bites. The food reaches me, and I put two on a napkin, the phyllo dough heating my palms through the paper.

Meghan nudges me. "Having fun?" She blows air at her bangs, sending them sparking up to the ceiling.

I gesture to my full mouth as I chew, swallow.

"Yeah, this is great. Thanks for inviting me."

"I know the girls can be a little…intense. But it's just because they love Adriana, they love her *music* so much. It gets the better of them. They'll loosen up once they get used to you."

My chest opens, a crack in the cloud cover. "Do you think they'll invite me back?"

"Oh my god, *of course*! Did you see how they reacted to your story about discovering Adriana? They were *touched*."

"But… I'm a new fan."

"We don't care *how* or *when* someone gets into Adriana. What matters is that they do." She winks, takes a conspiratorial sip of wine. Comradery washes over me in a shimmering wave. I'm bathing in the afterglow of a flame. I catch a whiff of smoke, a metallic burning, so strong it seems to come from within me. I'm so happy my insides are on fire.

When I turn my face toward the center of the living room, I see a different warmth: friendship, licking the walls in comforting flicks. Crystal and Pearl, hands linked as they bow their heads together and whisper like schoolgirls, Crystal's curls tangled in Pearl's abrasive strands. Veronica, braiding one of Jessie's black pigtails with sisterly tenderness, her rosy hands expertly weaving the plaits. The air smells of spiced apples and hot, female breath.

I dab at the corners of my mouth with a napkin to hide my maniacal smile. This. This is where I am meant to be.

We drink and snack. Stories escape from my knotted tongue, little confidences I can't remember sharing aloud before, not even to Stephanie. Meghan at my elbow, egging me on with encouraging gestures, a small smile, the cryptography of her twitching chin. Veronica's living room feels like the inside of a hearth, the walls crackling with heat. I realize the sound must be coming from an out-of-sight radiator. The wealthy pay for this concealment: all of life's unpleasantness, the heating mechanisms and homeless people, hidden from view. They have other things to worry about, like the stock market and getting your teeth cleaned twice a year and nailing (or paying someone else to nail) that perfect flat-on-top, wavy-on-the-bottom hairstyle favored by newscasters and women who work in the tall buildings on Park Avenue South.

Before tonight I would have said you lose something by living this way. A certain rawness, the rough edges that scrape at your humanity and keep you honest. But Veronica is so content in her pale living room, her life unruffled as the bottom of a milk bottle, ivory teeth clicking in the trembling light, long arms and legs pleasantly bare in the middle of January. I can admit that it's nice to be warm in the winter without having to think about why.

Veronica picks up her glass and lightly taps a fork against the side, cutting through the chatter. "It's about that time," she says. "Whose turn is it?"

Pearl raises her hand, then scratches the shaved part of her head, bone-white flesh visible beneath prickly hairs that remind me of a cactus. "I believe it's me."

She holds out her cell phone, presses a couple of buttons. There's a little beep from some unseen corner of the room and the lights dim, as if by magic. Slowly, the girls rise from their seats and come to kneel in a circle on the floor with the phone in the center. Pearl hovers over the screen, hands twitching, witchy and fevered as she makes her selections. I follow suit, kneeling between Meghan and Crystal. Even though this position makes me feel like a child and puts too much pressure on the delicate, shifting bones in my knees, I am comfortable. The plush carpeting cups my calves. I want to lie down and make little snow angels in the pile.

Veronica passes out silver candlesticks towering with unblemished white tapers. She lights her wick and uses the flame to ignite Crystal's and Jesse's candles on either side. By the time the circle closes in on me, the room is glowing. I light my candle with Meghan's flame and hold it away from my chest with both hands gripping the base. Then we place the candles in a ring around Pearl's phone. She presses a button and leans back. I expect the music to come from the phone, but instead, Adriana bursts from a nowhere speaker. She's in the room with us. The floor vibrates and pulses. It's the song about grinding on the dance floor. Adriana sounds lonely and sad. She's all *Closer, closer, closer.* Hip bones mashing together, skin and muscle flaking away, bones crumbling to dust.

Love me, she begs. *Dance with me. Love me. Love me. Love me 'til I break.*

Are those the lyrics? I can't remember. Her voice sounds brittle, like a thin layer of ice. But the lake underneath pulses like a heartbeat. A current so strong it could pull you under, hold you down until the final strains of breath leave your lungs. Her voice sounds weak only because it's so strong.

There's a strange wetness on my face. Is it raining? I touch my cheeks and taste my fingertips. Salt: *Oh.*

We're all crying now, tears falling unrestrained. Pearl is arched forward, palms pressed into the floor, the shaved wedge of scalp like a shard of cracked china. Crystal gazes up at the ceiling, arms straight in front and wrists bent back, zombielike, two rivers streaming down either side of her face and a steady whine shaking her throat. Veronica weeps above her candle, droplets collecting in the well at the bottom of the holder. I can picture her dabbing her pointer and middle fingers into the liquid, crossing herself as if with holy water, and maybe that's what it is, maybe these tears are sacred. Jessie bends forward like she's trying to grow a protective shell and gnaws her lip until it bleeds. A droplet winds through the cracks in her lips. She glances up at me, feverish.

Beside me, Meghan is subdued. She presses a tissue to her eyes and the paper comes away soggy, dotted with black mascara stains like crushed insect limbs. We've all been possessed. Adriana runs through our veins, taking control. She spins our heads three hundred and sixty degrees. She makes us vomit sweet, slick bile. She sings us a lullaby and puts us to forever sleep.

Then the song ends, and the spell is broken. The lights come back on. The candles are blown out, trailing ghost flames. Meghan passes around the Kleenex and we wipe our eyes. Jessie helps Veronica collect the cooling candles and their waxen holders. A white wicker trash can, empty but for the crumpled petals of our tissues, moves around the circle. Everything in the room is so white. It's blinding.

I turn to Meghan. "What just happened?"

"The Growing," she says, as if it makes sense.

"And the candles?"

"They add atmosphere!" Veronica says, her voice loud. I'm startled; I thought we were whispering.

I have so many more questions, but Veronica is herding everyone toward the door, handing out winter layers. Now they're hugging each other and hugging me, saying, "Pleasure to meet you" and "Please come again." *Come, come, come. Come again.*

And now I'm on the street, alone. Where did they all go? I spin in a lazy circle, but the street is empty. I search the sky above the quiet buildings, wondering if I'll see broomsticks crosshatching the bulbous full moon.

Where am I? I spot the street sign overhead: *Driggs Ave.* Williamsburg. I point my feet in the direction of the subway and start toward home.

Adriana has a sore throat. She has to cancel tonight's performance at the Turn On the Light benefit concert for homicide victims. There's no option. But she's donating $500,000 to the cause, in Sophie's name. Her eyes filled as she wrote out the check, thinking about that poor girl, her broken and purpled and soiled body abandoned in a drab alley. She hopes

Sophie's last moments, the horrors she endured, were blotted out by something sweet, something like Adriana's own face on the billboard outside the arena. *One night only!* Hazardous *World Tour.*

Adriana doesn't actually think her own face is that great, can't imagine it being the last thing anybody sees before they die. But for a fan? There's surely nothing better. They tell her as much when they beg for it daily on the internet. They say, *Murder me, Adriana. Ugh, step on my fucking face.*

She's so perfect I could die, I will die, I am dying.

Comments like these appear by the hundreds under every selfie, every performance video, interview clip, campaign out-take. When she cries, they say, *even when she's sad I want her to break my fucking neck.* When she sings, they say *her bb5 just burst a blood vessel in my brain.* When she kisses Nolan for the cam-era they say, *I'm not even gay but if she were mine, I'd fuck her to pieces until she shattered and then I'd crawl inside and live in her skin.*

Men are simpler. It's all sex with men, the straight ones, anyway. Men are: *Do you think she whistle tones when she cums* and *I'd like to see her out of that crop top* and sometimes even just *Tittayyyyysss* which makes no sense because she doesn't really have much by way of a chest. She's forever foisting her small breasts toward her chin on red carpets, trying to give the il-lusion of more, to fill the gaps in the top of her bra. But the men want to see *tittays*, so *tittays* are what they imagine. She's seen some of them estimate her at a C cup, even though she's more of an A. Maybe a B, when she's on her period.

With the girls, it's about possession. Her female fans want to consume her, flay her alive, play in her organs, drink her blood. Even the ones who speak of her in sexual terms have a bent of brutality about their language. They want to become her and to destroy her in the process.

Adriana rolls over in bed and hacks into her open palm. She

grabs her phone, scrolls through her messages, hoping to see one from Nolan. He's performing in Birmingham, Alabama, tonight, some up-and-coming hip-hop artist showcase where he agreed to make a special appearance, boost the event's cachet. He flew out yesterday in a private jet, delayed because he didn't want to get out of bed, where she was. Adriana gets nervous when he goes a while without texting, even a few hours. The images that begin to swirl in her head if she's not careful. White dust, bloodshot eyes, flashing red lights. Relapse.

It's not that she doesn't trust him. She trusts *him*. But she doesn't trust his addiction, which is part of him. Though she's dabbled in very few substances—alcohol on a late night in the studio, a hit or two of weed when she and Nolan were alone, no cameras—she gets a taste of addiction whenever Nolan comes close. His smell, a blend of expensive cologne and stale cigarettes. His skin, rough in places, soft in others. His tattoos, creating a topography of his body.

In the cool, black pool of her phone's empty surface, her mind projects these images, a horror slideshow, a PowerPoint from hell. Gray-green foam spittling his mouth, flecked with red. Splayed limbs. Powder dusting a grubby carpet. Inside her, there's a sick twisting. A river of hot mucus runs down her throat. She curls inward like a beckoning finger and buries her face in the cushions on the bed.

Charlotte always looks like she should be chewing gum when she isn't. This is what I'm pondering as I cradle my head, heavy with tannin residue, in my right hand and respond to editor inquiries with my left. Charlotte's awakeness is making me angry. Her dark circles neatly, effectively concealed, her cheekbones frosted, she smirks at her laptop, opens her mouth slightly. Blows an invisible bubble. *Smack.*

I turn the volume on my computer up to drown out Charlotte's existence, but Adriana's voice sends a spike into my brain. I wrench out my headphones and try to focus without the music. The clacking of keyboards tickles my eardrums. I clear my throat to get the itch out. Rising from my desk, I nearly knock over a towering fern, crunchy and brown at the tips, on the engineering table behind me. Even Tom glances up. I careen into the bathroom, splash some water on my face. Blinking at my damp reflection, letting the water run in rivulets down my chin. A crusty substance speckles one corner of the mirror. On further examination I decide it is dried toothpaste.

I'm still standing there, nose an inch away from the mirror, face dripping wet, when Lexi appears in the doorway. An aura hovers around her, the light from the hallway milk-blue like a skinned-over vein. We stand like that, like we are at the beginning of a standoff. Someone has to make the first move. I lift an arm, attempting to wave while I rub a sleeve across my cheek to sop up the excess water.

Lexi blinks. If I were on fire, if I were drowning, she wouldn't save me. She nods, steps into the room. "See you at the meeting," she says.

She shuts herself into the handicap stall. I hear the lock gasp into place.

Outside the bathroom, face stripped dry and newly cold, head still pounding, I am nose to nose with the beauty closet. The edges are fuzzy and the room glows from the inside, heavenly. I palm the shoddy wood, beyond which rows of beauty products wait to be liberated. Moisturizers in curved glass jars and moisturizers in squeezable tubes. Moisturizers with SPF and moisturizers made of kelp treated with sound waves and moisturizers available at the drugstore. I want to smear them across my face, grab fistfuls like vanilla frosting from a box.

Head to toe, creamy and smooth, smelling like roses or lilacs or my grandma's perfume. Making me soft and supple, pliable.

"Is everything okay?"

A hand on my shoulder jolts me from my sunken stupor. Panicked, I lock eyes with the intern, Rae. She doesn't seem suspicious at finding me leaning against the beauty closet door, looking desperate and crazed. Mostly, her eyes hold concern.

She eases me onto the floor. My legs give out as if they're made of rubber. She's asking if she can get me some water and I feel myself nod. "I'll be right back, just stay here."

Rae returns with a plastic cup and urges it into my hands. I swallow the liquid in two solid gulps. It's like ice sliding down my throat.

"Can you stand?"

My voice cracks. *I think so*, I try to say, but nothing comes. I nod and start to reverse-slide up the wall, shoulder blades scouring the white paint. The skin subdividing Rae's eyebrows pinches together. "Maybe you should go home."

"I'm fine. Dehydrated, that's all."

She doesn't believe me, and I don't want her to believe me. What I want is for her to call my bluff. To say, *you're not all right, none of this is all right, we should all go home and stay there, and this website will close, and no one will miss us at all.*

She'll never say any of that, though. She's an intern.

I shrug her off. A few engineers glance up from their workstations as I amble into the room, slightly out of breath and leaning to one side. The functions of my body, the squelches and gurgles, are amplified, and I worry that my skin, my bones, won't be enough to hold all of me. In the kitchen, I get another glass of water, drink it leaning against the windowsill. I check the clock on the communal stove. The web production all-hands is in fifteen minutes. If I can just get through that, I can be silent and still for the rest of this day.

Time is up. I stop by the bullpen to pick up my computer
and join my team trickling into the Emerald conference room.
Ashley quivers like a feather pen as she waits for us to enter
and take our seats. Lexi comes in last and sits at the head of the
table opposite the big TV. Trapped in this fishbowl, a room
within a room, I am on display. I scan the wavy windowed
wall, searching for the source of this feeling. All I see are the
pale hair parts bisecting brown and red and blond and pink and
purple strands blinking out across the office like beady eyes.

Then, two real eyes. Shining. Rae on the intern couch.
Watching me with an expression that says she knows all my
secrets and she's going to tell them to everyone. Even my mom.
Even HR. My palms start to sweat. I rub them on my jeans,
leaving behind bleary handprints.

At the front of the room, Ashley finishes setting up and
starts talking us through the top stories of the month. "Traffic
to the home page is up thirteen percent!" She fists the air en-
thusiastically. No one responds. She drops her arm. Her smile
disappears into her rounded cheeks. "It's a testament to your
hard work and dedication that our home page is becoming a
premier destination. We're one step closer to our goal of being
the millennial woman's online living room!"

The millennial woman's online living room is a phrase the
higher-ups bandy about to impress upon us the magnitude
of our mission. They want—we all are supposed to want—
to make this website *the* essential place for young women to
get their news and entertainment. Where our peers come to
relax, and to learn.

Ashley prattles on about the top stories—a listicle of at-home
yeast infection remedies with commentary from Instagram-
famous gynecologist Dr. Jewel; a short write-up of an original man-on-the-street video produced in-house, in which
two writers with camera-friendly hair and teeth ask passersby

if they can name the first women to hold various positions in government; an explainer about the influencer who scammed her fans out of money by selling tickets for a creativity workshop that never happened; and a jointly written personal essay by a woman and her husband who live in separate houses. I have read only the yeast infection story, late one night when my body chafed all over. It turned out I didn't have a yeast infection after all, just an undefined itching and burning for which there was no cure, like bugs were crawling over every inch of my skin. I slept fitfully, and by the morning I was no longer inflamed.

Thinking about it now, I feel those cells waking up again. It happens beneath the top layer of the epidermis, deeper into the flesh. I scratch at my forearm, digging pale grooves. Flakes pile under my nails.

The hibernating monster of my computer screen wakes as a notification announces the arrival of a DM from Lexi: Everyone can hear you scratching.

I'm so mortified I could scream. In my peripheral vision she watches me coolly, eyes jabbing above the silver lip of her laptop. I take a deep, shaky breath.

Sorry, I type.

Lexi is already halfway out the door when Ashley ends the meeting. She passes my seat on her way out, a frigid breeze skimming off her like the airy stir off the surface of the ocean, seeping under my heavy sweater and the sheet of hair I'm using to pretend as hard as I can that I'm not looking.

Her observation (*Everyone can hear you*) has so finely taken me apart. My breathing comes in fits and starts, ragged. There's a hole in my lungs that needs patching. The team files out one by one: Carly, Emily, Tom, Ashley. I know I am supposed to follow, to fall in line. Mariah is last. She lingers with her hand on the door frame. A dark streak is the last thing I see before it all goes black.

★ ★ ★

Something hard and domed presses into my back. Above me the ceiling is white, spiked with pipes painted to blend in. It gives the effect of movement, layers shifting on top of layers. I push a hand behind me, and fabric the texture of Brillo scours me. It's familiar yet unreachable, the connection hovering just above my comprehension. I turn my head. A shock of purple comes into view beneath my thigh.

I'm lying on the intern couch.

I wonder, for a delusional second, if I've been demoted. Faces hover before me, coming slowly into focus. First there are four, then eight, then sixteen. I blink a few times and my vision settles. Meghan, Ashley, Mariah, and Rae. Groggy, I sit up.

"Thank god! Are you okay?" Meghan grips my left hand with both of hers so hard her knuckles are blanched.

"What happened?"

"You passed out." This comes from Mariah. "I was leaving the conference room and you slumped over at the table like…you looked dead."

Meghan pulls a ringing phone from her pocket. She answers. "Hi. Yes, she's right here. She's awake." She hands me the phone, mouthing *MOM*.

Dazed, I accept my phone from her. "Hello?" I haven't spoken to my mother in over a month.

"Honey? It's Mom. Are you okay? Your coworker told me what happened."

"What…happened?"

"She said you fainted."

"I fainted."

"Why are you repeating everything I say? Does your head hurt? You could have a concussion."

"I'm fine, just a little bit dizzy. I don't think I hit my head. I was sitting."

"This happened once when you were little. On the soccer field."

"I played soccer?"

"You don't remember? You usually just stood there staring at the ball. You were in it for the ice pops at the end of practice. You really don't remember that?"

Right now, my past is a black hole that only becomes more nebulous as I peer into it. I really don't remember playing soccer, or ever eating a Popsicle. But I don't want my mother to worry about me, either. To get her off the phone, I pretend that it's all coming back, tell her I have to get back to work. The line goes quiet. I try to make eye contact with Meghan, to ask her how she unlocked my phone.

"I came running back as soon as I heard," Ashley says. Her eyes sparkle. She seems to be enjoying this, and why shouldn't she? We all wish for some drama to break up the monotony. I'm happy to provide that service today, even as my head and tongue feel sluggish and drugged.

I can tell that Rae feels vindicated in her rightness; she saw all along that I wasn't okay, but I didn't listen and now I've been humiliated the way I deserve, by fainting in front of everyone. She might be an intern, but she's cunning. I bet it was her idea to lay me down on this couch, my wrecked head resting on the cushion where she sits her ass day after day.

"Thank you."

"Take the rest of the day off. Work from home tomorrow, if you need to," Ashley says. Her brows strain toward each other but something prevents her forehead skin from creasing. I think of an article I published last month, about women getting Botox before thirty. They call it Baby Botox. A radical feminist blog then called us out for "encouraging women to fight the natural signs of aging" by "shooting up with toxins," but I actually appreciated that article. At least it wasn't a think piece saying that hyphenating your last name when you get married is feminism, or a love letter to pizza written by a woman who doesn't eat carbs.

Meghan helps me stand. I collect my things and leave the office, gliding over the city's rough terrain, losing myself in the familiarity of the commute. I'm hovering above myself, watching me make my way. My two halves don't reunite until I'm crawling under the covers, pulling my comforter over my head. I sleep, tossing around in bed, dreaming of missed emails and breaking news. Terrorist attacks and typos.

Hours later, I emerge. It's dark outside, but the living room light casts an anemic glow through the open French doors that doesn't quite reach the bed. I sit up, pulling my knees to my chest. Two figures hover in the doorway. My bed is situated in the far corner, underneath the window. The fire escape is on the other side of the window, should I need it. The grainy shadows surge forward. Muffled voices, vaguely feminine in tone. The figures are forcing their way in, stepping into the darkness, closer to me. Shadows stretching across the floor like vines. I risk ceding a few inches, creep toward the nightstand, and turn on the scarf-covered lamp.

My eyes adjust. Two heads, a dishwater and a platinum blond. Meghan and Veronica. I'm too alarmed to speak, and they must see it in my face because they are smiling warmly and coming closer.

"We come in peace," Veronica says, laughing. In one hand she holds something long and thin. She thrusts it into the light. It's a pink rose, skinny-stemmed, bowing forward with the weight of the bloom. I hesitate. Curling my fingers around the stem, I am met with a stab of pain. The flower drops onto my bedspread and blood beads to the surface of my palm, just above the lifeline.

"Careful! Watch for thorns," Veronica says.

Lifting the wound to my lips, I suck.

"Let's get more light in here," Meghan says. She wanders back toward the door and finds the overhead switch, flicks it upward. Only it's not connected to any circuitry, and so we remain suspended in an eerie chiaroscuro.

"The living room is better." I push off the bed and lead them out. We stand awkwardly around the coffee table until I gesture at the couch. "Please, sit."

It's strange, the two of them in my shabby living room. I fill a tall mason jar, place the rose inside, and set it down in the center of the kitchen table.

"Sorry for barging in on you like that," Meghan says. "Your roommate let us in."

"Sasha?" She doesn't come home before ten or eleven most nights. How could she have let them in?

"She was on her way out," Veronica says quickly. "Anyway, Meghan said you scared her at work today."

"I must've had more to drink than I meant to last night."

"Strange," Veronica says. "I was just fine. But that's not uncommon for your first time."

"It wasn't…my…first…"

"Let me get you some water. Where do you keep glasses?" Meghan asks, springing back up from the couch before she'd fully settled down.

I point out the cabinet and tell her to use the tap. I stand, gawky and out of place, while she pulls out three mismatched glasses, fills one for each of us, and hands them around. We slurp wetly into the silence. The audible sipping makes me twitchy. "How about I put on some music?"

I connect my phone to Sasha's Bluetooth speaker, navigate

to my Spotify library. *Sincerely, Adriana* begins to play from the beginning, the familiar opening notes soothing me, a balm to the soul. Veronica and Meghan close their eyes and sway back and forth like Russian nesting dolls rolling on rounded hips. Two women captured by the spirit. I wish I could ride the wave as they do, let Adriana pick me up and drop me somewhere else, somewhere peaceful. But suspicion nags, keeping me grounded. I keep thinking about Meghan calling my mother. Wondering if she pressed my fingertip to the Home button while I was conked out. Feeling violated.

One song ends and another starts. This album was released only a few years ago, yet it feels like it's from a different era.

A clearing of the throat draws my attention. Veronica and Meghan have both fallen still and are watching me with matching tight-lipped expressions. They remind me a little bit of Carly and Emily with their pleading Grady twin eyes.

"You must be *starved*," Veronica says. "I'd love to cook dinner."

"Oh, no. Please, don't. I mean, you don't have to do that."

"I know I don't have to, but I want to. Friends take care of each other. And that's what we are: we're friends."

We go back and forth like this for several minutes. Exasperated, I give her directions to the grocery store a few blocks away. Meghan says she'll join her, and they insist on leaving me behind. I hand them my keys so they can get back into the building, though I'm tempted to lock them out, and then they're gone. Adriana's voice bounces off the wall above the speaker, amplified in the absence. Her vocals, normally smooth as peanut butter, chafe at my inner ears. I keep looking over my shoulder, making sure I'm really alone, that they didn't sneak back into the apartment somehow. I lower the volume on the speaker until she's little more than a whisper.

In the bathroom, I examine my reflection. My skin is sallow. I spot Sasha's Kate Somerville cleanser sideways on the edge of the sink. I squirt some out and rub the frothy mixture onto my complexion. By the time I finish rinsing, the front of my shirt is the splash zone at a public pool. I go into my room and change into a sweatshirt. A bleating sound crosses over the music, and my first thought, from another life, is that the record is skipping. It is, of course, not the music, but my phone's email app.

Footsteps, voices, and rattling keys alert me to Veronica and Meghan's return. I leave my phone and help them empty the reusable grocery bags (Veronica's—she always keeps them in her purse) and then I'm dragged to the couch for wine.

"Hair of the dog," Veronica says at least three times as she opens the bottle, fishes out more mason jars, and pours three servings, mine nearly full to the brim. Veronica shouts questions as she and Meghan chop and stir and bang wooden spoons against my pan rims. She wants to know the biographical details. I am touched, and I spout them like I'm reciting a shopping list: hometown, college major, first job out of school, favorite music before Adriana. There is only *before* and *after*. The kitchenette sizzles with the not unpleasant odor of charred oil. It's not too bad, being cared for by these women who seem to care so much despite knowing me so little.

Twenty minutes later, Veronica asks for plates and, when I move to stand, she holds out a hand. "Tell me where they are."

She digs out three plates and Megan portions the food. We sit at the kitchen table with Veronica's singular rose pinkly dabbing the center. It matches her complexion, and the pink-and-white angora sweater she pulled off before cooking and draped over the back of her chair. Dinner is sautéed spinach and salmon filets marinated in a Dijon mustard sauce. Everything melts in my mouth. Everything is delicious. Better than anything I've ever cooked myself. When I don't order takeout,

I make charred quesadillas and grilled cheese sandwiches, or sometimes just spoon the meat of an avocado from the skin and sprinkle it with hot sauce, eating over the sink in a mad rush. I wonder if she learned from her mother, or a nanny.

My utensils scrape the naked plate. *Sincerely, Adriana* switches to *My Whole Heart*. Veronica actually drops her fork and puts a hand to her heart during the opening notes of "Bittersweet Goodbye."

I clear the plates. As I wash them in the sink, Veronica suggests we close out the evening with a Growing, led by me. "Normally I'd never ask a new member so soon, but it's just us. Besides, you've more than proven yourself."

Meghan nods. "You should do the honors. After the day you've had."

They're looking at me with those doe-eyes, those swallow-you-whole eyes, and I have no choice. Selecting "Lunar," the first song off *Hazardous*, an enduring fan favorite that sends Ivies the world over into a dizzying mash of bloodcurdling screams and shrieking imitation high notes whenever she sings it live. We gather on the floor. In the absence of tapered candles, we linger above the cold phone light. The irritating, staticky quality I detected in the speaker earlier has vanished; her vocals are crisp and echoey. They sizzle like a layer of freezer burn hitting a warm tongue.

She sings of the moon, of stepping into its frosted silver glow to kiss a man. Closing my eyes, I don't see myself and Tom or myself and anyone I've ever met. I see Adriana and Nolan on a hill above Los Angeles. Or my version of Los Angeles, spliced from a thousand movies as disparate as *Mulholland Drive* and *Fast Times at Ridgemont High*. That flattened grid speeding toward a small spike of tall buildings, a ruffle of pine trees in the foreground. City of Dreams, City of Angels. I've always been drawn to New York more than any other American city, but

I'm startled by this clear-eyed vision of what could be waiting for me on the opposite coast.

The Adriana and Nolan of my imagination embrace. He
whispers something and she giggles. They kiss. There are no
flashbulbs or screaming fans. They pull apart, she rests her
head on his bicep. Their shoulders sigh.

The song ends and I'm ready to book a flight, pack a bag,
board the plane, embrace the sunshine. I blink my eyes open,
disappointed at the secondhand rug that meets my gaze. Veronica hugs her own arms, sheathed in a spotless white blouse
that is somehow pristine even after she spent half an hour waving her arms over oil-slicked pans. We don't make eye contact. Veronica and Meghan scramble to their feet, blushing,
and pull on their sweaters and coats. We mumble goodbyes,
and then they leave and I'm truly, blissfully alone.

I go to my phone, still lying on its back on the rug, and pull
it into my chest as the next song begins to play.

8

Five Adrianas march down the street. Her repeating face is
six feet tall and plastered to the scaffolding, the same tilted
chin, downward glance, and pillowed lips gently pursed as if
she's trying to half swallow you like a lollipop over and over
again. It's an ad for the new album. She's in a purple butterfly-
sleeved confection that drapes off the shoulders and a jeweled
choker. Her gold-flecked gaze trails me all the way to work.
I'm the only one in the elevator, but I feel the hum of it over
my shoulder, turn around to look just in case. My own bleary
reflection greets me in the chrome backdrop.

I step into the disco fever lobby, pausing to fix my hair in
the mirrored wall. I fully intended on taking Ashley up on
the offer to stay home again, but I woke this morning with a
restlessness in my bones and knew I wouldn't be able to sit in
my musty apartment all day with only reality TV and empty
rooms shrinking the longer I paced them. It would make me
crazy. Crazier. So, I did my hair with Sasha's flat iron again—
"This here is the Cadillac of hair straighteners," she said to
me once, as in: *Break this and you die*—and I spent my com-

mute worrying about whether I unplugged it. Trying to conjure the memory of the cord in my hand, snaking through
my grip, the moment of give as the prongs tug and fall away
from the outlet.

But the more I dwell, the more it develops the tenor of a
false memory, an image cut and pasted from my past into the
continuity gap from this morning. It disturbs me, how regularly I slide in and out of my own life.

The web producers' bullpen is empty, but I sit with a pin-
straight spine. I'll show them all that no, I'm not a woman
who faints at the office. Not *often*, not *usually*. Tom arrives
less than a minute later and half smiles through mucky egg
sandwich bites. *Morning*, I think.

I open my laptop. Piger dings.

How are you feeling? Mariah always uses unabbreviated
words and proper grammar in text communication like a
woman twice her age.

I tell her I'm much better. Add an exclamation point and
a smiley face. Delete the smiley, then the exclamation point,
add the exclamation back and hit Send. She sends a thumbs-
up in response. I click over to my email. Nothing important.
I check Twitter. Nothing important. I pull up various websites, tell myself I'm scoping out the competition, not wasting
time. More nuances of nothing.

Nine more hours of this; maybe I should've stayed home,
after all.

Meghan appears at my side, a steaming mug in her hands.
My cat-shaped mug. I start to protest, and she puts the mug
down next to my mousepad. "Hazelnut, right?"

A surge of love wells from my toes to my chest. "Uh…yes.
How did you know?"

She waves a dismissive hand in front of her face. "I've seen
you make it. How are you feeling?"

"Much better. Thanks again for dinner. And tell Veronica too."

"Tell her yourself at the next Ivy meeting."

"You want me to come back?"

"Omigod of *course*! The girls *loved* you. And Veronica let you lead The Growing—that's *big*." She pats my shoulder. Her skin is clammy and cold through my shirt, corpse-like. "Let me know if you want to grab lunch!"

She leaves. I check the time. Nine thirty-two. I sip Meghan's pity coffee. It's nice to have someone looking out for me. Bringing me hot drinks. Checking in. A friend, an ally. A work wife.

The second single off of *solstice*, "turn on the light," debuts with a twenty-second video snippet on Instagram. She dances and mouths the words in the foreground while the producer Petey Jackson sits behind her at the console, playing the track. The song is political, with an erratic, shouted sample of a man yelling at an anti-police-violence protest punctuating the frantic, jangly synths and sharp marching-band beats that underline spoken-word vocals. It's chaotic and scattered, a headache. Repetitive and thumping, the kind of music that takes control, bobbing your limbs without your input.

I tap my fingers sporadically on my thigh while I listen. Online, the reactions are swift and harsh:

"What is this trash?"

"I hate the sample. It would be so good without the sample."

"A repetitive mess."

"The talking in the background ruins the whole song!"

My phone buzzes sharply. It's the Ivies. They've recently added me to their group chat, after the day that I somehow proved my worth by fainting.

What is she DOING???

She has got to stop working with Petey Jackson.

The production is a mess.

They hate the song. I start typing, then stop. I'm too new to disagree. I begin to spiral, weighing the possibilities. If I say *nothing*, they might think I'm an airhead with no opinions, an empty plastic bag. Worse, they might forget I ever existed. *Didn't we have some other girl at a meeting once? No, that doesn't sound right.*

These women, they could be the only ones who matter, the key to my release from the prison of myself. If they no longer believe in me, it might lead to my actual banishment, a blinking in and out of corporeal reality, an ultimate exile, a purgatory for the uncultured. The website will barely notice I'm gone. They'll reassign my responsibilities without missing a beat. Carly and Emily will throw a small happy hour honoring me in the JonBenét Ramsey booth at Blinkers, a celebration under the guise of sadness. There will be a hashtag and a themed cocktail that photographs well in low lighting, and the dead pageant girl will be the only one who misses me.

The iMessage cursor mocks me, blinking cheekily.

It's…different. I hit Send and drop my phone on the floor beside my bed. I restart the song and let the jittering rhythms send me into a restless, unlovely trance, the ceiling above pulsing hypnotic yellow, blue and red.

The stage stretches forever in either direction. Heavy breathing, a low rumble, panting. An audience lurks beyond a layer of unfocused and impenetrable darkness, filling the room like green fog at the bottom of the ocean. They are hungry and waiting. My stomach shakes like a dying animal.

It's just me up here. Me, and the microphone, a mesh cone mushroomed above a spindly stand.

I take a difficult step, inhibited by a long dress rustling around my legs and a weighted fur jacket pinning my upper arms to my rib cage.

A light comes on above me and the audience springs to life. Everything before me remains blank, but on the opposite end of the spectrum, so bright I can't make out faces or the features of the room. I can't tell if the theater is lush and gold or a muddy downtown black box. A bright blue spot swoops out of the velvet recesses and dives toward my throat. As it draws closer, I make out the shape of wings and a beak. It's a robin. The drilling *whoosh, whoosh, whoosh* of beating wings grows loud enough to fill my ears, momentarily drowning out the screams. Then the audience sounds return to me, bigger than ever, shouts morphing from excited to predatory, running the spectrum of mob mentality. They love me and they will soon charge with pitchforks.

And I still can't see a thing.

The robin changes course, lands on my shoulder. *Sing*, it demands. Our connection is telepathic—the beak is clamped shut. I grip the base of the microphone with unsteady hands. The light changes again. Two people in the front row become incrementally clearer, as if I'm peering at them through a damp shower door, having wiped the condensation from just one spot. The figures remain oleaginous, but I make out a few defining details: the sharp mountain peak of a ponytail brushing up against the rounded edge of a cap. A thin shoulder jostling a muscled one.

My mouth opens. No sound at first and then a stirring deep below the gully of my throat. A gurgling, like the sensation of water newly at the boiling point. The bubbling moves higher and then it's spilling from between my lips, an airy pink cloud, a cumulus tasting of vapor laced with whipped sugar, remaining suspended even when my jaw slides shut.

The first post on Adriana's Instagram account is from Christmas Day seven years ago. She has one arm wrapped around an old woman's wrinkled neck as she kisses her temple. According to the caption, this is her grandmother. The room where the photo was taken is too dark, the resolution poor, both figures difficult to make out. These are the photos I like best, the ones that show her at her most quotidian. Like this fame, this talent could come for anyone with a grandmother and clear enough skin.

I scroll through her early updates—a beaded *Adriana* necklace trimmed with hearts, an iconic Tiffany's box that I'm confident holds actual Tiffany's jewelry, a pair of sparkly wedges with butterfly wings sprouting from the heels, a macaroon-printed dress acting as the main subject of a mirror selfie. She used to be so over-the-top girly, the human embodiment of a piercing station at Claire's, all glitz and rhinestones. A twelve-year-old's idealized vision of celebrity and wealth.

Nolan's first appearance on her feed is as early as January of the following year. He's a heavily inked hand draped over piano keys, LOVE etched across his four right knuckles. Adriana's hand rests beside his, dwarfed, as her hands so often are, by a very long sleeve. The crop focuses on the space between their pinky fingers, as if purposefully drawing attention to the fact that they do not touch. The love is there already, coming to life in the space between their not-touching.

As I brush my teeth before work, I play an old video. It's just her, on a rumpled bed lined with pink pillows, practicing whistle tones, a somewhat private moment inviting the viewer to wonder what Adriana Argento is like when she is actually alone. The clip repeats on a loop, until the notes start to sound like cries for help.

Watching Adriana, I am reminded of a certain type of girl

from high school. The special girls, the ones who held themselves apart, distinguished by matters of bone structure, by the honey-drip way they moved through space. Heads followed them as they walked the halls between classes. They weren't really friends with each other, always surrounded instead by girls less attractive by degrees. Still pretty but diminished enough to make the shining ones appear even more lustrous. Their groups created pockets of effulgence clustered along the dingy enameled halls.

Special girls existed in every social class: special girls among the theater kids, the jocks, the English lovers, the artists. Not only did they have looks, they had talent. I'd often wonder which came first—did their skills in mathematics or painting turn them beautiful, or was it the other way around? It was an important lesson, learned early, in how utterly unfair life can be.

Most days, it's easy enough to pretend I'm happy. If I avoid my reflection, I can even forget for hours at a time that my skin is dull and nearly lifeless, that the pores around my nose are visible in certain lighting, that my body is as limp and inelegant as uncooked spaghetti. Looking at Adriana, like looking at those special girls, I begin to want more. That wanting is a danger.

I'm not sure what, exactly, I'm jealous of when it comes to Adriana. Is it the mind-altering drug of her beauty, or is it her voice, big enough to draw a stadium of people to their knees? Singing in my apartment when I know Sasha is not home, that's the only time I'm brave enough not to hold back. I guess, then, what I'm really jealous of is this: being so good at something you know you'll never truly embarrass yourself.

Fandom is about worship, yes, but it's also a reminder of all the ways life is unsatisfying for the regulars. Perhaps the riskiest part of staring directly into sunlight is not how it burns your eyeballs and whites out your vision; perhaps it's more about the way it makes you consider your own insignificance.

★ ★ ★

Over the closet door, an Adriana *Hazardous* sweatshirt is stretched to its full height and nailed into place, resembling a chalk outline, a two-dimensional torso, a figure hung on the cross. I ask why Pearl doesn't wear it. She blinks like my idiocy causes her physical pain and rubs her shaved scalp. She doesn't like me, but I get the sense she'll tolerate whatever Veronica tells her to tolerate. They all do. And Veronica wants me here.

"We're her *fans*," Jessie says. She's cut her black hair into a bob since I last saw her, and her hands keep reaching for the empty space around her neck that the pigtails used to fill.

We're slung about Pearl's bedroom, on her mattress and floor. Her roommates are watching a game, a whatever sporting event, in the living room, so the Ivies are crowded in here like teenagers avoiding the watchful eyes of their parents. Veronica sits in the only chair and I'm on the bed with Meghan, who finger-combs the ends of my hair. Our friendship has progressed to the level of constant touching, mostly initiated by Meghan. She's always linking an arm through mine, squeezing my shoulder, tucking a lock of hair behind my ears. It made me jumpy at first, this sharing of my body, but I've grown to rely on the knowledge that I am no longer only my own.

"Does being a fan of hers mean we get to dictate the art she makes?" I hear myself say.

Jessie reddens under her bronzed skin. It's like I slapped her. They all turn to stare. I feel their eyes crawling over me like ants. We're discussing a recent *Elle* interview in which Adriana dismissed some of her older songs as "hits designed by the pop machine." In the same article, she said that *solstice* is representative of the music she feels she was always destined to make. I think that can't be a bad thing, but the Ivies don't agree.

"All I know is that if the entire album sounds like this last single I'm going to be pissed. And it doesn't seem like a smart idea, alienating your biggest fans." This comes from Crystal, who faces away from me, her curls sunrising over the edge of the mattress. She's dyed the tips orange.

"But she doesn't know us," I say.

Meghan nudges my upper arm with her chin and suppresses her volume. "I get what you're saying. But we want her to be at her *best*."

I drop it, sinking into Pearl's mildewed cushions as the Ivies continue to grumble like disgruntled union members. The meeting wraps with Jessie leading The Growing with a song from *My Whole Heart*, "Adriana's most underrated album," which I take to mean *her worst album*.

We kneel, light our candles, lean hopefully toward the center waiting for the magic to hit. Pearl lowers the lights and closes off our lopsided circle, sliding in between Crystal and Veronica. I don't expect the tears to come, not this time, my ego bruised and my mood sour. But my cheeks are flooded before I realize what's happening. Someone whimpers, possibly me, possibly all of us, even Adriana, our mouths moving as one giant mouth, our plaintive little moans like the mewls of stray cats in the alley of trash cans next to my apartment. This is it, the reason I return again and again, the reason I tamp down my dissent; it's all for the moment we turn our thin-skinned inner wrists to the ceiling and open our veins to the sky, martyred to the cause of her voice, letting her fill us. The song ends, the lights return, and we blow out the candles one by one.

Emily is the one who asks this time:

Come out with us after the team dinner tonight? We MISS you!!! Xx

The team dinner is somewhere between mandatory and not. It's been on my calendar for weeks and up until she messages me, I still think I'm going to talk my way out of it. I was planning to fake an illness, but now I see how hard that would be to pull off, a lie that would just keep growing, new problems popping up like weeds in the sidewalk cracks of my story. What kind of sick would I be, and for how long, and what symptoms would I still have tomorrow and when would they finally fade?

So tonight I would be eating overpriced, overly cheesed Mexican food and drinking too much sangria at a trendy place downtown with Ashley, Lexi and all the rest. I haven't said more than ten words to any of them since I started spending more time with Meghan and the Ivies. Whatever threads held us together have long since been cut and I understand now that we had nothing, are nothing, without work and petty bullshit binding us together.

I consider, one last time, putting Emily off with a transparent excuse, the kind that would preclude me from ever being invited again, that would cordon me off as *not one of them* even as I am, plainly, one of them. It would be simpler that way, the way it should've been all along. I'd do my work and I'd go home, and I'd be quiet for the hours in between.

Emily sits way down at the other end of the table, on the opposite side, across from Carly. I notice her absentmindedly chewing on her hair, a habit that disgusts and fascinates me in equal measure. This feels like a trap. Still, I say: Ok—I'm sure I'll be dying to digest whatever happens at dinner with you all!

Dos Amigos is a chain restaurant that looks and feels like a chain restaurant. But the Manhattanized version of a chain, lightly polished with brass fixtures and artfully arranged plating. The food is mediocre, as divorced from real Mexican culture as it can possibly get. Lightly insensitive artwork featuring sombreros and full-skirted dancers lines the walls, and pitchers of cloying, sugary sangria languish on nearly every table, including ours. I'm seated between Mariah and Emily, with

Ashley and Carly facing us. Tom is at the head of the table; I would need to turn halfway around in my chair in order to see him, which I will not do. Lexi sits on the other end, next to Emily. We've just placed our entrée orders and the energy is already strained; I feel it, taut as a pantyhose leg stretched over my face, suffocating.

Lexi smiles using only one side of her mouth and half-heartedly joins glasses with Emily when Ashley yells, "Cheers!" Glass meets glass in a trickle around the table. The waiter wheels over a cart piled high with avocados and tomatoes and onions and limes and begins mixing medium-spicy guacamole with a mortar and pestle, a task that requires little skill and seems to be there only to show us how *authentic* this guacamole will be. Our stilted conversation screeches to a halt as we watch her work. I notice a small crescent moon inked in black with a hollow center next to the knob on her wrist. The tattoo reminds me of Adriana, as everything now does, and I long to be alone with her computerized image, boxed in with the cool dark of my bedroom, watching her exciting and glamorous life unfold, instead of here, living my own, wedged between people I barely like, at a restaurant I'd never choose. The problem with saying yes is that it puts the fate of your dinner in other people's hands.

I slide my cell phone out of a side pocket in my purse and hold the lit screen under the table. A text from Meghan decorates the screen, below Adriana's pointed chin, a tour image saved as my wallpaper. Below that, an email from a food delivery app expressing concern because they haven't heard from me in a while.

Ignoring the notifications, I let my hands take me on a tour of Adriana's social feeds. There's no need to be this surreptitious; the others all have their phones sitting out on the table, faceup beside the silverware, the screens blinking on and off every few seconds. But they are performing *work*, while I perform superficiality.

The guacamole hits the table and we fight for space with the brittle edges of beige, blue, and red tortilla chips wielded like swords. I can't tell if we are truly starving or just that eager to fill our mouths with something other than words. All but Lexi, who waits until we've each retracted our impatient hands, then gingerly plucks a crisp triangle from the fluffed pile. She spears a reasonable amount of lime-glazed guacamole with a sharp corner, bites the chip in half, and drops the remnants onto her plate with a chatter that sounds, to my ears, like breaking glass.

Ashley glances nervously around the table. She knows this night is her responsibility. She clears her throat and, in the manner of a peppy camp counselor, begins: "So, uh, thank you all for coming tonight! I wanted to take the time to celebrate all the success we've had this past year. You know, now that things have calmed down post-holiday season. I know being a web producer isn't as *glamorous* a job as some of the others in editorial, but it's an important one. The website wouldn't attract as many readers or run as smoothly as it does without all of your hard work and dedication. Thanks to you, we *will* become the millennial woman's online living room.

"Teamwork makes the dream work!" she concludes, and claps her hands.

Beside me, Emily turns a snort into a cough. I bite my lip to keep from laughing. Everyone looks down. We clink glasses in a chain around the table once again. The mood settles and loosens, expanding like dough spreading lazily beneath a rolling pin. As the sangria sinks lower down the pitcher, we begin to talk more, and even to laugh a little, softening as gum does when it's held against the inside curve of a cheek.

I remain aware of Lexi the whole time. She commands attention. She watches us with furtive eyes tracking above her bubbling enchilada. Every so often she interjects with a word or two, but mostly she observes. I get the sense that she's evaluating us all, watching for missteps. It puts me on high alert until the moment when the waiter drops the check. We all look at the bright rectangle of white paper as Ashley fumbles in her wallet, searching for the company card.

"Shit, I can't find it," she says and flushes once she realizes she's cursed in front of Lexi. "Where *is* it? I know I put it in my wallet before I left."

Collectively, we hold our breath. Lexi moves very slowly, reaching in front of Ashley, eyeing her as she places her own personalized company card down on the tray with the check. It leaves a metallic click. "I got it," she says.

Ashley's lips vibrate as she breathes out through her mouth.

"Thank you," she says, flattened. Her normally shiny skin is matte and lifeless. Her hair is slightly collapsed. She resembles a soda can trampled by the wheels of a truck. I genuinely feel bad for her. At least until she perks up and plasters a stiff grin frozen as rigor mortis on her face. Claps her hands together, and says, "Well, this was fun! I expect to see you all in the office at the usual time Monday. Hangover or no hangover!" She pauses. "Ha ha."

She actually says the words *Ha. Ha.*

I can't help myself; my eyes lock on Tom's. He reaches up to scratch behind his ear with the arm closest to Ashley and smirks into his wrist, keeping his gaze drilled on mine the whole time. I smile back.

Ashley orders an Uber, and we wait with her on the sidewalk, shuffling our feet, small talking our way through the final moments of this torture. A black Toyota Camry pulls up to the curb and Ashley hugs us each goodbye. Lexi stands apart, texting or emailing on her phone. My phone dings; she's posted a message in Piger. She looks up when Ashley disappears into the car, says, "All right, then," and walks off toward Broadway as if that's goodbye.

Carly breaks the silence: "What a clusterfuck."

The dam cracks and the laughter and discomfort I've been holding inside for the past two hours flood my head with light. And then we're doubled over, howling, hands on our knees, tears streaming down our faces. Emily and Carly hold each other's shaking shoulders. Mariah sits right down and buries her face in her knees, not even worried about all the spit and piss on the sidewalk, the crust of the city. I cover my eyes with both hands, cackling as my cupped palms echo my giggles back to me. I lose track of Tom, but his energy hovers somewhere to the left and I won't pretend it doesn't feel nice. I'd forgotten how good being near him is: not perfect, like listening to a song by your favorite artist for the first time or seeing that Adriana has posted a new photo on Instagram. But good like the first bite of hot pizza is good: the temptation and the beginning of the plunge before the regret.

Maybe we can start over. Be whatever we were trying to be, before. I catch my breath, lower my hands away from my face. Tom is watching with a mischievous smirk and a lightning flash in his eye.

It's going to be a weird night.

Obsession, as defined by the Merriam-Webster dictionary, is "a persistent disturbing preoccupation with an often-unreasonable idea or feeling." *Obsession*, as defined by me, is the itch under my skin, the unrelenting shiver ticking up my vertebrae, then back down when I'm waiting in line to buy lunch or ringing Veronica's doorbell or opening a mysterious package.

Am I obsessed with Adriana Argento? I'm sure most people would agree that I am. And sure, she is the first thing on my mind each morning and the last at night. Sure, I check in on her throughout the day, in the low, wasted moments. But our relationship is one-sided, and I believe that makes all the difference. If things were reciprocal, if she knew who I was and cared for me in turn, the way that Meghan does, the way the Ivies do for each other in lieu of a friendship with their idol—well, surely people would call us best friends instead. Wouldn't they?

This is what I'm thinking about as we slide into our booth at Blinkers and I find myself eye level with JonBenét, leader of the army of the unfortunately famous. Her child's face in the mask of a woman smirks out from under those Dolly Parton curls and I feel a tug at my heart. I cover her photograph with my hand, leaving the specter of my fingerprints like rings of smoke around her small body.

Tom sits next to me, on purpose. His shirtsleeve is rolled up and his forearm keeps brushing mine and I don't move away. A tattoo is partially visible on his inner wrist, some kind of round-edged leaf. While the others are at the bar ordering drinks, boldness overtakes me, and I place my fingertip directly on the dark green puddle of ink. My skin is cold, his is warm, and it creates a jolt between us. "What's your tattoo?"

He rolls the sleeve up to the elbow. "It's a poison oak leaf."

"How is it different from a regular oak?"

"See the edges? They're rounder. And the leaves are bigger."

"And it's poison?"

"That, too."

I put my hand, tingling with the hiss of JonBenét's poltergeistian whispers, over the colors embedded in his skin. "Is it contagious?"

Tom looks down at his opposite hand, which is clenching and unclenching a pulverized napkin. His voice catches. "My wife has—had—a matching one. It's a reference to one of her favorite songs. We got them the night I proposed."

I stiffen at the mention of her; improbable as it seems, I'd forgotten about the wife. The wife with the matching, possibly now covered-up tattoo. The one who got there first, who meant something more to him than I will likely ever mean to anyone, even to Meghan. I feel a certain sense of responsibility towards her, a kind of womanish kinship, even if she is now his ex-wife. I withdraw my hand from Tom's forearm. Scrub the flattened length of my palm along my pant leg.

Mariah pulls out her chair with a loud scrape and slams her beer on the table, effectively bursting the moment. "Hello, lovebirds."

Tom crosses his arms and I lace my hands into my lap.

"Oh, come *on*," Mariah says. She leans forward. "You're not fooling anyone."

Tom and I pass an uneasy look between us, but just then Carly and Emily resurface holding fresh margaritas, the salt licked off and cracking their lips, and we resume talking about work.

"Dinner was so awkward. I mean, what else did I expect, right?" Mariah says once they've settled down. "And what was that bit at the end with the company card? Did Ashley actually *lose* it?"

"If she did, she's fucked. It wasn't even her card; she borrowed the editor-in-chief's," Carly says.

"As if they'd trust her with her own," Emily says. "You know, Ashley told me they might ask us to start pitching stories," she adds.

"What? Why?" I hear the tremor running through my voice. This would be a dream for so many. Surely some of the people sitting at this table, Tom and Mariah especially, have hoped for an announcement of the kind. But the thought of presenting my ideas for evaluation makes my face burn.

Mariah licks a beer foam moustache off her upper lip. "Because our jobs are fucking pointless, if you haven't noticed."

"I think it's pretty cool, if it's true," Tom says. He's right to add that qualifier; our bosses are always telling us about upcoming changes and not following through, pretending they never mentioned whatever it was in the first place, acting like we are the crazy ones for asking. Denial is the main management strategy.

"Maybe they'll just lay us all off instead." Carly pouts at her cell phone camera, snapping a selfie as soon as she closes her mouth. She's wearing a black tube top even though it's freezing outside, shoulders hiked toward her ears, and her skin is lightly bronzed, as if she's spent all day in the sun.

"Oh god, don't say that. Some of us *need* this job," Mariah says.

The mood at Blinkers tonight is darker, the usual buoyancy chased into the shadows. All the sounds, the shouting and the loud music, are thunderous and threatening. The girls in their bandage dresses, displaying their fleshy spillage, seem desperate and sad, the buttoned-down men leaning a little too close. I fade out of the conversation, sipping my drink, letting the alcohol bathe me in soft sorrows. I can't bring myself to try or to care or to respond like I know I should.

While the other women debate the possibility of layoffs, the pros and cons of severance versus continued employment, with varying degrees of passion, Tom whispers in my ear, "Do you want to get some air?"

And that's how I wind up outside, alone with him. Once the air hits my face, I know we won't be going back into Blinkers. We've been paying for drinks in cash, so there are no tabs to close and our goodbyes can all be left unsaid. The cold is refreshing after the muculent interior. It shocks me awake; my eyes are wide open. Tom takes off in a random direction, and I follow without asking questions. He fumbles in his coat pocket and produces a pack of cigarettes and a red Bic. He presses the end to his lips and lights the flame, closing his eyes as he takes a grateful inhale. "I didn't know you smoked," I say. Smoking, I understood, was no longer supposed to be cool.

"It's a bad habit," he replies, as if it's an answer.

I note that he's no longer wearing his wedding ring and he notices me noticing, shoves his left hand deep into the pocket with his American Spirits.

"My wife..." he starts to say.

"You split up, I heard."

Tom shakes his head. "It's not that. She, uh. She died. It happened before I met you, almost two years ago. Car accident. I don't talk about it much."

I stop moving. He keeps on for a few beats before he realizes I'm no longer in step with him. There's a sheen to his eyes when he turns to face me, a slight quiver, like he's about to cry.

The moment to say something, anything, passes.

He goes on. "I'm sorry. I should've told you before. At the holiday party, or earlier, even. It just seemed like you liked me, and I didn't want to ruin it by bringing up my dead wife. I realize how dumb that sounds, because I ruined it by making you think I was a cheating asshole instead. But being with you...talking with you...it's the most *normal* I've felt since before I got a phone call telling me she was never coming home. I just didn't want you to look at me like—well, like you're looking at my right now."

My jaw has migrated downward without my consent. Horrified, I snap my mouth shut with a painful click. Tom's smoking hand is at his side, a feather wisp traveling from the burning end. I should be thinking of what to say to make him feel better, but all I can do is wonder where the smoke goes when it vanishes, where anything goes when it vanishes.

He's waiting.

There are several ways someone might respond to the knowledge that their maybe-crush has a dead spouse. They might, for instance, say they are sorry for the other person's loss. They might cross the distance, touch his arm, reveal themselves to be sweet and attentive, the way a girlfriend should be. I bet Adriana would do one of those things, if she were here. Bake him some cookies. Kiss his cheek. Sing him a song so beautiful he would be raptured and reborn and forgiven and absolved, his grief disintegrating in her mouth.

She's not there, but I am, and what I do is spin on my heel and run.

My lungs are on fire.

I don't, as a rule, run. By the time I slow down, on the outskirts of Union Square, there's an ache in my side and I'm breathing so hard that even the man with holes in his sweater asking for change at the subway entrance seems concerned. I flop my head over my knees, hair raining down either side of my head, and take a few deep breaths, keeping the oxygen flowing as smoothly as possible. In and out, as I've done since birth. He would've caught up by now, if he were coming.

I look up at the sky, navy and starless. My eyes are tight and dry from the late-winter wind. Yet I'm not ready to go home, to be alone with myself, to think about what I've done or not done. I circle the park to the wide, flat steps, where half a dozen people loiter despite the weather, smoking cigarettes or pot, talking and laughing, fearing nothing, these people for whom cold is preferable to home. I take my place among them, between a group of teens passing a joint under a mushroom cloud of sweet, earthy smoke and a cluster of dancers practicing their breaking choreography around a circular speaker. My blood stops rushing, and my ears adjust to the ambient noise. I can finally make out the music, some thudding trap beat.

I watch the boys dance, their skin flashing in the moonlight, their braided and dreadlocked hair flying, ropey torsos contorting like rubber bands finely calibrated to snapping. The song ends and they wipe supernatural sweat from their brows with crooked knuckles. Imagine, sweating in this cold. The effort it would take. I clap with the few other spectators who have gathered, adding a dollar to the upturned baseball cap when it gets passed under my nose. The boy holding it gives me a fist bump.

"You were amazing," I tell him, meaning it. He smiles wide. He can't be older than fifteen. I want to ask him if his mother knows he's out this late and, for the first time, I understand what it means to feel old. To sense the way time has begun closing down exits until soon there will be no choice but to stay on this road.

"Thanks," the boy says. Then he's gone.

The park empties out. I check my phone. It's after eleven and there's a message from Carly, received thirty-seven minutes ago: Where'd u gooooo? Miss uuuuuuu!!! Her hatred for me—for the way I continue to disappoint her, abandon her at every opportunity—drips out of the phone, heating the metal in my hand.

I call Meghan.

"Are you still in Union Square?" she asks.

"Yes."

"Don't move."

Meghan lives on the top floor of a Park Slope brownstone. Her apartment is one sprawling bedroom, a small living room, and an even smaller kitchen. The bathroom is a toilet and a showerhead screwed into the wall and a ridge of tile to prevent flooding. The place is cramped with old-fashioned charm. Run-down fixtures, the finishes chipping at the edges. Prewar. My apartment is roomier, but with less character, a newer development, though not exactly *new*. And then, of course, there's Sasha. What I wouldn't give to live alone, decorating everything to my liking, wandering from room to room without occasion. And how can Meghan afford to do so, on a digital editor's salary?

When she said she'd come, I assumed that meant she lived nearby. I didn't anticipate Park Slope, which is only a few stops closer to Manhattan than my neighborhood. She came from nowhere and we left together. I didn't think to ask where she'd been.

I glance out Meghan's window as if the dead buildings across the street can tell me anything and think about how night looks the same in every season. "I want disco fries."

Meghan pulls up her phone, opens an app, presses a few buttons. "It is done."

"How much?"

"Don't worry about it."

"I'll just Venmo—"

"I *said* don't worry about it."

She continues to not ask me what's wrong. We are quiet until the food comes, then she pulls two foggy plastic containers from a moist paper bag and we crawl through the window in the kitchen to sit on the fire escape, socks on our feet and a blanket over both our laps, torsos tucked into puffy coats. It's very, very, cold but not unpleasant under the layers. I hover my hands over the hunched mass of congealed cheese and gravy to warm my numb fingers.

I'm happy to be outside, looking down on the quiet street,

not doing much, but participating. Even New York City quiets
after midnight, especially in the neighborhoods like this one,
occupied mostly by families and the kind of young adults who
think late-night television and takeout make for the perfect
weekend night. Meghan holds up a finger, drops her container
of fries on the grate beneath our feet, and slithers back through
the window. A tendril of heat escapes from the apartment. She
disappears behind the refrigerator door and returns clutching a chilled bottle of strawberry André. The bottle appears
on the windowsill, followed by Meghan's compact body as it
threads back outside. She slides the window almost completely
shut, with just a sliver of space wide enough to fit our hands.

"Thought we could use a drink." The alcohol is sweet, ar-
tificially fruity, with the taste and appearance of seltzer with
a strawberry Jolly Rancher dissolving inside. The booze hits
my head slowly, a steady reverse nasal drip, reigniting my
earlier, neglected drunkenness. First, a small vibration at the
back of my neck. Next, an unraveling. Third, everything
turns golden at the edges. The freckles on the right side of
Meghan's face stand out in the peach glow leaking from her
partially drawn curtains. She scrapes at her bangs, and the hair
falls back in place the moment she moves her fingers away.
Still, she doesn't ask.

"You know Tom? From work?"

"The guy you kissed at the Christmas party?"

"The guy I kissed at the Christmas party."

"What about him?"

"He has a wife. She's dead."

"Before or after the kiss?"

"Before. But I didn't know. I thought he was trying to cheat
on her with me, because he still wore his ring all the time.
And tonight, he was hitting on me again. This time he got
all serious and told me about her. Being dead."

"What did you say?"

"I ran away."

"You mean, like, metaphorically?"

"No, I literally ran away. I left him standing on some corner."

Meghan draws the bottle toward and then away from her lips, rhythmically sloshing champagne. She's quiet long enough to make me nervous, like maybe I've ruined whatever was building between us these past few weeks by revealing how pedestrian, how wantonly cruel, I am.

But then she goes, "Wow," like she's impressed. And I know we're gonna be okay.

"I feel like an idiot," I say. We trade the bottle.

"So maybe it wasn't the most mature reaction. But think of it like this—he unloaded some heavy shit on you and he never asked if you were okay with carrying it. You get to decide if a dead wife is something you can deal with, you know? You're, what, twenty-four?"

I nod.

"If you're not careful, men will have you internalizing all their shit. They do it so we can deal with it instead of them. Like, go to therapy, dude. I swear, if you let them, they will take over your entire goddamn life. Next thing you know, you'll be twenty-five and scrambling Tom's eggs every morning. Is that really how you want to spend the rest of your youth?"

Meghan is a year older than I am, but she possesses a loaded wisdom that slopes her shoulders and draws her eyebrows together. Meghan knows what she thinks about everything, and what I should think about everything. I suspect that's why our friendship has moved so quickly. I need someone to do the deciding, and Meghan loves to decide.

Below us, a car alarm bleats like a troubled whale. I close my eyes against the row of brownstones across the street and allow myself to take in the sounds of New York I usually ignore— the scratch of traffic in the distance, music and footsteps in the apartment above us, a shout that comes, at once, from a few streets over and right next to my ear.

"I doubt he'll ever speak to me again."

"Do you even want him to?"

As my eyelids flicker open, I'm almost surprised to see that the sky is still dark, that Meghan is still next to me, holding the André, the line separating wine from glass inching closer to the bottle's concave floor. Night reads differently in the city, where there are billboards instead of stars and it's all an endless stamp of blankness, a skip in the atmosphere, a light that goes on forever. Just a shift from bright to brighter, blazing onward, blurring the demarcation between the days. Hours could've passed with my eyes closed, undetected.

"I want it less than I did before I met you. I haven't had a really good friend in a while." I think of Stephanie, her veggie burgers and untouched fries, unsolicited advice. Her theory that everything she wants is hers for the taking if she only imagines it. All the things I wanted from her, the ways I tried to see beyond her actual traits to find a person I could still love underneath. I reach to dislodge a fry with the aid of a plastic fork. Meghan and I smile at each other for such a long moment that the expression loses all meaning and then comes full circle and becomes grotesque.

"Let's go in, it's freezing," Meghan says.

Adriana Hula-Hoops the bruised galaxy, purple and blue and halcyon, circling her narrow hips. She swims in a water lily pool of floating color, milky lavender and pink tie-dying her body in a pastel dream bath. She sits, a giantess on a platform of marble, the ivory buildings framing her while small, angry men hurl physical insults at her body. She sings in a gospel choir, the only one rendered in vivid color. She spins atop the Earth and moves the clouds. She gives birth to the universe. When the video ends, we're both crying. Meghan's laptop burns our knees, but still we play it again.

Sun or the smell of coffee wakes me to the sound of Meghan walking around her apartment. She opens and closes the fridge, pours liquid into a glass. Then she appears in the doorway, two steaming mugs in her hands. She looks like my mother rousing me for school, a bathrobe cinched around her waist, a maternal aura hovering around her. It's as though she wants to take care of someone and doesn't particularly care who.

I'm trending toward moderately hungover, too exhausted to reject her kindness. Daylight meets me filthily: my lips are sealed with sleep gunk, my armpits are slick, the corners of my eyes are crusty. I take my time sitting up and accept the coffee gratefully. The mug's rim is chipped on one side, the cream-colored surface printed with a lattice of curling fleurs-de-lis and a large cursive *M* stamped in the center. "Thanks."

"No problem. I'm an early riser."

Based on the light from outside, it could be anywhere from midmorning to early afternoon. "Have you been up long?"

"Only about an hour or so. You looked so peaceful, I wanted to give you more time." She sits on the floor, back against the nightstand, legs stretched from her poised hips. The coffee cup balances between her bony thighs, tipping dangerously.

"Five-star service." I raise my mug and drink.

"I try. Maybe I should open a bed-and-breakfast."

"I'll be first in line." The morning light casts us bare, dragging long angles across the floor. We're starting over, with none of the ease of the previous night.

Suddenly, I really have to pee. I'm about to say as much when Meghan asks what I'm doing for the rest of the day. "Wanna get brunch or something?"

It's Saturday. There are things I could do. Errands I don't want to run and will probably put off anyway, laundry I should fold, emails to get a head start on, jobs I could look for, books stacked on my nightstand half-finished.

We get brunch.

There's a forty-five-minute wait at Rose's on Seventh. The vestibule is crowded with impatient couples, so we give the hostess my phone number and move outside.

The weather has warmed slightly since last night, so we pace up and down the block a couple of times, ducking into a bookstore on the corner. Meghan goes to the magazines; I meander to Notable Paperbacks, where *The Goldfinch* takes up sizeable real estate. I think of Stephanie's book, now rotting in a landfill, and feel a little bad. I'm searching the copy on top of the stack for where I left off when my phone chimes at full volume, the alert that our table is ready. It startles me so badly I drop the book. It hits the edge of the table and falls, spine upward, pages splayed to the floor. The woman next to me glares and turns to the New Releases. Cowed, I pick up the book, smoothing out the pages. A few are dog-eared from the impact, so I bury that copy at the bottom of the stack.

Meghan is sucking on the web of skin between her right thumb and forefinger when I find her by the magazine stand. Her other hand clutches *People* featuring the cast of *Fuller House* on the cover. A ruby smear bloodies Candace Cameron Bure's forehead.

"Paper cut." She tucks the issue at the back of the pile.

Hands in our pockets, we shuffle to the restaurant. I kick at the blackened snow trimming the sidewalk. The hostess seats us by the window in a screened porch that's colder than the main dining room but not so cold as to be unbearable. Meghan takes off her coat. I leave mine on, unbuttoned. We peruse the menu for a minute, and then Meghan pulls out her phone. She shows me a short clip of Adriana on *Fallon*. I'm embarrassed by the noise we're making, but she doesn't seem to notice. It is remarkably easy to forget, from my side of the screen, that Adriana is a real person, with lungs and a heartbeat. I ask Meghan how she got involved with the Ivies, because they're all so different. She tells me Veronica used to run a popular fan account. She made some money off of it, even had some sponsorship deals with a few merch companies. Adriana liked a couple posts early on, so she got attention and grew quickly.

"I used her as a source for articles at my old job; she was always first with gossip, even before other news outlets. I still don't know how she got her intel, but sometimes she'd tip me off on a scoop. It was almost creepy, how accurate she was; she predicted that Adriana would fire her old manager and sign with Scotty months beforehand. Some older accounts were jealous of her success and started writing all this abuse in the comments, saying she was a liar. She got sick of it, said she didn't want to compete with a bunch of thirteen-year-olds anymore, and founded the Ivies." Over pancakes and coffee refills, she describes the early meetings, the fevered head rush of finding her *people*, the first time they lit the candles and cried.

"They're like my sisters," she says, and it intimidates me, this ferocious dedication. They all share something bone-deep that I'm aware I will always lack for not being there from the beginning. And I allow myself to wonder what it is she sees, they see, in me.

By the time we finish eating, we've run out of things to say. I hug her outside the restaurant, using meal prep as my excuse, pulling from the deep well of saved-up traits I wish I possessed. I have never once done "meal prep," but the idea came to me while we were paying and, suddenly, I could think of no better way to spend my afternoon. Why couldn't I become a prepper of meals?

Leaving Meghan's neighborhood, I meander a path to the subway, darting into shops every block or so to keep warm. I plead with the cosmic weatherman to have some mercy: *It's almost March*. At the grocery store by my stop, I pick up lettuce, tomatoes, peppers, cheese and dressing. The apartment is empty, Sasha off at some weekend work event or outing with friends I've never met, and I take over the kitchen, luxuriating in pleasant loneliness.

With Adriana on Sasha's speaker, I methodically chop the salad ingredients and load them into mason jars, dressing first, reversing the order so the salad will waterfall out of the jar, a complete, tossed, ready-to-eat lunch.

The jars line both refrigerator shelves, a rainbow. A sense of pride swells within me; I am taking responsibility. I am feeding myself. I snap a photo before I shut the door, a reminder of what I can accomplish when I put my mind to it, when I buy groceries and think ahead. A reminder that I don't need to waste away, clinging to life on the other side of a dimly lit screen, offering my clenched fists to a gossamer girl in California I will never, ever meet.

I can be a real person in the world, two feet planted on the ground and a week's worth of lunches in the refrigerator.

My stealing habit worsens. I still stick to the beauty closet at work. Traditional store merchandise holds no allure; I only want to take from the place that takes from me. It's never premeditated by more than an afternoon, the decision made in a moment of discontent. Charlotte's voice pierces the dense air like a syringe, or another pastel parcel is placed into her manicured hands, or I'm asked to complete another mundane task that kills a few extra brain cells and something inside me unravels. Then, like clockwork I find the cold doorknob turning in my hand as I nose my way into the warm, poisonous enclave of creams and oils and powders designed to make me stunning. I take my time, swatching lipsticks on my inner wrist, scrubbing them raw with makeup wipes to hide the evidence, running my fingertips across the supple pans of cheek highlight and blush, the powders crumbling beneath the pressure, trailing mica on everything I touch for days. It never washes off.

My bags are loaded with cosmetics I will hardly use. I lay them out on my dresser like precious jewels pressed into brilliance by my spite. I touch them rarely.

Once, I overhear Charlotte gushing about an eyeshadow to Ashley: "It's like your eyelids but *better*." I get home and unpack it, rub the shimmery beige powder onto the skin above my lashes with a dry finger. There's nothing very obviously different about my reflection, but my eyes catch the light in a new way. I wish I'd learned this trick sooner, back in school, when I'd look at other girls and wonder *why them* and *why not me?* I wear makeup, sure—a little mascara, a little lip gloss. This is something new. This is manipulation. Playing with shadow and light to change the shape of my face. If I'm not yet beautiful, I'm closer. Maybe Charlotte knows something I don't, after all. I think, also, of Emily and Carly, girls who know the power a face can have when you dress it up and tilt it at the right angle.

Mine is not unpleasant. It's angular in the right places, soft and round in others. My lips are plush, and my cheekbones tent noticeably under the skin. My eyes are the best part: hazel with flecks of gold at the center. Like a beach at sunset. Like

Adriana's, now that I think about it. Next to the eyeshadow, the irises are filigreed. I realize how dead I normally look, how I'm a zombie walking through this world, repeating everything. A hamster spinning a torturous wheel for something to do with its feet.

I smile at my reflection. Blow it a kiss. Give it a wink. I'm that saucy, happy, flirtatious girl. No, a *woman*. That saucy, happy, flirtatious woman, needing nothing and no one. My room spreads out behind me in the mirror, a fun house version unspooling toward a hopeful tomorrow. And I begin to understand the risk I will take.

I will wear the eyeshadow to work.

9

It barely feels like spring in New York, but it's perpetual summer in LA. Adriana and Nolan walk her dog, Esmé, through a sunny parking lot under a banner of palm trees. The camera focuses on the puppy, trotting along, her cream-and-coffee coat gleaming in the sunlight. For me, the video is about what's happening in the background: laughter. Hers, a melodious twinkling, and his, a short hacking, like a cough.

Cut to the three of them indoors. Adriana's house is recognizable by the wintery interior, white walls and snowy countertops, the rooms sparsely furnished. It's as if she's just moved in, though she's lived there for at least three years, according to my careful research. The granite island in the center of the kitchen is littered with silver dog bowls of various sizes. Nolan appears, holding a bag of Wellness Complete Health. He tips the bag and sends a stream of pellets tumbling into the nearest bowl.

In the next video, he bows extravagantly, placing the food in front of Esmé, his opposite arm bent behind his back. "Your dinner, good lady."

That laugh of hers pulsates, and the hand holding the phone shakes.

Pop stars are unknowable by nature; when you're known to everyone, you're known to no one. But that laugh, so alive and remarkable, a spontaneous extension of her music, trilling like the harmonies that back her powerful vocals, tells me everything I need to know. They are in love. It is serious. It is maybe forever.

Adriana cackles again as Nolan meets her eyes, and, by extension, the camera. A smile cleaves his face in half. He comes right up to the lens, grinning wildly until he disappears, and his chest engulfs the lens, dwarfing my view with black fabric. The last thing I hear before the video ends is her laugh.

I close my eyes. In my head, his arms swallow her diminutive body. There's a wave of scent, a cologne tsunami. I see him kiss her forehead. They take a few stumbling steps backward as Esmé skitters out from underfoot. I'm not naive. I know he spent time in rehab, the most recent stint ending right before he and Adriana became official. "She showed up for me during the darkest time in my life," he told *New York Magazine* in his first interview after they went public.

It's not hard to imagine how it must have happened. They'd been friends for a few years already, they were both newly single. Maybe she visited him any chance she got in his sleek ivory tower of health and light, bringing fresh flowers to decorate his room or homemade brownies and cupcakes she'd labored over herself in that glorious kitchen. Maybe he hugged her harder and longer each time, inhaling the musk of her hair so that he could return to it at night as he watched the moon climb higher and higher along his tall barred window and thought about home. Maybe their first real kiss was on the rehab grounds, under a canopy of cheerful trees in a cautiously optimistic garden and maybe it felt, to both of them, like a returning. Like opening a book, tossing aside the scrap of paper that held your place, picking up where you left off. And when he checked out, a new man, they would be together, a couple, finally.

Addiction snags in the blood. Even someone as beautiful as Adriana, with the voice and smile and eyes of an angel, a smile you want to ride like a wave to safety, can't dissolve it from the cells so easily. Still, I can imagine how holding that ball of hysterical energy could make you better, temporarily. As the weeks turn into months, my fascination with Adriana morphs into something less than romance but more than envy. I want what she has, that self-possession. And the talent: what I wouldn't give for a talent, any talent. Singing, dancing, card tricks, doing the cherry stem knot thing with my tongue—anything to make me stand out. Anything to make them say, that's *her* thing.

If I had an inkling of what I'd be good at, I would dedicate myself to it, monk-like, and then the path forward would be clear.

Tessa Graves is the most famous Ivy. This is because she makes videos showing her face, which is blandly attractive, a projection made up in Adriana's image: winged eyeliner, nude lipstick, strong contour, moonbeam highlighter hugging the horseshoe curves of both cheekbones. She dresses like Adriana too, in oversized sweatshirts and T-shirts, merch, hair sharply peaking, blond to match the blue-eyed, very pale rest of her.

She tried self-tanning at least once and documented the process in an old upload titled *"Trying Adriana Argento's Tanning Routine!!!!"* followed by three emoji versions of *The Scream*. From the few minutes I can stand to watch, I glean that Adriana Argento's tanning routine consists of rubbing greasy liquid resembling car oil all over her body, washing her hands, and not sitting on anything white for several hours. Something tells me Adriana has professionals to do this for her, but Tessa gleefully ignores this fact for the sake of clickbait.

At the end of the twenty-three edited and jump-cut minutes, Tessa does not look any more like Adriana Argento, just an incrementally more orange version of herself.

I can tell the Ivies, my Ivies, are jealous of Tessa from the rabid way they claw toward Crystal's television as we cluster in her living room, flipping through the videos on Tessa's YouTube channel. They sink their fingernails into the carpet or the couch armrests, their breathing tuned to low-level growls. Veronica holds her glass so firmly I hear the stem splinter into hairline cracks under her grip. Meghan gnaws a close-cropped Bordeaux nail down to the quick, shaking her bangs off her forehead. Crystal hacks away at a chapped lip with a sharp incisor. Pearl scrapes angry red crop circles into her shaved scalp. Jessie seems placid, but in a way that scares me, as if she might snap at the slightest provocation, like a strong wind could send her into hysterics.

If I'm on edge, it's only because of the taut mesh of tension casting a net across the room. I'm actually excited for what we are about to do, which is dip our buckets into the vast well of the past and watch all twenty-seven minutes of *"MEETING ADRIANA ARGENTO!!! + Goodbye Sophie: My Hazardous Tour Experience."*

For the other Ivies, it's about due diligence. For me, it's about reclaiming what I lost by being a latecomer to the fandom.

The thumbnail shows Tessa on one half, clutching the sides of her face. Her mouth hangs open in a pose that mimics the screaming emoji from the self-tanner video, a pose that seems tasteless given the mention of the Sophie Heffernan. The other half of the thumbnail is taken up by a still of Adriana onstage, bathed in a sea of siren-red lights, her matching leggings and shirt twinkling.

Tessa did not meet Adriana in any organic, serendipitous fashion. She didn't run into her in the bathroom at Katsuya or outside Tiffany's at The Grove. No, she paid $1,000 for the privilege, the price of a VIP ticket that included a seat at sound check, a goody bag packed with exclusive merch, and a three-minute meet and greet. On the edge of a well-appointed bed, the white metal frame of which is trimmed with white twinkle lights, Tessa perches like a waiting cockatoo, her ponytail making for vibrant plumage, as she welcomes us back to her channel.

"If you're new here, I hope you stick around and subscribe!"

Today's video was *highly requested by you guys*, and she says it so convincingly, the *you guys* is so warm and inclusive, that I can almost feel myself, in a previous incarnation, doing the requesting. "It's all about my experience *meeting* Adriana Argento at the Los Angeles stop of the *Hazardous* World Tour." The *r* in *tour* unleashes a high-pitched tire squeak. She fans her mascara-charred lashes at the ceiling, a quiet prayer of gratitude.

Then she lowers her voice like she's telling a ghost story, letting us in on a joyfully scandalous, delightfully horrible secret. "That was also the night our poor Sophie was killed by a violent psychopath near the Staples Center."

Tessa didn't know her *personally*, of course, but don't we all, us Ivies, share a connection, a knowing that goes beyond acquaintance? "Losing an Adriana fan *during my show*…it was just so awful. Like, *it could have been me*." She pauses for a haunted beat, letting this really sink in, and a many-voiced groan rises up throughout Crystal's living room. Veronica digs her acrylics so deep into the couch cushion that she almost draws fluff. Beside me, Meghan huffs.

Tessa honestly can't believe it happened, it still doesn't feel real, and the farther she gets from the concert, the less real it becomes. It's unclear whether she's talking about Sophie or meeting Adriana. But then she says, "She's so cute in real life, like exactly how she is in all the pictures," and it becomes obvious. Anyway, she's getting *way* ahead of herself, and if we want to hear her *personal observations* about the night Sophie died, plus a description of the sound check and meet and greet, *plus* plus concert footage, we should *keep on watching!*

"Do we really have to watch this whole thing?" Crystal asks from her beanbag chair on the floor. Veronica admonishes her with a sharp *shh!* and a dismissive wave as Tessa plows through the process of purchasing tickets online, laying out her credit card *just so* on the desk, memorizing the number in advance so as not to waste precious seconds. "I was so panicked because it took a while for the transaction to go through and I thought I might lose my order and have to start all over again. But once the page refreshed, I saw the confirmation. I think I actually screamed.

"So then, fast-forward to six months later and it's my concert date!"

A photo splashes onto the screen, Tessa, looking very much the same as she does in the video, wearing a black crop top, denim jacket dotted with pins, and a high-waisted black skirt, standing outside the arena next to a life-size banner of Adriana's face. The photo dissolves and her animated expression returns to the foreground. She's holding the jacket from the picture. She details her exhaustive collection of Adriana pins, then flips the jacket to the reverse side, where an elaborate stylized rendition of the *Hazardous* album cover fills the entire back panel, shoulder to shoulder and hip to hip. Adriana is pictured from the chest up, lips parted, her strapless top cresting over the white border. A diamond choker frosts her collarbones, and her ponytail waterfalls over one shoulder. A gloved hand creeps into the frame, clambering up the side of her face. The jacket was a commission from the Instagram artist Cherry Halloway. I recall that she was recently hired to paint a mural tribute to Sophie on the wall behind the dumpster where her body was found.

Next, Tessa shows footage from outside the arena, sped up and set to a soundtrack of generic elevator music. Fans trickle in a long line from the door, a chain of tall hair and roomy outerwear. Most of them are young, in their late teens and early twenties. Tessa's own age is unclear. She never mentions school, work, boyfriends or girlfriends. Her face is nonspecific, unlined but not overly bothered by pads of youthful fat, and the lens filter she uses turns her features blow-up-doll perfect. Her money seems to come from nowhere, and everywhere. She could be any age between fourteen and thirty.

Back in Tessa's bedroom, I imagine her flammable, artificial hair dipping into the five-wick candle alight on the nightstand and going up in a quill-shaped flame. Tessa is the only thing truly in focus as she describes entering the VIP lounge, using her drink ticket for a cocktail at the bar (Surely, then, she must be at least twenty-one?) and chatting with the other guests. She appears to have attended the concert alone, without friends or guardians, unless she's omitting them from the telling.

Tessa and the rest of the VIPs are herded into the arena for sound check, where Adriana is sitting onstage, surrounded by dancers, looking *ohmygod, you guys, so* tiny. As small as she is in photos. Smaller. So small you could put her in your pocket. So small you could pop her in your mouth and chew her up like gum.

"A little fairy princess," Tessa sighs.

The sound check includes a question-and-answer session. Tessa declines to reveal some of the information Adriana

shared on the grounds of it being "too personal" and "a violation" of the trust she paid to obtain. She does tell a story
about Adriana discovering she's allergic to kiwi. "She was so
cute and laughing the whole time! But she's bummed about
the kiwis. That's her favorite fruit."

"No, it isn't," Jessie murmurs.

"What?" I ask. Veronica administers another *shhh* like a
knife, and I lean my face into my hands, trying to die.

Sound check ends, or Tessa gets tired of talking about it,
and she reveals that security locked her phone in a special case
that prevented her from accessing it during the sound check.
She says it with an air of superiority, as if having her cell re-
voked by Adriana's entourage makes her somehow chosen. The
VIPs are organized into a queue for the meet and greet, and
Tessa ends up near the back of the line, but she doesn't mind.
She chats with the people around her, makes a few concert
friends who she agrees to find during the show. She twitches
as she talks, as if the excitement has returned in the retelling.

Then it happens—she's next in line.

The security guard at the front leads her through a sectioned
maze of thick curtains. I imagine her plunging deeper and
deeper, striving to reach the warm, beating core at the center of the Earth. Finally, the curtains spit her out in a room
Tessa calls *gray, but in a warm sort of way.* Her description makes
it sound chicly empty and blandly modernist, like what I've
seen of Adriana's house. There's a leather couch on one side,
heavy with the bodies of Adriana's friends. Esmé rolls around
on the floor, slobbering on Adriana's best friend Claudia's
Yeezy Boost 350s.

One corner of the room has been curtained off with a separate swath of slightly darker gray velvet. Bobby, Adriana's
head of security, emerges from a gap in the fabric and beck-
ons Tessa inside with a stoic, "She's ready for you."

"So, I walk in and she's sitting on this bench with that, like, curvy cushion. What's that called? *Tufted.* She's sitting on this tufted bench and the room, it's just like a regular photo booth but slightly fancier. Adriana looks totally normal and chill, like a normal person with really smooth skin. I'm not convinced she has pores, honestly. I got as close as I could, and I didn't see any.

"So, the first thing I do is, I hug her and tell her I love her."

Adriana says she loves Tessa back and Tessa believes her.

"I could tell she really meant it, you know? She was completely genuine. But there was this weird, kinda intense energy coming off her. She seemed a little agitated, almost like she knew what was coming. The air in there, it smelled like burnt smoke, I swear. Like an electrical fire or something." Tessa pauses for a long moment, reflecting on the memory, their unfettered connection.

She takes a deep breath and continues. "But anyway, it was fine, I hugged her, and that was amazing. She smelled *amazing.* I think she was wearing Cumulus by Adriana. Or maybe it was Chanel No. 5."

Adriana guides their shoulders in the direction of the camera while Tessa fumbles for more conversation. They smooth out their matching ponytails, and Adriana coats her mouth with another layer of lip gloss. Tessa thinks she might offer her some. She longs to press her mouth to the soggy applicator, and if it happens, she swears she'll never wash her mouth again, she'll die with Adriana's DNA clinging to her lips, a shiny, lacquered, almost-famous corpse. But Adriana screws the lid tightly back onto the tube and angles her chin toward Tessa and purses her lips just as the flash goes off. Then she says, in her voice like a dozen dropped pennies, *we almost kissed just then.*

"I was like, ohmygod, did we? And I'm frantically trying

to find our pictures on the iPad but there are like a million of them and then she's hugging me kind of from the side with one arm and, like, *pushing* me, just gently, and then I'm outside the curtain again. And she's on the other side." Tessa's face drops, a lampshade just after the bulb goes out, and she glances down, forgetting her invisible audience, letting go of the illusion that we are in the same room, friends gathered for a casual chat. I'm struck with the conviction that it's similar in some ways, what she and Adriana do. The phantasm of closeness, the facade of intimacy.

Sadness almost overtakes Tessa, and I have to assume she's thinking about how she'll never really know her idol, how they are not friends, how she's been forgotten already. But she recovers, a true performer, a smile puffing her cheeks.

"Guys, it really was an unforgettable night," she says.

I wait for her to get to the part about Sophie, but she tells us to enjoy the concert footage, to *like, comment, and subscribe*, to join her next time. The rest of the video is an oily blur. The image trembles and skips like the hand holding the camera has been shot through with cocaine, and Adriana is a gyrating dot cat-walking around the stage, singing her heart out. The sound quality isn't as good as other videos I've seen, and her voice warps as it tips up at the highest notes. Tessa cat-wails in the foreground, sounding like she's the one being murdered and left behind in an alley.

The final frame, Tessa almost-kissing Adriana, a good two inches of flat, gray space between their lips, burns a black hole in Crystal's television. The two women resemble figurines, ageless and fragile, their features obscured by the blurring black-and-white lens filter so that they appear nearly identical.

This flattened version of Adriana, this stilted pop princess, this life-size cardboard cutout, has no soul. It leaves me—as a siren outside punches a canyon in the silence, tearing the mesh and releasing our held breath—with a strong conviction, stronger than any of my political beliefs or personal definitions. It's this: I will never meet Adriana Argento. I will never humiliate myself by standing before her cut-glass brilliance, stewing in my averageness, stuttering a sad maid-of-honor speech about how she *means so much to me,* how *her music saved my life,* how *I don't know who I am without her.*

"That was insufferable." Crystal turns off the television and chucks the remote onto the coffee table with a loud clatter.

"Don't you mean it was *amaaaazing?*" Jessie mocks, taking a swig of Blue Moon.

"It's like we didn't even attend the same show." Veronica delicately crosses one slim calf over the other, flashing her ivy tattoo.

"You were there too?" I ask. They all look at me, coiffed heads swiveling like searchlights on long-stemmed necks, catching me in their glare.

"We were *all* there," Meghan says. She puts a hand on my arm and looks at me pityingly, as if I'm a child, too young to understand. Her bangs rest heavily across her overplucked eyebrows.

"Did you see anything?"

"We saw *everything*—we were in the pit."

"No, I mean…did you see the girl who *died.*"

The Ivies stiffen and look at each other like *should we tell her?* And then they look at me like *no, she's not ready.* "Who knows," Crystal says. "It was crowded."

I have so many questions. Namely, why did they fly to LA when she played Madison Square Garden a week later? Instead, I say, "Did you meet Adriana too?"

Pop stars are contractually obligated to say they love their fans, to pen florid love letters to the people who follow them and spend their money to keep them in the business of making music. I believe they mean it, in their own way. After all, fans make them who they are. Fans fill seats, buy records, validate the belief that this is what they are meant to do. And yet, the way they love us, it's nothing compared to the way we love them.

So, I'm not surprised, not in the slightest, when Jessie blinks up at me from her cross-legged crouch, shakes her bobbed hair, and says, "No. No, never."

As if the very idea of meeting Adriana Argento in person is cursed.

"You have Adriana's perfume."

Meghan circles my room. She's walking with the even, measured gait of an inspector examining a crime scene, flicking her fingers over the odds and ends that line my shelves, forming the shape of my life. I've hidden most of the stolen goods from work at the bottom of my closet, but I must've forgotten the perfume because it's still there, alongside seashells and fogged bits of green glass from family vacations on Cape Cod lining the windowsill. Ticket stubs from indie rock shows at small venues clustered on the outskirts of New Jersey and eastern Long Island tucked into the mirror frame. Makeup and jewelry and movie posters.

The ephemera seem both more and less significant in the line of her scrutiny. I feel as though she's trying to decode me using scattered clues. I take the Cumulus bottle from Meghan, debating whether to tell her the truth about how I acquired it. Her face is open and trusting. "I… I found it. At Housing Works."

"Lucky find! A bottle of this stuff is like sixty bucks."

"Sixty-five, actually."

"What did you pay for it?"

I toss the bottle onto my bed and turn back to the pile of laundry I've been folding.

"I, uh, don't remember?"

Meghan's gaze prickles down the side of my neck, but she lets the lie go. She crosses the room in two long strides and flings her body sideways along my mattress. Propped up on an elbow, she plucks a sweater off the mountain of clothes and begins to fold it, rubbing a knuckle across each crease. The gesture's meaning is plain—she does know, she sees my lie for what it is, solid as the dresser across the room, and she's prepared to drop it. She places the sweater, now a compact rectangle, on top of the pile of folded tops, flops onto her back, and closes her eyes.

I take the opportunity to really look at her face. The better you know someone, the less you see them. Meghan's freckles have deepened with the increased exposure to sunlight that comes as winter retreats, and her eyes are creased with smudged pencil eyeliner. Her bangs are pinned to one side with chunky barrettes made of clouded pink plastic, the white swirls like veins of soap running through bathwater. Meghan's lids swim open. Her gray-blue eyes are on me, and all I can do is smile.

Laundry folded, we go out into the living room, order takeout from the Thai restaurant around the corner, and argue over a movie to watch. I vote for *High School Musical* and Meghan wants *Heathers*, so we compromise on *Mean Girls*, the natural halfway point. Even this mild, noncommittal fighting is pleasant, a reminder that I'm no longer as lonely as I once was.

Sasha comes home shortly after the food arrives. She stops dead by the coatrack, looking from me to Meghan, Meghan to me, like she's just seen a ghost.

"Hi, Sasha," I say once I realize she's waiting to be introduced. "This is Meghan. My friend from work. Meghan, meet my roommate, Sasha."

"Pleasure," Meghan says in her way that could disarm even the most fervent gun-toting Texan.

"What are you watching?" Sasha asks, kicking off her shoes and padding sock-footed over to the refrigerator. She opens it, peers inside, and closes it again without taking anything out. The movie is paused on an iconic early scene, and Lindsay Lohan's red mane fills the screen. She looks a little like Meghan, actually. Same full, Irish cheeks and innocent-yet-knowing expression.

"Wait, have you never seen *Mean Girls*?" I say.

Sasha looks at Lindsay's frozen, speckled face. "No, I haven't."

"What!" Meghan and I yelp at the same time.

"Everyone has seen *Mean Girls*," Meghan adds.

"Not me," Sasha says. She opens the fridge a second time, takes out a can of watermelon beer, cracks the seal and sits down at our small dining table, propping her feet up on another chair.

"Sasha hates fun," I say, with a playfulness that alarms even me.

"Shut up, I do not *hate fun*," she says, but she's smiling. "What's it about?"

We give her a brief summary of the movie's events thus far and start it from where we left off. I settle deeper into the couch. Meghan's presence balances the energy between Sasha and me, sanding down the edges that normally bump against each other, creating tiny fissures on our skin. On-screen, the Plastics gush over Lindsay Lohan's prettiness, sounding as though they want to peel back her skin like an orange and play dress-up inside it. Contentment drops over me, a blanket.

Beside me, Meghan smiles, repeats the line about *thinking you're really pretty*, like she's saying it right to me.

10

Stephanie meets me outside the Pret a Manger on Seventh Avenue and Twenty-Seventh. She's fresh from work, wearing her dressiest white polo and pressed slacks. A blazer is folded over her left arm, and she's holding an honest-to-god attaché. Her loafers are a brand-new pair of those Gucci ones with the gold horse bit detail. A gift from her boyfriend, no doubt.

We amble several blocks to a wine bar, where we settle onto leather stools at the counter. It took some finagling, but the Ivies agreed to let me bring Stephanie to our meeting tonight. She's been texting me for weeks, wondering where I've been, asking if I've finished *The Goldfinch*, if I've tried manifesting a better life. I panicked and told her about the Ivies, or, as I called them, *some girls I met through a friend at work*.

As we sip our drinks, as Stephanie twirls the little gold ring with a miniscule sailor's knot in the center on her index finger, I'm fully aware this plan could backfire. That's why I took her here, to this place with a leather-bound wine list the size of my upper body and a votive in front of every place setting, for the hour before we need to be at Jessie's in the East Village. That's why I made a reservation even though the bar is nearly empty. To show her, no matter what is to come, that I can be responsible, too.

Stephanie tells me about the new book her boss has acquired for half a million. "It's transcendent, the next *Goldfinch*. You haven't finished reading that yet, right?" She asks what I am reading, if not that, and all I have to tell her about are articles we've published on the website. One of our reporters debunked a conspiracy theory about doctors at Planned Parenthood selling aborted fetuses on the dark web. I start to describe the article and Stephanie's eyes go dull, get bored, and travel to her cell phone lying faceup on the bar, so I tell her I'll text her the link. She says, "Okay," and checks her email.

While her head is down, I survey the bar, wishing we were at Blinkers. This place is too clean, there's nothing to latch onto, no interesting people to watch. The air smells of Le Labo Santal 33 instead of sour cherries and fermentation. Everyone stands or sits at a respectful distance and keeps their voices down. There's no groping. No murdered pageant queens or disgraced White House interns on the walls. Even the music is dignified.

Stephanie could have been born here. She matches the color scheme. The diamond studs in her ears capture the flickering candlelight. I remember the one time we went to the classy cocktail bar in our college town. We dressed up in heels and short skirts, red lipstick. I was so nervous my teeth chattered as I decided what to get, but I needn't have worried. No one would dare imply that Stephanie was underage. In fact, she ordered for us, making eye contact with the bartender, daring her to ask for ID. Which, of course, she didn't. Not even mine.

We finish our drinks. I insist on paying, as well as picking up the wine on the walk to Jessie's. I don't even point out that *she's* the one wearing $700 shoes. That's how good I'm being tonight.

"Remind me what we're doing?" Stephanie asks as we turn onto Fifth Avenue.

"We're going to my friend Jessie's."

"But it's for some kind of fan club, right?"

"Not a *fan club*. We all just happen to be into Adriana Argento."

"Oh, right. That again."

"I don't know what it's like where you come from, but here on planet Earth we do things like *listen to music* and *watch movies*. There's this little website called Spotify."

Stephanie rolls her eyes. "I watch movies," she says.

"Yeah. Like *Citizen Kane*."

Jessie lives in a fourth-floor walk-up on Seventh Street between Second and Third. I'm out of breath when we get to her front door, which is covered in old green paint. Stephanie reaches for the bell and, when her fingers graze the door, it swings inward with an ominous creak. The apartment opens into the living room, where the Ivies are piled on the sagging furniture. They remind me of neglected coats left over on a department store sales rack near the end of the season.

Veronica greets us as if she's the host. She gives Stephanie a long-lost-sister hug, a separated-at-birth squeeze, and shoves her inside. They do, in fact, look a bit alike. Stephanie could be Veronica's Hitchcockian brunette twin. I bite down my jealousy as Crystal and Pearl make room for Stephanie on the couch, preening for her, relegating me to a fold-out step stool set up next to the TV. The plastic cuts into my thighs.

"My roommates are out, so we have the place to ourselves," Jessie says. "Make as much noise as you want." She places an order for pizza and uncorks my wine. We drink from pint glasses; mine says Barnard Class of '14 on the side.

Stephanie looks prim and uncomfortable wedged between Pearl and Crystal, who both wear band T-shirts with small rips in the fabric and boyfriend jeans. Crystal's is a Hole shirt with *Doll Parts* rendered in pink Barbie script. Her hair is adorned with plastic butterfly clips, and Pearl's has been freshly buzzed on the shaved side, giving the skin the pearlescent gleam of a newborn's eyelids. Stephanie is hunched slightly forward, hands shoved between her clenched knees. I don't think I've ever seen her with less than perfect posture, at least not while sober.

Another sip of wine calms my nerves. Stephanie will be fine. They don't bite.

"So, Stephanie. Tell us what it was like growing up with this one. She says you're her childhood bestie." Veronica jabs her thumb at me and peers down at Stephanie from her high-born perch on the arm of the couch. Stephanie raises an eyebrow at *bestie.*

"Please, tell us. Did she decapitate her Barbies?" Meghan asks. "She seems like the type."

I wonder what Stephanie will say. Truly, I'm not sure what growing up with me was like. I'd love for her to tell me.

"One time she stuck gum in her hair on purpose, just to see what it felt like. That was how she learned that hair can't feel," is what Stephanie says.

I actually remember that: my mom washed the gum out with oil, and I cried for hours wondering how something so integral to my sense of self could lack pain receptors. Ultimately, I think it came down to jealousy; I wanted to be so numb. "I got a pixie cut after that," I say out loud.

"Your first haircut ever," Stephanie adds.

"Do you guys have, like, a psychic connection? Can you tell us what she's thinking right now?"

Stephanie flips her palm and pushes it up like she's tossing a tiny ball. "We're not twins; we can't read each other's minds."

Oh, but we used to, back when we were close. We'd sit next to each other in class and have silent conversations, referencing them later on the playground or at lunch, forever on the verge of telepathy. For so long, she never had to ask me what was wrong. It saddens me, thinking of it now. The gulf between us has grown so large I can barely see her on the other side. I vow to buy her a new copy of *The Goldfinch*, write a note of apology on the inside.

Meghan says, "I'm not in touch with anyone from before high school, thank god."

The Ivies murmur in agreement; they are glad there's no one left to remind them who they used to be. Stephanie says, "What's wrong with holding on to the past? I like to remember where I came from."

Crystal giggles and lays a hand on the top of Stephanie's head. Then she takes her headband and shoves it over her own flowering curls. "Where have you been hiding her all this time?" she asks me.

"Flatiron," I say, because that's where her office is.

Stephanie's hands flail by Crystal's head, trying to reach the headband without rudely touching her hair. Crystal keeps turning her head so it's just out of reach. Stephanie makes desperate eye contact with me and I mouth *STOP*.

"Reddit thinks the new single is coming soon," Jessie says, returning with the pizza balanced on one hand. The box tips and the paper bag full of plates and napkins resting on top slides to the floor. Veronica's foot swings forward and gives the bag a petulant kick. She seems moody, like she's jealous of the attention the others are lavishing on Stephanie. I stand and pick the bag up, following Jessie to the kitchen. I put the bag on the counter, open it up, and remove the contents, helping myself to the first slice from the pie.

One by one, the Ivies rise for pizza and return to their seats. Veronica doesn't stand, but Meghan brings her a slice. The Ivies descend onto their food with ferocity, slurping and gagging, shoving the pizza as far down their throats as it will go without choking them to death. Stephanie bites into her slice with a desperation I haven't seen in so long, since she read *The Secret* and started believing that you could smell your way to fullness.

"I'm not ready for a new single," Pearl says, tugging her silver daith piercing. "I'm still recovering from the last one."

"I don't want to talk about it," Crystal says. She adjusts Stephanie's headband.

"It could be good," Meghan says. "You never know."

"Her single choices are always wonky," adds Pearl.

"But it's not just her," I say. "Revolving Records has input."

Veronica blows air out of her mouth. She smooths her already smooth white-blond hair. She, too, is wearing a headband. Hot pink. Like the bubblegum version of Stephanie. Stephanie Spice. "I have faith. This will be the song we've been waiting for. The one that tells us what the album will *be*."

Stephanie's eyes bug out from her head as they flit from Veronica to Meghan to Crystal to Pearl to Jessie and, finally, to me. Crystal tosses the headband onto the coffee table and Stephanie lunges. With the headband back in place, she recovers her regal posture.

Suddenly, Veronica stands. The Ivies get quiet. She paces the length of the apartment, dipping into the kitchenette and back, kitchenette, and back. Jessie crosses and uncrosses her spindly legs, casting disapproving glances around her apartment, which is, frankly, a hovel. It is entirely unworthy.

Veronica stops in front of Stephanie, her calf grazing Stephanie's knee. Stephanie jolts, as if Veronica's skin is charged, and Veronica reaches into the pocket of her caramel slacks. She pulls out a lighter, holds it parallel to her chest, and it flicks on.

"Stephanie," she says, looking into the flame. "Help me light the candles."

No one, not even her mother, tells Stephanie what to do. She hesitates, then stammers. My powerful and commanding friend is reduced to a moth under a magnifying glass. She flutters. Then she takes the lighter and follows in a tight circle as Veronica sets out the tapers in their tarnished silver holders. They leave a trail of tiny fires in their wake. A seventh candle has been lit, for Stephanie. I grab her wrist, keeping her close. "You don't have to—" I start to whisper.

What is going on? Stephanie mouths. I shake my head. *You'll see.*

Meghan selects the song for The Growing. It's a ballad with dark, heavy percussion. One of my favorites. At the first swell of Adriana's voice, my chest heaves. The Ivies are curling forward and drawing circles on the floor with their flat, searching palms, tears splattering the scarred wood. Pearl yelps, a wave of emotion bubbling over, but then I see her sucking on her index finger. Not magic. A splinter.

The Ivies are whining, keening, thrashing. They are one with the music, it's in their bodies like a fever. They are angry and sputtering and weeping. The world has wronged them, they believe, and here is their permission to do something about it, or, at least, to react.

At first Stephanie's presence tugs at me, preventing me from losing myself inside The Growing. But I forget her. She fades like an old photograph, like something from the distant past. Then, and only then, do I let the tears come.

"What the fuck did I witness in there?" Stephanie pulls me to a stop halfway down Jessie's street.

I'm drunk and wavering. "My friends!" I run ahead and leap, turning midair. "Tonya Harding!" I say. "The first American woman to land a triple axel." My ankle wobbles. I glare at it. "Nancy Kerrigan," I scold the offending appendage.

Stephanie is standing still, arms tightly crossed. Not amused. She charges, reaching me in three long strides, and grabs my upper arms so that I stop moving. It rained while we were inside, and the ground is a blue damp. I kick at a shallow puddle and droplets lick the crisp hem of Stephanie's work pants, splattering her loafers.

"Why are you *sober*?" I pout. I'm taunting her. I want her to slap me or shake me. To lose control. During The Growing, she sat completely still with her hands in her lap and her mouth twisted into a grimace. Ruining the mood. I can tell she wants to give it up now, can feel the capillaries breaking under her hands.

She grips me tighter and then drops her hold. Puts her head in her hands. "You joined a cult!" she moans.

I laugh. "A cult? They're my *friends*." I am, in this moment, astounded by her hypocrisy. I can only think of her cross-legged on her bamboo meditation mat chanting *I will what I want* into the predawn murk of her Yorkville apartment. "At least they're real."

"They're *nuts*," Stephanie says, like she didn't hear me. "I mean, what *was* that? Why was everybody crying? It's just pop music."

She's not joking. I take hold of a strand of Stephanie's smooth, straight, dark hair. Growing up, we fought like sisters. I pull hard. She screams. I'm running, pushing past a startled couple, waving for a taxi.

A yellow cab slams to a halt, bumper crossing the curb, and I scramble inside. Stephanie catches up. I try to shut the door on her leg, but she gets her whole lower body into the cab, and then the rest of her.

"Ladies," the driver says. "Are we gonna have a problem?"

"No, sir. My friend here had a little too much to drink and needs to get home."

His eyes narrow in the rearview. "No vomiting."

I don't feel sick. I feel lightened by my anger. My body floats out of the cab when we pull up in front of my building. I get inside the lobby before Stephanie is finished paying the driver. Pushing the door closed, I watch Stephanie through the fogged-over glass as she shuffles across the sidewalk in her fancy shoes. She pauses to watch the cab turn in front of the park. The taillights catch her in their gleam and it's like she's a stranger. Her face collapses as if she might cry. She takes a deep breath, rolls one shoulder at a time towards her spine, and walks to me.

No one, not even Tessa Graves, is prepared. The third single off *solstice* drops with no promo, no lead-up, no fanfare. We fall asleep in a world without this rhapsodic, blissed-out music, a simpler, less sparkling world, and when we wake up, it's waiting. Three minutes and eighteen seconds of choral harmony, Adriana's voice at its most angelic, piled on top of itself dozens of times, echoing like a hymn throughout an empty cathedral. The sound tiers fill me to the brim and then some, running over the whorls of my ears, gathering at the pointed ends of my earlobes, dripping a galaxy of stars. I want to hold the notes somehow, to contain them within me, but all I have are these ears and these hands, the ability to press Repeat. I am meek and useless and human.

Strictly speaking, this is a song about getting laid. To put it another way: it's a song about how Adriana is so good at sex she'll have you converting to Christianity or thinking she's the second coming of Jesus or something. The words, the meaning, they're secondary to the main event, which is her voice and the instrumentals. The combination crests under me, carrying me away, so far above everything that I forget my name, my face, and my address. Who am I, again? It doesn't matter. The song ends and I'm washed up on a bone-white beach with no identity, no possessions, and only the lyrics on my lips.

I listen three times in a row, my limbs starfishing to the four corners of my bed. I feel crucified. This is the closest I've ever come to reaching the impossible climax of becoming a brain without a body. It's a feeling I crave often, when my bra's underwire digs into my rib cage and the sweat collects in the dark places and I get a little winded on the stairs, too hot in the jacket that, outside, didn't keep me warm enough. The corporeal form is a curse and the only escape, save for death, is the sublime moment when a piece of art or an act of nature or a nip of alcohol helps you disconnect from yourself.

Listening to this new song is like staring down the basin of the Grand Canyon, tracking a scattering of stars above the tree line on a summer night, searching for meteorites. It's an inhale. It's the suspended seconds between sleep and waking. It's the instant your alarm rings and you realize it's Saturday and you've got nowhere to be. It's heaven.

The Ivies fucking hate it.

Grandiose, but in the wrong way. Distasteful, after Sophie. Just another song about sex.

"But you love her songs about sex," I say.

"That's not the point," Pearl snaps.

On the subject of Sophie, the Ivies are cagey. They speak about her with reverence normally reserved for deities, almost akin to how they speak about Adriana. She was *special, an angel, taken too soon.* But as far as I know they never *met* her.

"This song is so special to me." We're watching Adriana on *Nightly with Poppy*, sleeping over at Meghan's because she's the only one with a cable package. She needs to watch TV too regularly for work to rely on streaming apps. The website doesn't pay her bill, but Meghan says she doesn't mind, it's a tax write-off. Besides, she gets to watch shows when they actually air, a treat I haven't experienced since I last lived with my parents the summer after college.

"Stefan Mitchell came to me with a chorus already written. He'd recorded a few demos with other singers, but none were quite right. Sometimes, for whatever reason, a singer's voice or image might not mesh with the material; it's happened to me the opposite way a few times. But I was so flattered when he brought me this song. I mean, it's so *big*, between the lyrics, the instrumentals, the melody. A total flex. And I'm…" She gestures to her legs, which wouldn't reach the floor without the aid of the giant platforms attached to her ankle boots.

The audience laughs.

"*Yeah, yeah, we get it Adriana, you're short.* But anyway, I sang a few riffs based on what he had, and it just clicked. I said, let me take this home and work on some verses. Most of what I wrote ended up in the final version. We just nailed the recording. One day of studio time, and bam! It happened that quickly.

"Sometimes everything just comes together. In music and in life." A glance, almost imperceptible, at her ring finger, which is bare. I wonder if the other women notice, but no one speaks.

"And the video," Poppy says.

"What about it?"

"First of all, it's incredible."

"Thank you, Poppy."

"How'd you come up with the concept?"

"Jim Jones, our director, had some ideas sketched out when we met. It just so happened that we were both independently playing around with the concept of the cosmos, the theme of a woman as the universe. Because you worship in church, right, or some people do, but you can also worship in nature. And a woman *is* nature. Women are creation. All women. It's not about reproduction, but about power."

Poppy nods like she gets it, but I'm not sure she does. Do I get it? I don't really care; I just want to listen to the song again.

"The song is not about motherhood, clearly, but it is partially about acknowledging women's essential role in, you know, keeping the universe going! So that's where the space imagery and the religious imagery come from. And it helps to get people talking, of course. Not to say we were courting controversy but…we were aware of what the reception from certain circles would be like."

"Speaking of, what *has* the reception been like?"

"Oh, incredible. Absolutely incredible. Fans love the song, and I think the attention and the critical response have brought new people to my music. There's been some backlash, which we anticipated. That is going to happen anytime you reference religion in an unexpected way. So yes, I've been called sacrilegious and I've been told by strangers on Twitter that I'm going to hell a million times over, if that's what you're asking."

"Does that response to such a positive song upset you?"

"Let's just say, if it's between me and some dude hiding behind an egg avatar, telling women he's never met they deserve to be flayed alive because of a bop, who do you think is gonna end up in hell?" She smiles and it's clear as day—she's won.

Meghan mutes the sound as the show cuts to commercial and says, "Ugh, she's *such* a queen."

"Too bad the song is so tacky," Crystal adds. She pulls a wiry curl straight, lets go, recoils as it springs at her cheekbone like an angry snake.

There are nods around the circle and when it gets to me, I

move my head up and down in agreement. I could assert my opinion, but I prefer to stay quiet; it's like talking about the music would cheapen it somehow. Despite my involvement with the Ivies, I'm not loud about my Adriana fandom; I don't comment on her Instagram photos, reply to her Tweets, or otherwise advertise my appreciation for her work as if I expect her to notice me or to care what I think. There's another aspect to this, one that is too silly to admit aloud, which is that no matter how big she gets, I understand that she's still a person. She may be impossibly beautiful and astronomically talented, but she's not a goddess. She's a woman, just like me, and I love her not because I see her as so much better, but because I see her as not so different. It's as though a hand flipped us: she was heads, and I was tails. She landed on top, that's all.

The commercial break ends. Adriana stands in the center of an empty stage, just her and her mic and three backup singers in black pantsuits. "Here we go," Veronica mutters, disdain coloring her voice.

The lights flicker blue and lavender. Adriana closes her eyes, breathing deeply, and unleashes that wild, incredible voice on the live audience. It takes root deep in her throat, climbing like so much plant matter through her mouth, covering Meghan's room in joyful foliage.

We migrate to the foot of the bed, a pile of enthralled fans, limbs encroaching on limbs, forgetting to act like we're too cool to care, ending up on our stomachs with pillows or each other's heads and shoulders clutched beneath our chins. They can say they hate it all they want, but I hear the way they are breathing, feel it against my back. My eyes water against the bracing chill of Adriana's galloping vocals and I blink to keep from crying. One tear gets out, crawls down my cheek, sluices around the incline of my chin. It lands, becoming a dark spot on Meghan's robin's-egg pillowcase.

Adriana performs the entire song with her eyes clamped shut, her thick eyeliner tugging the line of her face into an elongated mask. Her cheeks look slightly gaunt, but her fresh tan is healthy. You can tell she loves this song, that it means a lot to her even if it's ostentatious and not particularly personal. She reaches the crescendo, whistle tones rocking her body, and opens her eyes, arms splayed in an arabesque, beaming at the cheering crowd.

Poppy comes onstage and hugs her. "Everybody, give it up for Adriana Argento!"

They keep talking as the credits roll, though we can no longer hear what they're saying. They look like mimes.

"Damn," Meghan says. She reaches back as Jessie hands her the remote and clicks the television off. "That was incredible. Say what you want about the song, but our girl can *sing*."

I'm too stunned to speak, but I can always count on the Ivies to fill the silence.

"That's what I've been saying all this time. She has *such* a voice; it's a shame she doesn't know how to use it."

"*Using it* is not the problem. It's the lyrics. They're not *about* anything."

"They're about boning."

"Anything *real*. I want to know what's in her *soul*."

"Tell us what's in your *soul*, Adriana."

"Your soul!"

They are mewling like kittens, nuzzling into the soft crevices of Meghan's bed, their little cotton shorts and lace-trimmed sleep camisoles riding up to expose molded hips, the curved junction of glutes and thighs. Those green ivy tattoos coil around their legs, a rainbow of white and pink and tan and brown flesh.

Veronica leans coolly against the headboard, slightly apart, and sucks on the inside of her cheek. "I don't think it's about the lyrics," she says, and they all stop purring. "It's the *production*. Her lyrics are actually pretty brilliant in their simplicity. They can be about anything. Nothing and everything. The production is what can take her songs to the next level. She needs to go back to her usual team; Petey Jackson is too experimental. The message keeps getting lost.

"That's not to say she's blameless," Veronica continues, folding her arms behind her head in a complicated knot. "Obviously, she chose to work with him. She keeps telling us this will be her most personal album yet, and I'm *not* seeing it."

Veronica shakes her head to indicate just how shameful she finds this, how unacceptable. How dare Adriana not make the music that she, Veronica, wants her to make. The music she, Veronica, thinks is *her most personal yet.*

My own voice rises up, an uncertain dust storm. "Well, I mean. Maybe these songs are her most personal. We don't know her, right? Not really."

The Ivies blink and blink and blink.

This is the end, I know it. They're going to kick me out. I'll have to change back into my jeans and T-shirt, out of the matching peach pima cotton pajama set Veronica gave me to wear so we'd all match. Stumble home in the dark, if I can remember how to get there, it seems so far, another planet.

Then, suddenly, Veronica starts laughing. And then Crystal and then Pearl and then Meghan and now they're all laughing, wiping joyful tears from the corners of their eyes, rolling around and balling Meghan's sheets in their slippery hands.

"Ha?" I say, like it's a question, which it kind of is, because I didn't think I was kidding.

Crystal flops up, still clutching the sheet. She pats my knee with the other hand. "You're *so* funny."

"Really, Meghan. Where did you *find* this girl?" Veronica

asks, lolling her towhead on a throw pillow. "Are all your co-workers this clever?"

"Hardly. Most of them are boring. They take a lot of selfies and spend all their time on Twitter. But this one right here—" Meghan ruffles my hair "—is a keeper. She has *ideas*."

Relief relaxes my stomach. I smile. "Everyone at our work *does* take a lot of selfies. As if anyone cares. They're not *famous*." I think of Carly and Emily, taking themselves so seriously, documenting their days, and then I join the Ivies, my friends, in laughing for real. From the belly.

We grab sweaters and move to the roof, which can only be accessed by climbing the fire escape and hoisting ourselves over the lip of the building into a valley of concrete. My hip aches from where it hits the floor on the way down. It's late, and Park Slope twinkles like a nursery rhyme. Meghan drags a picnic basket from one shadowed corner and pulls out two bottles of red, a corkscrew, six glasses, and a checkered blanket. We sprawl out, a many-limbed creature, a Cthulhu of young adulthood, elder girlhood, and I lose myself in belonging.

From the fine mesh of a speaker, produced from the pockets and folds, from the shadowed corners of the roof, emanate the opening notes of *Hazardous*. I'm not sure who starts singing first, but one by one our voices add to the body of sound and then we're howling at the navy blue above us, an off-key melody, rocket-launched into the sky, tumbling and overlapping. The fabric of our chorus mostly trembles and wavers above Adriana's own driven, focused vocals, but every so often it all intersects, and, for a sublime instant, we are not just *one of*, but actually, literally *one*. We drink and sing until our insides are ravaged raw and our lips are wine-bruised. I'm resting on someone's rising and falling stomach, eyes heavy, almost lulled to sleep, breathing in the smoke of the Ivies' tangled perfumes, musk and cracked pepper and lavender and vanilla and patchouli.

Glossed lips glimmer from the darkness and graze my ear, smelling like strawberries. "We did it," the lips say. *Did what?* My tongue is too swollen and thick to form the words.

"Sophie," the lips say. "We killed her."

My left arm is gone. Numb, and buried under Meghan's head, colorless in the early-morning, middle-of-the-night darkness. The peach shorts from my sleep set are twisted, and the little eggshell bow has migrated from under my belly button to my right hip bone. The moon shines into the room through the parted curtain and someone snores through her mouth.

We did it. Sophie. We killed her.

The words return to me like a childhood memory, something so far buried it can't possibly be real. I was drunk; I must have imagined it or dreamed it. I can't even remember who said it, or who I think said it. The voice, in remembrance, is tuneless, like the eerie whisper of the monster in a horror film.

I sit up. There are three of us crammed into Meghan's bed; she's closest to the window, I'm on the outside, and Pearl is strewn over our feet and curled up like a cat, no blanket. Her ivy tattoo seems to shift and expand, growing up her leg. The leaves rustle and flutter as she softly snores. I shove the heels of my hands deep into my eye sockets, trying not to see. Pearl moves in her sleep, tightening her eyelids, crinkled like the creamy petals on the pink rose Veronica brought to my room after I fainted at work. She is vulnerable and sweet in sleep, her guard down, and I'm filled with tenderness for her. I move to cover her with the discarded top sheet. Pearl curls into the layer of warmth, giving a satisfied moan as she turns her face into the moonlight. Her lips are slick as patent leather. Could she have been the one?

But why would Pearl tell me anything? She doesn't even like me. Maybe she just wants to scare me off. I shake my head and smile. It's silly, the whole thing is silly. They couldn't have *killed* anyone, these wispy girls. My new friends.

Could they?

11

"Thank you for meeting so early on a Monday," Lexi says. She doesn't sound thankful; she sounds like she's reciting a speech from a teleprompter, a speech she didn't even write. She stands at one end of the Emerald conference table, leaning forward onto both hands.

The web production team is spread around the room, taking up as much space as possible. Everyone is here, except for Ashley. Rumors have been flying all weekend, ever since Emily saw Ashley and Lexi disappear into Karen from HR's office late on Friday afternoon. She loitered outside, listening to the strained sounds of sniffling, whining, and lowered voices.

It sounded like my parents fighting, she texted to the mostly defunct group chat, breaking the cocoon of silence that had fallen around me since the night I left Tom standing on the street.

The air in Emerald prickles as Lexi sighs and taps a finger. Her nails are short, and so it makes only a dull thump on the table's surface, slicked with varnish. Then she says, with mild regret, "Ashley's last day at the company was this past Friday.

From now on, you will report directly to me. We will also be asking each of you to begin attending the weekly pitch meetings starting next week, with ideas prepared."

There's a sharp, collective inhale. I glance around the table at the reactions from each of my teammates, searching for clues to how I should act. Tom straightens and furrows his brow, a soldier at attention, preparing to take his appointment seriously. Carly and Emily focus on their computer screens, typing like mad, obviously to each other, not trying to hide it. Mariah stares up at Lexi, her expression blank, unreadable.

And then there's me. What do I do? I google *Adriana Argento* and gaze at her dimpled face until my heartbeat slows to normal.

"Any questions?" Lexi says.

Fragmented queries swirl in my head, but the one complete, fully formed question that blazes through them all like a flare in the night is not one I'm prepared to ask, and it's this: *What the hell am I supposed to do with my life?*

I shake my head to clear the sediment. Lexi takes the gesture as a sign that we're all finished here and dismisses the meeting with a curt, "You're free to go."

Mariah sidles up behind me as we bottleneck at the door, each trying to be the one to get out fast enough, so no one has to be alone with our new overlord. "What the fuck?" she hisses. I shrug.

Carly and Emily are whispering behind us. "I heard she was stealing from the beauty closet. Expensive perfumes and shit. Charlotte was so betrayed, she *cried*."

I stop. I feel sick. My body is jostled from behind.

"Watch it!" Carly snaps. I keep moving.

Ashley normally sits at the management table with Lexi and the other members of the editorial top brass. Her former workstation is conspicuously empty, cleared of picture frames and strangled hand lotions and dried flowers, gifts from publicists. The flat black surface where her computer used to sit is an omen. One by one, we eye her vacant chair as we pass.

I drop my laptop at the bullpen and run for the bathroom, which is mercifully empty. In the handicap stall, I flop to my knees in front of the toilet, hovering as if I'm going to vomit. My stomach clenches and shudders, my eyes water, but nothing comes out. I roll off my legs and end up leaning against the wall, knees tucked into my chest.

Ashley may have been fired under false pretenses, shouldering blame for what I did, but I'm surprised it took this long for the company to be made aware of what we, the web producers, have always been able to see: her utter redundancy. And yet, of all of us, Ashley was the one who cared the most by caring at all. She *needed* this job. It's always been legible in her openness, the expansiveness of her face when she ran a meeting, and in the double or triple exclamation points scattered throughout her official correspondence. Her frequent recitation of her favorite phrase, *teamwork makes the dream work!* Ashley loves this website; she wants it to succeed. That she should be the one they let go of first, the sacrificial lamb, is an impossibly cruel twist of fate.

I could trade my place for hers. March into HR and correct the record, tell them that it's me they want. She doesn't deserve this, but I do. I'm lazy and self-indulgent. I waste precious office hours online stalking a pop star who has nothing to do with my job. I take what isn't mine. I couldn't be less diligent if I tried.

My phone is sliding halfway out of my pocket. I straighten my leg and dig it out of my jeans. The bank app glows green on the home screen. I shove my phone back in my pocket and go back to my desk.

* * *

I notice the diamond right away, a living thing on her finger. All eyes and teeth, a snarl. A large oval fenced in by a border of smaller diamonds. The ring seems to drag down the entire left side of her body, causing her bones to sag beneath the weight. Shortening her by several centimeters when she can't afford to lose one. She's even tinier with the diamond dancing in the middle of her left hand. A lake nestled between the second and third knuckles on her ring finger, floating above the vena amoris, shooting straight to her heart like a poison arrow.

There has been no announcement, no explicit public mention of an engagement. In fact, one gray sweatshirt cuff partially obscures the ring in the paparazzi shot on the top of the *Us Weekly* home page. As if she's trying to hide it, but we will not let her: a circular insert casts her left hand in extreme close-up, a magnifying glass inviting the viewer to scrutinize, like the answer can be found in the faceted jumble of stones.

There are thousands of comments under this one article and TMZ, *People*, *Star*, and my own website of employment have picked up the story, Meghan's byline dancing neatly under our headline: *"Are Adriana Argento and Nolan Lynch Tying the Knot? Here's What We Know."* Each subsequent report cites *Us Weekly* and the grainy photo snapped by a lucky freelance photographer on Rodeo Drive as the original source. The entire internet is overrun with relationship timelines and in-depth song lyric analysis. Adriana Argento and Nolan Lynch have not responded to any requests for comment.

In the days following the photo's release, their public manner does not change. In photos and interviews, they act normal. No talk of flowers, wedding dates, white dresses, tailored tuxedos. Just that ring, a signal flare, the beam from a lighthouse.

I respect their privacy, in theory. But I read every article and fan theory, of which there are thousands piled on top of thousands, a latticework of speculation. Journalists and amateur sleuths alike itemize the relationship like a receipt. Parsing out each detail, rearranging the facts to fit the narrative they want to create. The hunger for information gnaws at me. One website puts the cost of the ring at close to $100,000. The figure makes me wince: twice my salary for just a few inches of pressed carbon and metal.

Less than a week after the ring first appears in public, both stars are asked *the question* in separate interviews. In a conversation with NPR, Nolan dodges the subject of a wedding. "I'll just say this: I'm young, happy, and very much in love."

Adriana gives *E!* a canary-eating smile, her eyes two cups of inscrutability, and says, with finality, "Let's get back to the music."

Veronica paces her snowy living room. She's holding a cigarette, but not smoking it. Every few seconds she lifts the unfiltered edge to her nose and sniffs.

"She quit when she was twenty-one," Meghan whispers. "The smell calms her down."

The Ivies are worked up, picking at themselves in a vast demonstration of self-soothing ticks. Pearl nibbles at a splintered cuticle until it bleeds. Crystal tugs the edges of her spiraled hair taut, winces at the tug of her follicles. Jessie traces the top leaf of her climbing ivy tattoo, pressing down with a nail. Meghan keeps refreshing apps, alternating between Piger and her work email. I sit in the middle of the floor, flexing and curling my hands, imagining how a diamond ring would feel, whether I would ever get used to the weight.

"How can she do this? *Right* before the new album comes out," Crystal moans. Veronica stops walking, glares at her, and resumes walking. The plush carpet is thinning under the grip of her fuchsia-polished toes. She hasn't said a word all night.

The Ivies hate Nolan. They think he's too gruff, unkempt, vulgar. They hate his tattoos, like the one of a peacock on his thigh and the *HATE/LOVE* ink on his knuckles and all the other ones, even the cursive *AA* he has behind one ear, a joint reference to Adriana and his sobriety, two essential elements of his life that are linked. They hate his music, the references to hard drugs and straight liquor and depression, the way it all eats at the soul after midnight. They hate to be reminded of pain.

I nod along with their proclamations, a pebble of guilt rattling in my stomach. *Yes, he is rough around the edges* and *no, we can't be sure he'll stay sober forever.* It's all true, even if our conclusions are different. Where they see flaws, I see honesty worthy of tenderness. Once, months ago, I defended him by saying his addiction shouldn't define him, that he still deserves love and, clearly, she really does love him, and they looked at me like I suggested we all shoot heroin with our breakfast.

"But what if he *relapses*?" Meghan had said, and I folded the duplicity away for later, deep in the dough of my core, and stopped trying.

I had avoided the Ivies for about two weeks after that sweaty, feverish night at Meghan's, begging off her invitations to get lunch or go for an afternoon walk, heading straight home from the office. But I'd forgotten how lonely I was before and when Veronica texted earlier that afternoon, I set aside my reservations. It was just a dream. There's no way these waifish, well-coiffed women flew across the country to kill an innocent teenage girl and leave her lifeless body next to a dumpster. No way.

I ignore the blaze in Veronica's eyes as she swings to face us, illuminated by the fading spring evening through her tall living room window. The sunset tinges her translucent hair, giving her a golden, Greek goddess glow.

"Do you think they're actually engaged?" I say.

"They're engaged." Jessie builds a hack of phlegm at the back of her throat, aims it like a teenage boy spitting at the asphalt, then abruptly swallows. "Why else would she be wearing a literal engagement ring?"

"It could be a *promise* ring," Meghan says.

"Don't only Christian teens wear those? The ones who've taken vows of celibacy—"

"And the Jonas Brothers, they had them."

"Those are purity rings."

"Oh. Right."

"But who spends $100,000 on a ring just to say *I think you're cool, let's keep hanging out indefinitely*?"

"If anyone would, it's Nolan Lynch. He's *soooo* rich, remember? He loves being rich."

"All rich people love being rich," Pearl says, her cheeks flushing when she remembers that Veronica is rich, if not $100,000-promise-ring-rich, and that Pearl is currently, gleefully availing herself of Veronica's rich-girl furniture and rich-girl Bordeaux cupped in rich-girl crystal.

Meghan takes a swig of coffee from a paper to-go cup. She straightens the curve of her spine and looks around the room before leaning toward me, a conspiratorial smile tugging her mouth wide at the corners. The rest of the Ivies are distracted by their anguish, and I wonder why Meghan never seems as emotional as the rest of them. She has a reporterly frankness that holds her at a distance. Even though she loves Adriana like a true fan, her duty, first and foremost, is to the story. At least that's how it seems to me, watching her stretch her limbs and let the others fight about what this diamond means for *our girl* and *her future* and *the charts*.

But then, there is that tattoo, a permanent mark of devotion on her skin, reminding me that she's just as fanatical as any of them. She just holds it closer to the chest.

The first signs of spring have been building, with the slow spread of sunshine on the first warm day, and now it's May. The air holds the sting of nail polish remover, that alcoholic floral that makes me think of long-ago evenings at the end of the school year, any school year. Always that same smell. There's a memory of a memory of a memory in that smell, something ephemeral and already fading by the time it's buried in my lungs. I take the walk from the train to the office slowly, sloughing my feet along the concrete, watching the scruffy birds take flight over my head. They give me that feeling of being alive in nature, even if they're only pigeons mottled by dirt and car exhaust. The same with the trees that struggle to bloom on the barren streets lined with bursting trash bags splitting at the seams like an oil spill. This diminished pace allows me to actually look at the magazines on the newsstand a block from the website's headquarters. Adriana's doe face blinks from the cover of *The Fret*, her silver-white ponytail pale lightning on the black background, natural roots exposed at the top. Her makeup is pastel—lavender eyeshadow, faint melon lip gloss, iridescent cheek highlight. She wears a black denim jumper and matching jacket slung so as to reveal a slice of burnished shoulder the color of slightly overdone toast, polished collarbones. She's winking, lips parted, in the classic pin-up expression of pop stars in photo shoots, an expression all girls are born knowing how to replicate, with varying degrees of success. I myself have tried many times to copy this look since childhood, in foggy bathroom mirrors and reflective restaurant tables. Somehow it never achieves quite the same effect. Less come-hither, more dumbfounded.

I flip through the glossy pages until I locate the cover story at the center of the issue, scanning the blurb at the top of the page. It's superimposed over a photo of Adriana sitting on a kitchen table eating a forkful of rainbow cake in front of a gingham backdrop like a trap-punk Dorothy in a fucked-up remake of *The Wizard of Oz*.

"Adriana Argento is starting over. The pint-sized starlet with a larger-than-life voice has been through enough tragedy to last a lifetime, but she's making her triumphant return this summer with a new album and a brighter outlook on life."

The article describes *solstice* as *deeply personal*, says that it's like *a glimpse inside the superstar's diary*, and *the most accomplished work of her career*, citing the experimental influence of producer and hip-hop legend Petey Jackson.

"He really pushed me to expose myself on this record in ways I haven't been brave enough to do before," she tells the reporter over lunch at a bright Beverly Hills café. Lunch. A casual, everyday activity propped up on a delicate wire structure of publicists and emails and scheduling conflicts, all of it invisible to the reader, yet still so *present*. I imagine sitting across from Adriana Argento as she chews, that masticating reminder of her mortality, proof that beneath that flawless epidermis there are layers of muscle and bone swimming with blood and bile, all the life-giving liquids that comprise the body.

The rest of the profile is refreshing in its professionalism. The interviewer focuses mostly on the art and not her doll-like beauty or her relationship with Nolan, though surely the conversation took place before the engagement rumors began swirling.

I close *The Fret* and fish my phone from my pocket, snapping a photo of the cover with the toes of my scuffed brown boots visible. I have social media profiles registered under my real name, first and last, no flourishes. Though I hardly use them, lately I've gotten the urge to inject more of myself into the ether, to prove I exist, that I'm not a collection of pixels, the tiny cells keeping the internet alive. As soon as I tuck my phone into the outer pocket of my bag, it buzzes twice. I point the toes of my boots south and head to work.

Charlotte reaches the coffee machine first. Today, her hair is braided in a long chain and threaded with fresh pink streaks that may be extensions. I watch her insert the coffee pod and press the lever, listening to the hiss the machine makes as the water heats up. Her lips and cheeks are flushed matching raspberry. Hers is the kind of pretty they manufacture on assembly lines.

She smiles to the right of me as she waits for the coffee to finish brewing. I've never been sure whether she knows how to connect my name, which she interacts with on Piger when she needs something and only then, with my features, and her vacant expression confirms my suspicions: she has no idea who I am. I step around to rinse my mug in the sink, catching a whiff of masculine floral. Funny. I expected her to smell sweet. She grabs my outstretched wrist as I'm holding the mug under the faucet. A charge runs through me, voltaic and sizzling. I see the mug slipping from a slackened grip, the adorable cat face fracturing into pieces, a lone eye staring up at me, unblinking, accusing. Frozen in death as in life. Like JonBenét.

My senses click back into place; the mug is still in my hand, whole. The faucet is still dispensing water, a wasteful stream flowing down the drain. Charlotte's pink nails press into the veins on the underside of my wrist. She let's go just as swiftly when she registers the bare shock on my face.

"Oh my god, I'm so sorry! I don't know what came over me." She shakes her head and smiles again, genuinely this time.

I'm too caught in the heady Cinderella-ness of her, the

perfect teeth and the whites of her eyes, to respond. I twist the faucet knob, plunging us into silence. The Keurig stops churning.

"I just wanted to ask what eyeshadow you're wearing. It's super pretty," she says.

"It's…uh…"

"Oh, gosh!" she smacks her forehead with a flat palm. "I always forget that not everyone pays attention to makeup like I do. You probably don't even remember what you put on this morning, right?"

It comes at me like an insult. I *do* remember. I will always remember. The plastic compact, white with a silver label. The brand name three lowercase letters. *Your eyelids, but better.* I flip the compact over in my mind and the shade name emerges from the fog.

"Tobacco Road."

"RMS! I love them. *Such* an amazing clean beauty brand."

I bite the corner of my lip. "Yeah."

"Well, anyway. It looks great on you! See you around."

With a little wave over her twisting spine, she's gone. Back to pretending I'm a robot on the other side of the screen, an extension of LIZZIE. I roll my eyes at the highlighted fritz of blond as it disappears around the corner and turn my attention to the task at hand, my coffee. Charlotte's spent hazelnut pod is still settled inside the Keurig, condensation collecting on the punctured foil. I discharge it from the moist cavern, toss it in the garbage, and reach inside the hazelnut box for another.

My hand grazes air. Of course. Charlotte took the last one.

The interaction with Charlotte rattles me, elevating her, in my estimation, from merely bubbleheaded to prophetic. She doesn't even realize what she knows, but the incisiveness of her gaze, her cunning flash of a smile, tell me everything.

She suspects, on some level, that I've wronged her, wronged Ashley, and she'll catch me one day.

I take my coffee to the bathroom to calm my racing mind. The flower is still there, etched into chipped paint the same color as the soft, ticklish underbelly of a pale infant's chin. I trace the pencil marks with my fingertips and try, again, to picture the artist. I'd love for her to tell me what she knows about survival. The drawing is a clear means to an end, the end being the proverbial six o'clock, the twilight of dissatisfaction, more real than the ticking hands on a clock, more solid than the other-worldly glow of numbers. Does she illustrate her notebooks and napkins, leaving a trail of ink to mark the endless days? Are the sides of her palms permanently graphite-stained? Is she hopeful about the future, whatever future there might be? Scientists warn of rising sea levels, the sun boiling the Earth's surface. Just the other day, I read a *New York Times* article about an airport in the South grounding all flights due to the heat. Sometimes when I picture the future, all I can see is beige. Beige where there should be grass, beige steam rippling the beige air, a beige, cloudless sky. And all around me, absolutely nothing for miles. I'm not arrogant enough to believe I'd be the lone survivor of the apocalypse. But the vision is telling me something, speaking to some larger purpose I've yet to discover.

Leaving the handicap stall, I flush the toilet and let the door swing shut. In the mirror, I close one eyelid, then the other. Watch the mica particles cresting at the center of each tightly shut eye, intensifying and dispersing on either side. I wet a paper towel from the dispenser next to the sink, wrapping it around my forefinger and swiping the pointed end in windshield wiper motions over my lids. When I pull my hand away, most of the tawny color is gone, leaving behind a few scattered flecks of burnished brown sparkle.

I feel clean, renewed. Like myself again.

★ ★ ★

"What do you think of Charlotte?"

Meghan and I are sitting side by side in a booth at the diner in her neighborhood, scrolling through #AdrianaArgento on Instagram, looking for signs of The Ring. "Charlotte, as in the beauty editor from work? She's fine, I guess. We don't interact much."

"But isn't that weird? You're both editors. Isn't there, like, a secret code?"

"You said it yourself: no one talks at the office. Besides, I'm just an associate. I think my section leader probably knows her better than I do. Why?"

I shrug, maintaining nonchalance. In front of me, Adriana Argento sits sidesaddle on a chestnut horse, her seafoam-green gown lush with embroidery frothing over its gleaming hump, weather-beaten cowboy boots tucked into the stirrups. The caption tells me it's from a 2013 *Elle* magazine shoot. Jabbing my thumb at the heart icon under the photo, I keep scrolling. "Nothing. She just seems sort of...rude?"

"Everyone we work with is rude, if you haven't noticed. Except you, of course." Meghan gives me a loving nudge with her elbow. I stick my tongue out and a laugh unspools from the pit of my throat, releasing Charlotte to the edges of my consciousness. Who cares, who cares, who cares.

"She just seems to have it in for me, I guess. Since Ashley left."

This is, strictly speaking, a lie. The only real conversation we've had was the one at the coffee maker, full of praise. But I'm always on the lookout for the ways a compliment can be weaponized.

"I wouldn't let it get to you. The beauty editors at every publication I've ever worked at have had a chip on their shoulders. Something about staring at your face all day in a mirror really warps your mind. Hey, remember when pop stars on horses were a major editorial trend?"

Meghan shoves her phone in my face, blocking most of my screen with hers so that the hem of Adriana's dress, her cowboy boots, and the horse's legs, appear doubled. I examine her plaintive stare over the off-the-shoulder billow of the dress. She is glamorous and untouchable. *Her face, but better.*

"She looks so pretty there," I say. "But did you notice she and the horse have matching ponytails?"

I turn my screen to face her so she can see that we are looking at the same image. Meghan laughs and withdraws her phone, placing it on the table next to her milkshake. Clotted white cream clings to the sides of the glass. She sucks at the straw, slurping the last of the ice cream clean.

This is as good a moment as any. "Hey, so… I had this really weird dream when we all slept at your house the other night."

"Oh, yeah?"

"Yeah. Someone told me that the Ivies killed Sophie Heffernan. Isn't that wild?"

Nothing about Meghan's position explicitly changes. She keeps her lips pressed to the straw; she grips the base of the glass. But there's an overall tightening, a rigidity like a spear running through her limbs.

She lifts her head and the straw lolls to one side, cocked in curiosity. "Wow," she says. "Weird."

She doesn't seem at all surprised.

On the first truly hot day, I take off my jacket and walk into Stephanie. I haven't seen her since the night of The Growing at Jessie's; she stayed in my apartment until I fell asleep and was gone in the morning.

She's coming out of Eataly across from Madison Square Park, a funereal blur on the landscape, and I'm looking down, shoving my jacket into my tote bag, misjudging the distance between myself and the oncoming pedestrian traffic. My feet graze soft leather flats. My shoulder thuds into an upper arm. A white shopping bag hits my hip and lands heavily on the sidewalk, emitting a warm, garlicky scent.

"Watch it!"

"Sorry, I—Steph?"

Her expression dissolves. She hauls me into a suffocating hug. "Ohmygod, *hi*! I didn't even recognize you." We pull apart. I pick up the fallen Eataly bag, my mouth watering as the oily aroma crosses my nose, and hand it to her.

My armpits are sweating through the spare fabric of my T-shirt. I bought it on recommendation from girls at work, stupidly believing myself to be someone who could wear white without staining it. Not that it was specifically recommended to me, but rather that this particular T-shirt from this particular internet-famous brand with one slate-gray storefront on Prince Street, a line out front, and an iPad-based checkout system, was owned and raved about within my earshot by seemingly everyone at the website. After just two wears, the cotton was already pilling. After today, I'm sure the underarms will be stained yellow.

"I haven't seen you in forever! How have you *been*? I'm just so busy with work lately I haven't had time for *anything* else. I got a promotion, did I tell you?" Stephanie chatters. "I meditated on it for months and it finally happened."

I adjust my tote, pulling the handles toward my collarbone. "No, you didn't. Congratulations."

Stephanie tosses her shiny hair off her shoulder with a haughty smile. There's not a drop of sweat visible on her. Her black shift dress and matching blazer are spotless, and she smells heady and claustrophobic, like warm conditioner residue lingering in the bathroom after a hot shower.

"It's a big responsibility, cultivating new writing talent. I've acquired a really exciting manuscript already. Can't talk about it yet, though."

"That sounds…great. A perfect fit for you." My voice is coming strained and high, each word an effort. I think I know what she's about to say and then she says it, giving the moment an unsettling clairvoyance.

"You know, my old job is still open. I could put in a good word, if you're interested."

I can imagine it: riding an elevator through a sculptural lobby, wearing starched clothing from the same brand that made my T-shirt, walking with purpose. A pile of manuscript pages on my desk—my real desk, shared by no one—aflutter in the breeze from the open window. A *window*. Speaking in meetings, offering opinions. Connecting with authors and agents, the people responsible for making books. Hands on my keyboard, a slim smile stuck on my face. Like Edith.

"That could be…"

"Oh, and I almost forgot the best part!" Stephanie says. "I'd be your supervisor."

I'm seeing Stephanie, really *seeing* her, with her pinched lips stained red from the Revlon she applied this morning, the rest of the color having long since traveled her digestive system on the wave of yogurt and granola and tooth-staining coffee, eyes a little too close together, her desire to boss me around, take me under her wing, palpable as the fresh spring humidity in the air. I see her like this, my friend who once open-mouth sobbed, leaving a trail of saliva in my bed, over a boy named Chad, and I know I can't say yes.

"I appreciate the offer, I really do. But I'm happy where I am." Stephanie's features screw up so tight I fear they might collapse into the center of her face, a vortex swirling around her nose. I hold my breath and plunge onward. "It's not official yet, but I'm also about to get a promotion. They're talking about making me a lifestyle editor." The lie flows so freely I almost believe it myself. And then it feels so good I lie some more: "By the way, I'm almost done with *The Goldfinch*. Great book."

Stephanie doesn't seem so convinced, and I'm scared she's going to press for my opinion. "Oh," she says, and puts on a renewed appearance of happiness. "That's great. Let me know what you think when you're done. And if you change your mind about the job—"

"I won't. Anyway, great to see you." I turn downtown, angling my body toward the train. She's standing there, nursing her scuffed loafer, when I turn to blow a kiss over my shoulder and say, "Talk soon!"

Stephanie is so still, and she speaks so quietly, that I almost don't hear what she says next. "It's about time you stop sabotaging yourself."

Then she calls my name, but I'm already walking away, choosing to read her words as congratulations. I consider the possibility that this might be the last time I see Stephanie.

Spring gives way to the slow IV drip of summer. I am fully awake for the first time since late October. The city heats from the ground up. First, the subway platform simmers to a boil, sultry underground catacombs where the breeze can't reach. Then the sidewalk, scalding the rubber at the bottom of our shoes. We, the dwellers, shed our layers, exchanging heavy coats for diaphanous scarves and stiffly creased denim jackets.

Meghan and I spend the precious few splendid days in late May and early June, before the humidity and the trash stench set in, outside. Eating cheese and crackers sprawled on blankets in the park, sneaking sips of wine. Splitting tapas at sidewalk cafés. Linking arms as we window-shop on Fifth Avenue, wondering aloud at who we would be in that shirt or this skirt, carrying that wicker basket. Meghan loves to try on silk floral dresses she can't afford at various boutiques, and I watch, serious-eyed, and give her my real opinions.

We are sometimes joined by the other Ivies, but mostly it's the two of us. Friendship, real friendship, shows me New York anew. The once oppressive skyscrapers twist and bend toward the clear blue of endless possibility. There are so many ways to pass an hour. Talking, telling stories from our separate pasts, trying to join our histories, laughing at shared jokes, undulating with anticipation for *solstice*, the album that will crack our lives wide open. I bitch about Stephanie too often, but Meghan never gets tired of mocking her self-serious nature and her meditation schedule.

Nothing much is different at work since Ashley left. At the web producers' bullpen, we continue our slow march through the weeds of content, now pitching ideas for essays and features at the weekly editorial meeting. Lexi rejects most before the section editors can chime in with their opinions. It's humiliating, but no more humiliating for us than for the others who were hired for this very purpose. We all turn red, get very interested in the tabletop, hold our breath and wait for it to end.

"They need to have a point," Lexi keeps saying. *"What's the point?"*

Earlier that same day, I hit Publish on an article titled, *"But Do Men Actually Wash Their Balls? Let's Investigate."*

I avoid eye contact with almost all of the web producers, especially Tom and except for Mariah, who still smiles from her post down the table and still asks how I am when we encounter each other at the bathroom sinks or waiting for the elevators in the lobby. It's the destruction of that one potential friendship that I regret the most, much more than everything that happened with Tom. With a little distance, I realize it wasn't him I liked, but the attention, the pheromones. And maybe the tattoo. Then, one afternoon, he sends a Piger message asking me to dinner, wanting to start over. *Third (or maybe fourth?) time's the charm?* I make a joke about HR and text Meghan for advice, or maybe permission. *Go, if you want*, she says. I tell him I'll think about it, but I do so with a winking smiley face.

To anyone looking through the window of my life, I have everything a person needs to be happy—a hobby, companionship, a paycheck, my health.

And in late June, the missing piece slots into place: a *solstice* release date. The announcement comes on Instagram and Twitter. Adriana floats upside down on a peach-colored background. The square image cuts off the side of her face, the focus on the snail-shaped cavern of her ear, blond wisps breaking the hairline.

"solstice. *Midnight EST, July 23rd. Preorder Friday.*" The fan accounts erupt, excitement bubbling like lava down my screen.

"This is going to be her magnum opus."

"Cryogenically freeze my body so I wake up at 11:59 p.m. on the 22nd."

"Is this bitch really upside down on her album cover? WE. FUCKING. STAN."

Meghan Piger DMs me mere moments after the announcement goes live.

Listening party at my place on the 22nd-23rd? We'll all be there.

Fuck. Yes.

12

I plug my headphones in as soon as I get to the office and jack the volume way up, the NA playlist on repeat while I do the day's emailing and spreadsheeting, the fixing of everyone's unnoticed mistakes. All four coffee breaks come and go, but I only stand once, to get a single cup and retrieve the salad I brought for lunch from the refrigerator. I eat the salad and drink the coffee hunched over my laptop in the flickering light of an old Adriana and Nolan performance on *Nightly with Poppy*. She wears a strapless dress patterned with roses and towering black pumps, as if she's fooling anyone. The top of her hair is secured with a rhinestone clip. Dancers kick-step in the background as she rocks onto the balls of her shoes.

Nolan comes out to sing his verses, receding into the wings for the choruses, remaining charmingly scruffy. I wish I'd been in the audience, feeling the energy between them as it swirled through the studio. All these years later and I feel it still, threatening to shatter my computer screen with its intensity. Nolan spins Adriana into the crook of his arm and they sway together, back to front, as he finishes rapping his last few bars. Then, suddenly as they come together, Nolan releases Adriana's hand and exits stage left. She's slightly unsteady on her feet without his anchoring weight, but she nails the impossible final notes in the whistle register, beaming.

I try to recall where I was around the time this was filmed. The years blur behind me in a gunmetal streak, the grind of rubber on asphalt. I spent my late teens and early twenties moving, zombielike, through college, then into the city, working odd jobs until I landed at the website. In California, Adriana Argento climbed the rungs from the Disney Channel to the Staples Center. While she was rehearsing for the Broadway show and then the television series that made her famous, I learned how to handle my liquor, underlined passages of Flannery O'Connor and Ernest Hemingway, and made out with tattooed boys on the campus green. While she was signing a deal with Revolving Records, cementing the start of her legacy, I ate bodega sandwiches and learned to navigate the subway buzzing on rosé and wine spritzers. In the studio, she recorded her first single. Across the country, I sent out résumés, cold-emailing and *just following up*, responding to job postings that made me want to die at companies that promised to make you *part of the family* and bought your loyalty not with a decent salary or career fulfillment but with monthly happy hours and free Chipotle.

And while she and Nolan Lynch were eating each other alive with their eyes in front of a live audience and Poppy Yates, I was kissing someone I met at a bar and running outside without ever asking his name. There are so many different ways to live a life.

The ring vanishes as quickly as it appeared.

A few days before it happens, Nolan and Adriana are photographed on a red carpet, wearing black attire like mourning shrouds. They stand close, clutching one another. Their faces are immaculate, made-up and blotted, completely oil-free. And yet I sense so clearly all the fluids and gristle that lurk, hidden by layers of skin. Flesh, bone, blood, tears, sweat, snot.

Adriana holds a black feather boa like a shield, and her eyes are lowered away from the flash. Nolan's face is stark and white, forehead creased, fastening his open lapel with a tattooed paw, eyes meeting the camera lens head-on, caught.

I search the peaks and valleys of their body language for a sign. What does it mean, for instance, that her shoulders are angled away from his, that his hand makes small indentations in her forearm? Could this be the night they splintered wide open, a grapefruit smashed on the ground, orange skin falling away to reveal the mealy pulp spilling from the exposed wound? Or maybe it was just the night they realized it was over, that it was time to stop fighting. The ring is not yet missing and yet already her hand appears small and frail and naked.

In a video from the event, an awards dinner no one cares about, they can be spotted in the background, always touching. Hand moving continuously between hand, arm interlocking with arm, one chin tucked to the other's collarbone. Whispers exchanged and breath measured. The posturing is sweet, but there's something vacant, a valley between them.

Sadness rocks through me. Her left hand snakes across the table, the diamond shooting like a geyser, creasing the tablecloth, fingers taut and overextended at the joints, reaching for him. But he doesn't see her, and her hand goes slack. Their shoulders touch, yet they are miles apart. I can smell the fissures, like petrichor after a rainstorm.

Veronica hosts a dinner. The table is set with pink-trimmed china, scalloped cloth napkins, champagne, a vase teeming with azaleas. This is my first time in her dining room, and it's even more opulent than I would've imagined, with an antique mahogany dining set and pink wallpaper with gold vertical stripes running from crown molding to baseboard. When no one is looking, I run my thumb over the wallpaper. It's thick, textured. The expensive kind.

I'm first to arrive. I've never been alone with Veronica, with any of them, and without Meghan providing a buffer, I feel stiff and uncomfortable. Like I've been stuffed into another person's skin. None of my bones are where I expect them to be.

A woman a few years younger than me, maybe twenty or twenty-one, circulates a silver tray laden with hors d'oeuvres, and on the credenza is a crystal dish piled with crudités, a fat dollop of sour cream and onion dip in the center. The server is wearing a white button-down, black pants, and a black apron that comes up to the waist.

"Oh, she's not a caterer," Veronica murmurs when I inquire. "She's an intern at my PR firm; interns are *always* desperate for extra cash." Clattering noises come from the kitchen, and Veronica stops me from going for a glass of water. "I'll have Anna bring it out."

Anna turns out to be the intern-turned-waitress. She emerges a few seconds later and hands me a tall, frosted glass filled with ice. It's so cold it hurts to hold. I sip recklessly, courting brain-freeze. Veronica flaps around, offering to have Anna fetch other things for me. I keep saying no, but I wonder whether, for Anna, standing there with nothing to do is actually worse. Maybe she'd rather feed me celery with a ball of pungent dip than shift nervously from foot to foot, balancing the untouched tray of spinach puffs on her delicate wrist.

Finally, the bell rings. Veronica rushes out of the room. I hear her pumps clicking on the stairs leading to the foyer, the vacuum suck of the front door opening, the birdcall of women greeting each other, always with a fervor usually reserved for soldiers freshly returned from war. Where did we get the impression that we need to be so full of excitement, so *gushing*, all the time? As though the simple occasion of meeting in a yellow-lit hallway is a cause for celebration. So eager to please we spill over our own rough edges, like champagne poured too fast.

I hang at the far end of the room, resting on a chair back's carved dowels, as Pearl and Crystal trail in after Veronica. I watch as she repeats the rituals with Anna, making her fetch them glasses of water and napkins and individual carrot sticks and cauliflower florets from the vegetable plate. "Dip? Anna, dip them in the sour cream and onion and put them on a plate, will you?"

Jessie and Meghan arrive soon after, one and then the other, and we're finally allowed to find our places. The seating arrangement has been delineated by folded pieces of cardstock, decorated with pink and purple watercolor and our names in black cursive, placed at intervals around the table. I pick my place card up and peer at the lettering. It looks hand drawn: the ink is darker in some spots than others. There's a heavy dot at the tail end of my name, as if the writer was interrupted. "Did she make these herself?" I ask Meghan, seated to my left.

She nods. "Veronica is nothing if not committed to aesthetics."

That much is clear from the meal, which is fit for the cover of a gourmet cooking magazine. A roast chicken, the skin browned and crisp, running with savory juices, the serving platter ringed with a thyme garland. A wide dish brimming with buttery mashed potatoes. Waxen string beans twined at the edges like witches' fingers. Anna juggles the oversized dishes as she brings them from the kitchen to the table. The serving spoon falls from the mashed potato bowl while she's lowering it, leaving a viscous oval of mush on the Persian rug, and Anna goes pallid, shoulders inching to her ears as she recoils from the spoon's path and stares in horror at what she's done. Veronica gets very rigid and hisses something tight and threatening. Anna runs into the kitchen and returns, red-faced, with a carton of baking soda and a roll of paper towels.

As Anna attends to the mess on the floor, Veronica declares that the food is getting cold and begins cutting into the chicken with a put-upon air, passing thick slices to each of us. With our plates loaded with food, she takes her seat at the head of the table and lifts her burbling champagne flute. "To Adriana's freedom!"

We cheer and sip. The others' effusiveness serves as cover for my hesitation. I feel a sinking sensation, the wrongness of going against my own convictions. Guilt bites at the inside of my cheeks as I drink. The champagne is cloying. It tastes expensive, like sucking on polished coins. One sip leaves me parched.

The feast commences. We shovel food in our mouths as if trying to satiate a need deeper than hunger. The meal, the candlelight, the lace tablecloth, the carefully drawn place cards, give me a holiday feeling. This is Thanksgiving or Christmas. It's easier to think that way than to acknowledge what we are really doing here—rejoicing in the end of a love affair between two people whose inner lives we can only begin to imagine.

The Ivies chatter. Classical music plays from hidden speakers. Veronica only believes in instrumental music at mealtimes, an old family rule she continues to obey in adulthood. I find it unsettling, the way the bare notes give me nothing to hide behind, nothing to sing along with under my breath. I remain mostly quiet, out of deference to Nolan and Adriana, whose imagined pain clings like a weight around my neck. The Ivies talk about the new album, their renewed faith in *solstice*.

"The breakup has obviously been building for a while. She must have plenty of songs written about what a deadbeat he is and now she's free to release them."

"But hasn't the album been finished? It comes out next month."

"You never know, it doesn't take long to edit a song if you already have the main elements in place. If the reports are correct and they've been on and off for a while, I bet she has some *savage* anti-Nolan music ready to go."

I am suddenly not in the mood for speculation. I knock back the rest of my champagne. Before the glass even hits the table, Anna is at my side with a chilled bottle, replenishing my supply. I give her a grateful smile, certain it's the first one she's received all evening, and she looks to the side before smiling back and darting into the kitchen like she knows she just got away with something secret.

Dessert is apple cobbler with vanilla bean ice cream, so fresh and cold it acts as a lozenge going down my throat. I wonder if Veronica has Anna hidden in the kitchen churning cream and sugar and ice into a thickly whipped paste as fast as her skinny arms can move. As I'm swirling the last of the ice cream on my tongue, Veronica bangs the tines of her fork against the side of her glass, calling us to attention. She stands at the head of the table, a broad grin bisecting her face.

"Thank you all for coming," she says, as if we would be anywhere else. "It's an exciting day for our little community. Adriana is finally *free!*"

They clap and I clap, softly, so I can convince myself it doesn't count. Veronica withdraws a sheet of printer paper and a long kitchen knife from under the table. I gasp, then clutch my hand to my mouth. Meghan touches my knee, gives it a firm squeeze. The Ivies flash in the wide gleam of the blade, all combed hair and frappéd dresses. I try to catch my own eye, but the reflection is smeared, like someone drew an elbow across a slab of paint before it had finished drying.

Veronica turns the paper so the image on the front faces us. A black-and-white Nolan winks at us from under the brim of a cap, his teeth lined up like hard little Chiclets. "It's time to officially put an end to this disastrous union," she says.

She stretches her arms, spreading the photo and the knife to opposite corners of the room. The blade points toward the kitchen, where Anna has crept into the doorway. She stands there, looking like she's about to cry. Veronica arcs the arm holding the paper and places Nolan faceup beside the azalea centerpiece. The Ivies stand and lean forward, straining. She lifts the knife, clasps the handle between her knotted fingers, and plunges the blade into the center of his face, pinning him to the table. The wood makes a horrible cracking sound as the knife breaches the surface, and the impact is so great that the tiered chandelier, pink-tinted crystals like frozen hail, swings on its axis.

The amplified creak of splitting wood becomes another feature of the room, like a curtain or a wall hanging. Veronica wipes sweat from her brow, breasts heaving. She lets go of the knife, leaves it sticking up like a sword jutting in wait from a stone, infinitely patient. It could hang there all night, it's no trouble. I want to crawl over the dirty plates, get my knees and my shins and the heels of my hands gummed up in the slick of ice cream and the apple crumb pebbles. Wrest the knife free from where it cleaves Nolan like a dart between the eyes. My hands crimp my skirt fabric. I can feel the marks my sweaty palms will leave on the schoolgirl plaid, like tire treads.

For a few long seconds, seconds in which stars explode, species go extinct, civilizations are born, die, and are remade, no one moves or speaks. Everything is quiet.

Then, a primal yell. A backbreaking scream. The Ivies move

as one, upending the table, sending the dishes sliding on an incline past Nolan's pinned visage. He watches, powerless to stop the chaos, a haphazard grin forever plastered to his face.

Veronica doesn't even wince as her dining set falls to ruin at her feet. I realize I only imagined the china to be precious, because it had the quality of an heirloom. These dishes, they mean nothing to her. She only wants one thing, a type of proximal revenge. She lunges, grabs hold of the knife strapping Nolan to the now sideways table. The blade clatters to the floor and his smile flutters after it.

The Ivies squeal and shriek and pile on top of him in a mad frenzy, Veronica on the bottom. I stand against the credenza, still set with the barely touched dish of crudités, feeling like Jane Goodall observing predators devouring a weaker animal in the wild. I want to leave, but I find I can't move, so instead I search the mound of wriggling bodies, hoping to see Meghan trying to calm them all down. I spot her sunwashed hair caught in Pearl's red-lined mouth. Someone yelps. Torn bits of paper fly like confetti. One lands near me and I pick it up. Nolan's crinkled eye bordered by a crooked ridge.

I fold the fragment, slip it into my pocket.

The kitchen door stands ajar on the other side. I creep around the wrestling Ivies, porcelain crunching under my boot heels, and into the room. Veronica's kitchen is clean and bright as a hospital operating room. In one corner, Anna is cowering. She's been crying, her mascara tracing thick paths down each rosy cheek. "What's going on out there?" Her voice is gooey.

I dig around in the freezer, emerging with a dented carton of Turkey Hill, then root around, opening drawers and cabinets, until I find a bowl and spoon. It's hard for me to believe this is the same ice cream I was just eating; it tastes freezer-burned and hurts my teeth. Out there it was fresh from the cow, nutty, with only a hint of sweetness.

I hold the spoon out to Anna. "Want some?"

She takes the spoon, cleaving a neat scoop of ice cream. We trade bites, the clean bowl abandoned on the counter, until we hit cardboard. Milky rivers run down the side of the Turkey Hill container, puddling in the crevices. Some of the ice cream leaks through a crack in the bottom and spills out onto the granite. There's a crash and a shout from the other room.

"Will they come looking for you?" Anna asks.

"I don't think so. They're...busy."

"What *is* this? Some kind of cult?" Anna's eyes are saucers. She jumps at a loud bang and a sound like someone stomping on shattered glass.

"You wouldn't believe me if I told you."

Anna sighs and pushes away from the counter. She bends, disappearing behind the kitchen island, and rises holding a black canvas backpack.

"I seriously need to find another internship." She goes to the door and opens it wider. A pair of shoeless feet attached to slim, dark calves kick into the frame. I hear panting and what sounds like a wild, drippy yawn.

Anna turns to face me. "Good luck," she says, as if I'm the one who needs it when it's she who is about to walk out there. Her halting, crunching footsteps reach me until they don't. I wait for a couple of beats to retrace her path. The dining room is in shambles. The rest of the Ivies are fallen tinsel strewn about the floor. Could they be sleeping? I kick aside a few broken plates. Stand over the pile of my psychotic friends, all the tangled hair and rumbled skirts, the inked plant matter.

"Hey." A silver platter levitates and falls aside to reveal Meghan's potato-mottled complexion. She shakes her bangs, and a white blob drops onto her chin. She swabs it with her finger, pops it into her mouth. A purple bruise blooms above one eyebrow and a long, shallow cut winds down her jawline.

"Hey. I was just about to…" I finger-gun in the general direction of the front door. "I've got a long subway ride ahead. Are, uh, are you gonna be okay?"

"Yeah, I'll be fine. You go. Someone needs to make sure these fools don't have brain damage when they wake up."

I stumble out of Veronica's front door and onto the sidewalk. The heat beats my flesh like an external pulse; I scratch at my arms, trying to claw through, to dispel the queasiness spreading through my bloodstream. I feel diseased.

I check the cost of an Uber, decide it's worth it, and walk to the corner to wait. I don't try to make any sense of what I just saw. There is no way to fit the evening into a tolerable narrative. But the scenes replay without my consent. One image in particular cloys at me: Veronica, her magenta tweed skirt bunched around her hips, raising the knife above her blond head. Over and over again she brings it down, prying the tip of the blade underneath the brim of Nolan's cap. Raising it and bringing it down, the chandelier and the dazed Ivies reflected in the metal. Me, doing nothing, trapped inside the inescapable curse of my spinelessness. And, under it all, sliding like a snake through tall grass, is the thought that scares me the most: whether or not the others are capable of murder, I now know, without a doubt, that Veronica is. There is murderous rage just under her placid, feminine surface.

My Uber pulls up, a window rolling down. The driver says my name as a question. I nod and climb in.

Adriana sits by the pool in her yard, the ginkgo trees bowing over her prone form like fallen lashes. The water, jewel-blue, diamonds flashing on the surface. The sun, pleasantly hot on her exposed limbs. She dips one blade-shaped calf into the pool and the water cools her entire body, sending an icy tremor from her toes to the crown of her head. Shivering, she glides along the marble tile and plunges into the pool, her pointed toes jackhammering straight to the bottom.

She opens her eyes against the chlorine, wishing, as she so often does, that she could float underwater for days. Not to die, but to be swaddled. As she floats, she remembers when she bought this house with her check from the first season of *Peaches*, the largest number she'd ever seen written down. Money you could use to build a life. The yard had reminded her of childhood. If she floats on her back in the pool and focuses only on the clear blue sky framed by the ginkgo leaves, the years fall away like so many ripped calendar pages. She can stay like this for hours, conjuring remnants of the past: her mom and brother singing show tunes in their old living room, the tangy smell of her grandmother's meat sauce.

The beauty and curse of fame, Adriana thinks as she rotates in the water, is how it insulates you from experience. A high iron gate clasped like a necklace at the foot of the drive, a copse of trees climbing above the peaked roof, five bedrooms and five baths cushioning both wings, the labyrinthine fortress of Beverly Hills sprawling. Her house is tucked on a hill with a view of more hills. The very geography of Los Angeles, with its canyons and wild tangle of neighborhoods, serves to cosset its elite.

It's rare she spends a day completely alone. There's always someone on their way over. Her mind flits to Nolan. Being with him has always counted as being alone, he understood her so succinctly, their identities fused together until there was no differentiating one from the other, until earlier this week when he packed his things and a long black car with tinted windows nosed up the drive like an oil spill and swept him away to *stay at his place in Silverlake for a bit* so he could *collect his thoughts*.

Adriana breaks the surface of the water, gasping. She hoists herself onto the pool deck and collapses, her lungs contracting madly, sucking in painful gusts of air. She hears a rattling in the distance. Maybe something has come unbuckled in her brain and she might die here. She can picture the TMZ headline: *"International pop star Adriana Argento: Dead at 26, Found Screws Loose."*

But the sound, it keeps getting louder, eventually attaches to a furry mound. Esmé is on top of her, panting and licking. "It's okay," she says, sitting up. "Mommy is okay."

She carries Esmé inside, the two of them trailing water down the hall, because they can, because someone will clean it later. In a gilt-framed mirror, Adriana examines her waterlogged face. Traces of eyeliner hug the top curves of her lids like the dashes on a dotted line, making her look drowsy and bored. Whatever formula her makeup artist uses, it takes days to wash off, settles into the creases under her eyes, reminding her that one day she'll wrinkle, one day she'll either be a has-been or a legend.

Esmé yips at her feet, toenails cracking on the tile. "Come, come."

Adriana rubs two fingers together and leads Esmé upstairs into the wide, sun-warmed kitchen. Esmé barks and jumps up and down as Adriana opens a can of wet food. As Esmé chortles and snorts, Adriana crouches next to her puppy, rubs the spot just under her diamond collar.

"My baby," she whispers. "It's you and me, baby, don't you ever forget it."

Nolan said something similar once, that night two years ago when he showed up unannounced, glassy-eyed and fresh from rehab. His first night at home and he reached for a drink, the last bottle of whiskey on the bar cart, staring flagrantly out like an amber dare. Instead, he picked up his car keys and wound his way from the squat bungalow in Studio City to her mansion in Beverly Hills, racing over the curves of Cold-water Canyon Drive, the path of Mulholland, snaking above the sequined city, until he washed up, breathless, at her door. This was the beginning, when they rushed at each other with chafed, naked emotion, before they were even really together. They stood just inside Adriana's front door for several minutes, hugging. Into the humid crook of her neck he muttered, "It's you and me from now on. It's just you and me."

The memory leads Adriana to her bedroom, full of overlapping cream and gray fabrics in different textures. *I want to feel like I'm on a cloud*, she told the decorator. She crawls into bed, her body a tumor under the sheets, or the lumpy impressions bones make in the skin. She feels like a virus, something sick and squirming. The bed's too big for one person, endless. She wishes she'd carried Esmé's food up here.

In her ivory tower, alone, she hears hardly any sound. She could be anywhere in the world. Anywhere, but she's here.

As the weather heats up, I forgo the bathroom for walks outside during lunchtime, each time leaving the office with the conviction that I will develop a fresh personality in the next twenty to thirty minutes. A new woman, coming of age in the heel-ground dust of the city. This new me will be confident and bold. She won't be afraid to shout her wildest ideas, so assured she will be that they are good enough and worth hearing. She won't flush and droop her eyes to her lap anytime Tom turns his head in her direction or Lexi sends a narrow glance her way.

The area around my office is dingy, populated by drab buildings and chain restaurants that seem to exist only to feed the cavernous maw of the nine-to-five crowd. We're about ten blocks south of Penn Station, on the border between Midtown West and Chelsea, one of the least exciting areas of the city. By the low West Thirties, the Times Square color drains away, the crowds thin out, the tourists disappear, and the remaining pedestrians turn serious and focused, dodging and weaving with eyes straight ahead, take-out lunches banging at their hips.

The one bright spot is the Fashion Institute of Technology, and that's where I walk. The campus is nothing more than a pair of beige buildings linked by a closed-off street barrier and a few outdoor patios where students gather when the weather is nice. I spend most of my break pacing either side of the street, relishing not having to look both ways, veering left or right onto Seventh or Eighth Avenue when the mood strikes. The FIT buildings are smooth and bland, with unforgiving windows that don't reveal the bursts of color I imagine can be found within. Yet the students, with their flamboyant outfits and thousand-yard stares, are inspiring. Today I've passed a girl with a chin-grazing green bob in a black tutu and lace-up boots; a boy with a rainbow Mohawk studding his scalp and a peacoat with emerald elbow patches; and someone androgynous in a full-skirted lavender trench, a piece of red gauze coiled around their neck. I picture them all working with needle and thread before a mannequin form, bending to swipe wisps of fabric from the concrete floor, twining them around the pale flute of its throat.

These students, with their colorful clothing, thrill me. I wonder how they got this way. Who told them they didn't have to be worried all the time? Sun bakes my bones, washing me clean from inside, a baptism. Music pounds against my eardrums, a drum tide and an angel chorus. I don't go anywhere without Adriana anymore, the wires tangled in my pocket and my finger hovering over the music player's logo on my phone. She's also the reason I don't hear Meghan calling my name until I'm just about to cross at the corner of Twenty-Seventh Street.

There's a tap on my shoulder; I whirl to the left, pulling the Y-shaped cord so the headphones drop from my ears, abruptly cutting the flow of the music. One fist is clenched at my side, as if I'm about to swing a punch. Meghan stands there, mouth agape, one hand raised in front of her face. I open my fist.

I've been avoiding her since the dinner at Veronica's. "Oh, hi. Sorry."

"I've been calling your name for the past block."

I gesture with the limp headphones. "Music. Were you following me?"

She shifts her weight from one foot to the other. "You haven't been answering my messages."

I check my phone, a nervous tick. Meghan leans over so she can see the screen and I instinctively rear back, pulling it toward my chest.

"I've been busy," I say. I have never, in the months we've known each other, been too busy for Meghan. She emits a nearly imperceptible twitch. If I didn't know better, I might have missed it. "And the other night…"

"Get a drink with me after work? Nothing has changed, you'll see."

Laughter sprinkles through the FIT quad, if you can call it that. We're standing in an overly exposed patch and the sun sears the virgin skin on the back of my neck. I should be wary of Meghan, of all of them, but I can't bring myself to turn her away without hearing her out. She is my best friend, perhaps the best friend I've ever had. She understands Adriana's appeal without me having to explain. All she has to say is: *That voice, you know?* And I do know. I know exactly. We are, all of us, inextricably linked.

"I know a place. Meet me in the neon lobby at six?"

Blinkers is full when we arrive, but the JonBenét bench remains empty, the overtanned women in pinched heels and ruddy-faced men giving the murdered pageant queen a wide berth. I wonder if the other patrons are avoiding her on purpose, choosing instead to roost near the lesser evils of Pee-wee Herman and Britney Spears's shaved head. Even O.J. Simpson and Princess Diana seem less depressing by degrees than a six-year-old dyed peroxide blonde in full stage makeup. She should be old enough to be one of these women in blistering shoes clutching a gin and tonic, but she's frozen in 1996. Death and white-hot, blue-eyed youth are the strangest, most disturbing bedfellows. People don't like to see them butted up against each other, so much decay and so much beauty.

So, what's wrong with me that I steer Meghan right to her, push her down onto the pleather seat so that her face almost grazes the photograph? JonBenét gives me a wave, tiny fingers splaying. I'm happy to see her; it's been too long.

I get us some of those treacly margaritas Carly and Emily like, with salted rims and tart jalapeños trapped between the ice. Meghan tries to smile but stops when she sees that my face hasn't changed.

"Listen, about the other night," she says. "Veronica…she just cares about Adriana so much, you know? We all do."

"I don't even know what I saw."

"A bunch of fans getting caught up in the moment. That's all it was."

I pause to take a fortifying gulp, steeling myself with gumbiting tequila and simple syrup. "Tell me the truth about something. I'll know if you're lying: What happened to Sophie Heffernan?"

Meghan's eyes go everywhere. She is so small and frail and lost. It reminds me of the very first day I saw her standing in the office kitchen, a briefcase dwarfing her torso. The truth is there, wrestling with her expression. I brace myself for whatever I'm about to learn, though, somehow, I already know.

"It started as a joke. At one meeting early on, we were at

Veronica's just talking about how Adriana really needed to ascend to the next level of artistry, otherwise she'd run the risk of fading into obscurity. Become another flash in the pan.

"She just needed that *push*, or her music was going to get stale. Someone, I think it might've been Pearl, made a quip about how maybe Adriana should experience a personal tragedy, you know, to encourage maturity in her songwriting? Veronica really latched onto that, wouldn't let it go. She got all serious and started saying all this stuff, like we could be the ones to make it happen and we owed it to Adriana, only whatever we did couldn't be *too* personal, or we'd run the risk of scaring her too much. We couldn't go after her mom, or Nolan. She'd be too broken up, maybe she'd stop making music altogether.

"Sophie was the owner of a minor fan account and Veronica knew her a little, from the internet. She'd interacted with Adriana a few times, posted screenshots of their DMs, which is a major taboo. If you're lucky enough to have direct correspondence with Adriana, you keep it to yourself. That's what put Veronica over the edge, that she'd shared their private messages. We flew to Los Angeles on a whim, got last-minute tickets to the show."

A dreamy expression crosses Meghan's face. Her drink sits, untouched, condensation puddling at the bottom of the glass. I get the sense that she's telling me all of this to absolve herself of a crucial sin. If she can relieve herself of the burden of secrecy, she'll be free. "I don't think I believed we'd go through with it, not until it was actually happening, and we had this girl with a bag over her head. We could've let her go—I wanted to let her go. I said it. I *thought about it*, at least. I think I did say it. But then Veronica stabbed her."

A flash, Veronica holding the knife over her own dinner table, the demonic slant of her body as she stoops forward.

Meghan is still talking, faster and faster, the story rushing forth. "The knife made this horrible suckling noise when it was in her. It made me think of my mom, of *nursing*, which is crazy, right? It's crazy, I can't possibly remember that. But I went deep into myself and couldn't stop thinking about breastfeeding. Sophie was crying so hard I couldn't listen to her anymore. The fabric over her face was moving in and out of her mouth. I got so much blood on my hands and I don't even remember how. I must've reached for her, but it was too late. One second she was just standing there, whimpering, and the next she was on the ground. She looked like a puppet."

She swears she doesn't remember the rest. "Veronica took care of everything. We owe her; she saved us."

Creeping dread slimes from my elbows to my hairline. What's she's saying, it's sick. It also doesn't make any sense. How could they kill a teenager, barely a teenager, in a crowded part of Los Angeles and get away with it? They're just *girls*. But they aren't girls, not really. They're women. Sophie was a girl. And anyway, girls can be monsters when we choose to be.

I wait until Meghan is finished. I'm calm as I stand, feel my way to the bathroom, twist the lock, and kneel in my tights on the damp floor. I open my mouth and let out a stream of stinging, pale green vomit. I flush and wash my hands.

At the table, Meghan slides her water to me. I rinse my bitter mouth, then swallow a little to slow the dizzy spin, the drumbeat in my nasal cavity. Blinkers tips and rights itself. Someone has upended the hourglass of my life. When it settles, I'm surprised to find Meghan sitting there as if nothing has changed. Same dirty blonde bangs. Same wide, perpetually smiling mouth. Not a murderer at all.

"Do you understand?" she says quietly, elbows on the table, crawling closer. "I never meant to hurt anyone. I didn't think it was real."

"But you went."

She nods. "I went."

"Don't you worry about getting caught?"

"Veronica took care of it. She knows people. In a few months, they'll arrest some man with a criminal record, someone who deserves it, a rapist, maybe, and then everything will go back to normal. We can forget it ever happened."

That man, he won't forget. Nothing will ever be normal again for Sophie. "But don't you think it's...suspicious? That you flew there to see her when you live in New York? She played MSG like a week later."

"What's suspicious? A few fans, going to see a show? We're not even much older than...than she was. Not really."

I don't answer. Ten years. It sounds much older to me.

Snippets of other conversations rise like oil bubbles over the crowd. *Did you hear what Denise... How fucking dare... And I told him, I said... Do vitamins have calories?* If I concentrate too hard on where they come from, the phrases fade into the static. I get a perverse thrill, thinking someone could've overheard pieces of what Meghan just told me and not understood a thing.

It's a long time before either of us speaks again. We finish our drinks and then Meghan says, "Ashley," and I can't have heard her right.

"What?"

"Ashley. I got rid of her for you."

"You..."

"I tipped HR off. About the stealing."

"But it wasn't...she didn't."

Meghan lifts a finger to her lips. She smiles. And I get it. She told them it was Ashley stealing the makeup. She did it for me.

Out of the corner of my eye I think I see Mariah in the crowd, talking to a skinny guy with a rash of pimply stubble on his jaw. I blink and see that it's not her, in fact it looks nothing like her, really. Of all the people on our team, Mariah is the one who most genuinely wanted to be my friend. When I met the Ivies, I understood I was leaving her behind for something better. Those heady nights in different apartments, furniture warmed by the presence of others, a constant supply of delicious wine, both cheap and upscale. Only the music I love on the radio, our own private language, all tied back to Adriana. And I like Mariah, I really do. She would take me back. I could text her right now, ask her to meet me at Blinkers if she's still in the area. But there's the effort I would have to make, and all that I would be losing.

I slide out of the booth. "I need some time," I say, and Meghan tells me to come when I'm ready. But then she adds, "I need you. You can't leave me alone with them."

It's hard to think of her as a murderer, this person who has coaxed everything out of me, all of my close-held secrets that, once shared, no longer seemed quite so haunting. Now, I see why. My inner resentments could never stand up to everything Meghan has been holding.

Walking to the nearest subway, I hardly care which one, anything to take me farther from the changeling I thought was my best friend, I check my phone, feeling powerful with the possibility of technology. I could tell someone. Call the cops. There's a Piger message waiting and right before I click, I allow myself the hope that it's from Meghan. Saying she was just kidding and to forget all that. Maybe it's some initiation ritual. A hazing, a test of loyalty.

Hey girl!! Can you add an update to the beauty influencer story tonight? The writer got a comment from a representative. Thanks!! Xx

I take my time composing a response, choosing each keystroke with care.

No problem, Charlotte. It's my pleasure.

Veronica is in front of my apartment when I get home. She makes the hallway appear flatter, drained, her vibrant dress drawing all the color toward her. In her hands, a bouquet of roses, sheathed in paper patterned with bloated cartoon flowers outlined in black. Her breast gently heaves, as if she's the heroine in a Jane Austen novel. I act like she's not there, wrestle with my keys in the sticky lock, the rusted brass mocking me as it protests. Veronica puts her warm hand on top of mine as I reach for the doorknob. I pull away, a little too roughly.

"How about we take a walk?" she says, and it's less a suggestion than an order. Besides, I don't want her in my apartment.

We go into the park. It's almost eight, but the lingering daylight makes it feel more like midafternoon. "I never get used to these changes in the weather," Veronica says, almost to herself. Settling on a bench by the handball courts, she presents the flowers. "For you."

I lay the bouquet on the bench between us as a buffer, an ineffectual moat, and lace my fingers in my lap expectantly. There is power in not being the first to speak, and I plan to retain at least that much of the upper hand. She has to cave; she has more to lose.

"Meghan told me about your conversation. What she told you. Sophie."

I nod once, to show I'm listening.

"You have to understand, I only acted with Adriana's best interest at heart. It was the same thing the other night, at my dinner. Nolan isn't good for her; you have to know that. Yes, we may have gotten a bit carried away—"

"You stabbed your own dining room table." As if that was even in the same realm as actually killing someone.

Veronica presses her lips together, a teacher losing patience with a difficult kid. She grips my knee, tight but tender. I want to fight her off, but she is so innocent in her precious sundress, the brown leather sandals twined halfway up her calves, following the pattern of her ivy tattoo. A mother and her young son toddle down the path a few feet away. He kicks a soccer ball, runs to catch up, and kicks it again, while his mom administers encouraging cheers, making sure he doesn't run too far ahead. If Veronica attacks me, I'll scream, and they can be here in seconds.

"Nolan isn't the right person for Adriana to be with," Veronica says. She shakes her head, like she pities me for my naivete.

"What about Sophie? Was she good enough?"

Veronica stiffens. Her hand retreats to cup her own bare knee, a few dry flakes on her legs the only evidence of her imperfection. I'd love to turn her inside out, show everyone what she's like underneath all that blond hair and pink skin and perfume. Then she smiles, showing her veneers. I wonder if she has lip fillers. It isn't natural for them to be so puffy and swollen. To look as if she's having a minor allergic reaction to fruit, something nonfatal. A shock to the system that makes her all the more beautiful, like those girls who are so pretty when they cry, all rosy-cheeked, dewy around the eyes, where I become blotchy and sunken, premature lines gathering at the corners of my lips.

"Sophie was *coddling*. She only would have gotten in the way," Veronica says, fingers flicking the warm evening air as if she's swatting a bothersome fly.

"Coddling?"

"She approved of *everything* Adriana did. Every single was

her *best single ever!* Every boyfriend: *the cutest couple ever!* She wasn't encouraging growth. She would've been happy if Adriana released *My Whole Heart* with minor updates every two years."

I don't point out the contradiction inherent in what she's saying; she, too, prefers Adriana's older music to the songs she's released more recently. That's not the point. These new singles are the *wrong* songs, that's the problem. It's the wrong kind of growth.

"You can't control her," I say, meaning Adriana. "She's a *person.*"

"A person, yes, but also a product. She provides us with services, and we pay for them: the real fans, the ones who collect vinyl and shell out for the best concert tickets. Wouldn't you be angry if you ordered pepperoni pizza and got a hamburger instead?"

"Art isn't pizza."

"Tell that to the guy who owns Gino's down the block."

I have nothing left to say. As far as I'm concerned, this conversation is over. But Veronica isn't done with me, not yet. She says what I've been waiting to hear since I saw her standing outside my apartment:

"I can't just let you walk away. Knowing what you know."

And how can I back out, return to the way things were? Happy hours at Blinkers, JonBenét Ramsey whispering and winking from the wall. Edith at night, the merry typist. So happy not to make a mess, to leave any stains. And even if I wanted to, it's too late. *Knowing what you know.*

Veronica continues, "If you stick with us, you'll be on the right side of history. Everything will work out. I promise. You'll be one of us, an Ivy, and we will always have each other. That's the point."

She lifts her arm, and as it hovers between us, my muscles

seize. Then she lowers it around my neck and says, "I'll give you some time to think about it."

With a squeeze of my shoulder, she vanishes. There's no trace of her in the park. The mother and son have traveled so far down the path that I'm effectively alone, though I still see them, still hear their gleeful shouts.

I pick up the roses and walk home.

Panic hits in the middle of the night. I remain calm all evening, buying frozen yogurt from the bodega on our corner, holing up in the apartment watching movies as the sun goes down. Sasha comes in late and sits next to me on the couch. I remember the night Meghan was here, the relaxed banter that unspooled between us.

"I had such a weird day," I say.

"Oh."

We sit for a few seconds, stewing in the unevenness of the moment: me, friendless and lost, Sasha, on an upward trajectory toward her dreams. Sasha stands, goes to the fridge, takes out a bottle of chilled rosé. She sets it on the counter and gets the corkscrew from the drawer. The wine makes a crisp sound as it hits the sides of the glass, like crackling ice. Sasha returns and places two glasses of rosé on the coffee table. The bases are slightly too large for the coasters, these wooden discs she brought back from a trip to El Salvador last summer.

"Thanks." We drink.

Sasha can be standoffish, but at times like these she's exactly the roommate I need. Right now, I appreciate her lack of curiosity. She won't ask questions, won't fish for information under the guise of support the way some girls, like Stephanie, would certainly do. Support as ammunition. To be deployed later, when it can do the most damage. We watch a reality show, women with glassy hair and desperately knotted lips

wedding-dress-shopping at a famous boutique on the Upper
East Side. After that, a Lifetime movie about a couple who
stalks and attempts to kill another couple for their money. We
order nachos and drink more wine; I fall asleep on the couch,
the living room on a lazy carousel spin.

I wake with a start and the room is half-dark, a square of
our cheap rug bathed in the warm glow of the muted television. Sasha snores softly behind her bedroom's closed door.
I sit up and my head swarms, the scenery dissipating like a
dozen tiny gnats. They come together to form the wall, the
window, the plants on the ledge. I swallow and my mouth is
sand. The clock on the stove reads 2:36 a.m. A knot snags at
the spot where my shoulder meets my neck. I rub at it absentmindedly as a wave of nausea hits me: tomorrow is Saturday
and I've nowhere to be, nothing to distract from the mess of
my life. A well of sadness pulls at my chest, an opening in the
space between my lower ribs. I want to tuck my hand under
the bones and touch my heart within its cage, make sure it's
still beating. In the static haze of the living room, nothing
seems real. I could still be sleeping.

Feeling my way into the bedroom, I plug my dead laptop
in to charge and flop stomach-first onto the bed. My text
notifications come through, six from Meghan and one from
Mariah that just says, We miss you at Blinkers, lmk if you wanna
grab lunch sometime! There's a message from Tom, asking if I
plan to take him up on that dinner offer. Out of habit I click
the Piger icon in the dock on the bottom of the screen, but
even the website's most eager worker bees are long asleep.

On Instagram, Adriana is counting down to the *solstice* release date—three weeks. She has on a frothy cloudy-blue dress
with ruffled tulle across the bodice and heavy Sharon Tate
bangs for a listening party she's hosting, playing the album for
some label executives. As my eyes adjust to the dark, I watch

a spider skip nervously across the scarf draped on my lamp-shade. It feels like the wrong season for spiders, but it's not. The night is cool, but it's early summertime, and there is turbulent heat propelling a warm breeze. Under the jittery skip of the spider's legs, the loopy paisley pattern blurs and shifts, curling like vicious snakes. I blink and the fabric stops moving. The photo of Edith is still there, but I haven't looked at it properly in months. The things you once loved eventually become the background noise. Her smile is maybe a little desperate. It says: *approve of me, love me, tell me my job was well-done.*

In the nightstand drawer, I find a year-old bottle of Xanax leftover from my brief stint with psychiatry. Before the first appointment, I steeled myself to convince the doctor I really was as panicked and frayed as I believed myself to be, that I really did need something to soothe my nerves. It was almost disappointing how easily she gave the prescription over, as if I'd geared up to sprint only to find myself stopping short at a dead end. I breathlessly described the tightening in my chest, delving into my lack of discernible goals and willpower, the way I felt shunted along, a passenger in the vehicle of my own life. "Sounds like anxiety," she'd said, filling out a script with a bored scrawl.

The pills rattle as I unscrew the cap and shake out an oval tablet, neon in the dim puddle of light. I swallow it raw, feeling every bitter millimeter as the pill chafes the sides of my throat. The effect is almost immediate, my body softening like an ice cube held in a closed fist, a placebo effect taking hold before the pill has time to dissolve into my bloodstream.

I lie back on the mattress, splayed over my astrology map bedspread, a holdover from the month I got into horoscopes, looking to the stars' arbitrary arrangement to give my life order and meaning. I'm limp as a corpse. A dead girl comes to me, abandoned on a concrete slab, but she cannot breach the plastic Xanax cocoon.

My eyes grow heavy, my consciousness gauzes and spins out.

Saturday. One of my wasted days, hours skulking by, lost to the dirty shuffle of unwashed sheets, the cry of my empty stomach. At 10:42 p.m. EST Adriana updates her Instagram with a grainy snapshot in her signature grayscale. She's in bed, alone. Her eyes are puffy. She's always thin, but now she's almost gaunt, her neck lanced with visible collarbones that protrude from the cratered neckline of her threadbare T-shirt, the uniform of the recently dumped. Her eyeliner hangs on, sagging at the very corners. One arm garlands Esmé's neck. Their two faces pushed together, woman and dog.

There's a click at the bottom of my throat and suddenly I'm sobbing, the muscles responsible for holding back tears surrendering, my mouth and nose and eyes turning to sediment over which my tears shudder and flow.

Through the crystalline blur of tears, I type Sophie's name into Google. I'm wanting to sharpen the pain, make it more acute. The most recent article is from three months ago, a short update. Police interviewed some witnesses who claim they saw a white man, approximately twenty-five to thirty years old, dressed in black, slinking away from the scene a few minutes before the body was discovered. The picture they use in the news, Sophie in her cheerleading uniform, the amputated arm of a teammate jabbing into the frame. Knife pleats circling her smooth, veinless thighs. A stiff vest top exposing a creamy stretch of midriff. A splotch of green cresting the top hem of her skirt, a crumbling temporary tattoo. Inky blue liner making her eyes small and squinty. She is both timelessly young and wise beyond her years, with a knowing slant to her chin and a watchfulness in her gaze.

I wonder about the girl who's cropped out of the photo. The girl who has seen her arm, the cut of her hip, on the evening news and the home pages of the *Los Angeles Times* and *People*. A mascot of morbidity, holding an invisible scythe. Were they even really friends? Did they hate each other? Take each other apart in that ferocious way teenage girls have, how they dismantle each other piece by piece?

Or, maybe. The most likely, and the saddest, possibility: they didn't know each other well at all. They were just passing acquaintances, the bottom and middle of the pyramid. The base and the flyer. The one who died and the one who lived.

Sophie loved cheerleading. She loved her turtle, Samson, and her cat, Petals. She loved Jane Austen, hanging out at the food court in the mall with friends. And, of course, she loved Adriana Argento. Every word of every song committed to memory. Had she survived to adulthood, she would surely slip into them later like an old comfy sweater, mumbling a tune as she washed the dishes or vacuumed her bedroom.

The concert was meant to be *the best night of her life*. She spent weeks planning her outfit, perfecting her makeup, practicing the installation of ponytail extensions. She was *just the nicest girl*, never said a bad word about anyone, never whispered behind another girl's back, they all said. I snort at that line; all teenage girls hide a touch of duplicity beneath their innocence, scabs and warts that come out when the moon is full, and the light is just right, and someone is passing around a S'well bottle of vodka stolen from their mother. *I love her, but you know she's a bitch, right? She's a great friend, but she's a fucking whore.*

I skim the details of the murder, my mind slotting the Ivies into certain roles. Veronica with the knife. Pearl approaching Sophie in the bathroom, complimenting her extensions, touching them. Jessie, yanking the black tote over Sophie's head. Crystal, tugging her by the forearm. Meghan, shoving at her from behind. All of them feeding off the malignant energy, the rot growing between them a uniting cancer.

My tears dry up, turning my face cold. Meghan texts me once, twice, five times. Near midnight, my phone rings. I let the messages and voice mails pile up like fish scales, slick and gleaming in the dark of my room. Finally, at two a.m., my body a dried-out husk, I fall, once again, into a deep, desperate sleep.

13

I'm underdressed. I should have checked the website for this place. I didn't even look to see what the restaurant was called when I pasted the address into Maps and pulled up the directions. It's Sunday. My hair is still damp from the shower, and the one thing I've done right is my face. The makeup from work, I'm wearing all of it. Piled on like a clown or a model. Tobacco Road, Lychee red lipstick, champagne on my cheeks, everything named for a food or a vice. Also, Cumulus by Adriana Argento.

Tom is already seated at the table. He looks good. A blue shirt, sleeves rolled up and the first few buttons undone to show off the spoon-press of his upper chest. The poison oak tattoo sets my heart racing, or maybe it's nerves.

He greets me with a kiss on the cheek, an air of absurdist adultism, and we sit. There's already a glass of rosé by my plate. The rest of the bottle chills in a silver ice bucket.

"Hope you don't mind, I got us some wine."

"I never complain about wine," I say like I'm pantomiming the heroine in a '90s rom-com. I've never been on a real date before. Not like this, anyway: a reservation at a restaurant, a set meeting time, a solid plan that's more than just *maybe I'll see you around sometime*. It feels ridiculous. We are actors on-stage and the restaurant is the set. Glass tinkles against my rings—stacks and stacks of them, so many rings I needed a photo from a jewelry store in Brooklyn's IG feed to figure out how to wear them, Anatomy of a Ring Stack—as I take a sip. Wondering if I made myself sound like an alcoholic just then, and then wondering if maybe I am one.

"I have to say, I was pretty surprised you agreed to come out with me."

"And I was pretty surprised you asked me out."

"Because of the running away?"

"Something like that."

Tom chuckles. His chuckle annoys me and then I think, *This is why nobody loves you.* "It's hardly the worst reaction I've gotten from telling a girl I'm a widower."

"You've had worse?"

"One time, a girl I went on a date with didn't believe me. She kept laughing and saying *you're so funny.* Hitting my arm, like, really hard. I had bruises the next day. Nothing I said convinced her. Even when I pulled up a wedding photo she said, *That's photoshopped.* But when I wouldn't drop it, she got angry. Dumped scalding coffee in my lap."

"No!"

"I have the scars to prove it."

I can't tell if he's joking, but I decide to believe him, if only to gain distance from the girl who didn't. The mood between us is surprisingly easy. Where, I wonder, did he learn to for-give like this. There's no trace of a grudge about him. When he invited me on this date, made the reservation, texted me the address, I partly believed this was a trap. I'd show up and find an abandoned warehouse instead of a restaurant. Carly and

Emily hiding among the rafters with buckets of pig's blood. Maybe he'd pull a simpler trick: he just wouldn't show. Me sitting alone at the table, poking my napkin, the server circling every few minutes like a hawk, dying to pick at my eyeballs, asking if I'm *sure they can't get me a drink* and *when did I say the rest of my party would arrive?*

But here he is, expansive and welcoming, gesturing with open palms as he tells a story. And then another story. And a third. The appetizer comes, oysters on the half shell, but I hate oysters and he's still talking about himself. Like, does he ever shut up? I pick up an oyster, add a heap of horseradish, bring the wide edge of the shell to my lips, tip my head back. Spicy sea liquid dribbles into my mouth. I suck and suck and the oyster pulls closer and recedes, stuck on the shell's nub.

I cough. Tom is still talking, going on and on and on forever about hazing at his state school frat. "They starved us for a week and made us drink their vomit."

The oyster comes loose and slides down my throat, gooey and viscous and salty as boiled ear cartilage. Horseradish burning my nostrils, making my eyes water. I cough again and the oyster threatens to pop back up, so I swallow hard and gulp the rest of my wine and somehow Tom is still talking.

"Are you okay? You look a little green."

"Excuse me," I mumble, and rise from the table. The oyster and the wine and the horseradish perform an uneasy tango in my digestive system as I locate the bathroom. It's single-occupant with opulently patterned black-and-white wallpaper and about a hundred tea lights dancing on every flat surface. So many tea lights it's like the room is on fire, but somehow also so dim I can't clearly see myself in the black-framed mirror.

My stomach settles. I soak a paper towel in cold water, dab it behind my ears and on my inner wrists. In the bathroom quiet I hear Adriana's whisper-singing and it's coming from my head and then it's coming from the speakers, it's really playing. The same song from Blinkers, the first of the *solstice* era. I inhale. I exhale. Cleansed, I leave the bathroom. There's a line. Three waifs slumped against the wall like a time-lapsed Kate Moss after a coke binge. They seem, strangely, wet. Beached mermaids with limp hair and scaly dresses. Their eyes narrow at me.

"Sorry," I say, "sorry." I keep apologizing all the way to the table.

I pause. A tumble of blond hair has taken my place across from Tom. The blond hair like a ray of sunshine, like a field of daffodils swaying under a warm breeze, runs a finger around and around the rim of my wineglass. The glass sings or cries. I hear it from my spot rooted to the ground, next to an older couple eating in silence, communicating with the *clink-clink-scrape* of silverware. Tom says something and the blond hair tilts its face down and then I see her.

Veronica. She's laughing at whatever Tom said, only not really, really, she's ironing her lips flat against her teeth and pressing three fingertips to the plush pink bloom of them. Really, she's covering her mouth. He thinks she's doing this because he's funny, oh so funny, but I see, as her eyes flick up to meet mine, that she's doing it because she's trying not to kill him with my fork. Then she smiles and does a wiggly-fingers JonBenét wave and I move closer.

"Veronica?" There's a bloody slab of lasagna I don't remember ordering in front of her, and a well-done steak with a bite cut out in front of Tom. The oysters are gone but my little appetizer plate remains with the single shell overturned like a dead potato chip.

"Hi, darling," she purrs. "I was keeping Tom here company while you were in the bathroom. Who knew there was *so* much vomit at state school!"

Tom laughs and hacks off a bite of steak. He didn't even fucking wait for me to sit down before he started eating. Veronica slides her shapely pencil-skirt-sheathed ass off my chair and stands up.

"What are you doing here?" I ask.

"I'm on a date." She lowers her voice. "Finance bro."

I look around but I cannot for the life of me see a single man sitting at a two-person table.

"Anyway," she says. "I wanted to say hi. Have a nice dinner."

She's walking away and I'm tracking her path, but then the server appears and blocks my sight line. "How are we doing over here? Is there anything wrong with the lasagna?"

"Oh, uh. No, thank you."

I sit. Lift my fork. Take a bite. The noodles are a bit tough but there's so much cheese smothering my plate that I hardly taste anything else. I smile weakly at the server until, satisfied, he leaves. Veronica has vanished. The dining room stretches on and on into the distance.

Tom says, "Where was I? Oh, right. The forest fire my junior year..."

My phone buzzes once, then twice. I pull it out of my bag.

A text from Veronica: Only serial killers eat well-done steak.

The next few days slink by, stretchy as taffy. I go through the motions. Coffee. Averted eyes. Coffee. Adriana Argento on repeat. Coffee. Keystroke after keystroke, a mountain of words like an M.C. Escher staircase leading nowhere. Coffee.

I ignore Meghan's messages, each more desperate than the last. Veronica texts only once, a single clock emoji. *Ticktock.*

The web producer group chat is still silent. I assume they've created a new one and left my number off, moved on without me. Maybe Tom is included this time, now that he's officially single and I refuse to respond to his texts and DMs asking if I had a nice time, did I like the food, would I like to get dinner again or maybe just lunch or even coffee? Stephanie tries to make plans and I don't answer, relishing the exquisite sting of my misery. Meghan sends a few more exploratory messages, feeling me out. I can hear the pitch of Veronica over her shoulder, dictating. I search for answers, but they slip out of my grasp, rubbery and metallic, shooting stars skating to the far corners of my vision.

I save a photo of Sophie to my phone and set it as the lock screen background, a sort of experiment. How much can I take? How much do I owe her? What will be my penance for fraternizing with her killers? If I return to the Ivies, am I better? Would it be any different from standing there in the flesh, holding the knife?

I don't know how long I sleep. It could be hours or days. Daylight creeps beneath my eyelids, waking me sporadically. At one point I think: *The longer I sleep, the less food I will need.* And then I slip under again. I wake for real and I'm sideways on the bed, head hanging off, blood pooling in my ears. Not a bad feeling. It sounds like the ocean is inside me. The ocean, and I'm the shell.

I sit up slowly, make a few loose circles with my sore neck.

My cell phone is on the floor next to me; I'm reluctant to check but I do. There are countless messages from my mom, who I texted just before the Xanax kicked in and then ignored for days afterward, and from Meghan. I'm coming over later, you can't stop me, the last one says.

The clock says 12:25 p.m. It's Saturday, again.

It's amazing how quickly life loses all of its meaning once

you step outside of yourself, floating above the parameters of commutes and meetings, friendships, office hours and salad bar lunches. You forget who you are and slip through a crack in reality, a liminal space. You're walking in a parallel dimension, watching the people in the real world go about their days from behind a cataracted scrim, but they can't see or hear you. Sometimes when they look, they blink for a few seconds, as if detecting movement. But they turn without acknowledgement, their attention falling away like tissue paper around a Christmas gift. In this way, I have finally achieved the impossible— a trait in common with Adriana Argento. We are both a half step behind the normal population, out of time, hanging back like specters, watching everyone else move on without us.

This is what I do:

I take the longest shower of my life, standing under the water until my hands prune. I lather every inch of scalp with frothy hydrangea shampoo, scrubbing with blunt fingertips until the nerve endings are shot. I drip-dry onto the ancient fake bamboo bathmat lined with mold while combing the knots from my tangled hair. I use copious amounts of Sasha's Kiehl's Creme de Corps to moisturize my limbs. I carry the stolen beauty products, which have become my most prized possessions, into the bathroom. Lipstick and perfume and blush and highlighter. I pile it all on, layer upon layer, until I sparkle.

Then I take my time getting dressed, meditating on the contents of my closet, touching each item with reverence. Pieces I've worn to work, happy hours, grocery runs and job interviews. All the cluttered moments in between. I pull on a rumpled floral dress that I stole from my mom and drape my décolletage with gold chains, cap my fingers with threadbare rings. I give a satisfactory wink at my reflection, returning to myself. Then I brew coffee in Sasha's French press, watching as the liquid turns from beige to chestnut.

I think, *I should buy my own fucking appliances and moisturizer.*

Maybe I'll leave New York, go somewhere warm all year, eliminate my seasonal depression. Everyone in New York acts like it's the only place, but there are so many other places, and things one could do in those places. I could open an independent bookstore, for instance. Finally finish *The Goldfinch.* Tape Edith up behind the desk, a reminder that happiness can be small, not explosive.

In my room, I crawl through the window next to my bed and sit on the fire escape. Nursing my coffee, I take a deep breath. A rancid spoiled milk smell unfurls, baking in the heat. Brooklyn is far from the ideal place to have a bad day, especially in July when the sun warms the sidewalk and unleashes a ghostly fog, the smell of trash and days-old sweat. Streets stained with crusted vomit and dog shit. Pigeons hooting like owls next to the window. When I've had enough, I tumble onto my bed, closing and locking the window, and crank the AC to sixty-one degrees. I allow myself to feel guilty about climate change, and then to liberate myself of that guilt. It's a natural response to the way humans have adapted, learning to seal ourselves off from suffering. Destroying the planet so as not to face the harsh truths of weather and distance and the real cost of a sweater.

The air conditioning provides white noise, numbing me to thought and emotion, a kind of spiritual North Pole. Coming back down, I find that Adriana has been relatively quiet on Instagram. While I slept, she posted a stream of promo shots and song snippets for *solstice*, all with the preorder link attached. I'm surprised to find myself bored by her. I hold my boredom at a distance and examine it with slight interest. Then I put the phone in a drawer and watch the ceiling. The hours follow an unpredictable, scattershot dragging and lurching pattern I associate with unoccupied weekend afternoons. Twenty minutes trickle by, marked by shifting purple shadows, and the next hour vanishes into a black hole, the same one where the years go.

I switch the air conditioner off as the day winds its way toward dusk, challenging myself to explore discomfort. Here I am, sweating on purpose when the AC is right there. Here I am, learning to sacrifice. I lie on the floor because it's cooler, the shadowed flooring next to my bed centuries older than the rest of the apartment, bogged with pleasant mustiness. Awake yet trapped in a fever dream, sweat crawling down the side of my neck. A bell chimes. I tug myself up using the drawer pull on my nightstand. Pulling the drawer out, I find my phone hissing and answer the call.

Meghan is outside. "Hey, come down. I'm here."

Downstairs, I open the door for Meghan. She troops through the cracked brown lobby like she belongs there, a black-and-gold plastic bag from the liquor store dangling from one wrist, the heads of two wine bottles swanning up to touch her forearm.

"A peace offering," she says, and shoves the bag at me as she pushes past, trusting I'll grab hold as she lets go. She swerves left, and jogs up the chipped staircase toward the third floor.

I follow with small, hesitant steps, bottles clinking, a guest in my own home.

"Wow, it smells like desperation in here. And coffee. Did you make coffee?"

Meghan stands in the center of my living room, in the narrow wedge between the reclaimed wood coffee table and the shabby-chic couch, as if she never left. She bends to pluck a *Bon Appétit* from off a stack of magazines and flips through the pages. Sasha collects the back issues for the photography; she doesn't cook anything more elaborate than pasta salad. This one has a beautiful, high-definition shot of no-heat puttanesca sauce on the cover. Cherry tomatoes and flecks of basil in the grooves between curled noodles. My stomach grumbles; I haven't eaten all day.

"You look like you need a sandwich. Have you eaten?" Meghan says, reading my mind.

"Meghan. What are you doing here?"

"I missed you," she tells the puttanesca in a suddenly meek little voice. Her confidence has vanished.

"Maybe you should've thought of that before you *killed someone.*"

"Not to split hairs, but *I* didn't kill her. At least, I don't *think* I did."

"Semantics." I blow a raspberry, ruffling the air with my lips. "But I missed you too." I'm so tired of hiding.

She smiles and pulls out her phone, starts rattling off a laundry list of cuisines, and just like that we're done with the homicide stuff. "Thai, Mexican, poke, sushi...is Rose's Pizza any good? Never mind, the reviews are weird... Oh! What about Joe's Burgers?"

"I've never been there. But I'm not really hungry, so just get whatever you want." My stomach does backflips in protest, an entire floor routine, but I ignore it. I'm not quite ready to sit across from my wild, complicated, accessory-to-murder best friend and act like everything is fine.

She pouts at me over the brim of her iPhone, but her fingers keep moving. Five seconds later she's placed an order for a "Hawaiian Burger," medium-rare, and fries. "You can have a bite," she says. "Let's open the wine!"

Side by side on the couch, we clutch golden orbs of chardonnay. I don't want Meghan here. I'm not done deciding how much I can forgive. But she is here, and I can't ask her to leave. The way she smiles so wide, her lips threatening to split at the corners. I remember her pleading at Blinkers, asking me not to leave her. Is that why she brought me into this? Because she needed an ally? It's possible she's scared of them, too. As angry as I am, I'm also touched.

Friendship is the unfortunate link connecting us against my will. I hate that she's made me an accomplice, that she's tainted the only thing I truly love with her brutal confession. But Veronica has made it go away. We have nothing to fear as long as I don't go anywhere. There's nothing to do but return to our uniting force. Meghan says, "Have you ever seen the *Hazardous Diaries*?"

"You mean, like Adriana's album?"

"Omigod you *haven't*! It's a video diary from the tour. Does your TV hook up to the internet?"

It does. I navigate to the YouTube app. Adriana's official channel has become more streamlined over time, the scrappy behind-the-scenes videos filmed on a camera phone giving way to polished Vevo-certified music videos and professionally shot footage from live performances.

Meghan takes the remote while I refill the wine.

She scrolls until she finds a trio of videos with pink thumbnails showing Adriana in black and white, wearing the outfit from the *Hazardous* album cover, head cocked to the right like the barrel of a gun.

Adriana lounges on a long couch in a drab backstage, wearing an outfit I recognize from poor quality fan-made videos on Instagram. It's a stretchy, long-sleeved black dress fitted on top and flowing out at the waist like a skating costume, the neckline crowned by rhinestones. A tiny princess lording over her court. From her reclined position, she opens her mouth and unleashes a riff from deep inside the swell of her throat. Maybe she sold her soul to the devil for that voice, stole a rose-breasted grosbeak's song, plucked it like a weed right from its throat. She's flawless, a beautiful dream. I don't know how I could love anyone more, anyone real, when a creature this impeccable exists. I want to swallow her down like a pill, take her inside my skin and fold her into me. It would feel similar to the Xanax I've been taking to sleep, a calming, just-slipped-under-a-bubble-bath feeling.

But I don't want to know Adriana, not for real, and the video diary is already too much. Adriana's faux-tanned skin and corny jokes are unsettling and bizarre. I glance at Meghan. She's staring at the TV, locked in a hypnotic trance, wide mouth pulled taut into a smile.

In the bowels below the stage, Adriana turns, giggling, always giggling, and says, "I posted a video of my warm-up on Instagram a second ago and my fans were like, 'Bitch, get on that stage.' So here I am, getting my ass onstage."

The video cuts to the audience view of the stage. House lights go down. Cheers fill the room like running water. Adriana kneels below the stage on a mobile platform and gives her videographer a little wave as she ascends. The dancers are already there, backlit by cold spotlights that dissect their bodies. Cut them to bits. Adriana arrives next, riding the platform. In the center of the writhing circle of dancers, twinkling synths and bells, a disco-inspired riot, she performs her most uplifting song. Then she walks off for a costume change, exiting through a tunnel of colored smoke, leaving an echoing void, a vacancy where she used to be.

This is what it means to be famous. To give complete strangers the same intensity of feeling they'd have for a lover or a parent, set it to music and a light show.

To make them sing.

Nolan floats in the background of several shots. He kisses the side of her forehead before she goes onstage, dances in the wings with Adriana's mom and brother, and massages her heel-battered feet after a particularly taxing show.

Adriana sits in her makeup chair while an artist swipes
powder on her cheeks. "I used to get headaches before I went
onstage. Now I just have these visions of flicking my head
to the side during the opening choreography and all my hair
falling off. Like, all of it. Not just the extensions. Bald as the
day I was born."

This is where she looks the most human, in a black bralette
and high-waisted yoga pants, slumped over, shoulders caving
inward and the middle of her spine pitched back, giving her
a childlike posture. She runs through a few notes, casually
belting like it's nothing.

Meghan and I don't speak as the video ends, YouTube
threatening to play the next, a fan-made compilation of Adriana's biggest onstage fails. I reach over and exit the app before
it starts, not wanting to see her as fallible.

One afternoon, I take the stolen beauty products into the
bathroom. I use a knife to scrape Tobacco Road from the
pan, watching as the mica-infused powder splinters from its
tightly packed rectangle and sprays dirt across the white porcelain. The splash from the faucet whisks the particles down
the drain until only a fine shimmer is left behind. Sparkles
that will never fully wash away, not as long as we live here.

The lipsticks are harder. I melt them with the flame from
Sasha's lighter. The smoke alarm goes off, the whole house
smells like burning, smells like a hunk of hot metal, and I
end up having to wipe the thick wax from the bottom of the
sink with a paper towel. I'm embarrassed that I thought that
would work. I craved something dramatic, an action with finality and flair.

Cumulus by Adriana Argento is next. I unscrew the cloud-
shaped lid and peppery musk hits my nostrils. I'm about to
tip the nozzle, let the blue liquid flow toward the open maw

of the drain, when there's a jingle. Click, swing, slam. Sasha comes through the door and I put the bottle on the window-sill behind the toilet. The pepper tickles my nose and I sneeze.

"Hello? You home?"

She finds me coughing in the bathroom. "Why does it smell like a thousand candles were cremated in here?" She sniffs audibly, a full crinkling of the nose. "Did you mace someone?"

"I, uh, had an accident? It's fine."

Sasha looks at me with such pity that it makes me want to fix my life just so she feels better. I try to smile, to reassure, but it hurts a little, and I can see from her expression that it's painful for her too.

14

At certain times of day when the light is just right, Adriana Argento likes to stand at the windows facing west and watch the back of her house reflect her face back to herself. Her outline wavers and the faint trace of her ponytail bobs with each breath. An inch up, an inch down. Through the window, the pool ripples, holding the upside down sky. A spray of green needles and a few black specks. She imagines them to be bloated, belly-up fly bodies. Makes a note to have the filters turned on.

The ponytail bobs up and down. Today is *solstice* day.

She could smash this window. Throw a vase right through the glass, or her framed platinum *Hazardous* record, which hangs above the couch. Watch the windows fall away like crumpled silk and splash into the water. The pool she paid for with her voice and her bone structure. Sometimes she just wants to destroy something, fuck up a pristine surface.

Instead, she presses all five fingers to the window, keeping them there for several seconds, as if administering a brand. This house has her fingerprints all over the walls. The ponytail slides up and down. *solstice* plays at top volume from speakers hidden in every room and connected to Adriana's cell phone. Later, these rooms will be teeming with family and friends, people with a stake in the business of being Adriana. But for now, she sits with her work.

Her body and the music she created, alone together for the very last time.

Each album release leaves new parts of her exposed, but this time is different. This is *a personal album. Her most personal album yet.* Muscles and veins on the outside, visible in all their ugly pulsation. The ponytail. Moving up, down.

She turns away from the window, extensions fanning. Her bare feet slap the tile. Why did she choose tile for all these rooms? It seemed chic at the time, and adult. The kind of flooring a pop star, which she was just starting to realize she was becoming, might have. And in her attempt to grow into herself, this new version who would be *known*, she chose tile without stopping to consider that she actually had to live with it, day in and day out. Her feet on the cold, hard ground.

Another thing about the tile: it makes sound carry in strange ways. She's always jumping, thinking there's someone else here, when it's just the dog walking around or the wind whistling through a crack in the foundation. It got worse when she went on that bender, reading everything she could get her hands on about Charles Manson after watching that one documentary. The house where his followers murdered Sharon Tate is not far from here. Once, Adriana made Nolan drive up the private road in his Range Rover. As they got closer to the gate blocking the former 10050 Cielo Drive from street view, she couldn't stop picturing the killers driving the same route, and she started to feel like maybe she even *was* one of them, her reflection on the passenger's side warping in the curved glass so that she looked less like herself and more like a mug shot.

Then she was hyperventilating, screaming at Nolan to turn around, and though the car was freezing, tinted windows keeping the sun out, she felt so hot she wanted to crawl out of her skin. She didn't calm down until they were back on Sunset, cruising toward Bel Air, Nolan's hand on hers, thumb cresting the summit of her knuckles, the gesture that could always be relied upon to still her panic attacks.

When they were together, Adriana and Nolan slept in the same bed every night they were both in LA. She preferred his place, cluttered with pianos and keyboards and posters and video games, televisions in almost every room, including the master bath. Like a college dorm room that had been decorated by a multimillionaire. Her house, the Wedding Cake on the Hill, as he called it, so empty and impersonal by contrast.

As she moves further into the upstairs living room, she swears the walls move with her. They swell and shrink. She hears a tinkling, the chandelier overhead caught in a draft, and she freezes, wondering if she left a window open somewhere. Track Eight, the song she wrote about Nolan one drunken night after a huge blowout, the first of many that felt like *the end*, is playing. Him, slurring his words on the other end of the phone. Her, screaming on the street outside the studio in New York, Petey waiting inside, Bobby's broad wingspan blocking her from the paparazzi's view.

Back in the studio, Petey took a look at her puffy eyes, handed her a notepad and a pen. "Sit. Write it out," he said, and cleared the room. The unblemished paper taunted her, like the mocking faces of the girls who made fun of her in middle school for singing show tunes in the cafeteria. The blank surface, clean as the wax sheet you sit on at the doctor's office. Something built at the base of her skull, the dark gray feeling that meant a meltdown was on its way, anxiety spilling over and tightening her throat.

She pressed down on the paper. Her heartbeat quieted. The ball of the pen cast a long shadow. The words started to flow.

Later, when things were good with Nolan, she would beg Petey and Scotty to remove the song she'd written that day from the track list. They had recorded it in one take, left the voice tremors in, the result of having an experience and creating a response within the same moment. All the years she spent fighting with label executives, begging them to let her write more personal songs and infuse them with R & B–inspired beats. She remembers one in particular, a tall man in a white suit, saying, *You're eighteen; what are you going to write about?* That was the moment she decided to become the biggest pop star in the world, so she could, eventually, stop being such a pop star.

But fame, she's come to realize, doesn't work like that. You can't turn back from celebrity. You can only fall or keep climbing.

She kept the song on the album.

Adriana pads downstairs and into the kitchen. She takes a used glass from the counter and pours from a pitcher of iced green tea in her fridge. Her eyes trail to the clock above the stove. Four o'clock. She lays her phone on the countertop, absentmindedly navigates to Nolan's Instagram. He's in the studio, teasing a few seconds of a song from his upcoming album. They used to daydream about planning their tours together, lining up the stops so they could share the occasional hotel, see each other perform. Watching from the sidelines as he starts the slow build of promo, puts the finishing touches on songs he wrote while they were together, songs she knows are infused with *her*, hurts like a splinter slipping sideways under the skin. She can't see it, but she feels it, a ridge of pain.

She feels worse than invisible. She feels like a fan.

Esmé nuzzles Adriana's knee with her damp nose. Adriana bends to lift her. Esmé wriggles in her arms, face ducking to the side. Her snout jabs the screen of Adriana's phone, leaving a wet splotch on Nolan's smiling face. Adriana puts her phone aside and looks into Esmé's searching eyes.

"Don't let anybody tell you that being famous means you can't also be lonely. Look at me—the biggest pop star in the world, that's what Scotty says, and I got nobody here but my dog. Aw, I didn't mean it like that, baby girl. You know you're all I need in this life."

Her knee begins to twitch in her squatting position, and she slumps to the side, landing hard on her tailbone. Sometimes she wishes she didn't have a body at all. She could be a soul only. Particles of her could float like vapor, coming together, parting as they pleased, omniscient. Once, she had believed being famous would take a wet rag to the whiteboard of self-hatred she constantly marked up inside, like a teacher standing before a class of hopeful faces. It hasn't worked out quite that way.

For one thing, she's too short. Plenty of celebrities are much smaller in person than they appear on camera; during Adriana's first red carpet, she spotted an aging '90s heartthrob a few feet down the aisle and he was so petite under the shimmering curtain of lights that she didn't recognize him until her handler whispered his name.

So, sure. Height doesn't matter too much. But Adriana is the kind of small that shows. The cameras can't hide five-foot-zero so easily. She does her part, with her tall boots and her ponytail protruding from her scalp like a wrecking ball, stretching her frame. Scotty used to yell at her for the sweatshirts—*you're beautiful and we want them to know it!*—until she printed out an article about the sexual harassment allegations against Harvey Weinstein, autographed it, and left it on his desk, weighted down with a stapler. He shut up about her clothes after that; he's happy as long as she shows a little skin for performances.

She checks the time again. The minutes move so slowly when she's not working. For now, she stands, brushes off her knees.

Even though there's no reason for Nolan to call her now, three weeks since she returned his ring, she carries her phone everywhere, turned to full volume. Just in case.

When the phone does go off, it isn't Nolan. It's Tommy Escobar, her makeup artist, telling her he'll be at her house in half an hour, unless the traffic is worse than usual, which it probably will be, because it's LA. But he's at her door in twenty-nine with his kit in one hand and a heart-shaped box of chocolates in the other.

He shoves the box into her hands. "For your heart," he says.

They go into her beauty room and station themselves in the customary way—Adriana seated on the velvet stool, Tommy looming over her, brushes in hand. "Make me perfect," she tells him before he descends. For fifteen minutes he wipes and daps, he pulls back and lunges forward, and Adriana watches the diamond stud in his ear grow larger, then smaller. He steps aside to reveal her reflection in the lighted mirror.

Flourishing his arms, presenting his masterwork, he says, "Stunning, as always. I hardly need to do anything to you, doll. You're poreless."

She looks, more or less, the same. Sharper wings, maybe, and fluffier lashes. Fuller lips. But still herself, still Adriana Argento, a little Italian girl from Sacramento. It never gets less disappointing, remaining herself after all this time. You would think something more substantial would change. She coos a *thanks, baby* and hugs Tommy, keeping her chin aloft to avoid rubbing makeup on his shirt, reflecting on the small damages of womanhood. Strained necks and golf-ball-sized knots from heavy loads and avoidances, extra time spent in the bathroom, money lost to skin care and lipstick.

Adriana goes to the mirror, taps under her eyes, and forces a smile. "Hey, Tommy?" She watches him packing his kit in the mirror. He doesn't turn. "Yes?"

"Do you ever think it's weird that women wear, like, these masks all the time? That we hide our real skin?"

Tommy gives off an exaggerated pout in her direction. "Oh, honey, it's not *hiding*; it's *enhancing*."

Her fingers find the phone in her pocket, travel the path to his number, and when she looks down, Nolan's name is glowing on the screen. She should delete his contact, but she can't. What if he needs her?

"Did you hear me, love?"

She looks at Tommy. "Sorry, I was distracted. What did you say?"

"I'm taking off, unless you need anything else. I've got another client in an hour."

"Nah, I'm good. I'll walk you out."

At the door, he kisses both her cheeks. "Remember, touch up that lipstick at least once an hour. And don't rub your eyes, it gives you wrinkles!"

Rubbing her eyes, her biggest weakness. Always itchy and bloodshot, no matter how many containers of Visine she pours into them. Her mother, and now Tommy, have been telling her to quit it for ages. But there's an itch that needs scratching and she knows no other way to soothe it. Besides, there's always Botox. There's always some way to correct the damage.

Adriana spends the next hour tidying her already impeccable house, fluffing pillows and washing the dog bowls. The housekeeper was here yesterday, but Adriana usually finds something that can be improved upon. Caring for her house, even in these little ways, makes her feel normal. You never think, when you're a little girl dreaming of sold-out arenas, that you'll crave normalcy. That you'll crave Windex and a roll of paper towels. But you do. Normal is the most beautiful thing in the world.

In her apartment-sized closet, Adriana changes into a creamy silk Balenciaga slip dress, a long gold necklace, and platform heels. She won't last long in this outfit before she shrugs on a sweatshirt like a shield. But at least she'll make the effort. Scotty will approve, tell her to post some pictures. *Show the fans how glamorous you are*, he's always saying. *Make them aspire to be you.*

Most of the time, she doesn't feel glamorous. She's like a child, shuttled from one place to another, overprotected, though you cannot, truly, be protected, not from the things that really matter.

"I wish I'd never become a singer. I wish I could take your pain away," Adriana remembered telling Sophie Heffernan's mom as they sat in her sunbaked Valley living room, a scrapbook filled with pictures of her daughter spread across their laps.

Scotty would be furious if he knew she'd said that, but it was true. She wished often, in the weeks after Sophie, that her voice would dry up like so much dust in her throat. It would be better if she hadn't been born with it at all. No dead teenage girls on her conscience.

The doorbell rings.

Her mother stands on the cobblestone steps, flamboyantly fuck-you-ing the heat in head-to-toe black, her short hair almost navy in the fading light. She pulls Adriana into a bosomy Chanel hug.

"Darling! How are you feeling?"

"Good."

"Ready for the fans to hear this album?"

Adriana thumbs the straps of her dress. They move into the living room. "They're going to love it, honey. It's spectacular."

"Do you really think so? It's not too much?"

"Too much what?"

"Too much…me?"

"They love you. Let them into your life a little. That's how you heal."

Her mother places a papery, fragrant hand on top of Adriana's smooth, tapered one and squeezes. She's suddenly very serious. "This album is going to make you an icon."

Adriana's phone flashes on the glass coffee table. An Instagram notification proclaiming that Nolan Lynch has posted a new photo. Every cell in her body screams, thousands of tiny mouths saying *nonononono*. She clicks, angling the screen out of her mother's sight line, hoping to avoid a lecture.

Inside the square-framed border, Nolan sits on a coin-operated wooden horse, his socked feet slipped into Nike slides. His eyebrows cocked as if to say, *fancy meeting you here.*

And it is fancy, so fucking fancy meeting him here, inside her phone.

A shadow grays the screen. Gently, her mother pulls the phone loose from Adriana's grip. At the same time, she lowers onto the couch and wraps her daughter in a hug. Adriana surrenders to maternal comfort, the original love. Her mother rubs circles on her back and kisses her hairline.

The doorbell chimes again. Her mother goes to greet her daughter's guests. Adriana slips down a small artery connecting the living room with a guest bedroom and into the nearest bathroom. She dabs her damp lashes with a tissue, drinks cold water from cupped hands, and reapplies her lipstick. *Good girl.*

In the living room, everyone cheers when she enters. Scotty hoists a bottle of Veuve Clicquot, condensation gilding the bottle's feminine curves. Flutes are passed around and the champagne is poured. Foam runs over Adriana's glass, and she laughs as the carbonation tickles her fingers.

Scotty insists on making a toast: "We are gathered today to celebrate one of the greatest musicians of all time. An icon in the making. I'm serious! Adriana, you are the real deal. Madonna, Cher, Michael, Mariah, Stevie…you're joining their ranks with this album. You and my pal Petey over here—" he gestures toward Petey with his glass, and they share a grin, the grin of two men who know when a woman is about to make them a hell of a lot of money "—made magic in the studio. I'm so excited to share this album with the world in just a few hours. But for now—we drink!"

Glasses are thrust into the air and lowered to waiting mouths, wet with anticipation. Adriana winces as the bubbles hit her tongue. The first sip is a shock that sends chills down her spine, goose bumps blooming down her arms. But she feels more relaxed already, as the knot at the base of her skull loosens and dissolves.

"Let's play the album!" Petey shouts.

They play the album.

Adriana watches for reactions. They've all listened to various iterations, but for most this is the first time hearing the entire record all the way through. Petey, of course, knows the record inside and out; he's doubled over, elbows on knees, eyes closed and fingers pinching the bridge of his nose. Scotty taps an energetic foot, even during the slow songs, this goofy grin on his face. Her mother purses her lips in deep concentration. Adriana's childhood best friends, Claudia and Noelle, bounce, clenching hands and squealing at the most impressive high notes.

While they're distracted, Adriana sneaks onto the patio. Lights illuminate the pool from underneath, making the water otherworldly. Adriana slips off her heels, lays them sideways on the tile so the red soles are exposed, and hikes up the hem of her dress. She sits with her legs dangling off the edge.

The water is still warm from the sun that has just recently disappeared over the horizon and into the dusk. Music thumps the walls of her house. The hills take the sound waves and fracture them, bouncing them back in a distorted pattern. Her own voice, her own beats, unrecognizable and garbled.

Adriana kicks her legs, the calm surface of the water rippling like a stream of satin. Her reflection beams up at her. She thinks, again, of Nolan. His image intrudes on her happiness. She's desperate to wash him off.

Slithering to the edge, she plunges into the pool and submerges. Underwater, she opens her eyes and holds her breath for as long as she can. Lungs threatening to burst, she splashes upward, head bobbing above the water's horizon line.

"Adriana!"

Claudia and Noelle are running toward her. They stop inches from where the tile slopes into the peaceful blue. She sees them noticing her shoes, watches their faces change as they realize what they're looking at: Adriana Argento soaking in a $2,500 dress.

"Hi, guys."

They exchange a glance, one that feels familiar, like they've all been here before.

"Is everything okay?" Noelle says.

"Yeah, of course. Why wouldn't it be?"

Adriana launches into a back stroke, feathering her legs.

"Um, well…we're all inside and you're…out here," Claudia says.

"I just needed a moment. It was weird watching you all listening to the album."

"So, you went for a swim? In Balenciaga?"

Adriana paddles over to the staircase, three stone steps that cascade into the shallow end. She climbs onto dry land and wrings out her ponytail. Her friends are bewildered, but they are both trying their best to act like this is something they see every day. Adriana is beginning to regret ruining her beautiful dress. She's chilly and she has no towel. Scotty will be pissed when he finds out that she hasn't even posted a photo of her outfit, and since the dress was a gift from the brand, he'll be getting an angry phone call. She fingers the hem. The silk is completely destroyed, chlorine eating at the fabric like a thousand moths.

"I'm going to get you a towel," Claudia says. She disappears into the pool house, which is across a short stretch of lawn opposite the main house, and returns to wrap Adriana's damp shoulders in terry cloth. "Thanks, girl," Adriana says.

Single file, they rejoin the party.

The night before *solstice*, the Ivies meet at Pearl's. They're displayed around the apartment like butterflies, papery wings spread and pinned to a board. Like they've been there for hours, or years. Pearl's silk kimono trails after her as she leads me into the bedroom. Uncorked bottles of wine, chipped teacups and crystal glasses, candles melting into wax puddles running over the rusted lips of candleholders and onto the furniture. The air smells musty, like an old book.

"Look who's back," she said when she opened the door and turned aside to let me in, the distaste in her voice an unacknowledged pleasure, a hard candy sucked until the melting point.

Meghan almost knocks me over with the force of her embrace.

"I'm *so* happy you made it." As if I had a choice. I don't see Veronica, but she must be here. She is never, ever late. The other girls are in various stages of private pre-going-out ritual, the makeup and hairspray and alcohol the charms they invoke to conjure a successful night.

Pearl spins to face me and drops onto the bed, sending shock waves through the trinkets scattered over the humps of the comforter, pushed back to reveal coral sheets, stained a touch darker in the middle from the natural oils in Pearl's hair and skin. I shift my weight from one foot to the other, cross and uncross my arms. Meghan has returned to her spot on the floor, where she sits at the foot of a full-length mirror and pounces a sponge soaked with flesh-toned makeup over her freckles. I take a seat next to her, feeling ungainly as I try not to flash my thong.

Pearl sees me struggling to keep my legs closed. "Relax," she says. "It's nothing we haven't seen before."

Unsettled, I give up and fold one shin over the other, exposing the stripe of my underwear as the hem of my skirt gathers near the hip creases. Sweat collects in my palms. I rub them along the polyester fabric across my thighs.

Crystal and Jessie are inside Pearl's closet, pulling vintage tops and dresses off bone-like wire hangers and tossing them on the floor, as if they're making a bonfire. The materials are starchy and flammable, shiny tops with tall lace collars and Jackie Kennedy shift dresses. We're listening to Adriana's catalog backwards, *Hazardous* through *Sincerely, Adriana*. The reverse evolution.

Pearl sings along while dabbing cream blush onto the apples

of her cheeks, not words but a series of runs and noises adding up to a melody. *Oh, oh, oh, oh, oh.*

Jessie shrugs out of her romper, a rosy flash of nipple and a deep belly button thumbprint marking her unblemished brown skin. She zips herself into Pearl's lamé jumpsuit with a low back and flared legs. Jessie is shorter, so the pants hit her in an odd place, just below the ankles.

"Thoughts?" She spins in a tight circle, flashing.

"Like the '70s puked all over you," Meghan says. It's the meanest she's ever been in front of me, but no one else seems surprised to hear the backbone ridging her tone.

Jessie stops spinning, crestfallen. She throws the jumpsuit aside like so much discarded wrapping paper and goes back to rifling through the closet mostly naked.

Someone passed me a bottle of wine while my focus was on Jessie and I sip straight from the bottle. It's been at least a few hours since I've eaten and the alcohol rips through me, disconnecting my head from my shoulders. It's going to be fine. Just fine.

The bedroom door bangs open and Veronica hangs on the doorway. Something is off. Her knees buckle at strange angles and her upper half is limp, as if it's too much for her legs and waist and spine to hold her upright. Residue collects on the rims of her nostrils. She wipes her nose with a dangling wrist and sniffs harshly. Adriana's singing is not loud enough to drown out the sound. We all turn to watch as she lumbers over to a wingback armchair and collapses into the cratered center.

I paw at Meghan with my eyes until she glances up from her makeup, a fluffy brush wedged in her lid crease. I jerk my head toward Veronica with a questioning eyebrow raised. *Coke*, Meghan mouths, her lips stretching on the *O*.

Pearl rises from the bed and walks over to Veronica. "I want some of what you're having," she says. They nestle together on the chair as Veronica produces a small bag of white powder. Pearl cuts two lines on a purple Lucite TV tray and snorts them both with a coiled receipt, a shiver coursing through her. Eyes rolled back, she sits up, shakes her shoulders, rolls her lips, and gives a pleasurable yelp.

Jessie and Crystal take turns shaking out their own portions of the coke. When the bag gets to me, I panic and swivel toward Meghan.

"Come on, don't be a little bitch." Veronica is venomous. A black aura encircles her hunched frame. Veins on her temples, leaping, squiggling worms. Mouth a devastating shade of peach. She's unkempt, a frayed '80s prom queen in a ruffled pink crepe dress and sparkly tights that hide her Ivy tattoo. I don't want to be near her, but I can't look away.

Meghan takes the drugs and the tray and distributes two neon stripes of powder. They seem modest in size, but I don't know anything about cocaine, about how much is too much. I watch the enlarged, gunk-filled pores on the bridge of her nose as the powder disappears into the bruised cavity of her nostril.

She passes the tray to me, pouring out a line. It's the head-to-toe pinprick of a tetanus shot mixed with the shudder at the tail end of an orgasm. My face burns, then the burning subsides, and I'm left with bliss, empty, hot-white nothingness. There's a rush. A stream of mucus is spilling from my nose. No, not mucus. Blood. My nose is bleeding. I touch the wet and my hands come away sticky and red. I smear the blood on my lips and laugh.

"Oh my god, you're a total psycho." Veronica is at my side, petting me, approving. Running her hand down the full length of my ponytail, gripping the base harder than necessary so the follicles tug at my scalp.

I feel like a horse. "Neigh."

"This girl, she's nuts."

"Totally one of us."

"Totally."

They're crawling towards me on all fours, knocking eyeshadow palettes and tubes of concealer out of the way, tamping down mod florals and prairie lace with the heels of their hands. Fingers press my lips. They lick at my blood, crazed witches under a full moon, cackling. Someone kisses me, a nudge, a powdery sweet tongue. We're all smeared, bound by fluid.

I'm buzzing like an electric razor, ready to cut something, anything. Veronica brings out a tube of body glitter and we rub it on our shoulders, thighs, the gentle mountains of our chests. We shimmer like technology. Androids, skittering to life.

Adriana's voice floods the room, cutting through me like a hot knife through butter. I taste blood on the tip of my tongue.

We pour out into the night, bloodied and effervescent, and the night is supportive. Open, like a loom waiting to catch me when I trust-fall, believing in the strength of eternity. I have no idea what time it is. I've never been happier to let someone else take care of it, hail a cab, tell the driver where to go, get me there. I don't know where we're going, anyway. I did, before, but I've forgotten.

The cab takes the turns at a brisk pace. Traffic parts for us. We drive for however long, clattering onto the West Side Highway. I think of the car crash in *The Great Gatsby*, and the moments before it all goes haywire. Music and laughter and alcohol and—*screech!* It should be an omen, but if there's any foreboding undergirding this evening's freedom, if there's any sense that this will all come tumbling down around me, it's buried so far down under layers of cocaine and wine and the sky reflecting the city's lights instead of stars, and all I think is that this is really it: I'm going to live forever.

Pearl snuggles her head on my shoulder in the back seat. Our arms are linked. Her oyster-shaped handbag rests against my knee, sparkling with tiny beads. A pearl and her oyster. She doesn't even like me, but right now we are in love.

The cab slows to a stop outside a club called River and bursts open, a raucous clown car. I don't know how we all fit inside, but here we are on the sidewalk, poised like Christmas ornaments. Tinseled. I can't help but think if we were men, the cabbie never would've let us all inside, drunk and high and dizzy as we are. Men would cause a fight, start a brawl, exercise their power. But six women looking the way we look now? Harmless. He never stood a chance. Just to be near us is to be chosen, blessed.

We join the line outside the club entrance. A marquee over the door advertises *Adriana Argento Dance Night!* And it all starts to make sense. Why we are here, what we came for. Girls totter in ankle-snapping heels, yanking at the tops and bottoms of their bandage dresses, that oozing toothpaste spill. Flesh trying to breathe. One girl at the front has pastel hair and blue semicircles painted above her eyes. Another, long dark curls and a clingy violet slip. A few are dressed as carbon copies of Adriana: extensions, matching crop top and skirt sets, over-the-knee boots. Painted-on replicas of her tattoos, or maybe even real replicas.

The line moves quicker than expected, bouncers ushering groups of five or six inside after checking IDs and slapping orange bracelets on their wrists. We're next, then we're inside, and River is a swamp pit and the girls are lizards and frogs and snakes and alligators, languidly gliding their hair and their asses and their long limbs through the quaggy air. Adriana's voice surround-sounding, her visage on every wall, a veritable shrine. A music video gyrates and twitches over a dozen television sets. Her image skips and repeats. Hip shakes and stomping feet, her back to us, the flick of her head as she glances over a shoulder, inviting us in, beckoning. A private moment shared not only with the people packed into this club, but with the millions who have watched this video in the three years since it was first released. What she does, it's not dissimilar from porn: she takes a sentiment, be it love or loneliness or anxiety or sexual desire, and she massages it into a song, and then she makes it yours and hers and ours. Singular yet universal.

"She's a genius!" I shout, not really to anyone, and also to everyone. Since River is so thronging with bodies, the words come out of my mouth and are swallowed immediately by the swell of other voices.

Meghan hears, though, and screams, "An absolute fucking genius. Somebody give her a Pulitzer."

And I know that's not how Pulitzers work. And I know *love me, love me, love me*, which is what Adriana says over and over—an incantation I have memorized even though I can't hear it—is not profound enough to earn her any accolades, though it's actually the most profound thing anyone could ever say because it's also the most true thing. But, still, I say, "YES!"

I don't think it's just the drugs, though it could be. The drugs are opening me up to the infinite possibilities in the world. They are a kaleidoscope spread before me, a buffet of *options*, and how can anyone be sad, ever, with so many choices? Choice is power and freedom and knowledge.

I'm spinning around and now I'm wrapped in Veronica's arms. Her mouth is open, and her teeth are blue. She makes like she's going to bite me, clatters her jaw in my ear and hisses instead. Then she pulls me into the crowd. I turn back, but none of the others follow, and I can no longer see them in the press of bodies. I'm afraid, but the fear is muted, the coke and wine coursing like silverfish through me, tingeing the club, the voices, the flash of Veronica's teeth, with magic and adventure.

We're in the bathroom. Veronica yanks me into a stall and slams the door shut.

"Lock that, will you?" I lock the door. She rambles as she shakes coke onto the dented toilet paper holder. "Didn't you miss us when you were gone? We missed you. We missed you so bad. You can't *do* that to us, not again." She straightens and narrows her eyes at me. "Never do that to us again."

"I won't." Veronica takes a step, grips the end of my ponytail in one white-knuckled skeleton fist. She pulls, forcing me forward so our noses are touching. "You're one of us now. Don't forget it."

She lets go and I limp sideways, almost putting a hand into the toilet's gaping black-lipped, goth princess mouth as I regain my balance. Veronica hunches, back to me, and I can just barely make out the desperate scrape of her inhaling a line, though maybe I imagined it. She hands me a rolled-up bill and I take mine obediently. My head aches.

The bathroom spits us up. We find our friends, writhing like pythons on the dance floor near the bar. They are so beautiful, and their beauty makes me angry, but tonight I am part of it. Crystal holds a beer. It foams out of the mouth of the can as she works her hips, swaying from side to side with the tick-tick rhythm of a pendulum. Meghan hops over, sandwiching me between her chest and Veronica's.

A man sidles up and leers at us. "Beautiful ladies. *Bellissima.*" He blows kisses, his lips smacking like firecrackers.

"You're disgusting," Veronica says, pushing a protective arm across Meghan's and my shoulders, shoving us out of the way.

The man becomes instantly hostile, his caterpillar brows darkening. "Bitch," he snaps, and walks away. Off to find some other women to harass. Women he hates because he sees them being happy without him. Happy only with each other.

Veronica laughs. "Pathetic."

We keep dancing. There is nothing left to do but dance.

Early becomes late becomes early. We're in the bathroom again. All of us, this time. Pearl sits in the sink, legs on the counter, bare feet in the opposite sink. Shoes on the floor, knocked over like dominos.

"My skirt is wet," she keeps saying. "My skirt is wet."

"'Cause you're *sitting* in the *sink*."

"You ever thought about how weird that word is? *Sink*."

"Sink, sink, sink, sink, sink!"

"Sinks sink." The last one is me, pushing onto the counter, leaning all my weight into my hands so that I hover several inches off the floor. The walls are mirrored. We've chased everyone else out of the bathroom. It's all of us, dripping like ivy from the walls. Veronica has tied a paper towel around her neck like a bandana. Jessie is holding her hands under the drier. When it stops, she pulls away and shoves them under until the motion sensor reactivates. The result is a constant whirring that makes me feel like we're inside a fan. I'm twitchy, as if there really are paddle-shaped blades slicing through the air. "I like my limbs," I say.

"What? You're so silly. This girl is soooo silly!" Meghan says, and grabs my wrist, holding my noodle arm aloft. I am a heavyweight champion, a master of strength and speed. And I'm going to be sick. I rip my arm away and her fingers leave skid marks on my delicate inner wrist as I crash into the nearest stall and void the contents of my stomach.

"She's puking!" someone yells from the other side.

Then, hands in my hair. Meghan is stroking my scalp. She's gentle, not like Veronica with her tugging and her scratchy

nails. She's *shhh shhh shhh it's okay*-ing me as I gag all the fluids from my body. My insides wring like a dishrag. The liquid coming out of me is dark, inviting comparisons to blood
or tar, but I'm too dizzy for comparisons, or to worry what's
gone rotten in my core.

I try to rest my forehead on the lip of the bowl, but Meghan
catches me in time, fingers pressing into the nape of my neck,
and says, "Easy, tiger. You don't wanna touch that. Is gross."

Meghan tugs me by my ponytail so I'm sitting on my knees.
She flushes, wipes my mouth with toilet paper, flushes again.
Stands me up and leads me to the sink, shoos Pearl's dangling
feet to the side so I can rinse my mouth with cold water. A
little of it spills down my throat. Pearl is sing-muttering the
words to an Adriana song that isn't playing, making the shape
of the lyrics without the enunciations. The whir of the hand
dryer starts up again. Jessie giggles. Her knuckles are cracked.
Hoop earrings dangle around her face.

I scrape my upper teeth against my lower lip and a hard
piece of skin flakes off. I chew on it, thinking of unpopped
kernels at the bottom of the popcorn bag. The blood from
earlier has dried into an uneven lipstick smudge. It hits my
tongue with a graphite tang.

"Where's Veronica?" Crystal asks, banging out of the stall at
the end of the row. I didn't even know she was in here. At the
mirror, she tufts her curls and readjusts the decorative rhinestone comb creating starbursts above the happy spirals. She
is radiant and I want to hug her, lift her up off the floor, but
I won't dare ruin her splendor with my sour, vomit-scented
affections.

No one answers. We don't know where Veronica is. Her
absence is a relief, the stir of a coastal breeze after a spell of
choking humidity.

"She's probably dancing with a *boy*," Pearl says, full of disgust. Feet in the sink, faucet still going from when Meghan turned it on for me to drink. Her cherry toes splash and flex in the quicksilver.

The bathroom door swings open and two girls with Adriana extensions, red and blond, stand there in *Charlie's Angels* posture, shoulder blades kissing. The Ivies freeze. The only sound is the *whoosh whoosh* from the faucet sluicing over Pearl's feet.

For a moment, I think something passes between us and them. A telepathic girl code, a territorialism: *This space is ours.* But then the redhead shoves past her friend with unnecessary brutality and clomps her Jeffrey Campbells into the nearest stall. The handicap stall: I feel a stale sense of possession, conjured from my daytime self, rising, but it's only more vomit.

I retch in the sink, right onto Pearl's moonstone, cherry-capped toes.

She shrieks. Jessie laughs, pushes her hands back under the dryer. Crystal walks out of the room, shaking her corkscrews. Meghan increases the pressure on the faucet. Chunks swirl down the drain. I stand there, skirt balled in my fists. The blonde Adriana snorts and leaves, abandoning her friend, who is so silent in the handicap stall I wonder if she's died. The Ivies, too, collect themselves and leave.

It isn't until the two of us are alone, the redhead's rubberized shoes poking out from under the door, that I find the words to apologize.

She's above the crowd spinning like a top, balancing on one foot, then another, a music box ballerina or a holographic image. Veronica. My kind-of, sometimes, maybe-so friend. My beautiful, seductive murderess.

The stage is a raised platform above which unfurls a white screen, Adriana hugely projected behind Veronica and the other dancers. They mimic her and ignore one another, each fighting a personal battle to be noticed. By whom, I can't quite tell. Most of the people on the floor are too focused on themselves to care, or too prone to resentment to give the platform dancers any attention. The rest are men who are wrong here, men in blue or checkered button-downs who have wandered in off the streets because they knew inside they'd find women. Women in too-small outfits with vacant, never-mind stares. Women who didn't come here for them and yet must endure these men and their naked leering, faces concealing nothing. They want to do unthinkable things. They want to hurt, to use their power on something, they don't particularly care what, as long as it's beautiful and reminds them of past rejection, of how much they've overcome, now they are the dominant. The ones with jobs on Wall Street, swollen bank accounts, puffed biceps. They are what they imagine women want.

But the women are not here, do not dance, for these men. They don't even notice them. And Veronica: she would destroy any one of them with a single look.

She's not looking now. Her eyes are squeezed shut in ecstasy as the pink and yellow lights flash across her body, carving her into tiny neon triangles. She floats on another galaxy, so innocent, girlish. I think of her holding a knife. Cramming it clear to the hilt in the middle of Sophie Heffernan. None of it seems real.

Someone butts into my side. It's Meghan, grinning. She forms a tent with our joined arms and spins me underneath the steeple. "I'm glad you came!" she yells over the din.

"Even though I puked on Pearl?"

"*Because* you puked on Pearl." She winks and pulls me deeper into the crowd. We're surrounded. I can't move without hitting a stranger. I almost smack a girl in the face, and she smacks back, playfully. But I love it; I want to be crushed.

Confetti falls, starbursts from canons hidden in the ceiling.

The paper strips are so thin they dissolve on contact with our sweat-slicked skin, creating a gummy film we wear like armor.

The Ivies come together like magnets. We clot at the center, forcing the other dancers to give us space, a ring of emptiness gathering around us. When we leave, we have been renewed from splashing in the healing Adriana Argento Dance Night waters. I forgive the Ivies for what they've done, for what they might do. They are part of me, as much as an extra limb, a nonessential organ that I would miss nonetheless if it were removed, like a second kidney or a less interesting toe. We crash through the doors of River and flail on the sidewalk, singing different lines from different Adriana songs, creating a musical Frankenstein's monster. We're off-key and rambunctious. The sky is rotating like a dinner plate on the end of a stick, but actually it's just me, spinning and spinning with my arms out, *the hills are alive with the sound of music.* My fingers tingle and my hands go numb and I'm knocked over and laughing in a pile of other girls.

"Get a room," a fratty finance guy in an Islanders jersey snaps at our heaving, cancerous mass.

"Fuck off!" I yell, gleeful, and the rest of the girls drag me under. We're all laughing so hard we ache. Laughing so hard the bouncer comes out from the throbbing club entrance, tells us to *scurry on home, it's too late for a bunch of pretty ladies to be out here by themselves.*

"We're not by ourselves!"

"We could *kill you*!"

"We wouldn't even think twice."

"We've done it before."

The bouncer has lost the kindly twinkle that lit his eyes just moments ago when he thought we were innocent. He wants his girls to be innocent or else they can choke. He's gearing up, the muscles in his thick neck twitching like organisms under a microscope.

Meghan jumps up, smiles that ice-melting smile, and pulls out her phone. "The Uber will be here in five minutes; let's wait on the corner."

We back away from the bouncer, snarling.

15

I refresh the clips on Instagram half a dozen times: Adriana's mother and Scotty bringing out a flaming cake while everyone sings *Happy album day to you* to the tune of "Happy Birthday"; Noelle, Adriana, and Claudia grinding to one of the raunchier songs; Petey crying as he tries to get out a champagne-fueled speech. In all of them, Adriana wears a large gray sweatshirt, and her hair is dripping wet.

The last video shows Adriana, eyeliner smudged, hair waterlogged, expressing a heartfelt thank-you to her fans. To me.

I can't wait for you to hear this album; it means everything to me. It's my most personal yet.

Adriana has been missing since her album release party the previous night, when we were out dancing. The evidence points to her having left voluntarily; security camera footage from the backyard shows her dumping her phone in the grass, walking calmly toward the edge of the yard. Party attendees note that she seemed *distant* and *spaced out*, but not *upset*. Claudia and Noelle, her two best friends from before she got

famous, those leeches who suck at the teat of her fame, admit
they found her going for a dip while fully clothed in her party
dress, a Balenciaga, of which there is no photographic evidence, earlier in the night.

"But she was fine," Noelle sniffs on the news. "I swear,
she was fine."

I don't find out until Meghan calls.

"Check TMZ. *Now*."

The home page is chaotic, so reminiscent of the '90s su-
permarket tabloids decorating the walls of Blinkers that it
takes my eyes a few seconds to adjust. Then I see it: a bleary
paparazzi photo from last year of Adriana shielding her eyes
from the cameras outside a club, Nolan's hand just visible in the
lower left corner. At the top of the screen blares the headline:
*"SINGER ADRIANA ARGENTO, 26, MISSING FROM
LOS ANGELES HOME."*

The all-caps make it seem like TMZ is excited about this,
and of course they are, actually, very excited about this. Bad
news brings traffic.

"Do you see?" Meghan is saying.

"Yeah. I see."

"They're still releasing the album at midnight. Scotty put
out a statement. So please come over, like we planned."

We hang up.

The curse of time is how it paces opposite to your desire.
It's like that embroidered throw pillow saying: *The days are
long, and the years are short.* But the hours are what really get
me. The hours are the hardest part. The hours are eternity.

I wade through them, shaky-footed.

I fill the excruciating minutes until it's time to leave for
Meghan's by stretching out menial tasks. A sink full of dishes
luxuriated over in the same manner as a bubble bath. The
vacuum excavated from the back of the hall closet for the first

time in months. Pillows are fluffed and sheets are changed. I walk a bulging sack of laundry half a block to the laundromat on Church Avenue. I have so many clothes I could wear something new for months, and so I often do, washing my underwear and socks in the sink, leaving them to dry on the unstable rack I've had since freshman year of college. I've knocked it over so many times trying to pee, socks and tights and delicate sweaters lying flaccid and abandoned over the dark grout between the tiles.

While a load of colors spins around the porthole of the washing machine, I duck into the café next door and spend $5 on an almond milk latte. My fingers tighten, just for a second, around the hard plastic debit card as the cashier tries to take it from me. I think of my dwindling bank account, the blank days until my next paycheck clears. The cashier—Ellie, reads the name tag clipped to her lapel—sets her mouth into a stern, lips-only smile and pulls until the card rips from my death grip.

Ellie swipes the card, slides the receipt and a pen across the counter. I sign, consider stealing the pen when she isn't looking, the ink so smooth it glides over my signature like an ice skater doing a triple lutz, decide against it and thank her as I step down the bar to wait for my drink. The barista is cute, a floppy-haired boy a few years younger with a silver lip ring. He winks as he nudges the latte towards me.

"You got my best heart yet," he says.

I examine the cup. Embedded in the quivering layer of foam is a loopy, exaggerated milk heart. "It's great. Thank you."

I take a sip and the heart wilts toward the impression my lips leave in the foam. I add a lid and push through the door, shielding my eyes from the sun. I've recently become aware of faint lines tracing my forehead, a map of my facial tics;

every time I squint, I imagine them tunneling deeper into my flesh, parasitic.

I move the damp clothes to the dryer and sit on a plastic chair, finishing my coffee. When I get bored of watching my wardrobe make psychedelic spirals, I check the latest news on Adriana. The only updates are crackpot theories by fanatical fans on Reddit, Instagram, and Twitter—*Nolan kidnapped her and sold her into sex slavery for drug money! Scotty murdered her because he was angry the album he had the least control over was set to be her first Billboard #1! She was abducted by a jealous fan!*—and only marginally less crackpot theories reported as real leads by journalists—*Possible Adriana Argento sighting at gas station on La Cienega! Former LAPD investigator claims that Adriana Argento disappearance is part of a plot by Charles Manson fanatics! Adriana Argento's security head wanted for questioning!* I don't check the website, though I'm sure Meghan's weekend writers are reporting on the disappearance.

I'm cattle-called to attention by the beep of the dryer. I'm the only nonemployee at Lee's Laundry. The near emptiness lends the room an uncanny, echoey quality that makes me feel like I'm being observed by someone I can't see. I check the dryer. The machines suck the way machines in public laundry facilities always suck. Some of the heavier items, a pair of pajama pants, a sweatshirt, are still damp. I shove everything back in my bag, cribbed from a wash-and-fold service I used once or twice during finals in college, before the guilt of adulthood started to set in, and trudge home.

It's somehow only a quarter after three and I'm not due at Meghan's until seven. I hang the not-yet-dry items on the bathroom towel rod's bare spine, fold and put the rest away. Then I turn the shower to scalding. Under the spray of steam, my anxiety blooms like a hothouse flower. I don't usually sing in the shower, but I try out a few experimental bars, anyway.

The pipes cheer and clank as I shut the water off. I stand in the sogged-over bathroom, letting the moisture soften and expand my skin, thinking that maybe I finally understand the appeal of a sauna. I slick my wet hair into a sloppy bun and shimmy into denim cutoffs and an oversized tank top with a tarot card printed on the front. The moon. La Luna.

I use a few coats of mascara, a coral lip stain that makes me look like I just ate a fruit pop.

My phone jangles, delivering Meghan's blustery, windswept voice straight to my ear. "Come over early. I have booze."

Yes, it was stupid. Stupid for Adriana Argento to think she could leave her property in the middle of her album launch party and not call anyone, not even Bobby or her mother, to tell them she was fine, it was not a big deal, she just needed to be, not *alone*, but *away*.

Of course, it actually was a big deal. A very big deal. Who was she to think she could just go? Without a plan. Without a team.

This has been one of the most difficult aspects of fame to get used to, having grown up normal, or about as normal as a kid actively pursuing a career in show business can be—losing her ability to act autonomously. The shift had been gradual; at first, only fans of her Disney series would recognize her on the street. Then the circle widened with the release of *Sincerely, Adriana* and rippled outward from there.

But that's not how she remembers it. No, in her memory, fame happened in an instant. One day, Adriana had been able to walk from her car to Starbucks and back again without being noticed. The next, she couldn't look out the window— any window, anywhere—without the swarm of flashbulbs and the echo of screams erupting at the mere flick of her gaze. She sees those lights, hears those whispers, whenever she closes her eyes.

So, for once, she wanted to play at being average. In a sense, this was another part, like the version of herself she puts on for stadium crowds. She sometimes thinks she should have a closet full of iterations. Just pull on the one you want to wear.

And so, she leaves.

Her voice follows her as she traverses the lawn. After the pool, she'd changed into a sweatshirt and leggings. She walks into the ragged brush lining the yard and places her right foot in the brick divot closest to the ground. Her skinny ankle wobbles slightly as she lifts the other foot and reaches up to find a hold higher up on the fence. The first few steps are shaky, but soon she becomes confident in her footing. It's not at all dissimilar to dancing in heels, all coordination and the timing of breath.

Adriana hops off the fence. She thinks she will go back, she really will, she just wanted a taste. But then she looks down, sees the hill and the ribbon of road beneath, slippery with early dew. She listens to the crickets murmuring in the shrubbery. And she feels so *free*.

Now she's in a Holiday Inn on North Highland Avenue. The oatmeal bedding is crisp at the edges. The air smells reused, devoid of natural fragrance. The artwork is soothingly bland. Comfortingly bad. A seascape behind the bed, umbrellas ballooning over a naked stretch of beach. A dog mid-catch on the wall next to the TV, above the desk. Molars exposed, and gums pushed forward, teeth clasping a red Frisbee.

She checked into the hotel using Scotty's name. They will find her, they always do. But for now, she enjoys the silence. Picks up the room phone and contemplates who to call, but she knows, of course she knows.

He answers on the third ring.

"Hi."

"Adri?"

Her heart trills at the old nickname. She snuggles into the word, a worn bathrobe contoured to the peculiarities of her body.

"I need to see you."

Nolan's exhale ripples, tickling her ear through the receiver. "You can't keep doing this to me. Are we broken up or not?"

"I just miss you, that's all."

He sighs again, but it sounds more like defeat. "I miss you too."

A soft beat pulses on the other end of the line. Adriana pictures Nolan in his home studio, clicking around Pro Tools, putting more finishing touches on his already finished album.

"They threw me a party. At the house. For my album launch."

"What do you mean at the house? Are you not at the house?"

"I left."

"What do you mean you left?"

"I hopped the fence."

He laughs. *"You hopped a fence?!"*

"Why is that so funny?"

"Just the image of you, a five-foot-nothing international pop star, climbing a fence. Tell me that's not fucking hilarious. Please, picture it."

"If you're just going to make fun of me all night, then I guess I'll hang up and enjoy this lonely room at the Holiday Inn all by myself. Watch some pay-per-view."

"Hold the goddamn phone—you're at a *Holiday Inn*? How much did you pay them not to tip the media off?"

"I wore sunglasses and used Scotty's card."

"Someone is going to recognize you, if they haven't already." He sighs. "All right."

"All right?"

"Gimme the address."

Less than an hour later there's a knock at Adriana's door. Nolan's in a black hoodie that conceals his most identifiable tattoos and a pair of reflective sunglasses, the kind that surfers wear. Topping his head is a floppy yellow bucket hat.

Adriana pulls him into the room by the sleeve and slams the door. "Are you alone? Did anyone see you?"

"Relax. You on the run from the Feds or sumthin'?"

Adriana rolls her eyes, but she's smiling so wide she can't hide it. The floral curtains are drawn and the room, though clean, smells damp. Nolan and Adriana stop laughing, and the silence turns murky. She's the first to look away as she flounces over to the bed. Her hair is down, her real hair, wavy and crimped from the dried chlorine. Discarded extensions are laid out on the dresser. Nolan wanders over and rubs the ends of her disembodied hair between two fingers. Even though it's not attached to her body, she shivers. He drops the fake hair and sits on the edge of the other mattress, folds his hands in his lap, both therapist and patient.

"So, why'd you make a break for it in the middle of your release party? You love that stuff. Pink champagne and shit."

Adriana contemplates the ceiling. "I felt weird. Like I wanted to put the music back in the studio. Bottle it up."

"You're not proud of the album?"

"I'm *so* proud of this album. That's the problem. How do you do it?"

"Hm?"

"Release such personal music. My whole career, I've been this manufactured blow-up doll. A singing sex fantasy, like silicone with lungs. And now it's like I'm screaming: Hey! Wait! I'm a person! Pay attention to my feelings!"

Nolan tucks his hands into his armpits, eyebrows reaching toward the brim of his ridiculous hat. "You just gotta grow a bit of a thick skin about it. People are gonna say shit. Critics are gonna review based on preference, not based on your life. Everyone is gonna pick the lyrics apart for references. Ignore it the best you can. Remember, they're reacting to the music, not to you."

Adriana props up on her elbows. "But what if the music *is* you?"

"You asked for my advice so I'm giving it to you. Yeah, it's gonna fucking suck the first time you see a comment online criticizing a song you poured your heart and soul into. And if *Billboard* and Pitchfork rake you over the coals, that'll hurt too. Although I don't think they will, because the album is really fucking good. You're an artist. Lean into that power. Now, really—why did you call me here? We could've had this conversation on the phone."

He crawls onto her mattress. She pulls at his shirt and they cling to each other, lovers on a sinking ship. The urgency between them has never faltered; every time they touch it's like the end of the world and they are alone and failing each other over and over again. But at least they have this.

Meghan, when she buzzes me in and opens her apartment door, is disheveled. Her hair sticks up at odd ends and her bangs are flattened to her forehead. I hold out a bag from the liquor store; the bottles inside clank as she dumps the bag on the dining table. She opens a drawer, fishes out the corkscrew, and wrenches the curved end into the red. Discarding the cork on the table, she draws the bottle to her lips and knocks her head back. Droplets cling to the side of her mouth as she pulls the wine away and swallows.

"Nervous?" I say as she passes me the bottle.

"You have no idea."

Adriana is on shuffle, volume low. There's a thrumming under my breastbone, an anticipation. On the subway over here I watched the other passengers staring at their phones. They were bored in a detached way, like they were uninterested in their own boredom. I recognized my old self in their glazed eyes, their slackened jaws as they clicked around their screens with a certain desperation, unsure of what they were searching for. I knew that it wasn't about the destination—the clicking was the point. The clicking was not a means to an end, but the end unto itself.

Being with the Ivies was the opposite of that. I was on edge with them at all times lately; I could no longer let my guard down. It made me feel engaged, all that proximity to death, the fear of making the wrong joke, wading into danger. Less relaxed, sure, but more alive, too. There was often a raw, sulfurous scent hanging around them, strongest when they were all together, an invisible shroud of stink. A particularly feminine stink, like the churn of raked dirt or exposed plant roots or period blood, verdant and sodden.

Meghan smells like that now. Her anxiety, about the album, about Adriana's whereabouts, is coming off her in waves. I sneeze.

"Bless you," she says, and drinks.

I sit on the couch with the bottle. Meghan sprints from one corner of the apartment to another, wielding a Swiffer duster. She stops each time she passes the couch to swipe sips from the bottle. By the time she's finished dusting, she's drunk.

A hangnail by her thumb starts bleeding, but she doesn't

notice. The blood pearls and runs into the groove between nail and nail bed.

"You're bleeding," I say. She looks at her thumb like it's a prosthetic and she can't remember losing a finger. She says, "Oh." Then she says, "I can't believe it. Where did she go?"

"I don't know. Maybe she just…left."

"You think she disappeared on purpose?"

"That's how TMZ made it sound."

"That doesn't mean nothing bad happened to her. She could've gone for a walk and gotten, I don't know, abducted. Or something." It sounds like another confession. About her own uncontrollable urges to take Adriana, maybe. To make her a collectible, an object housed in a glass case in one of those living rooms where all the furniture is covered in plastic and you're not supposed to touch anything.

"Oh god. Don't say that. I'm sure she's fine."

"Well what do *you* think happened?"

"I don't know. Maybe she's at Nolan's. They could be reuniting and just haven't checked in with anyone. She's allowed to go off the grid."

"No, she's not. She's a *celebrity*. And her family wouldn't have involved the police if they weren't *sure* she was missing, right?"

"You don't know that. I mean, she's famous, like you said. Hugely famous. And if she walked off without security and isn't answering her phone? They could just be worried. It doesn't mean she's…" *Don't say* dead. *Don't say* dead. "…hurt."

I breathe out and in, out and in. Getting in touch with my basic functionality, the life-giving instinct. Clearing my head.

"Are you hyperventilating? Do you need some water?"

I decline, touched that she can still be concerned for me at the same time that she's consumed with vexation for Adriana. The fact that someone could love me and love Adriana,

a veritable goddess, an angel of song, at the very same time—
it might even be enough. We are on the same plane: god tier.

I'm filled with a swell of love, for Meghan, for Adriana,
for all they've given me. I reach out and grab Meghan's hand
and hold it the way that really matters, fingers laced between
fingers, clasping. I squeeze and she squeezes, and we don't say
anything until the buzzer shocks the room.

Meghan stands and presses the button, asks who it is. The
person, who is Veronica, because of course she would sense
this moment and ruin it with her killer instinct for superiority, her need to be the ringleader, says, "Me!"

Meghan presses the button again and lets her in. Before
she reaches the landing and knocks on Meghan's front door,
Meghan turns to me, shares one last private thought: "Between you and me, I think Veronica's a little excited Adriana
is missing."

She goes to open the door. While her back is turned, I
rush to the bathroom. I didn't feel drunk before, talking to
Meghan, but now that I'm standing under the stark bathroom
lights, I am warm and woozy. My face doubles in the mirror
and then merges.

I look around for the source of a loud vibrating noise before I realize that it's my teeth chattering. I don't feel cold,
not on the surface of my body, which is damp with sweat. But
underneath all that, my bones are freezing. I turn on the hot
water in the sink, but I can't get it to cover enough of me. I go
to the tub and run my arms under the hard pounding water
flowing from the faucet. Still, I want more.

I crawl into the tub, fully dressed, and plug the drain. Water
fills the curved bottom, drenching me slowly. If I close my
eyes, I can imagine I'm inside a womb. Not my mother's
womb, exactly, but some clear exterior bubble, a womb I could
walk around in. There's a knock. I sit up, blinking as I take in

my surroundings. My legs hovering in the water. My denim shorts, the gentle sway of my shirt. Gripping both sides of the tub, I hoist myself up. My shorts suction to my upper thighs like a wetsuit. The water level rises and dips. The bathroom door swings open and Veronica is standing there. I'm still in the tub, the water cresting up around my calves.

"Sorry, I didn't mean to disturb you." Veronica doesn't sound like she's sorry. She takes in the bathwater, the soaked bottom half of me.

"I was cold."

Veronica steps into the room, shutting the door behind her. Instinct kicks in and I take a step backward, stumbling through the weighted tub splash, catching myself on the clammy wall. Veronica walks over to the toilet, lifts the lid.

I cannot believe this is happening.

She hikes up her dress, pulls down her underwear, sits. Her leopard print thong is stretched like a hammock between her smooth, hairless thighs. The fabric is tinted a contrived purple, trimmed with lace. I can't see the tag, but I know: Victoria's Secret.

This cannot be happening. I keep telling myself that until I hear the gentle *hissssss* sprinkling into the toilet. If I close my eyes, maybe it would sound like a rain forest. But my eyes are wide open, bulging, and I can only see it for what it really is: a terrifying wealthy blonde murderer urinating right in front of me. It's a display of dominance.

"Oh, come on," she says, peeing and maintaining steady eye contact that I would love to break and cannot seem to break. "You had to know I use the bathroom just like everybody else."

I didn't know that, not for sure. Veronica isn't particularly down-to-earth. Yeah, I get it; everyone pees. But if there was one person who didn't, it would be Veronica.

She pees for so long my feet start to wrinkle. The bathwater turns gray. I get a little worried, then hopeful. Maybe she's not okay. Her being not okay would solve a lot of my problems. But then she wipes with a neatly folded wad of toilet paper, pulls up her underwear, lets down her dress, lowers the lid of the seat, and flushes with a definitive press at the lever. I continue to watch as she rinses her hands (*without soap*), wipes them on Meghan's towel, and leaves the room, shutting me inside.

Meghan insists on offering me dry sweatpants and a tank top emblazoned with the Coca-Cola logo when I finally come out of the bathroom, lightly dripping. She asks no questions. She says, "We're all having a lot of feelings right now."

I change into Meghan's fresh clothes and rejoin Veronica and Meghan in the living room. They've taken over the settee, and now I must sit on a spindly chair that feels like it might crumble when I sit down. Like it's made of spider webs and string lights and everything ephemeral. I try crossing my legs, but I'm too short and my butt starts sliding toward the front edge of the chair. I tuck one leg under me, bracing the other foot on the floor, and pretend the folded leg isn't already prickling with pins and needles.

Meghan and Veronica are on their phones, scrolling for updates. I'm disappointed; I'd hoped to share this moment of panic with my best friend and now Veronica is here, inserting herself. Making Adriana's disappearance about her.

"I can't believe she did this on album release day. The day we—some of us—have waited *years* for. Years. Do you think it could be a ploy for more sales?"

"That seems crazy."

Veronica doesn't take her eyes off her screen. "Does it? She saw how the tragedy with Sophie boosted her media coverage."

I'm about to defend Adriana, to say she would never take

advantage of her fans like that, when Meghan's buzzer goes off. The rest of the Ivies are downstairs. Meghan rises to let them up, and while her back is turned, Veronica ignores me. Hostility comes off her in waves, angry vapors.

"Why do you hate me so much?"

Meghan whirls around, mouthing *Don't*. But it's too late; the damage is done.

I swear that Veronica's creamy roots lift slightly, as if preparing to strike. I do the worst possible thing—I keep going. "I didn't kill anyone. And I've kept your secret. What more do you want from me?"

"You didn't keep my secret; you kept her secret." Veronica jabs a finger at Meghan, who is glued to her spot on the floor. The bell rings and Meghan scurries to open the door. Veronica focuses on her phone once again.

Soon the room is overtaken by Ivies all talking at once.

"Did you see?"

"They found her!"

"Adriana's okay!"

"She showed up at home like she never left."

"I knew everything would work out. I could feel it."

"My tarot reading from this afternoon reassured me; I pulled the Ace of Cups."

Suddenly they notice that Veronica hasn't spoken. Nor has she glanced up from the screen, where she's pinching two fingers together and spreading them apart, as if enlarging an image. "She's wearing the ring," she says.

I look at the other Ivies, aligning myself with them so that I won't be alone.

"What?" Crystal says, as if we could have misheard.

"She's. Wearing. The. Mother. Fucking. Ring!" There's a brief, pure silence, a shining hush. Then Veronica reels the arm attached to the hand holding the phone. She hurls it at the wall like a pitcher making the throw of her life. It rotates midair and crashes through the window. Did it? Did it crash through the window? How frail the glass must be, and how heavy her phone case. Heavy as a bullet.

For a while, no one reacts. It's almost possible to believe this is a prank.

That's it, it must be a prank. The window is a fake, some trick of light and sound and plastic. And Sophie. It was all a sick joke.

I don't notice I'm laughing until Jessie, of all people, puts an arm around me. Tugs me close. I think she's being sweet; I allow myself to feel touched, but she puts a finger to her lips and says, "Shhhhhhhh."

Meghan rushes to the window and looks through the fragmented hole where the phone went. Then she turns to Veronica, disbelief slackening her face.

"You are all fucking INSANE," I yell. Jessie covers my mouth and shoves me onto my chair, which is now surrounded by pebbles of broken glass. Meghan fetches a broom, and begins to sweep the mess. Veronica is catatonic, working at her lower lip with her upper teeth. Jessie and Pearl stroke my hair as I rock and whimper like a child. Crystal takes Meghan's seat on the settee.

Sometime later, I'm no longer shaking. The living room lights are out, and a flickering glow emanates from Meghan's bedroom. Tender whispering, and music. It sounds a bit like a cocktail party. Far, far away. But the doorway is at the wrong angle and very, very small. I move my head and the room rights itself. There's a crick in my neck and pain down the side of my rib cage where the chair dug in while I slept.

So. A dream. It was a dream.

I stand. An unusual breeze stirs the peach fuzz on my upper

arms. I search for the source and see a streetlight shining too brightly into the room. Jagged edges framing the rays. The broken window.

Then I remember. The ring. The phone. The crash.

Adriana is found. She and Nolan are together again.

My eyes seek out a third source of light, the almost three-dimensional pulse of the digital clock on the microwave. 12:05.

The album is out.

As I approach Meghan's room, the muffled sounds get louder. Sniffling, maybe. A violin. A deep wail.

The Ivies are sitting on the bed, listening. They are not moving or speaking, possibly not even breathing. Those whispers I heard, they come from the speaker at the center of the circle. They are Growing to *solstice* without me.

As I step closer, their tears catch the candlelight. They do not see me, as if my breakdown has rendered me invisible to them. I sit on the edge of Meghan's bed and do what I came here to do; I listen to *solstice*.

The music takes me on a ride. I'm in the country one moment, the city the next. I'm in love, I'm breaking up, I'm dying. I'm a newborn crying for her mother for the very first time. Though I'm outside the circle, though I don't hold a candle, I soon find that I'm crying, too. The Growing isn't about ritual or circumstance or all the trappings we attach to it. It's not about candlelight, maybe not even togetherness.

I only require the music to Grow.

I am once again all alone, hearing whispers on the other side of the wall. Whether I slept or slipped into a fugue state is not entirely clear. All I know is that I feel lucid for the first time in months. I don't know what the Ivies have been drugging me with, slipping into my wine when I haven't been looking, but it's gone from my system and I'm thinking with my head on straight.

The police. I will go to the police. I will tell them what I know about Sophie's murder. Either they'll believe me, or they won't, but I'll be free. Maybe I'll leave Meghan out of it, or maybe I won't. She's not as innocent as she'd like me to think.

I can wash my hands clean of the Ivies, every last one, and start over. Mariah will take me back. This time, I'll be the friend and coworker she deserves. I'll go on a second date with Tom. I'll order the appetizer—no oysters. I haven't really done anything wrong, have I? It's not too late for me to be good, and pure, and right.

Resolutely, I plant my feet on the ground. Seeing my legs sheathed in Meghan's sweatpants sends the memories reeling through my mind—the bathtub, the cracked window. I search Meghan's room for my clothing, determined to leave as I came, as myself. I open drawers and turn over lightweight pieces of furniture. Nothing.

"Looking for these?"

Meghan is holding my shorts and blouse, folded in the manner of a department store display. She hands me the pile and I shake out the top. It's pristine.

"I hung them in the bathroom so they'd dry." The notion that she could be a crazed superfan, an accomplice to murder, and still fold a shirt better than me, fold it so the sleeves don't crease, and the middle doesn't rumple, makes me furious. I lift her Coca-Cola tank over my head and throw it at her face. The fabric hits her between the eyes and falls to the floor. She blinks, stunned. Like I'm the crazy one.

Standing there, topless, I say, enunciating each word, "I'm telling the police. I'm telling them everything."

She glances nervously toward the living room. "Be quiet! They'll hear you."

"Let them hear! I want them to know what I'm capable of, and that's destroying this fucked up little club of yours. I'm tired of—" For the second time in twenty-four hours, I'm gagged by a hand.

Meghan maneuvers me into the corner so we are not visible from the doorway. "I am *trying* to keep you safe and you are not making it easy," she whispers. "Veronica and the others will kill you and dump your body in the Hudson and they will not think twice. You think they feel guilty about what we did to Sophie? They are *proud* of it. They loved it."

Floorboards creak. The Ivies have stopped whispering, which cannot be a good thing. Sure enough, they inch into the room, eyeballs and hairlines and fingernails and socked toes. Vintage band tees and artfully ripped jeans and Greek-goddess–patterned slips and a white blouse with short puff sleeves like swan's wings. I'm surrounded.

I feel Meghan's hand at the small of my back. My back, which is bare, because I'm not wearing my shirt. I clutch the fabric to my breasts.

Veronica steps to the front of the pack, all Snow Queen, gliding on her puff sleeves. The room is hot, but I feel my skin frosting, turning crisp and cold under her tundric gaze. "Where do you think you're going?"

"Me?" I say, like an absolute moron.

Meghan saves me, as always. She wedges her shoulder between us, shielding me from Veronica. "She was just getting dressed so she could join us in the living room. To discuss *solstice*."

Veronica's eyes shrink and keep shrinking. She must decide that Meghan is telling the truth, because she rotates on one slippered heel and walks out, the rest of the Ivies trailing her. Meghan casts me a mournful, tender warning of a glance before shutting me inside.

Alone, I momentarily evaluate the possibility of escaping through the window. But the only fire escape is in the kitchen, and the drop from the window by the bed is too far to make it unscathed. I weigh the battle against hospital costs, my paltry health insurance, against the war waiting for me on the other side of the door.

I know how to talk about Adriana. I pull on my shirt.

Something is missing. Sound. The living room is curiously quiet, even as the girls chatter under their breath, mouths snapping shut when they see me standing next to the couch.

The album. They are not listening to the album.

They are not listening to *solstice*, the uncanny, quirky, beautiful, personal, political arrangement of thirteen songs that I knew before I'd finished the first rotation was not only my favorite Adriana Argento album, but my favorite album of all time. This collection of merciless seconds is perhaps the longest I've gone without Adriana's voice backgrounding my life since I first discovered her music, save for sleeping, and perhaps not even then, when I so often fall asleep with her discography on repeat, the soundtrack of my subconscious.

My brain fills in the lack, a tuneless parade of words in my head.

A large white poster board is propped on the chair I used last night. It's decorated with red arrows connecting phrases and rectangles. I make out the name of the website, the word *Adriana*, a crude sketch of a weapon.

"What's this?" I say, pointing a hysterical, doddering finger. But I know. I know what it is.

The Ivies are going to assassinate Adriana.

16

The plan goes like this:

Adriana Argento is coming to the website. She will shoot a cover story for our back-to-school digital issue, "Reinvent Yourself." Lexi has assigned Meghan the interview. When Adriana leaves the building, Veronica will shoot her from a vacant upper floor across the street. Apparently, she's an excellent shot.

I am privy to no other details. If I stay out of the way, if I stick to my routine, the Ivies will let me live.

They will also let me attend the intimate *solstice* Sessions, to which they've scored six impossible-to-get tickets, with them. "You have to kill to get these tickets," Veronica says, as she hands one to me.

One thing is very clear: the Ivies do not belong at Blinkers. Separately, it might work. I could see Jessie sidling up to a banker in a too-tight Hervé Léger knockoff, or Pearl at the bar knocking back shots with her Tulips bandmates. Together, they are so out of place it's funny. Veronica, in particular, reminds me, in her blue-and-white-checked tank dress, of Dorothy in the haunted forest after her banishment from the Emerald City. I've never seen her so small.

I brought them here to share greasy snacks and cheap drinks before our *solstice* Session at Irving Plaza. I longed to be on my home turf, somewhere I feel safe. As we entered the bar and pushed toward the tables at the back, aiming for my usual booth, it suddenly occurred to me that maybe the web producers would be there. I felt a burst of hope like sparklers in my lungs. But then I remembered: they'd all been laid off last week, and they would not come to Blinkers unless it was to complain about jobs they no longer had, or maybe to apply for a position behind the bar.

I was the only one left. Lexi had even given me a speech in the meeting where I thought that I, too, would be fired. I imagined perhaps they'd found out that it was my habit to steal from the beauty closet, not Ashley's, though I hadn't taken anything in weeks. Maybe they smelled it on me, Cumulus. Maybe Meghan finally told the truth. Her way of setting me free.

Instead, Lexi told me that she saw something of herself in me. She said my ideas needed work, but that I was excellent at uploading photos and pulling numbers for spreadsheets in a timely manner. That I was, in fact, the best at it.

My soul vacated my body when she said that, and I'd like to think that's why I'm here, allowing my psychotic friends one step closer to killing our idol without my interference. I'd like to think it's my restlessness, my desire to bludgeon the status quo, and that it's not about the concert, which I would not be able to get into without the Ivies, as it has been sold out since the first hour tickets went on sale.

JonBenét is already chattering when I sit down. It seems I don't even need alcohol to thin the veil between worlds. She greets me with a smile and a curtsey. I wink in return. I want her to tell me who killed her, and why.

Honestly, I couldn't believe it when the Ivies invited me to the *solstice* Sessions after laying out their plan to Mark David Chapman our Adriana. "You mean…you still want to go to the concert?" I'd asked.

"Of course!" they'd collectively shouted in descending order, like a wind chime.

Meghan sits next to me and squeezes my hand. "Can you believe in just a few hours we'll be less than ten feet away from Adriana?"

I shake my head. I really, truly cannot believe it.

Adriana is seated on a low stool. She wears a sweatshirt with her own face on it, Stuart Weitzman boots, a diamond collar. Her hair has been unleashed; it hangs down past her butt like bleached seaweed.

If I survive the week, I wonder if I'll finally get my ivy tattoo. I wonder how much it will hurt. Probably not as much as being *this close* to Adriana and not being able to touch her, to be her. Or to warn her.

We're pushed against the barricade. The venue was already packed when we checked in. Veronica maneuvered to the front and we followed. She kept her gaze focused on the stage, shoving people out of the way if she had to. Most stumbled to the side, dazed. They must have assumed she was important; she has that royal way about her. Just before the lights went down, Pearl tried to get us to go take lines in the bathroom, but Veronica said no, said *we need to be pure*.

Bobby is just on the other side of the metal bars, his head near the sole of Adriana's boot. He casts an imposing presence, like a boulder or a tall gate. The illusion of safety. I want to reach out and touch him, to vault over the barricade, to test his limits.

If I could reach Adriana, I could tell her to go. We could leave together; we both need some new friends.

Reading my mind, Bobby looks into my eyes. He raises a finger and, still staring, draws it in a horizontal line over the tendons of his neck. I wish I had taken Pearl up on her offer. I'm nervous. A live band and an orchestra clutter the stage behind Adriana, and a trio of backup singers. Pink and purple lights render her ethereal. There is no single spotlight. The room is transcendental.

First, screams. Then, a hushed silence. I feel as though I'm hovering at the galvanized lip of a UFO, waiting for an alien species to welcome me home. The first few notes of *solstice* ring out, like a drug in and of itself. Track One is the song I first heard at Blinkers, the song that saved and ruined my life in one go. Three minutes and twenty-five seconds of walking into a bright light.

She sings the entire album in order. No backing track, all the ad libs performed live and the harmonies overlapping with the help of the backup singers.

I dance and sing my heart out, as if I am alone. My throat hurts and my lungs feel like they might crawl out of my body and flop on the floor like slugs. The Ivies are mostly calm; they grip the top metal bar and occasionally shake it with passive anxiety, like they can't stand to be pent up, to be so close and yet so far. People push against our backs and at our sides, hoping for a shift in our formation. For one of us to use the bathroom or bend to fix a buckle on her shoe. But we stand our ground.

And I spin and jump and beat my fists, and when a song ends or Adriana smiles or giggles into the microphone or tells a joke, I cheer with the masses, finding pleasure in losing my voice among the crowd. No one is watching me, not even Veronica.

Near the end, as Adriana finishes crooning the slowest song on the album, the one we all know is about Nolan, Meghan leans over. "She really is amazing, isn't she?"

"Yes. She is."

The other Ivies are disheveled. Right now, they don't seem so scary. Pearl is scraping her Skrillex spot. Crystal is swinging onto the balls of her feet, using the barricade to float to the top of her toes like a ballerina, and lowering down, curls puffing around her shoulders. Jessie is dancing from the chest, pumping an exaggerated heartbeat, black hair flying.

And Veronica is standing completely still, save for her lips, which are continuously moving. In fact, they all mouth along, never missing a word.

At the end of the final song, the screams are deafening. Adriana's smile dimples her cheeks. "Thanks for coming out, my babies! I love you so much, you have no idea. I don't know what I did to deserve fans like y'all, but I never take it for granted. This album means the world to me and I'm grateful for this chance to share it with you."

The lights go down and we're in total darkness and, all around me, chanting:

We love you, Adriana!
We love you so much!
We love you!
We love you!

"I love you," I say, and it's the first time I've said it to anyone not related to me, and it feels so good I say it again and again until the lights come up and someone takes my hand and leads me away.

17

Just like that, the day arrives.

Why are the office lights always so bright? It's not the same as the sun, which keeps us alive with vitamin D, and they must know it, whoever designed this office space, whoever thought *yes, these fluorescent bulbs* and *yes, these lumpy couches* and *yes, this orange food*.

Yes, this is human.

They must know it's not the same, and yet. Those lights, how they buzz. How they hurt my eyes as they bleed out of their chemical tubes like ink, hot-white and violent. The web producers' bullpen stretches in both directions now that it's only me, a gleaming blacktop like a Lynchian highway, asphalt and the yellow lines forever and forever and forever, leading nowhere.

I feel Meghan two tables behind me and facing away. We are linked by the waiting. My part in all this is just to sit still and shut up. I'm sweating so bad my hands stick to the keyboard, leaving snail trails on the keys. I think I might be sick, but then Meghan sends me a winky face as a warning, so I know she's watching. They will kill me if I mess this up for them, this one chance at redeeming their fallen angel, their wronged savior who wrote and sang the music they didn't like, who wants to marry a man who isn't good enough, isn't cute enough, is so weak he needs to soften the blow of his own bloodstream with *drugs*, how disgusting. The not-good-enough man with a crooked, punched jaw grin and a problem.

I hear them in my head, their supernatural mantra: *Not good enough for our angel. No one is good enough; no song is good enough. We must put her out of her misery.*

The intonation goes on long enough that I start to believe it again. We are doing the right thing; we have to be. A Meeting reminder flashes across the screen, reaching out from another life, and for a moment I think maybe it isn't too late. I can tell someone. I can tell Lexi. My eyes seek her out, frantic, momentarily lost, but the chair is empty and spun away from me, as if she got up in a hurry. I go to the kitchen for coffee, Veronica's sugar-venom hiss in my ear the whole way: *Act normal. Do everything as you normally would.*

Cat mug, coffee pod, lever, button, *hisssss*. I picture the father-like man peeing, being careful not to stray from my inward routine either, as if the Ivies are reading my thoughts from their Bond villain positions up and down the street. Then my mind movie flickers and switches to my lost imaginary loves. They all look like Tom, which I hate, but I go with it, anyway. Fifteen Toms repeating and repeating and repeating up and down the floors of our drab corporate tower. Saying *Morning! Morning! Morning!* Like a busted cuckoo clock.

A bristle of excitement tickles my diaphragm. All this sameness coming to an end.

In the bathroom, I avoid my reflection. The handicap stall is occupied, and the air vanishes from my lungs. For a second I am utterly lost. I spin in a circle, hoping for another handicap stall to open in the wall like a portal to another world, an alternate bathroom where I can be a new person, one who isn't aiding and abetting her icon's assassination, one who took a path forward, followed the appropriate timeline, who stopped standing still. This other me, maybe she works at Stephanie's publishing house. Is content with a medium successful career in middle management. Goes for morning jogs in Prospect Park. Has read *The Goldfinch* from cover to cover.

But there's just me, frazzled and caught in the wall of mirrors.

I knock on the stall door.

"Someone's in here!" The voice is plaintive and unfamiliar.

"I really need to go."

"The other stalls are empty."

She's right; they are so empty the doors are wide open, welcoming me. I go into the one farthest from the handicap stall and, quiet as a mouse, I climb onto the lid of the toilet seat. I'm short enough, in my minimalist-chic flats, that my head doesn't come up over the top of the stall. If I keep a loose bend in my knees, I vanish.

Crouching there, the shoddy plastic lid sagging under my weight, I listen for the flush, for the metal clang as the lock slams into the wall and gouges a deeper groove in the plaster.

Then I hear a *whisk whisk* sound, like someone is methodically fluffing whipped cream with even, steady strokes. A curved shadow curls under the stall door. Wheels. Someone in a wheelchair. Leaving the handicap stall.

Someone in a wheelchair leaving the handicap stall.

"It's all yours." The woman's voice, which I've never heard before, not once, I'm so certain, I'm almost certain, comes from inside the very walls themselves, and I'm glad that I will never come back here after today, that I will never have to face the humiliation, to risk recognition. This woman, whoever she is, will never know that I'm the ableist bitch who hogs her stall, the urban equivalent of stealing the handicap parking space because it's closest to the store and it's snowing outside, and you'll only be a minute.

I climb down. The toilet lid almost snaps under my heel, but it doesn't.

I shut myself into the handicap stall, pink as an organ and smelling of chemical air freshener, and sip my coffee. A spot across from me, above the sanitary napkin bin screwed into the wall, is darker pink than the rest of the partition. Someone, perhaps a janitor, has painted over the flower illustration.

And I'm suddenly furious and so, so ready to enact my revenge on these people, on this world that doesn't understand beauty and therefore destroys everything beautiful.

Veronica is right. We aren't hurting Adriana. We're saving her.

Then I'm lifting my arm. Bending it back. Hurling the cat mug at the wrong pink on the metal fake wall because we are so barely human we have to shit and pee in these glorified litter boxes, just a few inches of dented steel and globby paint between us, so thin it doesn't even cover the sound, and the smells linger for hours, and is there anything less dignified than stewing in the aftermath of your coworker's bowel movement?

And the mug is flying, it's arcing through the Febreze-stifled air. It's hitting the partition, shaking the entire network of stalls like an earthquake. Coffee is splattering. The cat mug is falling. It spins midair and the cute little face turns to me, the pert nose and beetle eyes, pleading with me, saying *why* and *no* and I look away, tears in my eyes, and it shatters.

And I can't look at the mess I've made but know it's real because my face is wet with milky droplets and the ground crunches beneath my feet as I leave the stall.

At the bullpen, I listen to *solstice* on repeat. It really is a beautiful album, full of dissociative lyrics, lyrics that say, over and over in many different ways, *I'm there, but I'm not really there.* I allow myself to mourn Adriana as the artist she won't have a chance to become, the beginnings of the genius Veronica and her friends, my friends—*we*—won't let her discover. I give in to self-pity and let it pull me below the scintillating synths and layered vocals.

I have no right to sympathy, what with everything I'm about to allow. But I take it anyway, I take it and I gulp the salt water of it through my open, gasping mouth. I take this one private moment of despair and claim it for myself.

Adriana and her people arrive at eleven a.m. Her presence is announced by a hush falling over the entire floor; everyone knows something is going on, even if they can't see, aren't sure exactly what. A cluster of bodies shuffles into the hallway, greeted by Lexi, who has materialized out of nowhere. She is put-together. The edges of her pixie cut are electric-shock alert. Her leather boots hug her shapely legs, which her tight black jeans do little to conceal.

Peeking through the gaps, there are signs. Two needle-thin spike heels that slip between shuffling feet. A glossy bump sprouting from a crystal-studded hair elastic. The puffed-up hood of a down jacket despite the eighty-five-degree forecast.

Before I can get a good look, the herd vanishes into the Sapphire photo studio, the glass walls of which have been pre-covered with opaque black curtains.

When the door opens, I glimpse the website's talent co-ordinator, Gerald, holding out a sheaf of papers, releases for Adriana and her publicists to sign, and a photo umbrella arcing behind studio lights. The room is packed.

Charlotte and Lexi and the CEO.

Everyone but me, it feels like.

Meghan does not turn my way as she rises, holding her glittery Adriana Argento notebook, and vanishes into the conference room. Preparing for her big interview.

All around me, the rest of the website pretends it's business as usual. Nothing to see here. Just furnishing the living room of the internet, arranging a settee over here and a fainting couch over there. Maybe a fiddle leaf fig by the window. Faux, so we don't have to water. What do we think of slipcovers? Too much? But they make such cute ones these days. Not your grandmother's slipcovers.

I mute the volume on the music to see if I can hear anything coming from Sapphire. The typing is unbearably loud today, a bored marching band droning its way through "You Can Call Me Al" or "The Final Countdown" or "Smoke on the Water." Playing the hell out of those plastic keys, society's finest instrument.

Sapphire is on fire with the silver blaze of flashbulbs and the murmur of what sounds like a hundred voices but is probably only about twenty. I catch her for a moment, or I think I do, in a lower register than all the others, a calm whisper undergirding the frantic shrieks and shouts. Could she be— is she—singing? It's hard to tell but I think I hear a lilting, keening moan, a melodic growl. I want to get up, press my ear to the windowed wall.

But we've been told, in no uncertain terms: *Do not disturb our guests.*

And I've been told, in no uncertain terms: *Do not fuck this up for us, you hear me?*

So, I sit. I tap my foot. I get another coffee. I refresh my inbox. No new emails. No new Piger DMs. If only they knew this was their last chance. Last chance to have me *check this news story for typos* and *make sure the images look okay here?* and *upload this interview with the founders of feminist clothing brand WeREvryGrl to LIZZIE, would you?*

Last fucking chance.

I keep the music off, listening for the creak of the door hinges signifying the end of the interview, the return to normalcy, or so they expect.

To stave off boredom, I visit Nolan's grid. His most recent post is a grainy paparazzi shot, him and Adriana holding hands on a Meatpacking District side street. Nolan is *here*? In New York? Adriana licks a red lollipop and stares up at him with adoring doe-eyes.

The caption says, *My girl for life.* He doesn't know how true that is.

The unbelievable collision of sweetness and horror overwhelms me. I'm choking. Hands are closing around my throat. The laptop display tells me it's 11:55.

I spring out of my chair. I'm not sure what I'm doing as my feet track a path down the elevator-lined hallway, heading for the back entrance instead of the front lobby, only that I must do it, whatever it is.

I walk all the way to the end of the hall and wedge my body into the corner near the farthest bank. The one I suspect she will use, if I had to guess. I don't have to wait long. Voices soon echo in the hall, and a smacking that could be air-kisses. Footsteps. A long shadow distends into the archway. A pointed head, ponytail flip like a curled tentacle, sharp heels, a big puffy coat rendered in silhouette.

Two figures come around the corner and then I am alone with Adriana. Well, Adriana and a tall, angular publicist with a face that says she's angry at everything, especially me, though she's not exactly acknowledging my existence.

They're walking this way, just the two of them. My idol, her publicist, and me.

She has her head down, making fierce eye contact with the floor. Her diamond engagement ring, restored to her left hand, flashes in the darkened corridor. The publicist decides I can't be avoided and shoots me a glare, as if daring me to speak, a real *off-with-her-head* energy springing off her. She jabs the down arrow button three times in quick succession, as if that will make the elevator come faster. It comes when it comes, and not a moment sooner. We wait in tense silence as the red number on the display climbs higher.

Five, eight, ten. Adriana has not lifted her chin an inch.

Ding.

"Wait!" My hand is pressing the elevator door open. I look at it like *How did that get there?* Adriana's eyes widen in sheer terror and she steps backward, hugging one inflated arm over the other, as if she's trying to disappear. As if she will ever again be able to disappear, even in death.

"We told them no photos with staff," the publicist says sharply. She's all edges. She resembles an architecture blueprint, her suit folded and sketched over her body in clean lines. Lapels that could take an eye out.

Outside, Jessie and Crystal are sharing coffee at the outdoor hotel café two doors down, casting nervous glances behind each other's heads. Pearl is checking that the coast is clear, smoking a cigarette by the service door directly across the street. Meghan is back at her desk, dutifully transcribing Adriana Argento's last interview ever, the story that will make her career. Veronica is three stories up in the abandoned former Sharpstart office, the world's first (and probably last) "adulting" app, designed to help recent college graduates get on their feet, as if there's any hope for someone who can speak Latin backwards but still brings their laundry basket home to Mommy. She's on a pillar of exposed drywall, her pink tweed Chanel skirt suit collecting specks of plaster like forgotten snowfall. There's a tiny run in her Wolfords, right near the left ankle. She hasn't noticed yet, but she won't be happy when she does.

The rifle heats up, purring like a kitten, thrilling in her lotioned hands. Not a cuticle is out of place, and did you know she gets them done at a little hole-in-the-wall in Soho run by a family from Korea, *not* Paintbox, because that's where she takes business meetings and your personal nail salon should be your sanctuary, you know?

She peers out the window, which is really a clear wall, at the spit-mottled sidewalk. If anyone were to look up, they'd see what appears to be a very well-dressed mannequin left behind in the fallout shelter of pre-renovation clutter, and maybe they'd even think *poor plastic girl, she probably doesn't even have a head.*

No one will look up, though, because they are so busy, too busy, they couldn't possibly, there's no time. And Veronica, well—she does indeed have a very impressive head.

And me, I'm halfway into the elevator, hand pressing on the insistent door, my mouth opening and my throat constricting in protest. What am I trying to say? Do I really think I can *talk* to Adriana Argento? Using *English*? Aren't there special words? A new language that will come in the moment of opening my mouth, like speaking in tongues. Shouldn't some divine spirit pour through me, breathing life into my soiled veins, gilding my throat? Making me worthy? I'm a mermaid on land for the first time, walking on unsteady legs, and I have no voice.

And besides, Adriana won't even look at me.

Her publicist slams the Door Close button again and again, so forcefully she snaps a nail down to the quick on the final stab. (Paintbox?)

"Look what you made me do!" she yelps and jams the wounded finger in her mouth. I push the whole right side of my body flush against the door, forcing it into the slot from whence it came, wide open, feeling the insistent push as it fights my hold. A small laugh escapes from Adriana's clenched, powdered-sugar lips. She wears gold foil eyeshadow, left over from the shoot, the thick lines of her winged liner extending almost to her temples.

The half moons of her eyes slide up and up and then she's looking at me.

Adriana Argento is looking right at me with those solar irises floating on a white galaxy threaded with red. I expected to feel small, caught in the laser points of her gaze, yet her attention fills me with helium. I'm one of those giant balloons waving outside a car dealership: filled to the max with air, a permanent smile affixed to my primary-colored face like a hangnail that won't easily be bitten off, comforted by the knowledge that, hey, even Adriana Argento gets dry eyes.

"We have to *go* now, Adriana," the publicist says. "I told them *no photos*."

Then, to me, she snaps, "If you don't let us leave right this instant, I'm going to call the police. Do you have any idea how important this is?"

I'm not sure what she means by "this," whether "this" is some appointment she's forgotten to make me aware of, forgetting that not everyone is privy to the details of her personal planner, or simply Adriana herself, the most important person in the world to this woman, the one who keeps her in those pressed suits. I get the sense that if I stand here long enough, she'll hire me as an assistant just so she doesn't have to look at me anymore.

For once I don't care if I'm in the way. Right now, I don't want to be Edith, smiling above her reams of paper filled with other people's words. I want to be an inconvenience.

So I just keep staring into Adriana's eyes, begging her to understand, trying to will a telepathic thread into existence between us, this dead space an utter betrayal after all the hours

I've spent this past year floating around in the world she created with her music, a world I thought we shared.

She stares and I stare, and we keep staring and I keep saying nothing, but my eyes are pleading. They whisper *don't go* and *I'm sorry* and *thank you*.

A single tear escapes from the corner of one of her wide, oval eyes. Is there a surgery that makes your eyes look like that, perpetually awake and watchful? She really is, as Tessa described, perfect up close. Poreless.

I watch as the tear slides down her cheek, catching a rainbow of elevator light and making a prism. Very, very slowly, minutely, Adriana shakes her head. Barely there, but definite, a small jerk of the chin and a tilted little smile. She seems resigned. Gently, she places a palm on the publicist's upper arm, rumpling the crisp fabric, and pushes her aside. The publicist rocks on her kitten heels and stumbles sideways, nose crinkling in disgust. Adriana steps forward. The hollow stabs of her Givenchy heels make sucking sounds on the floor and I feel each one in my stomach like a knife. In, out. In, out.

She jabs her own finger on the button. Door Close.

My heart shatters, tiny fissures lacing throughout the knotted surface of hard, rough muscle, the essential organ at the core. There's a tightening in my chest, a corseting.

I release my grip. The elevator door tumbles out from exile, rushing at me, and I step out of the way just before it crushes me, turning me to pulp against the wall.

The last thing I see before the elevator seals shut is a varnished hair curtain slicing downward as Adriana turns her face away. A sliver of quilted olive. A fine-pointed heel.

The hallway is so many shades of gray. I notice, for the first time, that one of the bulbs in the ceiling has burned out. The red letters count backward as Adriana plunges down, ever closer to the biggest surprise of her life.

I see myself in the elevator's metallic, impenetrable surface, a phantasmagoric stain, the horror that haunts your nightmares.

I press my hand to the elevator, flesh meeting spirit. The red light blinks L.

And she chose; I chose.

★ ★ ★ ★ ★

ACKNOWLEDGMENTS

While working on this book, I developed a habit of reading the acknowledgments pages in my favorite novels to remind myself that writing doesn't happen in a vacuum. I'm so excited that it's now my turn to thank the people who helped put my debut in your hands.

To Maria Whelan, my dream agent. Thank you for your shrewd editorial guidance and for championing this novel every step of the way. Working with you has quite literally changed my life. To April Osborn, the best editor a writer could ask for—you understood my vision from the start and helped make this book the best it could possibly be. I'm so proud of what we've done together. And to the entire team at MIRA, especially Quinn Banting, Monica Espinoza Chavez, Ashley MacDonald and Justine Sha, thank you for taking a chance on this strange little story and launching it into the world with passion (and an unbelievably gorgeous cover).

This book owes an endless debt to the teachers who encouraged me to keep writing: Carolyn Ferrell and Mary Morris at Sarah Lawrence College for their kind feedback on my early work; Denise Hayden at Floral Park Memorial High

School for handing me a list of colleges with creative writing programs and telling me to apply; and Mr. Palladino at Floral Park-Bellerose School for introducing me to the craft in the third grade—and for never once calling my parents in alarm when I wanted work on my "novel" about a haunted house instead of playing outside with the other kids at recess.

To my dearest friends: "the Daves" (Bridget, Egg, Hope, Jojo, Kelsy, Liri and Shanicka), Emma, Erik, Katherine, Sarah, Zac and Zach. Thank you for all the laughter and commiseration throughout the writing process and well beyond. And a very special thank-you to Gaby, the Jessica to my Elizabeth Wakefield, for always being there and talking me through every anxiety attack. I'll meet you on Fear Street anytime.

Last, but definitely not least, to my beloved family on all sides—thank you for constantly cheering me on. Mom and Steve, thank you for never asking about a backup plan. Mostly, thank you for reading to me from day one and only very occasionally requesting I put the book down. I'll always be your bookworm.

And Benjamin, my great love. I couldn't have written this book, or any book, without you. Thank you for believing in me when I struggle to believe in myself and for being my most vocal cheerleader and biggest fan. I am your #1 stan for life.